DEAD STAR:

FROZEN MAGIC

DEAD STAR:

FROZEN MAGIC

a novel by

Gregory Mandarano

When the universe broke,
ONE clawed its way back.

His bare hands clawed at the snow.

He pressed his fingers down into the layer of icy pebbles and ash beneath, and with a final grunt, pulled himself to the summit of the rocky outcropping. For a moment, all Havik Davenport could think of was the chill of the bitter cold. It seeped down into his bones where the pain had transformed into a pleasant ache. *That is not good,* he reminded himself, as he pressed his hands into his ragged black cloak. He huddled against his chest and exhaled hot breath onto his fingers. The last thing Havik wanted was to lose his hands once he made it back to the ship. *If* he could get back to the ship. His hopes were that he'd be able to see it from the top of this rock, which would mark it less than two days away. Any further and he might not have the strength to carry on with the sled.

Havik rolled onto his back, closed his eyes, and rested against the flat ledge with a comfort he'd not known in days. *I wish I still had my gloves,* he thought, but instantly knew the better of it. Those clothes were stained with wolf blood, as well as his own. When the Silver Star rose in the sky after that fifth frightful night, he'd walked a full league East towards a chasm he'd seen from the hill. There, atop a fragile bridge of snow, he'd tossed the bloody cloths and furs, and cursed the beasts under his breath. With any luck they'd be drawn to the scent and fall to their doom, or at least buy him the time he needed.

It is unnatural how they hunt us. I know they are not starved. There was no shortage of game in the Lost Hills. Even here, near the gate to the top of the world, rabbits and elk, moose, possum, squirrel, beaver, and all manner of birds and other small game lived in the forest. On that first journey to the gate he had never eaten half so well. Their fires were tall and the meat plentiful. He still had his rum then, his squire, and his sanity. It was not for lack of food that the wolves pressed their attack. Each of the past five days and nights the pack hunted him. In truth it had been longer than that, but for a while he half believed he had lost them. Each day he made his way across the hills, and each night the wolves lingered ever on the horizon.

They're more vulture than wolf. It's as if they wait for me to collapse so I'd make an easier kill.

His following thought was more sobering, as he wondered if they were simply not hungry for the moment, and were drawing out the kill like a spider saves its prey. Havik had killed three of them before he lost the sword, but he dared not go back for it. Once sufficient blood had been spilled the wolves turned on their fallen pack mates like jackals. He watched them tear the flesh from their brothers, before his wits got the better of him, and he grabbed the sled and made for the hills.

Wolves do not eat wolves. He knew that from his studies. He knew far too many things from the books and scrolls his uncle forced upon him as a child. *It is your books that have driven me to this fate, uncle. To hell with your tales of star metal and your eyes for the throne. And to hell with you!* He regretted the words as soon as he thought them, and muttered a half spoken apology under his breath. Then he chided himself for not having his own strength of will to curse his uncle even here, half a world away from where his name, or his family, meant anything whatsoever. It all seemed so comical. His smile gave way to giggles, and soon he was laughing in full force, letting his mirth echo out across the snowy hills. *Dear Goddess I am going mad.*

His jovial mood ceased as suddenly as it began when his ears honed in on the hollow echoes of his laughter. A bolt of fear coursed through him.

They could have heard me. Now is not the time for rest.

Havik opened his eyes. Far above him, above the forest and the wolves, above all the world of Eldaria, the Dead Star sat transfixed in its own permanent throne in the sky. Black and cratered, with a vexing purple hue that shone night and day, the star never moved and never turned. Between Eldaria and its dark halo, countless mountains of rock drifted the vacuous Sea of Heavens. Sometimes they would strike one another like boats upon a storm, and send pieces careening up into the star, or down below into the top of the world. Star metal occasionally rained its hot death upon Eldaria, but there the Dead Star sat silently, and watched.

Would that I could sit and ponder the mysteries of Heaven, but then I'd be as dead as that star.

And with that Havik stood and looked out over the hills. Stretched out before him were endless leagues of empty wilderness, rolling lands of white, bearded with tall pine trees bearing great branches that created a vast under-forest beneath the snowy canopy above. It would have been unwise for Havik to enter the forest on his way back. While it would have offered protection from the wolves and weather, the roots of the trees would have made for treacherous travel with the sled. No matter how many times he told himself he should, Havik never once left the sled or its occupant behind.

Captain Jhev deserves a better fate than ending up as wolf shit, he swore when first faced with the decision of entering the woods or taking the long way round, the way that almost killed them every night when the wolves came. Although he was never sure if the good Captain would survive the journey, *at least his wife would have his bones,* he thought. Plus he dare not return without any star metal to show for his efforts. Havik and Jhev both had carried as much as they could when they left the Barrens, but it was only a pittance compared to the great sum that had been left behind. Even so, Havik would not mourn what could have been. He was glad he had his life and his Captain yet lived. His good fortune might soon run out, and he had once estimated it would take him seven full days to cross the Lost Hills and reach the ship.

A week of flight and fear.

That first day into the hills, before it turned dark, Havik had sought shelter against a mighty pine that once fell from its own weight. No trees grew around it in the snowy ashen ground of the hills, but there this tree stood, until some heavy fall of snow took its final toll. It could not have been too long ago as the needles of its branches were green and lush. Havik thanked the Goddess, and with his sword in hand, cut off branch after branch with the intent of making a shelter. It's not that the wind was bad, for the tree provided its own protection from the elements, but he hoped that if they were out of sight, perhaps the wolves might pass them by. *The snow will be falling soon,* he had told himself. *And this will cover up our scent.*

When he was done, Havik took a piece of cloth and tried to wipe the sticky sap from the sword's blade, but it was to no avail. He didn't even have a whet stone to sharpen it, let alone oil. With a moan of dissatisfaction he pocketed the cloth and sheathed his sword. It wasn't *his* sword, truly. He had taken it from Jhev's belt when first he fell victim to the fever. Havik needed it to make the precious sled that now carried him, and the small bit of heavy star metal ore they'd salvaged. As for his own sword...

No, you mustn't think of that! Strike it from your mind. You can cower in your cabin when you reach the ship, but for now you mustn't fear... Wolves can smell fear. He pulled the sled behind the wall of branches, and closed it up behind him. Pale white light poured through a hole aimed at the Silver Star. It shined brightly in the sky that day. If you could call it day. They were so far North that the Red Star never crested above the horizon. Instead, day was when the Silver Star rose and for a good twelve hours set its course across the night sky. Its reflected luminance of the Red Star bathed all the Northern world in a soft white glow. At least it did there in the hills. The Barrens held no snow, and there the world was purple and foreign. Smoke and cinder rose from open fissures and the air smelt of sulfur and ash. Havik Davenport was a man who feared neither man nor beast, but he shuddered when he thought again of that fell place. It seemed all he did now was fear. *I mustn't be afraid,* he resolved, but the experiences of the Barrens were fresh in his mind. He forced himself not to think of that place, but still the memories were there beneath the surface. They were rotting away at him from the inside out.

Havik was not a devout man, but there that first night he prayed to the Goddess to take his fear from him, and he looked to the Silver Star's reflected light with want for salvation in his heart. Only a few brief moments passed before it disappeared behind a distant hill and cast his world into darkness. *It is no sign, it is only the dark of night.* Though here even darkness was not true darkness. A foul lavender stained everything. It was a strange fluorescence that permeated all matter, including the branches and leaves above Havik's head, where the light of the Red or Silver Star would have cast shadow. He could see, but it was an unholy sight that all men abhorred. *The light of the Dead Star is a foul thing.* In the South where civilization once again tamed the wild world, the dark light did not overtake the shadows. There the Dead Star was no more than a great shield that hung in the Northern sky, but here it was a celestial temple that dominated all the view of the Heavens above.

Havik grabbed the branches and covered the hole securely. Tonight he would rest well should the Goddess be so kind as to grant him sleep. But first, his mind was on his hunger. Havik took a small satchel from the sled and thumbed at the food within. "Ten rolls of hard bread. Five slices of hard cheese. Four sausages... At least food won't be a problem."

He nibbled at the cheese and bread and ate half a sausage cold. He dare not start a fire to make a meager stew for fear it would draw unwanted attention, so he consigned himself to the beggars meal and ate it happily. When he was finished eating he took the large jar of rum from the sled and enjoyed a heaving gulp. *Careful. Too much and I will sleep too soundly.* They were lucky enough to have had wine on them when they first ran, but as Jhev's illness took hold he developed a fierce unquenchable thirst. Havik had resorted to watering the rum with melted snow in an empty jar. *This was Brackens' jar. The one he collected that queer salt in. Half Brackens poured in a circle round Narvis, and the other half I...*

Fool! Do not think of it! I told you not to think of it!

Havik cursed under his breath, took a swig of the watery brew, and tended to Jhev. For a long while he pondered whether to chew the bread or the cheese into a watery paste so he might force some food down Jhev's throat to keep him alive. The man had slept nearly a full day, and he did not want him to starve. Havik finally pocketed the roll and slice of cheese, and had decided on chewing sausage instead when Jhev's eyes fluttered open and he found himself awakening back into the world of the living. Havik shifted closer and sat beside his wounded Captain.

Jhev was a man born of Gulgari, the oldest and proudest of the merchant cities, and as such his skin was copper. His hair was an elderly silver with hints of the brown oak strands of his youth. His eyes were as blue as the waters of the seas he had sailed, with flecks of white sea foam. Havik once admired those eyes when he saw a storm brewing behind them, but now they seemed faded and old, and the whites of his eyes were reddened by his growing sickness.

Jhev was not a handsome man, and bore more fat than muscle in his elder years, but from his tales he was once quite comely, and had bragged of freely bedding as many women as ports in the Central Sea. Havik never had reason to doubt. Before they set sail from Astermount that fateful day, he had seen his wife, the lady he swore off all other conquests for, Lady Celinda Whitesteed. She was a beautiful woman of the Western Realm, with gold in her hair and the sky in her eyes. Such a prize would not have been won with coin alone. Even so, Davenport had no lust in his veins nor any desire to have the looks of an Islander. Nor did he have any love for a woman of the West.

The Davenport blood was watered with the old blood of the Eastern Kingdoms, but within their line was an Ancient. Those with the old blood, born of black hair touched with the empty darkness of the night sky, their eyes would always shine black like obsidian jewels on a field of snow. Their hair and eyes might change with each mixed marriage, but black hair meant black eyes, always. Not so for the Davenports, and other proud Houses that boasted an Ancient in their line. Sometimes it was *that* blood which rose to the surface.

Havik's hair was jet black, but his eyes were an unearthly violet with flakes of silver and gold, just like his uncle. His own father, Lord Envek Davenport, had black eyes and black hair, but Lord Hubert Davenport, his uncle, Lord of Witchblood Stronghold, and ruler of the Davenport House, his eyes were kissed with the Ancient's grace as well.

And rightly so, Havik once had thought, for his father was a cowering sycophant that would rather grow fat on the leavings of other, better men, whereas his uncle was the greatest man he had ever known, if not also the most deceitful and cruel. He had no doubt his uncle would propel his House towards heights his father could never fathom. *Even if I should never return...*

It does not matter that I am not his son, Havik had told himself while thinking of his uncle. It was on the day he'd first boarded Wandering Turtle, that sturdy Corsair which would take them on their voyage. *I have his eyes where his own sons don't. When I prove my worth and return with wagons laden with ore, he shall have no choice but to rain honors down upon me, and where then will all the mighty lords put their trust when Hubert dies? In his sons, by blood, or in someone who could lead them?*

Havik took the jar of watered rum and pressed it against Jhev's lips. "Easy now, no need to speak. Drink first."

Jhev had some strength left in him still. He grabbed the jar with his own hand and took a swig. It was all he could do not to spit it out, and his face bore his disgust as he drank it all down. When he was done, he gave away the jar and spit.

"What is this swill? If there's rum left, give it here," Jhev muttered.

"All that wine and your refusal to eat has led you to this sad state. If you've strength enough to complain, you've strength enough to eat. Here." Havik thrust some sausage upon him, and while Jhev ate, the two sat in sullen silence for a long while.

It pained Havik to see his friend so pitiful and helpless. He was accustomed to Jhev being the stronger of the two, perhaps even the more ambitious. Jhev had been born a slave, as was common in the merchant cities, though banned as savagery in the proper Realms. Jhev's ambition first led him to buy his own freedom, and within two decades he had built a profitable business and amassed near a score of trading ships in the Central Sea. He had made marriage with a reputable Western House, and even took their name, Whitesteed, for his own. He did not gain a lordship from it, but there was time for that yet. He fathered three children, two of which were young sons as proud and handsome as their father. He had even gone so far as to win the trust and friendship of a noble Davenport, something which Havik was not so quick to give, but gave to Jhev all the same. Granted Jhev's fleet had been lost in the Emerald Isles, no doubt taken by some pirate lord making a name for himself. Some day they might know the truth of what happened. The only reports they'd heard came from a man pulled out of the sea by a fishing boat. He was half drowned, mad from drinking the salty brine, and he spoke of a pirate who commanded Water itself, and took the octopus for sigil. The very waves they sailed obeyed the pirate's ungodly will. *Magic,* the man swore. He never lived long enough to see dry land again. *The fevered words of a dying man. Such words cannot be trusted,* Havik thought when he heard the tale. *Madness and nothing more.*

The loss put great financial strain on Jhev, and Havik knew he was partly to blame. Havik leveraged his friendship with Jhev to gain use of his ships for a venture he thought would make them rich beyond compare. He never expected pirates in the isles. That stroke of ill fate stained Havik's honor, and when his plan for mining star metal was hatched, Havik included Jhev to help repay the debt he felt was owed. Jhev knew the risk but was eager to gamble his fates once more. With his uncle's coin and blessing, Havik purchased a Corsair in the Northern port of Astermount, and put Jhev to Captain.

And yet with all Jhev's bold ambition, his fate had brought him to this sad end, awash with fever, sled-ridden, and his life in the hands of a Davenport. *Not a safe place to be, if truth be told.* Every instinct his family training had taught him urged Havik to abandon Jhev to the wolves and make time that much quicker with sled and star metal in tow. *I will not leave my friend behind,* he silently swore as if his uncle were there with them, objecting to his weaknesses.

"How far have we come, Havik?" Jhev asked, breaking the quiet.

"Not far. We are a day into the Lost Hills." A piece of him was unhappy that Jhev addressed him by his name, instead of *my lord* or *Lord Davenport.* But their bond of friendship ran deep, there was no one else to hear his words, and he would not begrudge a dying man for improper etiquette. Havik leaned over him and pressed his palm against Jhev's forehead. *Still burning.*

"I'm sorry it's come to this," Jhev said weakly.

"There's no need. You would not be here if not for me." There was much truth in that, though when Havik once expected cautious counsel, he was instead confronted by Jhev's lust for riches at the first mention of star metal. "Rest now. It will be a long while before we reach the shore, and I will not have the singers tell of my friend, the brave Jhev Whitesteed, who traveled the length of the world only to be slain by a flush. We have a long night ahead. Eat when you wake. There's water enough in that jar over there. And I've put a jar in your breeches. I'll not have you piss yourself and freeze to death."

"Is that what that is?" He coughed as he laughed. "I had thought my cock had frozen off and felt half a man."

They spoke for a brief while of the feasts they would enjoy, the honors to be pinned, and glory to be had when they returned with their princely treasure. It was not all that they had hoped for, nor that which they had even once possessed, and their fanciful visions of the future were marred by the bitterness of savored dreams lost, and tainted by words unspoken, even feared thought. He decided against telling Jhev that the wolves might still be hunting them. Havik had seen them with every flash of ethereal lightning that frequented the Barrens, and spied their silhouettes against that wicked sky. For two days he saw them approach from the horizon, but he lost sight of the pack once they passed through the gate. It was when he could no longer track their movements that he feared the most, and as luck would have it, that was when Jhev's feet would no longer carry him. As the first opportunity for wood presented itself, Havik used the sword to make his sled. From there only one day's travel took them to the crossroads, and one more to the sheltered tree. He hadn't seen the pack of wolves in all that time. *Six more days...*

Perhaps I've lost them, Havik had mused as he drifted off to sleep. *They followed us from the Barrens, that is to be certain, but game is plentiful beyond the gate. They are only animals, after all, and with the first scent of elk or rabbit, the pack would go off to hunt easier prey.* A part of him believed the words he told himself, but he could not forget the way they tore Brownbeard to shreds.

They've tasted the flesh of man, and now they hunger for it... Or is it something more? Havik shunned the thought. *No! Do not think of it. You must not think of it!*

His dreams were of a black empty wasteland where time had no meaning. It seemed the lightning of the Barrens haunted even his nights, for purple and gold streaks split the sky. Against the flashes Havik saw an endless mountain range that peaked with terrible edges and looked as if the world had been torn asunder. Then came the fear. A familiar stabbing that started in his chest and spread across his neck. He wanted to turn and run, but his legs were stone and refused him. He wanted to look away, but his gaze was transfixed on the horizon. That is where he saw it. Barely visible at first, but with each flicker of ethereal light in the skies above, the beast came into view. It lay across the black field as if a mountain itself, and when it rose, the mountains were eclipsed and the ground trembled.

Havik was uncertain how long he'd been asleep when he startled awake. The memory of his dream had left him, but he still remembered the fear. He found himself holding his breath, and slowly reaching for the sword. The only sounds he heard were the labored breathing of his companion, and the soft rustling of the fallen pine against a light wind. It had snowed while he slept, and a tattered white veil covered much of his shelter and the world beyond. Then came the screech, a blood curdling scream that whined with mortal terror and whimpered like a crying child. *A rabbit, most like, that's all it is,* he thought as he carefully listened. For just a moment he felt at ease, confident in his explanation. But his sleep fogged mind was coming to clarity, and his fear rose up within him again when the cries fell silent.

They're upon you, fool! Be ready!

Havik softly unsheathed the sword from its leather. It was a bastard sword, and heavier than Havik was accustomed to. All good Davenport men wielded the longsword and shield, as any knight would. Havik was a noble lord, but he was not a knight, and had never been ordained by the Honorable Academy. Even so, it was in his power to demand such a grace, as the influence of his House was strong. Havik was not a terrible fighter and was confident he could hold his own in a joust, even though he had never made the attempt. Still, Havik had no interest in the duties and melodramatic posturings of a knight, and had no desire to have *Ser* replace *Lord* when being addressed. *This will have to do.*

He gracefully approached Jhev and crouched alongside him. Havik was unsure whether he should wake the man, gambling that he might shout in his feverish state and risk their notice, or whether he should prepare his friend for battle. Jhev would want to die with a blade in his hand, not being ripped apart in his sleep. *A hunk of ore, though crude, would still be better than his bare fists,* Havik thought. *That is if he even has strength enough to wield it.*

The wolf removed the choice from Havik's concern when it began to growl not three feet away. He had not even heard the creature's approach, but in the dim purple glow of the Dead Star's aura, he now saw the outline of the hairy mongrel through the tree. The wolf's eyes shone a neon green, and all at once his fear peaked.

It sees me.

The thing howled, and he heard the others respond not a hundred yards into the hills. Havik froze with indecision. He couldn't out run them, and in the open he would be prone. But behind his feeble shelter he knew he would have more difficulty wielding the blade than would serve. He could hear his uncle shouting in his mind. *His fate is sealed! Use it to your advantage! Grab the sled and leave him to the wolves! Do not hesitate!* But there was no decision to be had. Havik had made up his mind a full day prior when he could have chosen the forest route. *I have come this far and made my choice. It is time to face the outcome of my folly.* Even as he thought it, he did not truly believe it was folly. Although he had also chosen not to be a knight, Lord Havik Davenport fancied himself to have an inner belief in the chivalric code that transcended any outdated institution like the Honorable Academy. He had no need for their rules and their rituals, but he could have his honor. *If I must die, then let my death be an honorable one.* That, above all, is what a knight craves. To live and die in service of a just cause he believes in. *If I will not live a knight, then I will die like one, or wrap myself in glory,* he told himself. *The day could yet be mine.*

And so, Havik took the blunted sword in his hand, and stepped from his shelter into that brisk Lost Hills night. He stepped well away from the entrance, and stood with his back against one of the thicker branches of the pine. *Better cornered than surrounded.* He didn't know the wolf was there until it was upon him. He fell to his side, and the sword flew from his hand onto the fresh fallen snow. The beast was nipping at his throat. Its breath stank of corpse and its drool was a warm wet lather that sprayed across his cheeks and into his mouth. He turned and let the thing wrap its fangs into his well padded coat. The teeth drew blood and he felt its warm pain stinging his forearm, but it was nothing more than a scratch. He praised his feint when his hand wrapped sweetly around the hilt of the sword. While the blade's edge was blunted, the point was sharp and deadly, and it pierced the wolf's side and scattered gore across the virgin snow.

The creature whimpered as it backed away, and the hate burned bright in its eyes. Havik's blood was hot and fresh. He hacked at its head, and with his aim true, bludgeoned its skull. The wolf collapsed to the ground with a sickening thud. Havik darted back, glancing every which way while he searched for another wolf.

Enough time passed that his breath slowed and his heart calmed, but that's when the dead wolf murmured a ghastly groan. *Abomination. How is that thing not dead?* But it *was* dead. He took a few steps closer to the corpse of the wolf. It had mangy black fur that was knotted with brambles and ash. The thing was no larger than any grey wolf of the proper Realms, but it had a wretched stench that made him taste vomit in the back of his throat. *Am I such a child, that I would lose my stomach to the smell of a kill?* Havik pondered, but he was certain that was not the case. He had first been blooded at the young age of eight when his uncle made him kill his whipping boy. Havik didn't feel sad that he couldn't remember the boy's name, but that was because he remembered so clearly the fear in the boy's eyes when he held the knife to his neck. *His eyes were like honey.* He had come to despise the boy in his memory. *Have I not suffered it long enough?* The choice had not been his own, and it was that memory which served him to live every choice he made thereafter to the fullest. Havik hated his uncle for a time, but he would never enter his uncle's private solar again.

Havik was blooded once more at the age of ten when he began his lessons in inquisition, a skill that every true Davenport was expected to have knowledge of. Though it wasn't until he was thirteen, when in his first true battle he took the life of a man who might well have taken his own. All at once it seemed to Havik as if he might not know the names of any men he'd killed, as he could not recall that one's name for the life of him. The names of the merchants and mercenaries he'd disposed of over the years were forgotten as quick as yesterday's business. But he did remember the taste of the wine, the feel of the girl's breasts after that first battle, and the following morning when he arose with such a pain in his head he thought it might burst like an overripe melon. It seemed he couldn't remember her name either, though it was her that his cock had blooded that night. She was his first conquest as well, and for a time he fancied he might have a purple eyed bastard, but later learned that Crescent Field and all the O'Brien holdings South of Dagger River were burned. Ser Jonathan Brimly rode his five hundred horse across the Crescent and put every field and standing building to the flame. Those that escaped the fires lived to dangle from trees and feed the crows. *The Heartless they called him,* Havik recalled. He was slain at the Battle of Rooster Pass by Ser Vincent Draven, Lord Commander of the Drakken Guard, the royal retinue of Dameon Draven, then King of the East. He mourned her sometimes when he prayed to the Goddess, but he never mourned the whipping boy.

That was nineteen years ago. Havik counted. *If I make it back by the Rat's Moon I will enjoy the twentieth anniversary of the peace. Quite the time to be draped in honors from my return.* But the dreams brought on by his triumph over the wolf were short lived. It was then that the wolf's chest burst open with a wet pop. Havik reeled as if expecting gore and blood to shower his face, but it was not the color red that fluttered before him in the chill night air. Thousands of tiny black feathery seeds puffed up into the breeze carried by miniature sails of dark silky strands. *No! It cannot be!* Havik Davenport meant to back away, but instead found himself pissing his breeches. The whispering winds of the North lands bit into his crotch with its icy fangs, and it took all his force of will not to surrender to memories of what happened in the Barrens.

Run, you fool! When you are safe in your ship, it will all be as if a dream. Stay here and die!

Havik turned away, his breath held in case one of those foul seeds found its path upon his inhalation. It was fortunate he turned just then, or he wouldn't have seen the second wolf either. It had been racing towards him, and all he could do was raise the sword and stand his ground. The beast leaped at his throat, but Havik was ready, and with the bastard sword wielded two handed, parried its lunge with the heavy blade, and broke its bones sounded by a loud metallic crack. Havik did not fall, and death came swiftly to the wolf when he plunged the sword into its neck and twisted the life from its cursed twitching body. When he turned again, he saw more wolves cresting a distant hill, their purple black shapes visible against the fresh fallen snow. Clouds gathered overhead and the wind picked up. Snow began to fall again as suddenly as the first wolf had appeared. It was a wet snow, sticky and heavy. *We cannot stay here.*

He started for the shelter, but as he cornered one of its branches, he spied a third wolf already clawing its way in. The unholy light of the Dead Star shone inside his hovel even beneath its snowy roof, and from the outside the outline of the sled and Jhev's body were plain to see. He didn't know why he thought the wolves might pass them by. Perhaps he had only ever really gambled they'd miss their scent, and never get close enough to see. But there the foul thing stood, looming over Jhev's body and sniffing at his neck. Havik thought himself stealthy as he strode towards the beast, but it turned and growled and bore its bloodied fangs. *This one killed the rabbit.* The wolf was not so quick to rush into a close kill, and it stalked cautiously towards him, foot by foot. He readied his sword and took a defensive stance, but began to lose his resolve as the other wolves drew closer in the distance. *Is this wretched beast biding its time, waiting for the pack to be upon me?* He choked at the thought. *Do not hesitate!* his uncle shouted, and Havik knew he had the right of it.

Havik charged and swung his sword wildly, deathly unsure of how to approach a wild beast. *But is it wild, truly?* The thought was wrenched from his mind as the wolf attacked past his swinging blade. Its fangs and claws tore at his chest and brought him to his back. The sword cut through its fur, and blood splashed over the wolf's head and his own. Its hide seemed thicker than the others, and the cut had only served to enrage it. *Not quite as starved. Is this the Alpha?* He almost loosed a laugh that he could ponder such thoughts as the wolf tore at his chest, but let slip a cry of pain and terror instead. His coat was thick and the wound beneath minor, but it would soon turn mortal if he lingered any further. He slapped the blade ferociously against the side of the beast, but the angle was poor and he could do it no harm. With one heaving push he turned the wolf on its side and managed to back himself away.

Whether it was anger or simple animal blood lust, he did not know, but the once cautious Alpha leaped with fangs bared wide. Havik stood his ground. He planted his feet, gathered support against his leg, and thrust the sword forward with all the strength he could muster. The sword parted muscle and bone alike and burrowed deep into the charging wolf's heart. He tumbled backwards as the thing died against his chest, with hot sticky blood spilling over his coat and staining the tunic below more red than it had been before. When he climbed to his knee, he saw the point of the blade rising up from the back of the wolf's corpse. Blood and ichor smeared its silver color away, and it shone malevolently against the light of the Dead Star's purple aura. The sword pierced through to the hilt, which itself was lost under snow and a hundred pounds of meat and fur.

Dead weight.

Havik saw the other wolves still approaching across the small valley towards the lone pine tree, and where once sturdy resolve hardened him, panic set in. He stumbled to the side of the dead wolf and desperately tried to roll it over. Just as he was turning the beast onto its side and saw the hilt rising from the ground caked with red snow, he heard the popping sound. Where the blade rose from the wolf, a burst of the damned black seeds fluttered up and mixed with the falling snow in a rising current of foul smelling wind.

Do not hesitate! Run!

But Havik only half heeded the words his uncle seemed to whisper in his ear, and he pushed his way into the shelter instead. With one arm he threw the blanket over Jhev's unconscious body, and with the other gained hold of the leathery straps. They once were their belts, but now served as a harness to pull the sled. He unearthed it from where it had settled, and scraped out from the shelter and into that crisp snowy night. Snow and seed rained upon him and his cargo, so Havik held his breath for as long as he could manage, and inhaled through his blood soaked clothes when at last he craved air. The wolf's blood tasted of salt and copper, and was not entirely unpleasant, but secretly he feared the beast's corruption might taint the blood as well. The thought of it suddenly got the best of him, and his world spun. He stopped, knelt, and retched the grim contents of his stomach upon the ground.

Havik soon stood and looked back the way he'd come. He was at the top of a small hill, nearly fifty yards from the tree. The pack had set upon the fallen corpses of the wolves he'd slain. Three fought over the flesh of the Alpha, while the rest tore the other dead wolves asunder. Rings of snow blackened with corruption surrounded each corpse, and the knotted furs of the living wolves were covered in the stuff.

It spreads...

The thought filled Havik with more dread than he could fathom, and he dry heaved until his nausea subsided. *Do not hesitate! They will not be sated forever.* The thought sobered him, and he stood once more to gather his breath. The wolves were busy with their meal, and as Havik regained his composure he discovered his hard roll and cheese in his pockets, the remainder of his own last meal.

The food! He made the words into a curse in his mind when he realized the satchel that contained their rations was left on the shelter's floor. He gazed at half a dozen wolves frolicking amidst snow of white, red, and black, then looked down upon the meager sum of food in his hands. Havik carefully tucked that prize under a cloak on the sled. *It is enough on its own, and there will be game to hunt,* he lied to himself. The Lost Hills would hold no hopes for game beyond that last tree. A chasm ran further South and Havik would need to skirt around it to reach the shore that way. His next shelter would need be snow, and that required digging. He groaned at the thought. *If you've got time to complain, you've got time to run.* With that he grabbed hold of the leather, and pulled the sled South.

The following four nights he had dug his shelters and prepared for an attack that never came. The wolves remained upon the horizon, circling them for the carrion they might soon become. Each night one wolf stalked their shelter, and circled it like a shark might circle its meal. Havik would wait and watch from within the meager snowy hole. Without the sword his only defense would be a stick, and a jar of rocks wrapped in cloth. But each night when he was sure it would come to blood, the wolf would scamper away and return to the pack.

They mock me.

Jhev was asleep most of the time and his fever was growing worse. *He won't survive to reach the ship,* Havik feared, but each time Jhev awoke he would tell him they were nearly there, and that they'd soon be in his cabin, warm, fed, and well wined. Havik melted snow in his jars for drinking water, though it left a bitter aftertaste from the pervasive ash that was present even in freshly fallen snow. He had finished the last of the rum, as he found it helped his mood and warmed his belly in the absence of food. He fed Jhev a paste of bread and cheese, and divided it equally, though his uncle told him he should take the lion's share for himself. *If you do not eat you will die. Better him than a Davenport.* His uncle had been driving him mad as of late, and he no longer possessed the strength to argue with him. Of course Havik knew his uncle was a thousand leagues away, no doubt plotting his next grand scheme, but he had no energy to rationalize with his own mind. When his uncle screamed in his ear, he had no choice but to listen.

What they want is blood.

But what if... What if their mind is not of the wolf alone... What if they're really...

I told you not to think of it! Never think of it! Your madness will not save you now! What they want is blood! Feed them Jhev, or you will not make the shore alive.

Havik knew his uncle was right, but he had *come this far,* and he swore those very words to himself again and again, almost in tempo to the beat of his legs. His feet had become blocks of ice and snow, packed down between layers of leather and cloth. His thighs were frozen pillars, and where he once wore his face in a thin beard, it was now overgrown with an icy patchwork of mucus and frost. Havik knew the luxury of a blade against his face would pale in comparison to the advantage one would bring when the wolves next attacked. Still though, his uncle was right. It was blood they wanted, and he would give it to them. He set his bloody clothes as ruse, then made his way South.

Havik had spent the rest of that day marching with as fast a pace as he could muster towards the rocky outcropping that marked the highest point past the chasm. *If I can see the ship from there, we are saved.* As he climbed it, Havik hoped with every last shred of his fraying humanity that his ruse had worked. He also prayed that his life would not come at the cost of his fingers. When he pulled the sled he kept them warm against his chest, but he needed his fingers to climb. A few torn shards of cloth round his palms were all that stood between him and the bitterest of colds.

After a brief rest atop that rocky outcropping, he said a silent prayer to the Goddess. His long, wistful gaze back upon the way he'd come had born no sight of the wolves. Perhaps he would not see them again. With one final prayer, Havik turned to look South, to see if his prayers had been answered.

There before him stretched the Sea of Secrets, and there, where water and sky met land, was the beacon fire. From this distance it was a quaint thing, and impossible to spot in the hills, but on the rocky flat lands that led from hill to shore it would be easy to follow. Snow had fallen across all the coast from the storms that passed. When they first arrived by ship the plains were brown with grass and the hills an ashen grey. Now everything was a dirty white that grew more virgin as the sea neared. There the sea was the color of home, and his heart soared anew with thoughts of sails unfurled and rum savored on deck.

Havik climbed carefully but quickly down the rock and came to a knee beside the sled. Eager as he was to tell Jhev of the news, he thought first to give him water and food. The task came easy to him now, as he'd done it what seemed a hundred times before. He changed his piss pot first, then, as he melted snow for water, he chewed a piece of cheese. This time, however, when Havik lightly removed Jhev's hood to look upon his face, he spit the food from the fright of it. Jhev's veins had become blackened with a strange pox, and his skin was sweaty and cool. His eyes opened and he weakly coughed black phlegm, then begged for what Havik could only assume to be water. He drank a good while before he again tried to speak.

"The ship... Could you see it?" Jhev's voice was weak.

Tears came suddenly to Havik's eyes, whereas until just then he had been stoic and fearless, just as he'd sworn to be. *I have to be brave,* he remembered, but he could not help but cry.

"Yes, Jhev. It's there. The fire is close, and the red and green sails of *your* ship are there too."

"*My*... ship?" he croaked.

"Yes, Jhev. Your ship. I'm giving it to you. I only needed it to get me here, and that part is done." Havik swallowed his grief. "When we return, Wandering Turtle is yours. A fine beginning to a new fleet. And a good business for your sons."

"My sons..." Jhev breathed deep. "Kalev was never the sailor. Give the ship to Jace."

"You can give it to him yourself, when we return." Havik had known Jhev might not make the journey, but each moment he could have spent preparing for his friend's death, was instead filled with resolve to reach the ship in time. Each step was a curse in the face of his uncle. Each step his own choice. Havik's tears grew thicker and froze against his cheeks. *Goddess... Please... Do not let him die,* he prayed, but he knew there was no hope for him. Havik had never seen veins like those that Jhev now possessed. They were marked with corruption and it made Jhev's face a waking horror for all men to look upon. Just then, however, all Havik felt was sorrow.

"Havik..." Jhev strained to speak, but his life was leaving him.

Jhev's palm was open and his fingers reached out. Havik gave him his bared hand. Jhev's fingers felt cool to the touch, like the ice and stone he'd climbed only minutes before. Jhev squeezed and looked up into Havik's eyes, silent as the grave.

"You'll be fine old friend, you'll see. We'll return by the silvery light of the Rat's Moon. We'll send a raven before we get there, so when we arrive they'll all be waiting for us. Those marble docks at Astermount will shine as bright as Lady Celinda's hair. Your sons will all be there, and so will my father and uncle. We'll feast in Salt Comet Hall and the singers will make praise of your bravery. Honors will be pinned, and all the Realm will know of the men who braved the gate and lived to tell the tale. Can you see it, Jhev? Jhev..."

But his friend was gone. The light had left his eyes, and even his corruption seemed lifeless.

Havik sat for a long while grieving for his friendship, which had been the only one remaining to him. The few friends of his youth were all dead, and everyone else was a servant, an ally, an enemy, or worse, family. *His sons will have his ship, and his wife will have his bones,* he swore, but that was when the fear took him. All at once he remembered the necromantic blossoms of the black seed. *Will he burst and corrupt me as well?* he worried, but he had made his choice, and was ill to turn back now.

Havik wrapped Jhev's corpse tight with cloth and blanket, then packed snow around his body on the sled. It would add to the weight, but there would be no more hills soon, and flat snow would be easy with the sled. *The snow will keep the black seed down, and when I reach the ship, we'll burn him and I'll have my bones. But what if it's not just seed... What if the blackness is really...*

Fool! I told you never to think of it! Your madness will not save you! What they want is blood! Do not risk black death for white bones!

Havik was too exhausted to argue with his uncle, and he should have rested near the rock before setting out. Night came quick upon him. He was dreadful tired, but he had reached the flat lands by then, and chose to spend hours more afoot. *The wolves might have heard me,* he cautioned himself. *Best get as far from that rock as I can.* His every step was fueled with grief for his friend and hope to reach the fire that burned on the horizon. He was filled with resolve for the choice he made, and his mind echoed with the ever present voice of his uncle. It ever urged him to leave Jhev behind.

Fool! He is cursed and you are tired! Leave his body to the wolves! You are too tired to drag him any further... You must leave him... You are too tired... Too tired... ... ...

THE MAN IN THE WOODS

He remembered the sound of a distant siren in the darkness. Even though he could not see, he felt a sense of desperation in the air around him. "Do you know your designation?" a man's voice said.

"Three four two." He felt himself say the words. *Is that my voice?*

He remembered a green eye. That image burned in his memory. He could see the nebula of the old man's iris as if it were the sum total of his vision. It blinked, and the eye became the old man. He had pale skin, but it was blotched with marks of age and varicose veins. His head was bald, and he wore a coat of pure white. He remembered the old man with such perfect clarity, but everything else was out of focus. There was a blurred symbol on the man's white coat, and the same symbol but larger on each of the grey walls behind him. Red lights flashed in the hall. He smelled smoke and fear.

"What is your primary objective?" the old man asked.

"My primary objective..." he heard himself say.

Then all he remembered was blue light and pain.

He heard the sound of water. It spattered all around him as it fell. Tiny droplets smacked into his face, his body, and the ground by his ear. He heard the sound of birds wings flapping. Insects were buzzing. The grass and the leaves rustled in the wind. Overhead a clap of thunder shook the sky, and the rain fell harder. He opened his eyes. It was day, but the light was dim under the storm clouds, and dimmer still beneath the canopy of the trees. *Where am I?*

"Dear Goddess!" The words of a man came from behind him.

He sat himself up, and discovered he had been lying in mud. His back and side dripped with the wet brown muck. He looked to the words and found coming out of the forest a man in a ragged brown robe. He carried a walking stick and by his step seemed to be elderly or crippled.

"Are you injured? You must be freezing!" the man said. "Here." The man took off his robe.

He heard the man's words, but he did not understand them. They seemed strange and foreign. Even so, he somehow knew, not suspected, but knew down to his core that the man could do him no harm. When the man thrust the robe onto him, he realized that he was stark naked. Goosebumps rose from his skin where his flesh was exposed to the wind and rain, and he felt an odd sensation coursing through him. His own skin was light cream, and his body was a muscled perfection. He looked up to the man, and saw that he had black eyes, and grey hair. He was old, but not as old as the man with the white coat. Underneath the man's robe he was wearing a brown woolen shirt with a history of patchwork and careful repair. The shirt had been dry, but was now getting soaked in the falling rain. He could tell the man was getting cold. When he fully stood, he discovered he was taller than the man by a foot.

"Go ahead. It's alright. Put it on," the man said.

He put the robe on over his naked body, and the man smiled and seemed satisfied.

"Now that's odd." The man had a look of curiosity. He followed the man's eyes down to the ground. The forest floor was dense with the greens of shrubs, ferns, and wild grasses. But the dirt where he awoke was a black scorched circle two meters wide. There was a small crater that indented into the ground nearly forty centimeters, as if a scoop of dirt was lifted up and carried away. The greenery at the edge of the circle was singed and burnt black, as if some great heat flamed for seconds, then puffed out.

Somehow he knew that this ground was dangerous. As he concentrated his gaze upon it, there came to be an unusual color that emanated from the seared dirt. It's not that he felt himself in danger, but somehow he knew it was unsafe for the man, so he took the man by the arm and gently led him into the forest.

"What's your name?" the man asked, but he did not understand. "Your name... Can't you speak lad?" The man sighed. "Was it bandits? Took everything and no doubt left you for dead, eh?" The man seemed sad. "Rotten bastards to pick on a simpleton." The man stopped and turned to face him. The man placed his hands on his own chest. "Darry." The man tapped his palms against himself. "I'm Darry." The man tapped those hands on his chest now. He looked down at them. "Who are you?" the man asked.

Is he telling me his name? His must be Darry. "Darry," he said.

The man laughed. "No, I'm Darry." He patted his own chest again. "Darry. And you?"

He must want to know my name. My name... It's... Why couldn't he remember? *Who am I?* Somehow he did not know anything. He remembered waking in the woods. He remembered... He remembered the old man, and the red lights, and the smoke... and his designation.

"Three four two," he said. *Is that my name?*

"What's that now? Treefort? Is that where you're from, lad?" The man shook his head. "Sorry, lad, but I ain't never heard of it." Lightning flashed overhead and it seemed the storm was growing worse. Darry took him by the arm and walked him North East. *How do I know it is North East?* he wondered. "Come on. You better come with me. That's my best robe, and I don't mean to have it run off and get lost."

What happened to me? he wondered as he followed Darry deeper into the forest. Everything seemed unfamiliar to him. The sky, the air, the man, and his language seemed foreign. It was all a wonder of new experience. Even his own skin seemed foreign to him. He felt himself walking stiffly at first, and a few times he stumbled in the muck. The man laughed at him and helped him up. Darry seemed kind and friendly, and it seemed he was leading them someplace to get out of the weather. He was unsure of how long they would have to walk to reach their destination, but he found himself hoping it was soon. Somehow he knew the man was growing colder by the minute.

"My son Gerry's gone to Tansville for work," Darry said as they walked. "But his wife Keeli and their children'll be home. I'm sure to get it something fierce for bringing back a stray, but I can't rightly have left you there like that, all bare to the wind. Can't say there'll be much to feed a big lad like yourself, but we've onions sure enough, and you'll have some good hot broth at least to warm you up. Don't you be feeling like it's an imposition now. I'm sure we'll find some way you can make it up to us."

He listened to Darry's words. Everything the man said seemed of perfect clarity and recollection in his mind, but the meaning behind the sounds of the words was lost on him. *Am I in a foreign land?* he mused. *Did I come from someplace far away?* He supposed he could think of ten to the tenth possibilities, but there was no point. He did not know anything at all, and felt like a child to the splendor of living. For now, he was perfectly content with walking in the woods, and feeling the wind upon his skin, the rain upon his face, and the cool mud and leaf under his bare feet. Even Darry's foreign tongue seemed a pleasant music to his ears. *I like this place. Is that why I came here? To get away from the smoke, and the flashing lights, and the panic?* He remembered the old man's question. "What is your primary objective?" the man repeated in blurred memory. *My primary objective... Is that why I came here? My purpose? I can't remember my purpose.*

Darry's voice trailed off to silence and they stopped. He did not know what made the man's demeanor change so suddenly, but the man backed up in his own footsteps. "Don't make any sudden movements now, lad," Darry whispered. "She'll tear those strong limbs of yours apart like bark off a tree." It seemed the man was staring at a creature in the bushes not five meters away. It was a large heavy mammal that sported a coat of luscious brown fur. The thing's bone and muscle were surrounded by bulbous layers of fat, and it seemed healthy and strong. It walked on fingered paws, and dug its snout at a pool of water as it drank from it. The mammal gave a soft groan, sniffed at the air, and looked in their direction.

Darry gave a quiet whimper. "Now just back away slowly, lad. And whatever you do, don't look in its eyes." He watched the man back away, but did not understand why he was reacting in such fashion. He looked back to the mammal. *It is large. Does it mean him harm?* He knew it stood between them and a Northeasterly heading. The mammal's curiosity was peaked as well. It took a few lumbering steps towards him, and snorted at the air.

The man gave a high pitched yip, turned, and ran. He watched him go, then looked back to the mammal. It opened its mouth and gave a long moan as it revealed its wide fanged jaws and lagging tongue. *I like this mammal,* he thought. *Its color is like the tree, and it is a handsome thing.* He heard the man behind him shout, "Boy! What are you doing! Boy!" He wondered if Darry was using *boy* as the word for run. *Why run?* he thought instead. *It is a fine animal.*

The fine animal rushed at him, and stopped its maddened charge not half a meter away. It reared on its two hind feet and stood at twice his height. The mammal gave a terrific roar as it waved its paws in the air. *Is it trying to communicate with me?* he wondered. He turned and saw Darry staring oddly at them. *He seems concerned about this mammal, and appears uncomfortable. Perhaps it means him some harm.* When he looked back the mammal was on its fours, and at equal level to his height, placed its face before his. The creature roared again, and released a pungent wave of hot sour breath upon his face. It kicked its paws at the dirt, and swept at the air before him. *I will set the kindly man at ease. I like him more than this animal.*

He closed his right hand into a fist, and took aim at the point between the mammal's eyes. With a fluid motion and speed that startled even him, he accelerated his fist into the center of the animal's head. Bone and cartilage gave way to brain. When he pulled back his arm the creature fell to the ground quite dead. He shook the pink bits of organ and blood from his hand. *This sensation displeases me,* he thought, as he wiped off the gore and cleaned himself in a puddle of water. When he stood again, satisfied that his hand was well washed, the man walked up to him.

Darry took him by the hand and examined his fist. The man gave him strange looks, and he no longer seemed as kindly, but took a somber tone. "Let's go." Darry walked away and he followed.

They traveled in silence for several thousand steps before the woods thinned and they emerged into farmland. The fields were fresh and wet with mud, but the tall stalks of plants were withered as if by drought. "This is the first rain we've had in months," Darry said with unusual emotion as they passed between the dead plots of land.

It was not long before they came upon a small house surrounded by trees. Most of them were dying from lack of water with nary a leaf, but a few stood proud and strong, and he thought their roots must go deep. The house was a simple structure, with a main section fifteen meters by twenty, and two smaller rooms on the North and East sides. He could tell the building wasn't very sturdy by the angle of the ground and the tilt of the load bearing beams. When they entered through the main door he caught scent of a curiously appealing vapor in the air.

"Keeli!" the man shouted. "Keeli get out here with some dry clothes." Darry stripped down to his bare skin, and stood shivering by the fire.

"Where have you been?" A woman with brunette hair and amber eyes stepped out from the adjacent room. "Oh no, you're freezing!" she cried. "Here, lets get you covered." She thrust a long shirt over the man, wrapped him in a fur blanket, and set Darry down on a chair near the fire. She looked up at him, and for a moment half approached, then stopped. "Thank you for bringing him back. Where did you find him?" He thought he liked her wooden eyes. They reminded him of the forest.

"It was *I* who found *him*, woman," the man said. "Naked as the day he was born, and left for dead in a ditch."

"And you brought him *here*!" She seemed excited. "Why would you go do a fool thing like that? Who is he? And what kind of *trouble* is he in?"

"I don't know for sure. He can't speak common." Darry laughed. "Now go do something useful and get us some soup!"

"Are you crazy?" she complained as she poured two bowls of

soup. "We don't know anything about this man. Darry, I want him gone."

"He stays," the man said.

"There's no way I'm letting a troubled foreigner stay under the same roof as my children, Darry!" she said. "Especially not when my husband, your son, their father, isn't here to protect us!" She set the two bowls of soup on a table near the fire.

"He stays," the man said again.

"I won't have it, Darry," she answered.

"I said he stays!" The man stood and almost looked to slap her. She winced anyway. "I'll hear no more of it!"

A baby cried. "Look what you did, you woke her up." She scurried away to tend to the child.

Darry motioned for him to sit, and pushed the bowl next to him. When Darry ate from his own soup, he watched. *The man eats. I suppose I shall eat as well.* He mimicked the man's movements, filled the spoon with broth and mixed plants, brought it to his lips, and tasted it. Never before had he experienced something so savory and delightful in all his life. He happily enjoyed three bowls of the soup while the man spoke to the woman in hushed tones.

That first night Darry helped him into new clothes, and gave him a blanket to rest in the chair while they slept. He closed his eyes, but did not dream, and soon it was morning. The rain had stopped by the next day, and the world was bright and new. He discovered that Keeli had three children. One was a baby named Lily, while the others were twin girls he came to learn were Rose and Kelly. The girls had the forest in their eyes and the trees in their hair like their mother. They were twelve years old and at the edge of their childhood. They took an instant liking to him, though Keeli made sure they kept their distance.

He was set to work in the yard, and dug ditches with a shovel while Darry showed him how. That afternoon they took more soup, and the girls laughed when he spilled his glass of water. When they finished the ditches, the man took an axe and showed him how to use it to chop at a tree. He took the axe, and on his first swing the blade cut with so much force that the axe handle exploded into a thousand shards. The tree was cut clean through, and fell away from the house with a crash. Darry was so taken by the event, that he started to call him *Axe* in place of lad, and the name stuck. *Axe is as good a name as any,* he had thought to himself when he took the name for his own.

The next day Darry fashioned for him an axe with an iron handle to accommodate his strength. It was not long before all of the dead trees were safely cleared and turned to neat stacks of lumber. The efficiency of his work and the innocence of his demeanor seemed to please Keeli, and it was not long before she warmed up to Axe, and allowed the girls to speak with him. It was the girls who discovered that Axe was no simpleton, and if anything, was a genius. Rose and Kelly spoke with him to such extent that Axe found he quickly deciphered the language.

For three weeks he spent his days working the farm. He cut trees from the forest and built a wagon that he pulled himself. He built a fence around the house and the onion patch. He built barrels and crates, and helped both harvest the onions and learn how to cook them in a dozen different ways. He spent his mornings and afternoons conversing with the children and learning the language. By night he would talk with Keeli and Darry, and learned of their family and heard stories of the land, but he never once told them of the old man or his strange memory. All they knew was *Treefort*, and he came to take his designation as the place he claimed he was from, even if he did not remember it.

He learned their farm had once been prosperous, but the drought took their crops, and the bandits took their animals. Darry's son took a job as a laborer in Tansville to support them, but was not expected back for some time. In the meanwhile they needed to purchase supplies, and that required them selling their onions at market for coin. And so one night they decided they would all travel to the nearby village of Hopsdale on the morrow.

That morning Axe loaded the crates and barrels of their onion harvest in the back of the wagon. Darry and the baby rode inside, while Keeli and the girls walked nearby. Axe grabbed onto the reins he had designed for himself, and pulled the wagon behind him. Darry was the one most impressed with Axe's incredible strength, but had told Axe to keep the story of the bear a secret. Even so, the feat of pulling the wagon was second next to the skill with which it was constructed. Keeli suggested Axe must have been a carpenter because of both his knowledge and finesse when it came to wood, but Axe was not so certain. The methodology of building a sturdy wagon that could be easily pulled came naturally to him, it's true. But *everything* came naturally to Axe once he'd set his mind to it, and he secretly wondered what great purpose had been intended for him.

Was the old man my father? he had mused each night while he rested. With all his thoughts of the old man, Axe had no desire to go off searching for the truth of his past. Whatever his primary objective was, it was forgotten to him, and was meant for a man who no longer existed. He was Axe Treefort now, and with each passing day he found himself more in love with the kindly man and his family. His purpose was to see their farm prosper again, and do whatever he could for them. It was not to repay a debt he felt he owed, but because they were all he knew, and all he loved in the world. Axe wondered if they might come to think of him as family, and hoped that when Gerry returned he would be pleased with Axe.

He learned from Rose and Kelly how much they missed their father, and he felt sad for them. Axe even considered going to Tansville himself to fetch Gerry and bring him back to his family. *If I am as good with carpentry as Keeli claims, then why should Gerry labor so far away?* Axe thought as he pulled the wagon. *Wood in the forest is plentiful. We could build wagons to sell, and use the money for fresh seeds to plant.* He fantasized about the future, and imagined himself building a new house for them, while Gerry worked in the field, and the children played in the garden. Keeli brought him onion soup, and Darry told him stories about his youth. *I will be happy here.* Axe smiled.

They arrived at Hopsdale before midday. It was no true town, but more of a swelling of stores and residences where three roads met. Rows of the tallest and oldest wooden buildings surrounded a centralized farmers market that stood in the town square. Axe marveled at all the different types of people, and animals, and plants that cluttered the marketplace. They had him stop where there was room to unload, and soon they had a stall ready to sell their onions. It was not long before Rose and Kelly were annoying Keeli, and she thrust a small handful of copper coins into Axe's hand.

"Will you take the girls to that Inn over there and see they're fed?" She pointed to a stout building where three large red brick chimneys puffed smoke. "Help yourself to whatever's left. Have some wine, Axe. You deserve a drink after all you've done." Axe wondered what sort of drink wine was, but had heard it mentioned a number of times by Darry, accompanied by one of his youthful adventures. *Whatever it is, it sounds like it will be fun to drink.*

He took the coins gratefully. "Thanks." Axe gathered the girls up and took Rose by the hand.

"Don't let them talk to anyone," Keeli said. "They can be a quite a handful." She smiled at him. "Keep them safe."

"I will." He nodded to her. "I promise."

The appetizing smells of the Dancing Sheep tavern overtook Axe's senses when he entered with the twins in tow. The enticing aroma of a hot bowl of soup was nothing compared to the scent of frying bacon, roast boar, and fresh bread from the oven. Axe sat the girls at an empty table and placed his hat on the chair he'd laid claim to. He asked the twins to wait while he approached the stained oak bar to purchase their lunch. A dozen other patrons were scattered throughout the place, but Axe's mind was on food and not the men eating it.

A fat woman with black hair tied behind her head, and a heaving buxom, approached him from behind the counter. "Yeah?" she asked. "What do you want?"

Axe was unsure. He pulled the four copper coins from his pocket and placed them on the bar. "I want to feed those two girls a good meal." He pointed back at the twins. "And I want some wine for myself. Some of that..." He pointed at the bacon. "And whatever else these coins can buy me to eat."

"Such beautiful girls." She smiled sweetly as she took the copper and batted her brown eyes at him. "Are they yours? They have their mother's hair."

Axe had come to discover that he had short cropped blonde hair, and light blue eyes. Keeli had described him as quite handsome, but said he had the look of a Westerner. "The color of your hair might be taken unkindly by some," she had warned him. "Although Midgard is neutral ground, the sea is close, and many men in these parts are from the East." She gave him a woolen hat that covered his golden hair, and told him to wear it while they traveled to be safe. Axe promised her he'd be careful.

"Their names are Kelly and Rose." He smiled as he looked at them. "And they're my sisters."

Before long the three of them were happily feasting on the assortment of foods the sweet lady had served them. Rose noted it was more than four copper ought to have bought, and Kelly suggested it was because she wanted him. He wasn't quite sure what Kelly meant by that, but was glad of it none the less. Axe was awash in a festival of tastes and sensations as he ate his meats and breads, and enjoyed a flagon of sour red wine. He was too caught up in the fresh experience of eating his meal to notice when the laughter and mirth of the establishment died to a sullen silence.

"What the fook do we have here?" he heard a man ask somewhere behind him. The twins froze with surprise from the shout, but Axe was more interested in the way the wine sloshed so pleasantly in his flagon before each delectable sip. It was when the man said, "Arsehole! I'm talking to you!" and knocked the flagon from Axe's hands, that he realized they were addressing him directly.

Axe swiveled in his chair, and found he was flanked by two gruff men with black hair and blacker eyes. They wore leather armor and long daggers hung from their belt. They smelled of horse shit and both had scars on their faces. "My name is Axe," he said to the man who had been speaking.

"Does it look like I give a fook what your name is, Westy?" the man replied. "I just wanna know what the fook you're doing in my chair." Axe watched with distaste as the man coughed up phlegm and spit in his stew.

"I'm here selling onions, and I don't want any trouble," Axe told him. "I just want to eat in peace." *That should appease them,* he thought happily. *Now that they know I mean them no harm, they will leave me alone.*

By now the other patrons had made for the door and left. The man kicked out Axe's chair from under him, and Axe fell to his backside. "Well it's time you took your onions and got the fook out of here. I didn't put up with eight years of blood and shit to have no Westies in my favorite winehole, whether I'm South of the wall or not."

"We'll leave," Axe said.

"The fook do you mean by we? I'm only talkin' to you." The man twice kicked Axe in his side, and spit on him.

"Stop it! You're hurting him!" Rose cried out.

"Leave him alone," Kelly whined. "He didn't do anything to you."

The second man circled beside the girls. "Fooking Westy's prick ain't satisfied with one old cunt, so he takes two fresh ones for his own."

"They're my sisters," Axe said, as he rose to his feet.

"Bull fooking shit they are!" the second man said, as he laughed in his face.

"They're our sisters now, Westy." The first man placed his hand on his dagger's hilt. "Now go run to your onions before there's any more trouble."

"You hear that lass?" The second man grabbed Kelly by the arm. "You'll have twice the cock to suckle on tonight."

Axe reached out and took the second man by the arm. "Don't touch her." His voice was soft but his hand was strong. His fingers gripped into the man's bone and broke it. The man screamed in pain, and Axe took the opportunity to grab the man's dagger from his belt.

"He broke my fooking arm!" the man cried in anguish. Axe might have made move with the blade, but the first man unsheathed his own dagger, stepped behind Kelly, and brought the cold steel up to her neck.

"Don't you even fooking think about it," the first man said.

Axe froze. "Don't you hurt her. I'm sorry about your friend, but leave her out of this."

Keeli opened the door just then and rushed in. "Axe? I saw people leaving and I got worried." She turned and saw the dagger at Kelly's throat. Keeli screamed and tore at her hair. "Don't hurt my baby! Please..." she begged them.

The second man threw her a dirty glance. "Fooking Westy has a whole slew of whores."

Axe raised his hand out to her. "It's alright. Stay back Keeli." He smiled at the two men. "It's me they have trouble with, and not the girls. Right?"

"Put down the dagger," the first man said, "and she can have her whore daughters."

Axe held the dagger palm out, and slowly placed it on the table. The second man scooped it up in his good hand. *I can't let them hurt the girls,* Axe told himself. *It doesn't matter what happens to me, as long as they're kept safe.* "Let them go."

The second man gave Rose a push, and she ran into her mother's arms.

"Now her," Axe said as he motioned to Kelly.

"I'll let her go, I promise." The man nodded to his wounded partner, who walked up alongside Axe with the dagger in his hand. "When you're dead." He smirked.

The second man lifted the dagger beside Axe, and although he knew he could stop him, he dared not risk anything that would see Kelly harmed. *The man promised,* Axe told himself, and he had learned the solemnity of a sworn promise from the twins. Keeli cried, Kelly screamed, and Rose hid her eyes in her mother's chest as the second man ran the sharp edge of his dagger across Axe's throat.

I'm sorry, Keeli, Axe thought as the blood drained from his slit neck in sheets. *I shouldn't have taken off your hat.* The blood was slick and crimson, and it spilled over his clothes, the table, and onto the floor. It did not spurt with the pumping of his heart, but instead poured steadily from his neck until it was completely spent. Even so, Axe did not fall to the ground, nor did he lose consciousness. He felt the pain of the wound, and the fire and ice of his split flesh, and yet he stood still as stone, waiting for the man to release Kelly from his grasp. The hate in their eyes turned to fear and confusion.

"What the fook?" the second man took a step back, and waited in futility for Axe, the man he thought he'd killed, to fall. The man even gave Axe a push, but he kept his balance to spite him.

"Fooking Westy don't even know how to die proper," the first man said. He threw Kelly aside like a rag doll to the ground, and she hit her head when she fell. Keeli's screams raised an octave. "I'll show you how it's done." The man cursed as he lifted his dagger and plunged it with all his summoned strength down into Axe's heart. The dagger sunk two inches through skin and muscle before stopping sudden with a resounding clang. The man's arm shook and his teeth clattered at the unexpected jolt. When he pulled his blade away, he gaped in horror at the sight of his iron dagger's blunted tip.

Axe looked down to where Kelly had collapsed. Her wound was minor, and not much of her blood had spilled, but she had not moved from where she'd been thrown, and Axe knew that her breathing had stopped. He was not sure if it was rage or panic he felt in that moment, but all he could think of was helping the poor girl, and first that meant dealing with these two men. Axe grabbed the first man by the sides of his head and lifted him into the air. His feet dangled thirty centimeters off the ground, and he let loose a cry of mortal terror as he slashed his dagger repeatedly against Axe's arms. But it did not change his fate. Axe squeezed until the man's skull imploded between his palms like an overripe melon. When he let go, the man's lifeless corpse fell to the floor.

The second man dropped his dagger and turned to flee, but Axe would not have him leave. He took the overturned chair at his side, and threw it into the man's back, toppling him to the ground. It was only seconds later that Axe stood over the man, and seconds more before his neck was snapped, and he too was dead.

Axe rushed to Kelly, where Keeli was leaning over her with tears in her eyes.

"Get back!" she screamed and pushed at him. "Get away from her!"

"She's injured," Axe whispered. "She needs help."

"I've had enough of your help!" she cried.

Axe pushed Keeli back and knelt over Kelly's body. He turned her over and saw for certain that she was not breathing. While Keeli slapped and beat her fists upon his side, Axe pumped his hands on Kelly's chest, then exhaled hot breath into her mouth. He repeated the process three times, but to no avail. Axe lifted her up, placed her back to his chest, and pressed his fists into her abdomen. After a few pumps of his fists, a hunk of meat spit from her mouth, and she coughed as her breath returned to her. Axe looked down at Kelly and felt himself overcome with joy that she was alright. But when she looked up at him, with his slit throat and blood stained clothes, she screamed.

Keeli pushed at Axe to get to her daughter, and Axe, stunned by the girl's screams, allowed himself to be driven away by her. "Mama!" Kelly cried as she fell into her mother's embrace.

Axe looked around the tavern. There was no one else present save for the sweet lady who served their food. When her eyes met Axe's she screamed, and ran from the tavern in fright. "We should leave," he told Keeli as he stood. "Come on, let's go."

"We're the ones who'll be leaving." She looked at him with hateful eyes. "Come on girls." Keeli grabbed her daughters by the hands and pulled them towards the door. When Axe followed she turned at him. "Don't you follow us."

"I don't understand," Axe said. "I can't come with you? Should I meet you by the wagon?"

"No!" she protested.

"So I'll see you at the house then?"

"Don't you get it, you stupid man!" Rose was crying, and Kelly wouldn't look at him. "I want you gone!"

"But..." Axe didn't understand. "I have no where to go."

Keeli had tears in her eyes, but Axe did not think they were for him. "I don't know what you are." Her tone was as cold as ice. "Some kind of monster. I'm thankful for what you've done, but I won't have you bring a curse down upon us."

"I thought..." Axe swallowed the blood in his mouth. "You loved me..."

Keeli was shocked. "You're just some stranger my fool of a father in law took in." She opened the door. "And I never want to see you again."

"Keeli, please." Axe took a step towards them. "Please. I thought we were a family. Kelly... Rose... Don't leave me!" But the children looked up at him with fear and stranger's eyes. Kelly clung to her mother's side, and Rose, after a lingering gaze, looked away. Keeli and the children stepped through the tavern door, and out of Axe's life forever.

Axe took the two daggers, and whatever pouches the men had on their belts, then ran from the tavern. Villagers were already swarming to see what the commotion was about, and Axe saw armed men approaching from the distance. Amidst their shouts, Axe took one last look at Keeli and her twins until they became lost in the crowd, then turned and ran away. *What am I?* he asked himself, as he fled from the marketplace, and from the only family he'd ever known.

CLIQUE

"It's time," Marcus said as he stepped into the cabin. He spoke in the sailor's tongue but Clique understood him well enough. The man his father had sent to fetch him was graced with the brown hair and blue eyes of the Gulgari, and had their sea legs as well. Clique was not so lucky. All the training his father had paid for didn't prepare him for stormy nights at sea. Fortunately that hell was four days behind them, and now was no more than a painful memory. The seas would be calm from there on out, and Clique was thankful for it. He didn't want to trip and foul up his demonstration.

"Just a few more," Clique said as he dragged the whetstone across the metal of his scythe's blade. It was nearly three feet of slightly curved black steel that came to a wicked point. The inner curve was where Clique honed the edge, while the outer ran into a sword guard that Clique knew could catch a blade and easily disarm the man wielding it. With a final stroke, Clique stood from his bed, and set the stone aside. "Let's give them their show," he grumbled.

"Shouldn't it please you, m'lord?" Marcus asked as he watched Clique fasten the blade onto the end of its iron banded wood handle. "There is fame to be had. The sailors will sing songs of it."

Clique sighed as he spun the scythe in his hand and checked its balance. The handle ran five feet long and was curved in the center where two metal bars were fastened for hand holds. "It's not for their songs I do this." Clique groaned as he fit a leather cap over his uncomfortably long hair. He had been at sea for almost three months now, and had sworn off shaving on the boat after his first attempt yielded blood and curses. His beard was of no concern, but hair in his black eyes bothered him, and he wouldn't have anything tarnish his first public slice. "The methods of the Guild are not meant for demonstration, but home is within reach, and I will see the good Captain who has brought me here successfully entertained."

Clique pushed past him as he exited his cabin and made his way to the deck of the ship. "When we reach Cliffwatch," Marcus said as he followed, "I have been promised a ship of my own."

"And what will you do with this ship once you have it?" Clique asked with feigned interest.

"I mean to sit it in harbor until you or your lord father has use of it." Marcus grinned.

Now that *did* interest him. Clique stopped at the base of the steps. "Why?"

"Well, m'lord. I've always thought a ship would be fine thing to have." Marcus shrugged. "But after half a year of the seas, I think I'll enjoy a taste of Midgard for a bit."

"Well, if my father's summoning me three years early is any indication, I would expect we will be entering interesting times in the Realm." Clique sighed. "If it is for nothing more than a celebration of the twentieth anniversary of the peace, I will have it in good mind to make myself an orphan with my second slice." Clique laughed at his father's expense, but Marcus did not seem amused. It didn't matter to Clique anyway. Truth be told, after being among the Devilkin for so long, any taste of humanity, even the droll politics of diplomacy, would be as if ambrosia to him.

Clique shielded his eyes against the brightness of daylight as he emerged from below deck to a rustle of cheers and hollers from the crew. There were nearly thirty men on the vessel, far more than were needed to sail it, but numbers would help if they were set upon by pirates. Clique was not a devout man, and had placed strong belief in neither the Goddess nor the red eyed gods of his masters. Still, during the worst of those storms, he found himself praying to every god whose name he could remember. He may not have feared the prospect of pirates when he first set out, but each day the rough seas turned him greener, and he found his fear rising up within him. He knew his chances of defending himself in such sad state would be slim. The voyage had been fairly uneventful however, and with the green shores of Midgard visible from the ship's starboard side, Clique felt his heart race with joy. *Silver Forest.* He smiled. *The only pirates in these waters are good Gracious men, and I will be home by nightfall.*

Strung from the boom was a massive spotted brown and white shark. Clique marveled at the size of the beast. It was nearly twenty feet long and was hung by chain. Most of its head lay flat against the deck, and a stream of guts and half digested fish had spilled from its open mouth. The thickest part of its neck was wider than the length his arm. As Clique approached the monstrosity he saw that its fins had all been removed. "What happened there?" he asked to no one in particular as he pointed at it.

A sailor with a green bandana laughed as he walked up and patted the shark with his palm. "They're the best part for eating, Lord Gracious," he said. "Mullbo's cookin' them up, you'll see."

The Captain of the vessel, a man named Fryer, stepped beside Clique and admired the shark. He was as Gulgari as the rest of the crew, but was not a day over twenty. Even so, Clique knew his father was a wealthy merchant, and better still, firmly in the pocket of his father's influence. "Are you ready?" Fryer asked, as he produced a silver hourglass with blue sand from his coat.

Clique nodded to him. "I'll have words first."

"Whatever you must do." Fryer and the sailor took a number of healthy steps backwards.

Clique turned round to address the men who watched with faces eager for a show. "What you are about to witness is not meant for tournament or farce. It is an ancient and deadly fighting style designed for combat with armored men." Clique made eyes with each man and showed them his battle scythe. "With weapons like this, the Southern Devils once waged war against the ancestors of men." Clique smiled. "Now they teach their art to any with the coin and dedication to learn their ways." Satisfied with the gravitas of his words, Clique gave a nod to the Captain. Fryer showed the minute timer to his men, and made a spectacle of preparing to overturn it. The crowd was silent. Clique steadied himself and held his weapon in a readied stance. "Begin!" Fryer shouted as he flipped the glass so its sand spilled to count the time.

All at once the crew began to hoot and clap to cheer Clique on, but he did not immediately begin. Instead Clique closed his eyes, took a long deep breath, and emptied his mind. When his eyes opened, he raised the scythe high, and set to the demonstration.

On the first cut the blade passed neatly through the base of the shark's head. Its body was wider than the length of the blade, and the corpse didn't move at the force of the blow. Clique circled around and spun his steel in the air. The second slice severed the head, and now the body hung clean by the chain. His third strike cut the shark only a foot higher than its severed neck, and it swung loosely. Clique made no attempt to sever the flesh that had split, and instead circled the beast while slicing higher with each attack. His blade made a spiral up the body, and each successive blow knocked the shark asunder. Soon it was swaying as if in a breeze with each passing of the scythe increasing its swing. Cut by cut he coiled the slices around the shark's core. Clique wielded the heavy weapon as if a dancer. He gracefully spun his body in circles and used the momentum of the blade to his advantage.

"Ten seconds!" Fryer yelled.

Clique cut twice more along the spiral then slapped the shark with the flat of his blade. At the apex of the beast's swing, Clique twirled and with great flourish brought the scythe lengthwise across the shark. His black steel carved its carcass perfectly along the spiral, and the shark fell from the chain in a shower of dozens of carved steaks. Only the fish's tail remained hanging above.

"Time!" Fryer shouted, and the cheers erupted in a frenzy. Clique lowered his scythe and took a much needed breath while the sailors exchanged coins and shouts of astonishment.

Clique held the black scythe aloft one handed, and used his other hand to call for their silence. In seconds a still quiet overtook the ship. "Now if you really want a show..." Clique pointed to each man as his gaze passed over them. "Next time you might try dressing the shark in full plate!"

The whole of the crew laughed fiercely at his jest, and the merriment carried on from congratulations to celebrations. In mere minutes there were rum kegs tapped and wine bottles uncorked. Half the steaks were taken away to be roast and stewed by the cook, while many took the shark flesh raw and dipped it in exotic spices. Shanties were sung, men danced, and for hours the crew ate and drank and celebrated the completion of their long voyage. In the center of it all were Clique, Marcus, and their young Captain Fryer, who had braved half the circumference of the Central Sea to return with their grateful lord.

Clique ate well for the first time in three months. Much of the journey he'd spent in brooding isolation within his cabin, and for him that meant more wine than food. What little he did eat consisted of stale bread and hard cheeses, anything that was easy to keep down and staved off the sickness of the storms. His mind had been on the men he'd called brother for a fifth of his mortal life, and how he would never stand side by side with the eldest of them to receive the proper robes of his graduation. In all likelihood, he would never see any of them again. Never would he meditate in the Garden of Sylphs, nor climb the Tower of the Umbra and practice his forms beneath the watchful eyes of their inhuman red eyed gods. Never would he achieve mastery of their devilish arts.

I do not care. He'd finally come to the conclusion an hour before he told Fryer he'd core the shark. *I have sacrificed more than most men or devil can even hope to achieve in their pitiful lives. And with the spoils of my offerings, the Devilkin have imparted most valuable lessons. I will return to my father with far more to offer than the peasant magic of a sharp scythe against armored flesh. After all,* he thought to himself at the feast, *under what but the rarest of occasions will I ever even use my skill with a scythe?* As the first born son of the Lord of Cliffwatch, Clique knew that he would probably see little of the battlefield in his life. His family was quite neutral, even where the peace was concerned, and he would have his own men to command. Unless Midgard ever came to war, Clique knew he would only serve his House through politics. And so it was the sharpening of his mind and other mental disciplines that had concerned him most when he first decided to study at the Guild. Clique smiled secretly to himself while he ate a second portion of the seared shark meat with a mash of beets and potatoes. *My mind and my senses have been sharpened in ways a civilized man cannot understand.* Clique savored the meal with thoughts of his imminent homecoming.

His musings were interrupted by Mullbo leering at him from across the table. "Yes, what is it?" Clique asked between bites. The cook set a steaming bowl of soup down before him.

"I heard you never had shark fin stew." He grinned through his crooked teeth.

Clique sighed. "To be honest with you, it does not sound all that appealing."

Mullbo was aghast. "Oh, no! It is a savory delight that is considered a delicacy across the eight seas." He wafted his hands over the steam. "Can you not smell its inviting aroma?"

Clique set his fork down and pulled the stew closer to him. He did indeed find its scent quite tempting. "Thank you, Mullbo."

"Mullbo is honored his lordship remembers his name." The cook grinned most convincingly. "Now, eat. Eat up!"

Clique glanced to his left where Marcus was playing *bounce the copper* with a few drunken sailors. To his right once sat the Captain, but he'd wandered off and was nowhere to be seen. Clique looked back to Mullbo's entreating eyes, and took hold of the spoon. "Alright." He gathered some broth and a bit of the diced fin in the spoon. When he lifted it the liquid steamed anew with heat, and Clique blew on it lightly.

"I chose the sweetest meat for you," Mullbo said as he watched the spoon near Clique's mouth.

Clique brought it to his lips, and while he meant to taste it, he found himself frozen instead. The world around him seemed to darken, and everything slowed down. He remembered the months he spent in the darkness of the Underhall, and the memories of those dark masters' lessons seemed to force themselves upon him. "How can one tell which scorpion is the most deadly?" master Vaelstrykh had once posed to him beside glass cages of the creatures. While Clique looked over the menagerie of scorpions, he asked his master how, and naively expected an answer. Instead, he was told he must choose one of the scorpions and allow it to sting him. Whether he lived or died would be up to him alone.

The puzzle may have confused him once, but by then he was an Acolyte of the Three Aspects, and was halfway towards his mastery. It was not long before he stuck his hand in one of the cages with a medium sized black scorpion. It looked hellish with red stripes across its tail and abdomen, and it had enormous claws that snapped as he approached it. When he let the skin of his wrist get pierced by the scorpion's sting, he did not wince in pain, but watched confidently as it injected its green venom. When he pulled his hand away his master was pleased. "Yes." Vaelstrykh smiled. "It is not whether the thing itself is large or small. The smallest child or the largest man can kill you. It is not even in the way it looks, for the brightest appearances may be death, or nothing but a mere shadow of death. It is how you weigh the size of the scorpion's hands against itself. When the strongest poisons are used, it will become relied upon too heavily, at the expense of all else. For scorpions, small claws mean death."

Clique had come to learn the ways a man might die as intimately as the Captain knew his ship. Any scent, any texture, or any color could mean the difference between life and death. And yet, it was not a mastery of poisons and herbs that the Devilkin taught to Clique. The Aspects were as intangible as fire, but like the flame, their imbalance would change a thing. "Change causes waves," he heard another master whisper in the darkness of his memory. *And waves can be felt,* Clique thought. *Even before they hit.* Clique had a sinking feeling, and he knew a wave approached. A more intelligent man might have questioned the soup based on logic, but the Aspects were not simple tricks in the realm of thought, and unlike logic, would never lead to unnecessary paranoia. Clique knew that if waves were felt, then something, or someone, had made them, or will make them, no matter what.

"Is there something wrong?" Mullbo asked as Clique lowered the spoon back to the bowl.

Clique looked all around him, and took in the faces and goings on of all the crew on deck. Finally he looked to Mullbo and smiled. "You have some first, Mullbo. And tell me if you think it is not too salty."

"You want... You want *me* to try some?" Mullbo acted confused. "I tasted it myself when I made it. I *assure* you it's spiced to perfection!"

Clique pushed the bowl gently towards him. "All the same. I would have you dine with me."

"You *would*?" Mullbo seemed quite surprised.

"Yes!" Clique stood. "Sailor!" Clique pointed at a man balancing a copper coin in his fingers as he readied his next shot at the goblet. He turned to Clique's attention. "Get the good cook a chair and seat him down!"

"Aye!" the sailor responded.

"I'm afraid I can't stay, m'lord. There's more cooking to be done!" Mullbo protested.

"Nonsense, Mullbo!" Clique proclaimed as the sailor brought the chair up behind the cook. Clique leaned across the table, grabbed him by the shoulder, and sat him down. "I insist!"

"Well, alright then," Mullbo said as he adjusted himself.

"Here!" Clique grabbed the Captain's plate, flung the contents from it onto the deck, and slammed it down on the table next to the bowl of stew. "You'll want a bit of everything now! Some shark!" He took a serving knife and impaled a seared shark steak and slapped it onto the plate. "And some mash!" Clique spooned a large heap of mash onto the plate. "And some bread!" He took as many rolls as his hand could grasp and piled them on top. "No meal's complete without some gravy!" He poured half the contents of the pitcher and smothered the bread and mash with it. "And some wine to help wash it all down!" Clique grabbed a bottle and sloppily filled a goblet.

By now the commotion he was making had drawn the attention of a number of sailors. Still, the smile on his face muddied concerns of whether he was acting all in good drunken humor, or if something more sinister was afoot. Mullbo was ill at ease, but tried to appease Clique with etiquette all the same. "You are *too* generous!" Mullbo exclaimed. "But what the hell! Let the sailors get their own damn seconds. It's time for *Mullbo* to have his feast!" Marcus and a few nearby sailors laughed.

Clique smiled anew and carefully passed his gaze across the deck. Mullbo took a long swig from the goblet of wine, but when he gathered some mash on his fork and made move to eat it, Clique took a nearby dagger and stabbed it hard onto the table. "The soup, first." Clique stared at him.

"If it pleases you..." Mullbo set his fork down and stirred the shark fin soup with the spoon. "I don't think it's quite so hot anymore." He never broke eye contact with Clique as he lifted the soup to his mouth and ate some. "Mmm!" he whined. "I wish I could eat this every day." Clique forced him to take a second, and third spoonful. Mullbo savored every sip of it. "Are you sure you don't want any m'lord?" he asked after his fourth taste. "I think I've had enough. You *really* ought to have some. It's... It's..."

Mullbo foamed from his mouth, then fell from the chair stone dead. The sounds of drink and song died as suddenly as Mullbo, and soon the ship was awash with curses and startled lingering looks. Unlike the rest of the men, Clique's eyes were not on Mullbo. He scanned the crowd and found his mark. One of the crew seemed unsurprised Mullbo had met his fate, and when Clique's eyes fell on his, the man started to make his way past the crowd.

"Mullbo?" The Captain pushed his way out from a group of sailors and frowned at the dead cook. "What the fook happened to him?"

Clique pulled the dagger from the table, gave it a little flip in his hand to check the balance, then threw it past the Captain's ear. Fryer ducked out of the way, men drew their weapons, and Clique jumped onto the table and walked off the other side. Fryer had a look of hate and confusion in his eyes when Clique approached, but Clique strode right past him. Everyone turned to where the dagger had struck the wall of the Captain's Chamber. It sunk two inches into the lumber, and impaled the marked man's cloak along with it. The man first pulled at it, then placed his back against the wall in fear of Clique.

"Going somewhere?" Clique asked, as he took the dagger from the man's belt. He was a Gulgari, and seemed no different from any sailor, but his waves were the measure of guilt.

"I was... I was just," the man fumbled over his words.

Clique threw the dagger down into the deck, where it stuck with a twang. He pulled the serving dagger from the wall and held it to the man's throat. "Who?"

"I don't..." Sweat beaded on the man's brow.

Clique took a step back. "Hold him," he said to no one in particular. Three sailors immediately pushed forward and took the marked man by the arms. He didn't try to fight back.

"Please, m'lord. I don't understand," the man complained, but his voice trailed off to silence when Clique took hold of his left hand, and rubbed his fingers across the man's palm.

"Rough hands," Clique said softly.

"Yes... Yes, it's from years of the rope."

"What's your name?" Clique let go of his hand.

"Wodkins." He smiled uneasily as he sweat.

Clique grabbed Wodkins' familiar green bandana from his belt and wiped his brow with it. "There, there, Wodkins. Don't be nervous." Clique glanced at the third sailor who missed the opportunity of grabbing one of Wodkins' shoulders. "Grab his wrist." The sailor happily complied.

"Who?" Clique asked, but the man was frozen with fear. Clique firmly took Wodkins' middle finger on his left hand, and dug the tip of the dagger beneath his fingernail.

Wodkins cried in agony as the steel point drew blood and scraped bone. "Please! Please stop, m'lord!"

"Who?" Clique asked again.

"I didn't do it. I," the man started, but was interrupted by his wails of pain as Clique twisted the dagger into his ring finger.

"Who?"

"I didn't! Please!" Clique pushed the dagger so deep the man lost consciousness. Clique reached out his hand and someone gave it a goblet of wine. He splashed it in Wodkins' face and woke him up.

"Who?" Clique asked one more time.

The blood drained from Wodkins' face when Clique dragged the bloodied tip of the dagger across the length of his arm, and with it sliced the smallest of cuts into his wrist. "He never told me his name," Wodkins whimpered, defeated.

Clique took a step back and tapped the dagger against his own palm in thought. "Then what use are you?" he asked.

"No, no! I saw his ring," Wodkins went on. "It was an octopus with seven tentacles and the eighth in its mouth. Gold on silver. I'll never forget it."

"There, Captain! You have your cook's killer." Clique returned to his table and ate a large spoonful of mash while everyone soaked in the man's confession. "A pity, too! Mullbo was so good at his job. Dare I say, he even made it an art."

The Captain knelt by the dagger in the deck, picked it up, and frowned at Wodkins. "String him up!"

One man hung a rope while another rolled over a barrel. The two sailors struggled to hold onto a squirming Wodkins while they dragged him to his hanging. "How much did he pay you, to betray the Sailor's Law?" Fryer asked, disappointed in the man. "How much to betray your Captain?"

"It wasn't like that, I swear!" Wodkins pleaded. "He knew my sister and her children by name. He said he'd kill them if I didn't do it."

"Why wait all this time to kill the cook?" Fryer asked.

Clique snickered under his breath as he drank deep from a goblet of wine. Marcus stepped forward. "The soup was meant for Lord Gracious, who made the cook drink it. Might have even been Mullbo was in on it."

Wodkins was aghast. "Poor Mullbo! I never meant any harm to come to him! I had only the poison the man gave me, you see. And his lordship didn't take no food from the kitchen. The feast was my only chance." The two sailors lifted him up onto the barrel, and one of the men slipped a rope noose round his neck.

Captain Fryer sighed. "Hang him."

The sailors cursed and spit at Wodkins and cheered the hanging on, but one sailor in the crowd spoke up. "Don't hang him Captain! You'll break his pretty neck, and I want to see him dangle." That drew a number of hoots from the crew.

"Very well." Fryer frowned. "Hoist him then."

"No... Urk!" The rope went taught as a few men grabbed hold of it and pulled. The boom creaked ever so slightly and Wodkins lifted into the air. His eyes bulged and his fingers grabbed at the rope in futility.

Clique set his goblet down and spit. "Shit." He picked up his black scythe from the deck, and strode over to where Wodkins was having his life choked out of him. Before anyone could question him, Clique swung the scythe and cut the rope. Wodkins fell to the floor in a heap and gasped for breath.

"What's the meaning of this?" Fryer asked, legitimately bewildered. Clique wondered if the man found himself confused by something every day of his life. "The cook's death demands–"

"I know what it demands!" Clique interrupted him. "But unfortunately Wodkins must live." Wodkins might have thanked him for the kindness, but Clique placed his boot heel on the man's cheek and pinned him to the floor. "Don't worry, my good Captain." Clique unbuttoned his breeches and drained himself over Wodkins' face with a long stream of yellow urine. "He'll wish he was dead soon enough. My father's men have a way with their words." Clique finished and pulled up his pants.

"Cliffwatch! Ho! Cliffwatch! Cliffwatch!" The crow's man pointed and cried from his nest.

"Marcus!" Clique glanced at his father's servant. "It's time for us to pack."

"Yes, m'lord." Marcus scurried off.

"Captain." Clique stepped away from Wodkins. "Put him in a crate. I want to properly present my father with his little gift." Clique kept the green bandana, and went below to get ready.

When Clique emerged it was late afternoon and they were first entering port. His scythe had been broken down, and the pole was slung over his back while the blade was sheathed in leather on his belt. He wore the finest noble clothes he had, which was no more than an old suit of cloth and silk with the plain black and grey colors of his family. Cliffwatch was a great city and castle that overlooked the sea from the a height of over a thousand feet. A wide and deep cove dug itself into the rock cliff, and in some elder day, perhaps even by Ancient hands, the cliff itself was chiseled away and a channel dug to allow all manner of ships to enter the cove. Therein the cove was protected from any storm that might ever assault the cliffs from sea, and all that concerned men were the tides. The solution for this was a vast array of floating docks with a patchwork of ladders and steps that led to a veritable sailors haven built into the cliff face. Cliffwatch Port boasted a resident population of near three thousand people, even though the mighty steps that led to the city took near two hours to ascend without stopping. The port had room for a hundred large ships to fit comfortably, though in times of bad weather it would be crowded beyond reasonable capacity. While the Red Star had not yet set, hundreds of lanterns had been lit in the cove, and for Clique, it sparkled of home.

The ship passed between the Stone Gates and made its way towards the docks. As it neared its slip Clique saw the grey and black cloaks of his father's knights flapping against the light breeze. A half dozen men in their finest doublets and wools stood waiting for his arrival. "They expect us. My father must be anxious to speak." Clique knew it was no pleasure to descend and climb such a length in armor and sword. *I am his first born son, and after seven years, such honors are to be expected.* Clique smiled at the pleasantry. *It will be the first of many to be pinned. Thirty seven years is far too long for a noble lord to grace his life and have only two pins to show for it.* The Honorable Academy kept strict record of every new honor awarded throughout the Realm. While honors could be traded or given, new honors could only be awarded by lords or knights of a certain fame or position. Upon the moons of the Cat and Monkey the Academy would deliver newly crafted unique pins to those who had been awarded new honors. Each and every honor to exist in the world, whether received by trading, gift, or proper reward, could all be traced back to the event surrounding the honor, and to the person who properly awarded it. Such was the mastery of the Honorable Academy's pins, that they could never be replicated, and thus retained perpetual value. Clique now wore his two honors upon his left breast. Each held a story for their gaining, and each properly awarded by his father for Clique's actions. But that was a lifetime ago, and Clique was no longer the same man as he was back then.

Marcus set his travelers trunk down next to Clique with a huff and smiled. "I sent a raven."

Clique pointed at the crate that contained Wodkins. "Make sure that gets brought up with the rest of my things. I'm going to see my father straightaway."

Marcus nodded. "I thought you might." They stood there waiting as the ship pulled alongside the docks. "Be sure to look for me if you're ever in need of a ship," Marcus told him. "By all accounts, it should be the finest this port has to offer."

Clique extended his hand. "I will, Marcus." He shook hands with his father's leal servant who had been his companion those three lonely months at sea. "Though I hope it will be a shorter journey."

"As do I, m'lord. As do I." Marcus smiled, and with that he went off to speak with some sailors.

When the ship stopped, Clique stepped off and met with the group of knights. He came to learn the elder one, a man with grey eyes to match his old grey hair, was Ser Walthaus Shade. He had been appointed the head of his father's Honor Guard when Ser Rimolt, the knight he replaced, had died in his sleep three years before. Clique mourned the man when he heard news of his passing. *I wonder who else has died,* Clique thought while they escorted him up the steps. By the time they reached the Iron Gate, which led directly to the castle's courtyard, Clique was so tired he thought *he* might be the next to die. *I have been idle too long in a cabin.* Clique promised himself he would train more diligently now that he was on solid land. In truth, it felt strange to him, and though the ground beneath his feet was still, at times he could feel the shifting of waves. He almost fell twice on the ascent, but each time caught himself, and was grateful for it.

When he entered the castle he was beset by familiar smells, and all at once he wanted to go looking for his brothers and sisters that he'd not seen in so long, and rest in his bed that he'd dreamed of for so may nights on the ship. When he suggested he might visit the kitchen, Ser Walthaus, who had remained at Clique's side, objected. "There will be time enough for you to replenish yourself, my lord. Your father was insistent that I bring you to him immediately upon your return."

"Very well." Clique sighed. "And where might we find my dear father?"

"He is awaiting us in his solar." Ser Walthaus led him through those stone halls and stopped when they reached two wide blackwood doors. He remained outside while Clique pushed his way in.

The solar reeked of incense and smoke. The walls were covered by ancient tapestries, with countless shelves of books and scrolls. A small fire burned in the fireplace, and his father sat writing at an ornate desk. The windows that overlooked the courtyard and sea, as well as those that viewed the city, were both closed and shuttered. The light was nearly too dim to write by, and even from the door Clique saw his father's once black hair was now dusted grey with time. Clique shut the door behind him with a thump.

"Is that you, Henry?" Robert set his quill down and rolled the small piece of paper up. "Take this up to the rookery see it sent out right away."

"If I can remember the way," Clique quipped.

His father turned and looked, but his eyes seemed distant. "Who are you?" He pulled a dagger from his sheath and stood. "How did you get in here?"

Clique was astonished. *Is it possible he does not remember me?* "Father. It's me. Clique."

"Who?" Robert took two careful steps towards him with his dagger, but before Clique could respond, his frown turned to a mischievous grin and he laughed. Clique smiled too, and after Robert tossed his dagger aside, they hugged. Robert took a step back and admired the man that stood before him. "You're so old!" He patted Clique's cheek, and smiled. "You're even greying." He tussled Clique's hair with his hands. "And you look ragged!"

"I stopped shaving after the first day on the boat." Clique set his pole and scythe on a nearby table and poured himself some wine. "Where's mother?"

"She's at the Lookout with most of your siblings." Robert sat himself back down.

Clique took a long drink of the wine and savored the taste of it. "Most?"

"Yes. Samantha is in Braxton where she's married Lord Garton's son Harold. Felicia is in Blackstone pregnant with Lord Kenzig's child." Clique took another sip of wine and listened. It had been two years since he'd received word from home, and news of his family was well appreciated.

"Kenzig?" Clique asked. "Felicia is so beautiful. Would she not have made a better match for Kefka's second son? Their heirs would be four places closer to Blackstone."

Robert snickered. "The boy has refused to marry, and some say he's gone mad. Kefka's line relies solely on Vincent." Clique scratched at his beard. Lord Kefka was the head of one of the six Great Houses of the Realm, and was sworn to the King of the West. Their House controlled vast wealth and had at one time commanded a mighty army, but the accords of the peace demanded concessions by both East and West. Kefka dismantled his army, and his first born son Vincent was given at the young age of six to the wardship of Dameon Draven, then King of the East. Dameon died five years ago without heir, and his younger brother Harloque had assumed the throne. But while Dameon was dead and buried, Vincent remained ward of the Dravens at Aztoz Castle. Clique laughed at the irony of it. *One of the most powerful men in the Realm, and his peace has cost him both his sons. One to madness and the other to a life of Draven lessons.* The boy would certainly have had a proper education, but the Dravens were of the old men and worshiped the djinn, while the Kefkas worshiped Scientos. These opposing ideologies, in part, were at the heart of why the nobility kept up old grudges and made peace so unlikely for hundreds of years. For the peasant folk it was always just about blood and land.

"I leave for a little while, and you marry half my sisters away." Clique finished his wine. "What of my brothers? Is Evan here? Has little Kevin made knight yet?"

"Evan is at the Lookout. As for Kevin... He's near a man grown now, though still too small to handle any sort of plate mail." Robert gave a sigh and shifted in his seat. "He's been squired away to Envek Davenport's first born." He lit a pipe with a bit of burning waxed string, and puffed on it. Fragrant smoke filled the air.

"Davenport..." Clique went over the name in his mind.

"Yes. He was going on some polar expedition, and I thought it would be a good opportunity for Kevin to prove himself. It also strengthens our ties with Witchblood, and gives me close watch on their activities." Robert coughed and took drink from his water cup. "Susan opposed the squireship of course. She's hated Envek since she was a girl, and wouldn't have her son be corrupted by him, but I set her straight. His son's a good lad, and smart too. Kevin will stand to learn a great deal from him."

"I'd half expected to see mother at the docks camped out and waiting for my return." Clique refilled the goblet and sat down next to Robert in one of the plush leather sofa chairs. *I'd forgotten the comfort of home.* "Am I expected to visit the Lookout to join them?"

"No." His fathered straightened in his chair. Clique expected as such. He had not been summoned home three years early and sent directly to audience for a homecoming party with his brothers and sisters. Clique set his goblet down and leaned forward.

"What's going on, father?" *I will have my answers.* "Tell me."

Robert took Clique's goblet of wine and drank from it. "The last few years have been rough on the peace. Fighting's broken out a dozen times, and some *very* old blood feuds were reignited." He shook his head sadly. "The forced peace has become so bloated that everyone expects it to burst. King William and King Harloque summoned their banners, and amass their forces near the border. Some say near a hundred thousand men on each side."

Robert took a few puffs of his pipe, while Clique fetched himself another goblet of wine, since his father had stolen his. He was unsure how to take the news. "So then it will be war, will it?"

"No." Robert coughed out a plume of smoke, and Clique wondered what scheme he was plotting. "The situation has been dire, but my good brother has thrust himself fully into the spotlight as an ambassador for peace in the Realm. He met with the Kings' diplomats separately, and has negotiated a summit."

"A summit?" The pieces clicked into place in Clique's mind. *Neutral ground.*

"A peace summit." Robert said. "Davik suggested that Stormbreaker Stronghold would suffice as proper neutral ground for the meeting."

"It makes sense. Stormbreaker's upper hall is the most defensible place in Midgard, and each King would feel safe enough to meet behind closed doors," Clique remarked as he sat back in his seat. "But how would they get there? By ship?"

"No." Robert frowned. "East and West alike have been banned from having any ships within a hundred leagues of the Starfire Sea." He finished all the wine in one gulp. "They're walking. And with them walk the full might of their armies."

"They can't mean to!" Clique protested. He balked at the thought of two hundred thousand foreigners crossing the wall and marching through Midgard. "It's been over a thousand years since there's been an army South of the wall!"

"Oh, but they do mean to." Robert smiled just then. "One army South down the Cloak Road, and another East by the Wind Road. Each will camp outside of Stormbreaker's walls for the duration."

Clique nodded. "Yes. I can see it. Draven's men would camp by the bluffs and have the high ground. Tarnell's South by the shoals where they have easy retreat, and can fortify against counter attack. No ships, mean no undue advantage."

Robert was impressed. "It's good you remember your lessons. You'll have need of them soon." Clique sat up and his father continued. "I'm sending you to my brother. The Rat's moon is less than a fortnight away, and by its light two armies will be at the doorstep of our family's ancestral home. Davik has need of the skills you've learned. Tell me..." Robert gazed at his son. "Was it worth it?"

Clique nodded and smiled. In order for him to train for a period of ten years, the time the Guild demanded for each of its disciples to reach mastery, Clique was forced to give up his birthright. It was a strange price that was negotiated with the Devilkin ambassador during the petitioning process for entry into the Guild. Right to Lordship of Cliffwatch would pass to Evan, his father's second son, and Clique's younger brother by a year. Cliffwatch would ever be his home, but it would never belong to him. Such was the sacrifice he made for his training. In truth, Clique did not care. He only wished to serve his family, and if he would rule, it would be someplace else. He loved Cliffwatch, and all it had to offer, but Clique wanted to make his own way in the world, and to him, that would mean someday making a new home for himself. No doubt once this peace business was settled, his father would marry him off to some choice candidate. Clique was unsure if he'd agree to a union of any sort, but was not entirely opposed to the idea. He imagined he would have a family some day when he thought of the future, but for now he was only thirty seven, and wanted to put the skills he'd learned to good use. "It was an easy price to pay," Clique finally said. "Though some have already tested my learned skills and failed."

Robert was displeased. "What do you mean?" Clique told him of Wodkins with the green bandana, and Mullbo, but when he explained how he detected the poison, his father was not at all as surprised as Clique thought he'd be. "The devil who took you told me some of the things you would come to know," Robert explained. "It was said you'd be able to sense death before it happens."

"Not just death." Clique grinned. "A change in the Aspects can mean much more." Clique went on to tell of his inquisition of the man, and described the seven tentacled ring. Clique hoped his father might know what the signet represented, but it was unknown to him as well.

"I doubt it will yield anything more, but I will have this Wodkins inquired upon none the less." Robert grimaced. "I will not suffer an attack against my son... Rest assured, I will look into the origin of the ring."

"Yes, father." Clique knew the pain Wodkins would soon face, and cast him from his thoughts.

"Now go. I've instructed Ser Walthaus to escort you to Stormbreaker tonight. There is no time to be wasted." Robert stood.

Clique stood in response, and stepped around the desk. He hugged his father goodbye, but something did not sit right with him. "Why should you and Davik want peace?" he found himself asking. "Midgard would have nothing to lose, and everything to gain from any conflict the Realm might have. I would have thought you'd both be stoking the flames of war and putting Gracious forges to good use smithing steel for both sides."

Robert laughed. "You have a sharp mind, Clique. I have never doubted it, but your understanding of the Realms are antiquated at best. Peace is *paramount* to Midgard's future, and it's best you put your tongue towards nothing *but* peace from here on out. There is no telling what spies have infiltrated our lands with the summit so soon upon us. Our words are ever for peace, but yes, Clique, yes. I have cooked up a special dish that my brother will serve our guests. You may even be doing some of the cooking yourself." Robert patted his first born son on the head. "Davik will explain it to you in good time. Do everything he commands, no matter what he might ask of you."

"Am I to be his errand boy?" Clique asked, not altogether dissatisfied by the notion. His uncle had the most brilliant mind in Midgard, and was equally blessed with unparalleled charisma and ambition.

"No." Robert smiled a wicked grin, and Clique was taken aback by it. "Davik was to tell you, but you may as well know now. While you can no longer be heir to Cliffwatch, we have decided, my brother and I, that you will be given new privilege befitting one of your stature."

"And what might that be?" Clique's eyes shimmered with possibility.

"Davik's son is a boy of four years, and his wife is yet pregnant with another child, though the sex is unsure. I am giving you over to Davik's line. You are your uncle's heir now, and second in line to the Lordship of Stormbreaker Stronghold until more sons are born to him. You are to command Davik's Royal Huntsmen, and sit his council as Lord Chancellor."

Clique was truly astonished. The gravity of such an honor was not lost on him. "I'll serve our House faithfully, father."

"I do not doubt it."

"You will not be coming to the summit?" Clique asked. He now fully understood why his family was at the Lookout. *It is safe there should it turn to war.*

"No. There is much that remains to be done here. But, if the peace accords are signed, there's to be a celebration, and I will be there for it." Robert stepped back. "Now off with you. And tell my brother he was right. He'll know what it means."

Clique bid his father goodbye and exited the solar. Ser Walthaus met him with news that dinner had been prepared, though he must be ready to leave shortly thereafter. Clique set the good knight off to do his duties, and thought of future honors to be gained. Late that night, Clique, Ser Walthaus, and the five other knights set off on seven beautiful white destriers, which Clique believed to be the finest steeds Cliffwatch had to offer. His father's Honor Guard would only be bringing him to Stormbreaker Stronghold, and thereafter it would be up to his uncle to decide whether he would be given a squire, or have other men placed under his command. He wondered if he would even keep the steed he rode upon, as fine as it might be, and thought he might take a look at his uncle's horses before making his decision. After all, he was to command the Royal Huntsmen, and that meant having a fine horse.

The Royal Huntsmen were famous for fighting by horseback, and their seal was a sword and steed. They were a respected order that had existed since the founding of the Gracious House so many centuries ago. It was a group composed of the twelve finest men in Midgard, and the seat of their strength was Stormbreaker Stronghold. Though called the *Royal* Huntsmen, since Midgard was not a kingdom with a monarchy, but a series of provinces ruled independently by governors, they were Royal only in name. Lord Davik Gracious and his extended family did not own the land, but controlled three cities and two of the main ports, and with them the majority of Midgard's economy. In turn the Gracious Household provided security, economic stability, and an unbroken continuance of leadership to keep the governor lords in check. The Royal Huntsmen answered to no one, and followed only the command of the head of the Gracious family. Their charge was simple. The Royal Huntsmen were tasked not with war against any foreign enemy, but with the keeping of peace in Midgard and ensuring the safety of its citizens. War and thievery might lurk North of the wall, or East and West in the Realm, but in Midgard all would sooner or later answer to the Huntsmen. Their sense of justice and duty to the citizens of Midgard had over the centuries proved a strong deterrent to any corruption from within the local governments. Clique knew that by commanding such an order, it would not be long before some bandit or miscreant found himself on the other end of his black steel. He could already taste the heat of battle, and he hungered for it.

Cliffwatch disappeared behind them as their party traveled the white cobblestone of the Feather Road that rambled over hill and plain. *My lord uncle's castle is the most defensible place in Midgard. And whether by peace or by war, from its terrace will be seen either a celebration to rival all others, or the makings of a battle that will shake the very foundations of the Realm itself.* Clique smiled. *And I will be in the center of it all.*

In that moment, Clique felt himself the luckiest man alive.

HAVIK

Havik did not remember falling asleep. He didn't even know if he was dreaming, or if his thoughts were the memories of a man freezing to death in the snow. All he knew was fear as he once again marched alongside his companions towards the gate to the top of the world. Jhev was there. As was Brownbeard, his belly rolling with laughter at the jokes he'd often tell. There was Brackens, the grizzled Gulgari first mate, and Narvis, the kind Abreegan woman with skin black like tar and eyes like emeralds. There was also Jaxon, Horoway, Nimmet, and Flint, four stout Gulgari sailors who signed over with the Wandering Turtle. All in all, each one of them, even the woman, had been brave enough to make the journey. They were braver still for risking life and limb in the task of mining the ore. Each one knew that by being on the range their share of the profits would be ten-fold that of the other sailors who resigned to stay on the ship.

Also with him was Kevin Gracious, the squire recently appointed by his uncle before they departed Witchblood for Astermount, and the North. Though Havik was no true knight, as a lord of a noble House it was in his rights to have a noble squire. He had never taken one before, and he could all but assume his uncle believed that a man trained in the Litany of Honors might help to curb Havik's more entrepreneurial ways. A man in truth by age not deed, Kevin Gracious was sixteen years and looked even younger. His hair was black and his eyes black, just as any man of the Gracious family. His father was Robert Gracious, the proper Lord of Cliffwatch, though he himself was his fifth son. With no chance of inheriting Cliffwatch, and far removed from the marriage opportunities afforded his nearer born siblings, it was left to becoming a knight for young Kevin Gracious to gain his honors and rise within his House. Their family controlled the Southern Peninsula of Midgard, a vital piece of land perched between the East and West Realms. Midgard had no King, but was ruled all the same by Kevin's own uncle, Davik Gracious. Havik secretly enjoyed the similarities between their names, and knew it was because he was named for his mother's grandfather, a good Gracious man. How fitting that Kevin and Havik's uncles both outshone their fathers. Havik took an instant liking to Kevin, but treated him with caution just the same. *Gracious men are no fools, and he may yet be his uncle's cat's-paw.*

Davik Gracious controlled Stormbreaker Stronghold. That mighty citadel counted amongst the oldest and most envied of castles. Aside from the Barrows, it was the most impregnable, and had never once been conquered. Havik knew it was built by Octavian Greyson, the first born son of the Lord of the Grey. Over a thousand years ago he built the stronghold as the seat of his power, and with his first born son there began the Gracious lineage. Their House was not one of the six Great Houses of the Realms, but they were sworn to neither East nor West, and the wall they built to protect their lands spanned from mountain to port. For centuries they grew rich from trade. As in wars past, Midgard remained neutral in the War of Woe, though it fought its battles just the same. Havik's own House, the Davenports, were sworn bannermen to the Dravens. The fact the squire chosen for Havik was from a House far greater than his own reinforced his hope that his uncle truly believed in both his quest and his worth. The honor was not lost on him, though none was pinned, and Havik was certain his uncle plotted and schemed alliances with Cliffwatch and Stormbreaker, and the rest of the Gracious brood. *Kevin Gracious makes a fine squire indeed.*

He's dead you fool. They're all dead.

The ten of them made a handsome party of rangers, and each rode a garron, mighty steeds with thick hides and a penchant for the cold weather. Three extra garrons were brought just in case. They also led five drays, solid work horses that pulled two wagons behind them. All manner of tools and supplies had been brought with them, all bought and paid for with the courtesy of Lord Hubert Davenport, but money spent was of the least concern. Their voyage by sea had taken them three months, and they knew they were blessed by the Goddess all the way. When they needed wind it was there, and calm seas were broken only by mild rains. Deep Northern waters were known to them only for a few weeks before they spotted the shores of Fenria. That land was marred by harsh hot deserts and bore no trace of human life for as long as the Realms remembered. They followed its coast for near two months, a measure of time for the waxing and waning of the Silver Star, and watched the desert give way to mountains. The colors were first spun gold and bronze of sand, copper and oak of mountain, then grey slate wastes until all was white.

The marvel of the strange Northern lands was tempered only by the foreboding brought on by the steady disappearance of the Red Star. Each day they saw less and less of it, until when they left Fenria behind, they saw it no more. There the world was cast into a night that belonged only to the Silver Star, and the Dead Star, which grew in frightful countenance as if a living thing as they sailed further

North. Before the Silver Star was full for the third time, the Wandering Turtle entered the Sea of Secrets, and they found their hidden cove. The map his uncle had copied for him was worth its weight, and Jhev had sailed their turtle true. With fortune smiling upon them, how could each of the ten rangers not have visions of grandeur? *Star metal! That means gold! Gold! All the gold you can wish for!* Though Havik knew *all* the gold would be paid from Davenport coffers, and the star metal sold straight into Davenport forges.

All they saw in his eyes was gold, but in his mind's eye Havik saw the promise of *power.*

The gate to the top of the world was no true gate. The forests gave way to a mountainous ring that encircled all the North. It rose from the ground a thousand feet and higher in a jagged cliff, and was all but impassable. It seemed to them like a godly wall, as its outer face was sheer and unclimbable. On the inside the wall tapered down in a light curve. *It is like a castle. Easily traversed from the inside, and impossible to scale from without,* Havik once mused. *But what demon would call this place home?*

Fool! There were no demons until you loosed them.

The gate was no true gate, just as the wall was no true wall. Havik had made the jest of calling the place *Demon's Wall*, and Brownbeard, ever the jester, made such note of it that the name held. Even so, Havik preferred to think of it as a ridge wall. In truth the place had no name. There was just the gate to the top of the world, and the Barrens beyond. *A Demon's Gate for a Demon's Wall. Was it out of superstition that no one ever named this place?* he mused as they made their way to the gate. Havik did not believe in demons, nor ghosts, nor even magic. He was a noble lord, and was well educated in the greater truths of the world. What men called magic was truly the work of what the Ancients called Scientos. He knew of the latest mechanical arts that made clocks whir with gears and springs. And he knew that those who lived before the Doom had things of Scientos that would be a marvel to behold. It had been six thousand years since Doom took the world and broke the weather, as all men knew. Amidst the generations that braved the Age of Snow, and the line of their children who braved the Age of Ice and Sorrow, the mysteries of Scientos were lost. Only now in the proper Realms was civilization taking a foothold, and the veil of superstition and belief in the mystical giving way to Scientos and rational thought. Havik knew, as well as any man who lived in the Realms, that the djinn were all frozen. If ever magic was real, it was now as dead as the djinn in their prisons, the dead ice that never melts nor breaks. And yet, as Havik Davenport, the man who feared nothing, approached the gate that first time, his heart sunk heavy in his chest. He could not help but feel that if elder magic existed anywhere in all of Eldaria, it would be found there. In the distance, a wolf howled.

Fool! You were mad to brave that place.

The gate loomed before them nearly half a league across. It was a great tunnel that bore its way into the ridge wall and led with a gentle slope into the Barrens. The snow line ended here, and where the rock above met the tunnel, great vines of black moss hung hundreds of feet in the air. A pungent, sour smell clung to them, and Jaxon retched. Thick mist clouded the tunnel, and their path was often blocked by pools of silvery muck that bubbled and stunk of rancid meat. No insects nor other living thing was seen within the gate, save for mosses and mushrooms and other ghastly flora. Not one of them dare pick or even go too near any of those foul plants, save for Brownbeard, who was queer when it came to all things that grew. He claimed some were valuable and suggested a stop to recover them in bulk, but Jhev refused, and would hear no argument. No one objected. It took only a few hours from entrance to exit, but that passage through the gate seemed an eternity. Havik wondered whether this place had no name for need of it being left unremembered and unsung. *Some places are better forgotten.*

Narvis, the Abreegan girl, sung strange hymns, and told a tale of how the gate came to be.

"Eldaria will one day be as dead as the star above," she had told them in the common tongue. "Eldaria is both Mother and Father. She was born, and she will die. She has a navel where the Delvers dwell, breasts across her many mountains that milk the world with water, and here at the top of the world was her cock. Now she bleeds. One day Doom will come again, and with it her death, and ours."

Havik marveled at how little her Abreegan accent tainted her common. She was Jhev's choice for first mate when they had initially discussed getting a crew together to man whatever ship they would buy once they reached Astermount. "Narvis was a pirate Captain's daughter once," Jhev had whispered. "I say once, cause the bastard turned his back on her. She never told me why. Made her walk the plank, he did. Afterward she took the black robe for her own, and been a dark wizard ever since. She knows a thing or two about piracy, if you gather. 'Specially useful since we'll be having precious cargo and the like."

"There are no pirates where we're going, Jhev," Havik had told him in stern fashion. He knew that Jhev would soon protest, so with firm eyes he drew his gaze. "I want Donner Brackens to be your second." Jhev's heart raced and his temper swelled. Havik softly placed hands upon his good friend's shoulders. "There is blood between you, but I'll hear no more of it."

The memory of it faded with the men's laughter.

"This world has no cock love, but I've got mine right here!" Brackens grabbed at his crotch and gave Narvis a lude smile from his horse. "Come and take a look! Get real close now! It won't bite!"

If Narvis was amused, she gave no sign of it. Her tone was solemn, and her words seemed prepared, as if spoken to her first by foreign elders. "Where Eldaria's cock once stood, she now has only the Barrens. The Doom carved it from her groin, and the gate remains from where one of her hairs burned away. Perhaps I'll carve out your cock and make you like the Mother."

Brackens ignored the insult and pressed on. "What in blazes does a world cock look like, let alone one of its hairs?" he barked.

"It was a tree," spoke Brownbeard, his demeanor as sober as Narvis. "The life tree whose leaves once graced the Heavens. And it was no hair, but a mighty root that carved such a hole. Though some say the wall rose round it."

"Aye, and who says that?" Brackens whined.

"Some say it. Somewhere," Brownbeard answered, and with that they all fell silent.

No one spoke until they reached the gate's end. At last the tunnel rose up, so all ten of them, wagons in tow, pushed up a small hill and crested it together. The Barrens beyond lay within an indented pit dug into the ground as if scooped by the Goddess herself. From here it seemed like they might see all the way to the other side of the ridge wall, if not for the clouds of black smoke that lingered in the air, and the perpetual motions of a lightning storm ever brewing above those cursed lands. Here it was much warmer than before the gate. While the North was deathly cold, and the gate a moist hole in the ground, the Barrens were an ill tempered scar, red, hot, and wrathful. At times a terrible chill wind would blow from the sky, and freeze one's spit before it reached the ground. Other times it was as hot as the desert in day, with dry winds that seared cloth and kicked up ash and dust. The air itself there was toxic with fumes.

Havik's gaze drew upwards, and he saw above him the fury of the Sea of Heavens eclipsing even the Dead Star in the sky above. He knew the view was not altogether different from the other side of the gate, but here his perspective seemed changed. He could almost feel the weight of the Heavens themselves bearing down upon his shoulders.

"Here is where the world ends and the Heavens begin," Havik declared.

Fool! This is where Doom is born!

The plan was simple. They had made it this far with all of their supplies in tow, and that was truly the difficult part. Now they need only follow the plan, and in a few weeks time, they'd be on a boat back to the Realms, rich men. Horoway drew out the face masks for the horses and fastened them over their bridles, while Nimmet and Jaxon passed out masks for the men. Brownbeard took from the wagon a heavy jar and applied his paste across each of their masks.

"It smells like shit and vinegar!" Brackens complained.

"You can choose not to wear it, if you prefer, but you might find the stink preferable to the yellow cough," Brownbeard said plainly. Brackens groaned in complaint, took some on his finger, and smeared it over his mask himself.

When it came time for his own mask to be applied, Havik did not complain, and instead found himself pleased. *From here on out, this will be the smell of star metal.* Some paste was applied to each man's mask before sleep and upon rising, and each were given an ample sum of it. Their horses were always masked except for when they were watered and fed. The pools of water and worse were to be avoided, as was anywhere steam and smoke rose from the ground. Sometimes the Barrens shook and the rock floor split to release heat and flame. Time spent in the Barrens had no discernible night or day. Even the false day of the Silver Star was lost here in the circular valley below the ridge wall. Its light neither graced sky nor ground, but here the accursed dark light of the Dead Star burned brighter than anywhere in all of Eldaria. And yet, even within its unearthly glimmer, there was a shadow. Cast beneath the Sea of Heavens upon the center of the Barrens, there was a shadow, round, and wide, and dark. Not pitch and black like a Silver Starless night, but foul and tainted, with black ash for ground, while the remainder of the Barrens was grey, stained purple only by unholy light. They avoided the shadow by circling well around, and all felt the better for it.

In the two weeks they braved that place only once did they lose a horse to the flame. Horoway's garron roasted, and the meat smelled savory. Brackens and Flint argued over its rump and made crude jokes, when Brownbeard swore, and would let no man eat from its flesh.

"That horse is cursed!" the once jolly man had piously proclaimed. "Leave it to the Goddess."

Horoway meekly claimed one of the extra garrons and took it for his new mount.

Humor has no place where even jesters kill jokes, Havik thought grimly.

By then their wagons were laden with enough ore that the drays were having difficulty pulling the wagons across the rocky Barrens. The process of mining it had gone smoothly enough. Star metal fell from the sky, it's true, and while they were there they saw some crash not two leagues away. A great eruption of fiery death spewed from the gaping maw it left in the rock, and black tar bubbled and spit flames all around it. They were not there for fresh star metal, it would seem. The Barrens were pocked with craters from where the metal had fallen, but not all rock that fell from the Heavens contained their coveted metal of choice. Many were iron and other strange sorts of stone. In some places the rock was fastened as if it were once forged by man. Heavy sheets and girders struck from the ground like pins in a map. Some were even black with writing.

The Ancients leave their eldritch marks even in this lost place.

Star metal ore was distinguished by the silvery flakes found in the dirt surrounding its deposit. Much of his time had consisted of scooping dirt with a long shovel from horseback, and idly examining it for silver. They would walk in a wide vanguard, and when someone found the flakes, they'd shout and wave hands. Soon everyone was digging with their hearts in their mouths. The first few deposits elicited hoots and hollers of joy, but eventually it only meant hours of hard labor, followed by brief meals, hard sleeps, and more searching for silver. By the time their wagons were near full, every one of them was sated with glory and had had enough of their adventure.

You had succeeded. Fool! You should have left it be...

"It is time for us to go home," Jhev told him, as they shared some wine that night.

Havik nodded in agreement. He knew it was time to go, and yet, there was something which had caught his eye, and his thoughts were found to linger on it.

"My friend... Had you taken to notice those Ancient pillars we passed?" Havik queried.

"I and all of us. And what of it? The Ancients are no strangers to the isles."

It was a fair question. Large unwieldy pieces of Ancient metal were scattered across all of Eldaria. All useless of course. Old iron and steel not fit for weapon or horseshoe, and oddly unfit to smelt. It was no wonder the Ancient's remains were all rusted and broken and their mark on the world all but erased. *Poor steel,* Havik once mused, but he knew that was a lie. It was just that they had *so much* steel, even a poor man could build a castle. And a rich man, well, a rich man's steel was Ancient indeed, and only a precious few weapons that came from Ancient forges remained known to men. It was said of Ancient weapons that their edge never dulled. They were feather light, unbreakable, and were impervious to smelting or being reforged. They always felt cool to the touch, and when they came upon armor, would slice through as if silk. Each one was said to be worth a kingdom's price.

Havik's uncle owned two.

"Their spacing intrigued me. I've been plotting it out, and I think they might have at one time been corner castles for a great wall." Havik took a swig of wine and leaned in. "Look here."

He took his gloved finger, drew a circle in dust on the ground, and poked at it. "This is the Barrens. Standing steel can be found there, there, there, and here was the large one spied yesterday. It's clear they once connected!" Havik looked back to Jhev, excited with his words.

"A wall then. And a wall for what?" Jhev asked, unmoved.

"The shadow."

Jhev did not like that answer. He shook his head, and shifted himself uncomfortably. "No, Havik!" He passed his hand over the dust, and erased the map Havik had drawn. "No, it is folly and I will not abide it."

"We need not bring the wagons," Havik told him. "Stay by them near one of the standing steels, if you must, and I'll take any man who will not fear."

Havik could have gone on to say how he dreamt of home that night before. He could have described how in it he could not bare the shame of puzzling out the shadow's wall to his uncle, and explained how he left that place without ever investigating the shadow out of fear. Fear was one thing Hubert Davenport could not abide, and it was something even his own father had drilled out of him when he was a boy. "Well before my first inquisition, my fear of death was sated!" Havik had whined to his uncle in his dream, but Hubert was not moved.

"Yet when put to the mace, you buckled like a balsa shield!" Hubert laughed.

I have shamed my House, Havik had thought deliriously, as he threw himself from Witchblood Stronghold's solar, and fell to a watery grave below. When Havik awoke, his sweat pooled in his small clothes, and he begged for air and water. It was then that Havik was faced with his choice, and by the time he'd mentioned the shadow's wall to Jhev, the choice had already been made.

"Go then, and be damned," Jhev cursed, but they both knew he did not mean it. Jhev was not as fearless as Havik, a thing which they both knew well. He had captained the ship sweetly, and dutifully played his part on the range, but the Barrens had taken its toll on Jhev, and some of the strength was gone from his eyes. *Maybe it is only this accursed light.* A paleness had taken hold of Jhev's face, and he knew the man was frightened bone deep.

Havik's choice was put to the group. The sailors, Horoway, Jaxon, and Nimmet, all chose to remain with the wagons. Jhev would remain behind as well. Brackens would not pass up the chance at additional spoils or glory, and Flint, ever Brackens man since the journey began, elected to stay at his side. *He looks to serve him for advancement,* Havik noted of Flint. He and Brackens grew fast friends once they had entered the Barrens, and some small part of Havik was wary of a betrayal. Brackens could Captain the ship himself, and Flint could support him. Flint toyed with his daggers from the first moment Havik laid eyes on him to that very day. Flint was no stranger to steel, and his fingers juggled a blade with a master's precision. Even so, Havik was not truly the least bit concerned. *Only a fool would dare harm a Davenport,* Havik comforted himself, but a part of him thought they were all fools for making such a voyage.

They're dead! All dead! And you were the more foolish of them all.

Narvis was deathly curious as to the mysteries of the shadow. As soon as the question was posed she was eager to go. She claimed her order had no knowledge of the black spot, and that its mysteries and some of the shadow's ash could alone be worth the voyage. Brownbeard's own fear had risen, but he would not be outshone by a woman, and agreed to go as well. Kevin was ever at Havik's side, and did not even address the choice. He simply took his sword from the wagon and belted it round his waist while the others spoke. *Should it ever come to blood, Kevin Gracious will be leal to me,* Havik hoped. He had no reason to wear his blade in the wilds of the Barrens, so it was in the wagon too. A part of him feared some beast or denizen of darkness might lurk inside the shadow, but Havik reminded himself that monsters did not exist, and Scientos explained the mysteries of the world. *Still, there could be some stranger manner of life.* He struggled briefly about whether he should fetch his sword or not, but finally cast the thought aside. *Kevin Gracious is all the sword I need.*

Havik and Kevin, Brownbeard and Narvis, and Brackens and Flint, all left the wagons at the standing steel and pressed onward towards the shadow. It laid three hours away by a slow trot, and as they approached it a grim solemnity took hold of them. No one spoke, and no one smiled as the field of ash grew larger before them, and soon enough they were beside it. They came to a stop when Narvis unhorsed and knelt at the edge where dirt and dust met black. The shadow itself was not perfectly formed. It seemed to be a fine black powder that at first lightly scattered the ground, then grew thicker as it went further in. Narvis believed it would do them no harm, and ran it through her bare fingers to show the truth of her words. Narvis filled several jars with the foul stuff while Havik unhorsed to examine it himself. At first he expected it to be ashen, like burnt wood or volcanic ash. But when he pooled it in his palms and rubbed it between his fingers, he found it more akin to metal than soot or rock.

Black rust... Havik repeated the words in his mind. *The cock was a tree of metal.* All at once he imagined a tall tower that gloried the sky. As he looked up and beheld the sight above him, he thought perhaps it was a bridge of Ancient iron that spanned the Sea of Heavens itself and met upon the Dead Star. *Could it have been so long ago, the Dead Star yet lived?* Havik dismissed his thoughts as the fancies of a starstruck child. Scientos was the answer he had come to understand, and the distance between Eldaria and the Dead Star was unfathomable. *Although...* he argued with himself as he looked over the vast distance the shadow covered, *there are leagues upon leagues of it... If I knew how deep the rust was, and how far apart its center, a man could calculate the size of what once stood in this place.* Havik knew such knowledge would be the apple in the roast he meant to serve his father and uncle when he returned with his prizes. *Oh, how my cousins will be green with envy,* Havik gloated. *Mysteries and metal, a fine dish to serve.*

Fool! You will only serve them death, and the rest of Realm along with them!

"Gather your courage. I mean to walk length of it," Havik declared. "If it becomes deep enough that the horses can't tread, we'll turn back."

His men did not complain, and when Havik first rode his horse into the shadow, his mount stirred and reared, but with a few kicks and whistles Havik coaxed it forward. The shadow seemed to be only a thin coating on the ground, but it clung to it as if of some ethereal attachment. *Magnetism,* Havik mused. The base secrets of magnetic elements were not unknown to educated men, and though costly, magnets had their uses. Myth would have it that men once used magnets to know direction, but all men in the North could tell their position by sight of the Dead Star. In the far South, beyond Eldaria's hips, where that dark star did not shine, sea travel was perilous indeed. That was a realm of two stars, much as this place. "What kind of land is so foreign that even the accursed light of the Dead Star dare not tread?" Havik had once asked an elderly sailor, who in his life had rounded all the Central Sea.

"A land where men are not alone," the sailor answered, and with that puffed his pipe.

In the Southern most reaches of the Central Sea, the only stars visible were the Silver and Red. Apart from the Red at day and the Silver mixed between day and night, the Heavens were a veil of empty darkness. In the light of the Dead Star, the world was the realm of men, the seat of which were the proper Realms. But in the South, there were other things neither man nor beast, and it was in those places where men dare not tread that they made their home. *Delvers in the deep, and Devilkin in the forests. My place is the Realm.*

Fool! Your place is an icy grave.

Here though, the darkness was the very ground they tread upon, and the Dead Star's purple aura kept the scary things that go bump in the night at bay. Here the fears were men and beast alone. *And no beast would tread this place.*

Within half a day they were beyond sight of the shore. When it seemed they must be nearing the very heart of the shadow itself, the light wind, which was ever present elsewhere in the Barrens, died down to a vacant stillness.

"Even the air dies here," Brownbeard said with a sigh, but they had all thought the words.

"This is our Mother's wound, covered with the tears of the

damned," Narvis chimed. "Look how the lightning does not strike."

They all looked above at the abated storms, and saw it was true. The sky threatened, but it never lashed. Throughout the Barrens the lightning was ever present. But not here in the heart of the shadow. Here there was a strange calm that reeked of caution.

Narvis reared her horse and turned to address all five of them.

"In this place, no lightning strikes. No fires burn. No water falls. No wind blows. The icy chill of the North is well removed, and even the ground is dead. This place is a sacred crypt of holy import, bound beneath the unholy light of the Dead Star. In *this* place *nothing* has power, and we should pray to the Goddess that *nothing* will be found. All we shall find here are ghosts and bones, and the graves of Eldaria are best left to the dead." Wind or no, her hair seemed to sway with the intensity of her speech. "Let us turn horse and leave this place. You have your distance from shore to center."

After a pregnant pause Brownbeard spoke, "I say she has the right of it!"

"And I say she's afraid of a little dead cock!" Brackens snorted to lift the tension, but the joke was ill spent, and no one laughed nor smiled.

For a brief moment, Havik regretted bringing Narvis along, as he found her words unusually disturbing. He was sure even Brackens felt the fear, and was overcompensating for it with jest. But Havik would not have them run when he needed their hands. After all, his choice was already made.

Much to the disappointment of his companions, Havik reared his horse forward a step past Narvis. "Grab your shovels! When we reach its shadowy heart, we dig." Havik expected them all to follow, but Narvis would not go, and even Brownbeard was taken with disobedience.

"Bugger that!" Brownbeard chortled, as part his old jesterly self returned. Havik knew then that the man had reached his limits, and in making the choice to not cross that final line, had given in to his fear. Flint was ever his silent self, and Brackens seemed unmoved by her speech. Havik knew the prospect of buried treasure played at the greed in their hearts, whereas duty tugged at Kevin's honor, and he thanked the Goddess he would not have to dig alone.

"Go. Come. I will dig myself if I must." Havik pressed on with a trot.

"Do not go, my lord!" Narvis shouted. "It is unwise!" But he paid her no heed.

Brownbeard started back while Narvis stood and watched. Flint, Brackens, and Kevin hesitantly cantered forward. It was only moments later that Havik's horse reared and threw him from it head first. To the others it must have seemed as if he disappeared into the ground and was swallowed whole, for Havik found himself fall slowly as if through quick sand. Then, as if by some magic, he emerged into a layer of air beneath and fell a good ten feet onto a hard dusty ground. Havik wiped his head and tried to gather his wits, but everything was a pitch black around him, and the aura of the Dead Star gave no illumination. He guessed his direction by the sound of the whinnying horse, and made for it cautiously. The ground sloped up, until his head passed into the layer of black rust. He ducked down and shook his head instinctively, letting the dust fly from his hair, but he felt it pull upwards rather than fall over him as it flew off. *A layer of magnetism! Scientos, not magic!* Still, it was a clever trick to hide whatever lurked below, and it was frightfully queer that the rust allowed no unholy light. *I need a torch.*

It took a few minutes of explanation once he had emerged from the pit to convince his men it was safe to go down below. Try as they might, however, the horses would not be led. It was not long before flint met steel, and Havik lit the hooded lantern his squire had brought with him. The fire seemed dim, even though the wick was tall and the oil pure. The torches would not take to flame, and the oil, though flammable, would not light unless behind the heavy glass of the lantern. Brackens and Flint begrudgingly followed in the darkness behind Havik as they were both refused the privilege of holding the lantern. Kevin readied his naked longsword, even though there was no foe to be seen. *My squire is afraid,* Havik mused. *But I pray he will not drop the sword when pressed.*

Fool! You should have been afraid as well! Some things are meant to be feared.

The dusty rock of the ground tapered low and lower until they believed themselves to be several hundred feet below the black sands above. By the time the ground leveled it had become chiseled white granite cobblestone, which further gave way to a wide flat expanse of polished marble that lay two steps lower than the cobblestone before it. A thin layer of dust covered the floor. Each one of them, save for Flint knelt, and ran their hand across the surface of the marble slate. Faded beneath the dust was a fine marble pattern of veined silver and gold. The marble was a treasure, and for farther than they could see, it was the very floor itself.

"This place is a marvel," Kevin whispered. "Do you think there is a temple?"

"The Ancients did not build temples," Havik answered with a quiet certainty. "Their gods were here." And with that he tapped his index finger upon his own temple.

"What about the djinn?" Flint asked, and Havik was amused by the question.

"Djinn... Man... Both are their own gods, in truth," Havik told them. "What magic a djinni has, can be outdone by a man's mind when put to action."

"Men have no magic. Men cannot be gods," Flint pressed.

"That is so. Men do not have the powers of the djinn, but they have their wits to accomplish great feats. And what one man can do, another can do. When new heights are reached by one man, every man is raised in turn." Kevin, who had been listening, seemed satisfied with Havik's answer, but not Flint.

"Djinn are gods!" Flint exclaimed. Something about his tone angered Havik in that moment.

"Djinn are gods, *my lord,*" Havik said softly.

"Djinn are gods, m'lord." Flint smiled through his teeth. "Men can only play at god. No man has ever been magic, and no man ever will. What every man can do, any one of the djinn can lay to ruin."

Havik graciously consigned to defeat in the argument. There was no logic to be had with a true believer in the djinn. The Goddess and her love were as real as the stars in the sky, but the djinn were dead and caged, their magic forever frozen in the icy altars that littered the proper Realms. *Why pray to a statue, when you can pray to the Goddess?* Granted, the Goddess was not as tangible as an icy slab that any man could see or touch, but Scientos proved the right of magnetism, and that could neither be seen nor felt. Havik could feel the truth of the Goddess in his heart. Even as far removed from proper faith as he was, some did yet lurk within his soul. *Faith is a strange thing when misplaced,* he considered.

They moved onto the marble and clung close to Havik as they pressed on. The light of the lantern seemed to dim further, and it was so silent that each one of them could hear their own hearts beating. There they walked into an empty abyss that stretched out in every direction with only a whispering flame to guide them. The flat marble went on and on into the hollow tomb, and soon even Havik felt fear replace the Goddess in his heart. He toyed with the thought of turning round and declaring their search for naught, when they spied against the light's edge a crater in the floor. The marble circled, spiraled, and cracked around a pit of white sand not five yards across. It was not as if star metal crashed and cratered this spot, but the pattern of the spirals and cracks instead shined with the masterful skill of the stone masons that carved it. He marveled at the shape of the pit, and walked round it as he studied it closely. *This place is the heart of the shadow.* Havik knelt at its side, leaned over the white sand, and spilled it betwixt his fingers. To the shock of his men, Havik even tasted it.

"Salt," he declared. "It's only salt."

"What's that there?" Brackens asked, and pointed. When he heard the words, Havik's hairs stood on end, and he felt the fear pass through him.

They all saw it. *What is that?* Havik wondered as he inched over the sand.

It is Doom, you fool! You should have left it there as Narvis said!

There, nestled in the sea of salt, was a black orb the size of a pumpkin. Havik's mind raced, and he found himself holding his breath as he cautiously approached it.

Brackens fearlessly knelt and picked it up amidst a chorus of gasps.

"It's lighter than it looks, and it looks like a giant hazelnut," Brackens said. "Only black with age."

Havik and Kevin alike gaped in awe as Brackens shook it beside his ear, and shrugged. Havik passed the lantern to Kevin, and Brackens handed the orb over. The nut was smooth and seemingly made of shell. There was no seam, nor stem, and when he shook it to his ear as Brackens had, he neither felt nor heard anything shake inside.

Brackens bent over and filled a large empty jar with salt. "This will fetch a fine price," he muttered. "Spice your soup with Eldaria's cock, m'lords? Only fifty doubloons a rattle!"

Havik's thoughts were lost upon the curiosity in his hands, but at the mention of soup his stomach growled and his mouth watered. He was thirsty as well. *Had it always been so hot and dry in this fell crypt?* he wondered. *How long have we been down here?* When he reached for his wineskin and it was not there, he made his decision. Whatever they might seek to find in this forgotten place, it was now in their possession, and so it was time to leave.

He wrapped the nut in a bundle of cloth and passed it to off to Brackens. *Better him sated with the treasure than my squire without a sword in this place.* Not that Havik expected any duplicity from his men, but they were far from the Realms and beyond the influence of any House. Even the smallest caution was a token consolation in such places. *A Davenport trusts no one, but relies on the honor of dutiful men.* He could trust Kevin's blade as he'd seen his skill with it first hand in practice. The boy was small, but that could be always a virtue in sword play.

Brackens let the salt jar hang from his belt, took the nut with a grim smile, and held it close like a newborn mother might cradle her babe. The four of them left the crypt back the way they'd come, and made haste through the darkness. The trip out seemed shorter, and they were all relieved when they broke through the ceiling of black rust and saw Narvis with their horses nearby.

No one spoke as they mounted up, but Narvis did not once avert her gaze from Havik's eyes. He briefly wondered whether it might be best to keep what they had found a secret from the others. Brackens was his man, and Flint, Brackens. Kevin was his squire and would not be a concern to the crew. Still, this woman knew strange things of this place and more, and what Havik knew, was that *a wise lord hears the counsel of his men.* Narvis was not a man, though, and wore strange robes. Somehow that unsettled him. Finally, with a soft glance to Narvis, and a hard look to Brackens, Havik kicked his garron and rode forth.

The air seemed to chill as they left the heart of the shadow, and as the shore of the shadow sea came within sight, Havik felt his own heart soar. Some part of him felt as if he were fleeing his fears and retreating from the dark as a child might run from a stranger. He rationalized it as a need for home. He, like everyone else in his party, was sick of that bedeviled land. Much were the prizes that awaited for him at the end of his journey, and he knew he was eager to taste the fruits of his victories. But deep within, Havik truly knew he was afraid. *What is it?* The words repeated half a hundred times in the hours he raced his steed. *Brownbeard will know.* And he held to that thought.

When they came near the shore where rust met sand, they discovered Brownbeard had fetched the others. Their horses, the laden wagons, as well as Jhev, Jaxon, Horoway, Nimmet, and Brownbeard all waited at the shadow's edge. *They are eager for home as well.*

Havik and his four followers slowed as they reached the shore. Havik came to a stop and dismounted. His boots sunk inches into the black rust. Brownbeard stood at the edge upon sand. For half a second it looked as if he'd make a jest, but when he saw Havik's face, Brownbeard frowned. "What did you find, my lord?" the once jester solemnly inquired.

Havik turned back and gave Brackens an icy stare. "Go ahead. Show the man what we found."

The fear was visible on the faces of all who watched as Brackens unhorsed, took the satchel from its pack, and cautiously approached. He gently unwrapped the covering as he walked, and soon revealed the black orb for all to see. The shadow's rust seemed to quiver about their feet with excitement as the unholy light of the Dead Star fell upon the orb, but Havik was certain it was only his fear poisoning his senses. *I will not fear,* he resolved. *A wind takes hold and nothing more.* But the way the rust loosed from its magnetic chains and flew upwards around them troubled him. The moment passed as Brackens crossed the threshold of the shadow's edge to tread on ordinary sand. He stood now beside Brownbeard, and all at once the rust seemed to settle.

Everyone looked to Brownbeard for answers then, as he was known to be familiar with all manner of plants, but no immediate explanation for the object came. The man took it in his hands and puzzled over its shape and shell. His eyes were not marked with familiarity for the thing.

"It feels like a shell of some kind," he declared.

"Aye, that's what I said," remarked Brackens. "Like a big nut."

Brownbeard scratched the shell with his fingernail, held the orb to his nose, and sniffed. "It has an earthly aroma." Brownbeard wrinkled his forehead.

"In what manner was it found?" asked Narvis, and all looked to her.

"In a bed of salt," Havik answered before Brackens spoke, "at the heart of the shadow's shadow, hidden in the dark, lay a field of flat marble. In its bosom was dug an ornate carved pit. Filled with white salt, that thing sat in the crux of it."

"A carved pit?" Narvis inquired.

"Yes, it was most carefully shaped and unusual to behold. Art or altar." Havik nodded, wondering what the import of it was.

"The carvings... Can you draw them for me?" she asked.

By this time the rest of them had begun to back away from Brownbeard, all satisfied with their close look at the thing. Kevin and Flint unhorsed and went to the wagons. Havik took a dagger from his sheath, crossed the threshold of the shadow's edge, and knelt to draw in the sand. Narvis followed close by. Havik drew the circle first, then added its eight spiky cracks. They were eight jagged fissures that forked out from the center. Each evenly spaced apart, they were broken and pierced by eight spiral tendrils that wrapped altogether around eight carved diamonds crowning one side of the pit. As he drew in the sand a gloom overtook Narvis' pretty face. Havik was troubled by her concern. *They are just shapes in sand.*

"I know this," she said, and Havik waited for her to say more. Her finger traced the circle. "Here is our Mother." She passed her hand over the eight cracks. "These are eight veins, that give her life." She pointed at the spirals. "These the eight winds that carry her life to all creation."

"And the diamonds?" Havik found himself asking, more curious than he ought to be of her savage mysticism. *This is an Ancient place, and old stories may yet hold grains of truth, or treasure.*

She pointed last at each of the diamonds. "The eight colors."

"Colors?"

"The colors of magic," she said, and with that used her palm to scatter the picture in the sand.

Havik was unsatisfied with the answer. "And what are *those* for?" he pressed.

"They are not *for* anything... They *are* everything." Her tone was soft and stern. "All that is, all that was, and all that ever will be, are of the color. Whether a thing is one, or some, or all colors together, no thing can be without color. When one color leaves a thing another takes its place."

"What does that even mean?" Havik complained. "Speak plainly."

Narvis took his hand with her own, and placed a leaf from her pouch upon his palm. "What do you see here?"

"A leaf." Havik answered.

"And what color is it?"

"It is green."

"You are looking with your eyes." She pouted. "Look with your heart."

Havik did not understand, but he puzzled it out in his head. "It is the color of the forest?"

Narvis was pleased. "Yes. And when the leaf is being burned to cook your meal. What color?"

Havik knew the game then. "The color of fire."

"And when the fire has left it, what then?"

"The color of ash," Havik answered proudly, but Narvis' disapproval was clear to see.

"No. It is still the color of the forest. You cannot change the nature of a thing. Fire was added to the leaf, and fire taken away. It is still the same color as the leaf."

"But it's no longer a leaf, it's ash," Havik pointed out.

Narvis smiled, and Havik believed she enjoyed feeling the teacher for once, whereas much of her life she must have been a student of her order.

"The leaf is born in ash," she said. "Fire has darkened it, so to again *appear* the leaf, it must be lightened. And how so?"

Havik understood. "With the color of water."

Basic chemistry, Havik concluded. By colors she was referring to the elements. *And what colors must I mix to turn lead into gold, pray tell?* he might have asked her, but thought the better of it. She took herself quite seriously, and such jests were best left outside the Barrens. Still, her esoteric nature held some fascination for Havik. The arcane teachings of her occultic order, whatever the black robes might be, seemed to have a unique and valuable perspective. She was quick witted, beautiful, and better at a blade than some of the mercenaries he'd employed over the years. All at once Havik felt she was a wise choice to bring so far North. He decided then to greatly reward her once they returned to the Realm. *Perhaps I will offer her white robes to replace her black ones, and name her priestess.* Havik knew that should he ever come to inherit a castle, no female would be able to sit his small council without a proper title. Havik would need people to rely on after this was all over, and he could count those he wanted on one hand. It began and ended Brownbeard.

Jhev will be off somewhere rebuilding his empire, and I'll be in need of counsel. I mean to keep one wizard. Why not keep two? Havik knew their adventure together would bind them close, and he would have further use of both of them. Brownbeard found his best niche as jester, and once Havik had rewarded him a lordship for his service, that would be *lord jester,* and no one would question his place. For Narvis the path was titled *priestess,* and was something he could bestow upon her himself by lordly right. *I hope she's not forced to wear those dreadful rags, and won't object changing them out for some nice sparkly white ones. She'd look quite the picture, her gown the color of virgin snow and her face obsidian shadow. Oh how my father would protest!*

All this considered, Havik could see why Jhev had suggested her for first mate. Havik *needed* Donner Brackens at his side, however. Jhev had been made to see that by the gravitas of Havik's words alone, and he was glad Jhev did not press the argument further. Brackens, once a first mate, had killed one of Jhev's Captains those years past when Jhev still had a fleet. The Captain had been Jhev's cousin through marriage, but the death was a clean and proper duel in Gulgari fashion. Jhev hated the man, but did not know the half of it. Havik had sworn to tell no one, not even Jhev, the truth. *Brackens is an O'Brien spy,* Havik forced himself to remember. After the duel, Brackens became Captain, took the ship and crew for his own, and left Jhev's fleet. Havik found it suspicious that soon thereafter all Jhev's ships were lost to piracy. *Some O'Brien plot no doubt. I must keep him closer than the others.*

Havik could take no credit for the ploy of bringing him along. The idea remained his uncle's. Havik could not puzzle out the tactical advantage of allowing an O'Brien spy to be part of his journey, and he could not help but resent his uncle for leaving him no choice in the matter. Havik had not wanted espionage to play any part of the voyage, let alone have to deal with a spy for a first mate. No doubt Jhev prayed each night that Brackens wouldn't challenge him to a duel in a repeat of the past. Havik wouldn't have allowed that to happen, anyway. Still, Brackens was more Captain than Jhev. This voyage Jhev wore the hat, but Brackens had crew and ship back home while Jhev had neither one. *That will soon change,* Havik had once thought. *A Captain's share outweighs first mate by five to one. Brackens might buy himself ten more ships, but Jhev will gain an Admiralcy.*

The first month of the journey Havik considered whether he might ignore his uncle's commands and try to turn Brackens' coat, but that was very risky. *Best not play your cards too soon. The journey home is the more dangerous leg.*

Fool! They're all dead! And soon, you will be too.

Havik cast the thought aside and found his mind returning in the reflection of Narvis' eyes.

"If you are so wise that you see in color, dear lady," Havik remarked. "Then what color, pray tell, is that?" And with his finger, he pointed at the nut, which Brownbeard was using his shirt to polish.

"*No* color," she whispered, and Havik felt the fear flow through him once more. "It should be returned to the shadows from whence it came."

Fool! You should have listened to her! That was the time to act! And now, it is too late.

But instead, Havik turned away. *A wise lord listens to the counsel of his men,* he remembered, *all his men.*

"So what *is* the thing, Brownbeard?" he shouted.

Brownbeard handed the black orb to Brackens, who had never left the thing's side. "A nut, most like."

"I *told* you it was a nut, m'lord!" Brackens proudly exclaimed. "And I'm no bleeding wizard."

Havik strode forward and placed a hand upon Brackens' shoulder. "No one doubts your wisdom, Donner." He looked to Brownbeard. "What do you make of this... nut?"

The jester scratched at his head through his raggedy brown hair, and shrugged. "Hard to say for certain, my lord. Only way to know for sure would be we treat it like any other nut."

"And how's that?" Havik asked.

"We crack it open..." Brownbeard answered.

"And see what's inside," Havik finished.

COLLIN

Collin rubbed the sleep from his eyes. He adjusted his sword belt and fidgeted with his doublet while he waited outside the door. He was quite relieved when it finally opened, and Amy stepped out. Even at such an early hour she looked as beautiful to him as ever. Her eyes were red like starset, and her hair even redder. "She's ready for you, Lord Commander."

"Please, Amy, you can address me as Collin." He smiled to her and said the words as he had every day that week. Amy was Keira's new bed servant for the final months of the pregnancy, and it was clear that she was still adjusting to being surrounded by nobility. She was fresh from Starcrown Cathedral where she'd been trained by priests in special healing arts. *Only the best for Lord Gracious,* he quipped to himself. Collin had become all too aware of his lordship's eccentricities and extravagant tastes. Still, the four years he'd spent at Stormbreaker Stronghold since Lady Keira's marriage to Davik Gracious had been the happiest of his life. Keira was happy here, and for Collin, that meant the world to him.

"Yes, my lord. I mean, yes Collin." She curtsied and stepped out of the doorway.

Collin nodded his head politely and entered his lady's bed

chamber. Keira sat by a tall silver mirror combing her long and lustrous red hair. Her blue and grey silk dress shimmered by the light of the hanging lamp. *O'Brien colors today,* Collin mused. Keira was always quite beautiful, but the glow she gained as she approached the birthing of her children made her radiant to behold. Charles, the four year old little lord, was fast asleep in his bed, but his younger sister Keira, a tiny three year old bottle of lightning, was already awake. She hopped up from the table where she played with her bowl of porridge and sprinted into Collin's arms. "Collin!"

"My lady!" He took her under her arms and lifted her playfully into the air. "And what have you got planned for this morning?"

"Keira and her brother will be joining me in the gardens today." Keira set her brush down and stood. "Keira go eat your oatmeal. Amy, would you see to it that Charles is dressed and fed?"

"Yes, my lady." Amy gathered up little Keira and brought her back to the table.

"Collin, would you walk with me?" Keira took him by the arm and led him outside onto the terrace. It was still dark outside and the Red Star was but the mere hint of fire on the black horizon. On this side of the upper castle the harsh wind of the sea was blocked by hundreds of feet of stone. The most pleasant of light winds blew and the wandering torches and lanterns in the courtyard far below seemed like fireflies to them. They stood for a minute in peaceful silence and took in the view.

"My lady, is there something special you require of me?" It was unusual for him to be called so early, though he knew that day was far from ordinary. He was expected to meet with Lord Gracious and his nephew that morning, and had also been told to summon the Royal Huntsmen for the occasion. The order had been given nine days ago, and his men had been gathered from the four corners of Midgard and readied. They'd have come anyway in anticipation of the upcoming summit, but would not have been expected for another week. Collin wondered if the reason for his calling to her side had something to do with their early state of readiness. "If it's about the summit?"

Keira smiled. "Yes, Collin. That's exactly what it's about."

"The Royal Huntsmen are at your disposal my lady." He stood to attention for her. "If there's anything we might do for you, simply name it, and it shall be done." Collin took immense pride in the fact he'd been named Lord Commander of the Royal Huntsmen, and while it was in no small part due to his noble birth, such an honor would never have been afforded to a man who could not handle the responsibilities of command. Collin O'Brien was fourth in line for Lordship of the Barrows, one of the most important castles in the Realm. He was the second born son of Patrick O'Brien, whose father Ronan was the head of the O'Brien family, one of the six Great Houses of the Realm. Collin's father Patrick was first in line, followed by his elder brother Liam, and Liam's son. Keira was Ronan's only niece by way of his sister Mary. Since the lineage of father to son passing would ultimately give the Barrows to Collin's elder brother, it fell to Collin to seek some other way to serve his House. He elected not to join the Honorable Academy, as he felt no call to the responsibilities of a proper knight, and at the young age of eighteen was unsure of what path to take in life.

The answer came to him when marriage was made between Keira O'Brien and Lord Davik Gracious. The joining of one of the three Great Houses of the East with the leader of Midgard was a bold political move. There had been some bad blood between the O'Briens and Midgard since the Battle of the Bridge almost forty years prior, and an unconventional marriage joining the Houses would finally put the matter to rest. There were and always had been six Great Houses and two Kings for the two Kingdoms of the Realm.

Tarnell, Kefka, and Brae stood for the West, while Draven, O'Brien, and Warne stood for the East. The Kingdoms stood for more than three millennia, but Midgard was carved out barely a thousand years ago. In all this time the bloodlines of the Great House's highest nobility never mixed with any outside of the six. But the past few decades had unsettled the balance of power in the Realm, and it was clear that Midgard was a rising star at the center of the civilized world. Far removed from the wars that plagued the Kingdoms, their culture had flourished and prospered, and the marriage could only serve to strengthen the security of the O'Brien name and heritage. Collin spoke with his grandfather, and in the sight of the three djinni of the Barrows, swore a sacred oath to serve Keira in all things. From then on, he would protect her and her children while she made a foreign land her home. Collin knew such service would last the remainder of his life, save only if Keira and her children died before him, and Collin pledged to never to allow such a thing happen. He would gladly die for his cousins and his House, and she knew it.

"It is not your Huntsmen I need." She smiled at him. "It is you Collin."

He nodded. "What would you have of me?"

"As you know, in one week's time the summit will be held." She sat down on one of the pillowed chairs beneath the terrace's purple awning. "Both King and Queen of West and East will be staying in the upper castle. West will stay in the Silver tower, and East in the Red tower, with us. The Queen of the East is our aunt, as you well know, and she has stayed there before. Each King also brings the head of their Honor Guard for protection, so it will be six foreign dignitaries in total that will sit the solar during the summit." Keira motioned for Collin to sit down and he obliged her. "My husband and I will sit at the table, and with us are allowed one man for our counsel, and two blades to counter their two knights."

"Yes, my lady." Collin smiled. "It would only be proper to enforce the peace, and keep the knights from coming to blows with each other. Ultimately the Kings place their lives in the hands of our House Guard. It's they who will be tasked with defending the inner castle from any that might choose to disrupt the summit. But the danger is not from some unknown outside force. It is each man sitting across the table with generations of blood spilt between them. I know the risks well."

"The Royal Huntsmen's Lord Commander holds the honor of sitting the summit, with one chosen sword beside him." Keira smiled.

"Yes, my lady. I know. We voted and have chosen Ser Ringley for the task." Collin was preparing himself each night for the art of diplomacy. He practiced his smile in the mirror each day as the priest had instructed him.

"Collin." She placed her hand on his forearm. "You were to hear it from Davik, but I wanted to tell you first. I'm sorry to say, but Davik's nephew is to be afforded the position of Lord Commander. It is his brother's wish, and Davik has agreed." Collin stiffened. "You will be set to groom him for the position." Collin didn't expect that at all. The look that Keira gave him was meant to console what ought to have been sadness and perhaps even jealousy. Instead Collin found himself strangely excited. *I thought this nephew to be just another Gracious lord. Another reader of books,* he mused while Keira rubbed his arm. "I'm so sorry, Collin. I know how much the position meant to you."

I don't know Lord Robert's mind, but Davik would never allow a man who could not fight to be a Huntsman. A Huntsman is no King to command from the rear, but will face a foe head on, and rely on his personal skill to protect himself and the lives of the men who ride beside him. Collin was no stranger to battle. Since a young age he had dedicated himself to the art of sword mastery, an ancient discipline that required endless training and study. He had worked his whole life to be given such a command, and the thought of someone else coming along that would so easily replace him, filled Collin with curiosity. "What about the summit?"

"That's what I wanted to tell you. Sheriff Baldric will sit counsel, but I was quite firm with Davik, and you will replace Ser Ringley's seat as Honor Guard. Clique will have the Lord Commander's seat, but I would not feel safe without you there."

"You honor me, my lady."

"Damned be honor. It's the truth." Collin sensed her words held some darker sentiment behind them.

"My lady, you know Ser Ringley is a most capable fighter, despite his age." *He is near seventy,* Collin thought, *but still could best any man alive if it came to it.* Collin knew the same might be said of the newcomer Axe Treefort, whose strength was something to be feared, but they all felt it best that a man with more honor, and renown in the Realm, sit the summit to appease the Kings.

"It's not that." She grimaced. "I would just feel safer in these delicate times with family protecting me. It's not that I doubt the honor or intentions of anyone else. You just hear things, about how the Kefkas have been known to change a man's heart."

"No Kefka will enter this castle, my lady," he told her. "The Honor Guard of the West is led by Ser Laurence, the Queen's own brother."

"Still, you will oblige me yes, and be my guardian?" She looked into his eyes and he knew he could never refuse her.

"Of course, I will," Collin said firmly. "It is my privilege."

Collin chatted briefly with Keira about her upcoming day in the garden, and other idle gossip of the goings on in the Stronghold and the preparations for the summit. When he took his leave of her he went to the kitchens and sunk his emotions into a chicken pot pie. He ate to his full with thoughts of Clique Gracious on his mind, and how he might properly test the man's abilities. *There's no point in fighting amongst ourselves like squires to match skill. The metal of a man is not to be found when there is nothing on the line. But where to first begin...* Collin came upon his answer. *It is to be a ranging,* he decided. *He will ride with us, camp with us, and hunt with us. Let him come to know his men. That is what's most important if he's to one day properly command us.*

By the time Collin finished his meal, his squire Samuel Gracious, Davik's cousin by extended family, had found him. "My lord," he said. "The Huntsmen are gathered and await your command." Sam was nineteen years old and now a man full grown, but he had been a boy when Collin first arrived and received him as squire. Back then Collin was the age Sam was now, but still Collin found it difficult to think of him as anything other than a boy. He had even been blooded half a dozen times, and Collin knew the lad aimed for knighthood, but still Collin did not think he was ready. As is acceptable for a lord from a noble House, when Collin joined the Royal Huntsmen so too did his squire. For now the title of Huntsman would have to appease him. Beyond Sam, nine other men were Huntsmen under Collin's command, which brought their total to eleven. Since their order was meant to number twelve, he had petitioned Lord Gracious to allow them to choose a new member. Collin now knew the reason they were denied, and he wondered if Clique Gracious would bring his squire into their ranks. *If he does,* Collin thought, *then for the first time in history, our order shall number thirteen...*

"Good, Sam." Collin finished his cup of fresh milk and sighed. "Tell them to come to formation in the courtyard and wait."

"Right, my lord." Samuel turned to go, but Collin stopped him.

"Also," Collin went on, "tell the stables to ready our horses, plus two."

"For a range?" Sam seemed delighted at the prospect. It had been nearly two months since the Huntsmen had rode together, and Collin did not fault the boy for his eagerness.

"Yes. If our lord permits, I mean for us to ride before the summit." He smiled. "Now go."

Samuel set off to his duties and so too did Collin. He found himself taking the long way round to the upper solar, and as he walked those stone halls he recounted his adventures of the two years he'd served as Lord Commander. Somehow the struggles he'd faced and victories he'd won seemed small and inconsequential. Every part of him felt as if the true ordeal of the Royal Huntsmen was yet to come. *I hope Clique is as wise as his uncle, and heeds the counsel of his men,* he worried. *I would not like to see my Huntsmen hobbled by weak command when their Lord would need them most.*

Collin also worried about whether Clique might seek to whittle the numbers of the Huntsmen should he wish to include his squire, or whether he meant to replace any one of them. Each member of the Huntsmen was either an influential lord, or an ordained knight of the Academy. Even Harold Wood, who was neither lord nor knight, was a bastard son of one of Collin's cousins. All were noblemen but for Axe Treefort, the man whose only history consisted of onion farming, and freelance vigilantism. Collin knew he would have to stress Axe's important contributions to the Royal Huntsmen almost immediately upon meeting Clique. It had only been six months since he joined, and in that time Axe had proven himself to be a veritable beast in combat. He also had a gentle temperament, and a strict moral code that prevented him from dueling with anyone other than a mortal enemy. Collin toyed with different ways of how he might highlight Axe's strengths. He truly believed that Axe would someday lead the Royal Huntsmen, or perhaps go on to be one of the finest knights in the Realm. And yet no one, save for the Huntsmen who had seen his prowess first hand, had come to believe in his potential. Ever since Collin gave Axe the late Ser Matthew's spot in the order, his place had been questioned a dozen times by numerous lords, including Davik himself. Collin suspected it was because of Axe's quiet and pensive nature, and Collin knew such an attitude did not exactly go hand in hand with politics. His refusal to make sport of his great strength was no help either, and stopped short several attempts by Collin and Lord Chase to sing the man's praises. Collin swore he would not let some new lord swoop in and take away both his position, *and* his protege. *Let him come to know his men,* he told himself again, and by then had reached the wide open entrance to the upper solar. With a final breath, Collin adjusted his hair, and his composure, and entered.

The chamber was sixty feet by thirty feet with high vaulted ceilings. The South wall had thick stained glass windows that caught the light of the Red Star and overlooked the sea. A tall mechanical clock encased in a heavy wooden enclosure stood at the center of the stained glass. Its clock face was two feet of mother of pearl with bright red numbers. It filled the solar with a perpetual soft clicking sound if you listened for it, and each hour chimed a sixteen note song, and played a tone for each number of the hour.

The East and West walls were covered in banners for both the East and West Kingdoms in honor of their arrival, and boasted three incredible oil paintings that were commissioned for the event. They had been delivered only a few days ago, and Collin spent some time admiring them after their hanging. Two depicted great battles fought by the men that first forged the Realm, while the third was the most incredible of all. It was a colorful mural of the Goddess standing beneath the open Gate of Heavens, and was masterfully painted on a wall of Redwood, a rare type of tree that grew only in Fenria, and was held sacred by the Goddess. The table sized Redwood wall had been painted elsewhere, and now stood propped for display against the grey granite of the solar.

The room had three entrances. Two were lesser iron doors against the back of the East and West walls, while the North wall boasted two metal bound black ironwood doors that served as the main entrance. Each doorway ultimately led to one of the three gates that separated the inner castle from the outer castle. Collin knew that the brilliance of Stormbreaker Stronghold was in its design. Even if some invading force managed to storm the outer walls and take over the castle, they would never be able to take the inner walls.

Each of the three gates that allowed entrance to the inner castle was a door of stone. The builders of the castle employed secrets of architecture that were no longer known to the Realm, and the castle walls themselves served as the doorways. They were controlled by levers from the inside, so it would require betrayal from within to gain access from without. Men might try to cut and chip away at the stone, and though such a siege would last years, it was still possible. From outside the castle itself, however, it was an impossibility. No siege engine that existed to man could damage the outer walls of Stormbreaker Stronghold, nor any of the elder castles in the Realm. Such arts remained lost to antiquity, though Collin heard some believed the advances of Scientos would soon reclaim them. Even so, Collin knew the future advances of mankind would not jeopardize security concerns for an event one week away. One might consider scaling the outer walls of the stronghold itself, but even the lowest level of the inner castle was three hundred feet above the jagged shoals and rocky shores below. Beyond just the difficulty of height, the walls were sheer with no place to gain hold, and most devilish of all, the location of Stormbreaker's construction provided its own protection. The winds from the coves and cliffs that littered the Southern sides of the castle were ungodly, and they blew around the circumference of the castle in a fiendish manner. The builders channeled the wind so that anyone attempting the climb would be subject to the whims of fate.

The inner solar marks the center of the inner castle. Collin smiled when he thought of the upcoming summit. *Should the peace be broken, even with their armies outside, this will still be the safest place in the Realm for my lady, with the upper towers even safer for my little cousins.*

In the center of the solar was an ornate wooden table suitable for comfortably seating a dozen men. It would seat eleven during the summit, but now held only Lord Davik Gracious at its head, and the man Collin assumed to be Clique Gracious to his uncle's left. The two shared a similar look, though Clique seemed more unassuming somehow, and Davik, even in his elder age, seemed far more handsome. Davik was a man of near sixty, and had the black eyes and black hair of any noble Gracious lord or lady. Collin knew that he had gone grey years ago, but had taken himself to the habit of dying his hair in exotic inks. Even so, his countenance was vibrant and inspiring, and he commanded the presence of any room he entered. With his dashing good looks and radiant charisma, Collin had witnessed first hand Davik Gracious charm every lord and lady he'd ever come across. Even so, as family, and cousin to his wife and children, Collin was privy to the private side of Davik that was revealed only to those he trusted most. The man was wickedly clever, and despite his warrior's physique was more well learned than any man Collin had known. His private library of rare books and scrolls was merely one of the many collections he poured his wealth into, but it was the one to which he gave the most attention. Lord Davik Gracious had more gold entering his coffers each month than Houses in the Realm collected in a year, but the gold was spent more quickly than it was earned. Most was owed to debtors of the many holdings that the Gracious House held across Midgard and the merchant cities, but all the rest and more served to entertain Davik's wild tastes.

At least the art is a sensible investment, Collin thought, *unlike those blasted mirrors.* For one reason or another, Davik had taken to collecting every antique mirror older than a thousand years from across Eldaria. His demand for them was well known amongst merchants everywhere, and in the span of the seven years he'd sat as head of House, and had command over all Gracious wealth, the price of old mirrors across the Realm increased a thousand fold. Each month the price seemed to climb, but still every ancient device that could cast a reflection was delivered to Stormbreaker. Collin had only been in the mirror room once, and regretted it soon thereafter when his dizziness forced him to run to the halls to spill his stomach. Collin knew people jested of Davik being so vain that he fell in love with his reflection, and that's why he buys so many mirrors, but that was nonsense. Davik never entered the mirror room at all. Instead, he would carefully, and privately, inspect each new mirror after they were purchased, then dismiss each one to the mirror room with disgust. Collin asked Keira about them, and questioned if his collecting had some sinister agenda behind it, but she laughed away his concerns. "I used to collect four leaf clovers and lavender roses whenever they bloomed," Keira had told him once. "I'd press them between pages of parchment and save them in my chest of treasures. It is like that, except he has the money to indulge in more expensive tastes. Didn't you collect anything as a child?"

Collin shook his head. "No."

"No, you've never collected anything?" she asked. "Hmm. Well, to start a collection you just pick something you like, and... well... collect them."

"I wouldn't know where to begin, my lady," he had told her.

"Well. What do you like?" she asked.

"Hmm... I don't know." He had no idea where to begin.

"Without thinking. What do you like?" she asked again.

"I like swords," he admitted.

She laughed at him, and he thought he'd blundered, but she convinced him otherwise. "Swords are a splendid thing to collect," she placated him. "And quite practical."

Since then Collin had invested a quarter of his money into his collection, and had obtained half a dozen fine longswords and a few short swords as well. They looked inspiring on his wall, but every day he struggled with whether he should abandon his collection and sell them off. *Perhaps I could sell them all, and purchase a single magnificent blade with the coin,* he had once considered. Collin slowly came to understand the temptations of collecting, but still the mirrors seemed an extravagant waste.

Clique and Davik spoke in hushed tones, and when Collin had gotten close enough to hear their words, he resorted to clearing his throat to gain their attention.

"My lords." Collin nodded to Davik.

"Collin. Have a seat," Davik said. "We were just talking about you."

Collin sat next to Davik and across from Clique. "Aye, my lord. Lady Keira told me that Clique is to be honored with the position of Lord Commander." Davik did not seem surprised.

"Yes, Collin." Davik smiled. "But what Lady Keira does not know, is the position will only be temporary."

"Temporary?" Collin could have laughed.

"Yes," Clique said. "After peace is secured, I am to be named Lord Chancellor." He smiled, but Collin sensed he was not altogether pleased. "It is to be from court, rather than horseback, that

I will serve my House."

"Even so, my lords, the Huntsmen are gathered." Collin leaned forward. "And if you would permit, my lord, I'd like to take the new Lord Commander on his first ranging."

"Now?" Davik protested. "But the summit is nearly upon us."

"Exactly, my lord." Collin grinned. "And if the Royal Huntsmen are to have a new Lord Commander, even if for but a brief time, at least let it be sung that he rode alongside them on a range, and camped in the company of his men."

Davik seemed unsure, but Clique seized on the opportunity. "We could take the Cloak road North. It would would be three days before we came upon their army's outriders. When we spot them, we can turn back, and assure our return before the Eastern King." Clique smiled at his uncle and nodded secretly to Collin. "And, as Ser Collin says, it makes a better song."

"Not Ser, my lord," Collin corrected him.

"You're not a knight?" Clique asked.

"No. I am Collin O'Brien, and fourth in line to the Barrows."

Clique seemed rightfully surprised. "Well then, I stand corrected, *my lord.*" In truth Collin was of nobler blood than Clique himself, but the influence of the Gracious family far outweighed even the O'Briens. Collin wasn't sure if there was sarcasm in Clique's voice, but if there was, it wouldn't have been altogether unwarranted.

"Very well," Davik conceded. "Enjoy yourself Clique, and make sure you do not parley with their army. I do not want it said that secret envoy met with East and not West."

"Thank you, uncle." Clique smiled.

The Sheriff entered from the Red Tower's side entrance and lingered by the door. The man was Baldric Vehement, and if there was one thing Collin did not enjoy about his stay at Stormbreaker Stronghold, it was having to deal with him. The man was a conniving viper that no doubt had his hands in every unsavory act any lord or governor dared to commit in Midgard. He was seldom seen outside of his pitch black leather armor, but had a number of elaborate black and purple robes that he wore over himself to cover his black haired and blacker eyed face in passing. He was a man to be feared and not one to be trusted, but still he sat as Sheriff to all of Midgard, and acted as supreme liaison between all matters of law and justice, and Lord Gracious himself. Collin might not have trusted the man, but Davik kept him closer than anyone else, even him. Davik rose when he saw the Sheriff, and rubbed his hands together with anticipation. "It was nice seeing you nephew. When you return from your range, come to me at once. There are some... important arrangements I will need for you to make before the summit."

"As you say, uncle." Clique rose and stood silent while Davik left the room with the Sheriff. "Now, you said the Huntsmen are in the courtyard, waiting?"

"Yes, Lord Commander," Collin said.

"Clique. Just call me Clique. If you're as noble as you say you are, there's no need for all these titles. We both know that I am no true Lord Commander of the Huntsmen, but if I am to be one of you, I would prefer I be called by my name." Clique smiled. "That is, at least, until you might call me Lord Chancellor."

Collin laughed. "You will find the others are not so giving. Every one of them prefers lord this, or ser that. I almost called the wine boy my lord at dinner last eve." Clique made his way through the castle towards the courtyard, and Collin followed after him.

"So who sits these Huntsmen, Collin?" Clique asked.

"Five knights, two lords, a bastard, a peasant, a squire, and myself."

"I can understand a bastard or two, but a peasant?" Clique fell right into it, just as Collin anticipated.

He went on to explain how he'd come to meet Axe Treefort one day while he was ranging with the Huntsmen. The small folk had been complaining of thieves that had made a nest for themselves near Frog Valley, but when the Huntsmen arrived to sort it all out, the people said a local hero had already sworn to take care of it, and they, moreover, *believed* in him. The Huntsmen tracked them to their hideout, and therein found Axe Treefort had slain nine of them, and left the tenth to tend to his dead. The man had laid down his arms and surrendered, and Axe showed him mercy. Axe himself was wounded, but seemed none the worse for it, and both him and his prisoner told the same tale. Axe walked right into camp one morning, and with a single iron axe took them all on at the same time. The man was as bold as he was fearless. It was less than a month later he became a Huntsman, where Collin and the others agreed he would be both put to use, and carefully watched. An independent vigilante that could stand down ten men to one should not be free to wander Midgard and left to his own devices. Axe wisely agreed to join their order, and Collin explained how he was becoming an outstanding Huntsman in his own right.

If Clique is to be a temporary Commander, I ought not share of Axe's strange affliction. Axe suffered from amnesia, and Collin knew if any Gracious were to find out, they might consider the low born man to be a potential spy. That was something Collin knew could not be the case. *The man truly remembers nothing,* Collin told himself, and if he was alone might have shed yet another tear for the sad tale of how Axe had come to find a home for himself, only to have it ripped away. Collin told Clique of the kind family, and how, when he killed some ruffians in a bar fight, they turned their backs on him because of his inhuman strength. He told Clique about how Collin and Axe had even ridden to the farm which Axe once called home.

They went to clear his name and show that he had become an honorable member of the Huntsmen. But when they arrived they discovered the farm had long since been put to the torch and laid to ruin. They found the remains of a man, a woman, and three children amidst the rubble. Axe shed no tears for his loss, and Collin found himself shedding them for him. When Lady Keira heard the sad tale she cried for days. Still, Collin knew Axe took their deaths to heart, and while a part of him died that day, Collin saw a renewed sense of dedication and purpose in Axe's eyes. Collin suspected the past month of inactivity must have been hard on Axe, who was always looking for a just fight, and he hoped that they would come across no bandits on the range. *Clique ought to know of Axe's worth, but if it comes to battle, he might recoil at the...* Collin toyed with the word in his mind while they walked. *Severity of his fighting style.* Collin knew that battle was bloody, but somehow when Axe met a man in combat, there was always just so much of it.

As they neared the courtyard, Collin stopped him. "Clique, will you be bringing a squire with you? After introductions we will leave straightaway. I've already readied two horses should you need them."

"No..." Clique decided. "I have my *own* horse, and my squire Janson has been mine for less than day. But if you'll wait here a moment, I will tell him I am leaving, and fetch my things."

Collin agreed, and waited no longer than ten minutes before Clique returned. He had a scythe blade sheathed on his belt, and had its pole strung across his back in two pieces. He wore a simple black leather doublet that bore his uncle's insignia, which was a black castle parapet on a grey sky. The Huntsmen wore brown leather, and their sword and steed symbol was in gold and silver. "I will have the armory forge a Huntsmen doublet for you to wear at the summit, my lord... Clique."

"Who cares about armor?" Clique laughed. "Let's go meet these famous Huntsmen of ours."

When the two of them entered the courtyard they were met by their ten men. Each of them were dressed in the brown leathers and cloaks of their order, but each had their own preferences when it came to weapons. "Huntsmen!" Collin announced, and they came to attention. "Allow me to introduce to you Clique Gracious, Lord Davik's nephew. He will be acting as honorary Lord Commander of the Royal Huntsmen until the summit, whereafter he will assume the seat of Lord Chancellor of Midgard! What say you Huntsmen? Shall we show our Lord Commander how we ride?"

The ten of them greeted Clique to hoots and the stomping of their feet.

"Clique." Collin turned to him. "Allow me to introduce you to the Royal Huntsmen of Midgard! There you have Ser Montgomery!" The man stepped forward and smiled with his full set of pearly whites. He was handsome with long brown hair and a sharp jaw line. "He's the finest jouster Midgard has to offer, and a better rider. They say he was born on horseback and he's lived there ever since. Next to him you have Ser Beribold, whom they call the Knight of Seasons." Beribold had black hair and blue eyes, and Collin knew that he was more intelligent and well read than any of his men, save only for Lord Chase.

"Why do they call you that?" Clique asked.

Beribold smiled devilishly. "Because I can always tell when the winds are changing, and it is time to advance or sound the retreat."

"There you have Harold Wood, my bastard cousin," Collin continued. Wood had red hair and green eyes, and was more O'Brien than those with their proper marriages between Houses. He was born to a beautiful follower that attached to the Eastern army when open fighting plagued the river lands, and found her way into his cousin's bed. "He's more ranger than any one of us, and could live for a week in the deepest forest, blindfolded, with his hands bound."

"It wouldn't have come to that," Wood laughed and scratched at his head, "if I hadn't gotten so damn blind drunk I lost the bloody key!"

"Here you have Ser Ringley, who I'm *sure* needs no introduction." Before he'd become a Huntsman, Ser Ringley had served as Honor Guard to Lord Robert, Clique's father.

"Ser Ringley, it's good to see you." Clique stepped forward and hugged him.

"Lord Clique, you've certainly come into yourself," the knight said as he admired Clique's physique. "Your training has given you a warrior's stature."

"Training?" Collin asked. *Why am I sometimes the last to know something?*

Ser Ringley looked for Clique's permission to speak, who allowed it. "Yes, Lord Commander, I mean, Lord Collin." Ringley's demeanor turned solemn. "His father permitted him to study abroad with the Devils Guild, and bring their secrets back with him."

Everyone, including Collin, seemed impressed, but Lord Haren was aghast. "Devilkin magic?" The man sported a strangely whiskered beard and mustache that always reminded Collin of an old cat. His hair was grey and black, and his eyes dark blue. "What sorcery have you brought back with you, to corrupt our fair realm from its second highest position as Chancellor?"

Clique laughed. "There's no such thing as sorcery. What one man can learn, any can learn. The secrets they imparted are nothing more than the ability of a man to use every tool at his disposal. Sight, sound, but most of all that feeling men get in the pit of their stomach." Clique smiled with some hints of his secret knowledge.

"See the scythe he wears!" Ser Beribold pointed. "It is the battle weapon of the Knight-slayer." Beribold's stern demeanor lightened and he laughed at Lord Haren. "Best not be tempting him, now."

"I'm not a knight!" Haren protested. "My own brother is Governor of the Snake Mountains."

"Knight or no, that curved black blade would split you like a pea pod." Beribold smiled. "And such bedeviled arts are welcome amongst us who serve Lord Gracious and not some ancient superstition." Beribold bowed deeply to Clique, and the lord seemed to enjoy the pleasantry.

"The man who fears your training is Lord Haren," Collin explained. "And you will find his skill with a long bow would rival even the Devilkin." Collin figured Clique doubted such a claim, but Haren was placated none the less.

"Lord Haren." Clique smiled through his teeth.

"Here you have Ser Thomas!" Collin motioned to the fifteen year old boy with brown hair, amber eyes, and a lack of facial hair. Everyone else save for Clique and Axe wore light beard or mustache in one fashion or another. "Do not let his age deceive you! Since the boy was five years old he has been hunting boar with spear. By the time he reached thirteen he competed in a tournament where anyone of high birth could enter, and to everyone's astonishment the boy bested them all!"

"It was in Jadespar, Lord Collin." Ser Thomas smiled gallantly. "And by *them all* you mean a score of the best knights there were to offer."

"Not everyone competes in trivial melees," Ser Montgomery chided him, but the boy had a strong ego and laughed away the comment. "The joust is where it's at."

"Here you have Lord Chase," Collin said as he motioned to an elder knight who stepped forward. The man's short hair was peppered with the black of his youth, and his eyes shone a strange purple. "He stands the wisest of all of us, and doubly so with a morning star. He completed the rites of wizardry at Starspire Sanctuary by age thirty, and went on to complete half the rites of a priest at Starcrown."

"It was more like one third," Chase quipped.

"Why didn't you finish, my lord?" Clique asked him. "Not a holy man, are you?"

"Lord Chase is famous in the melee," Collin interjected, "but was required to give it up while wearing the robes of clergy, and just couldn't keep himself from his glory."

"Do you regret not completing your rites?" Clique pressed. "I know that once you stop training in certain orders you can never return." He smiled. "Others are more lenient in their approach."

"I regret nothing, Lord Commander," Chase answered confidently. "I am a Royal Huntsman, and mine is all the order I need!" Collin and the rest of the Huntsmen hooted and stomped their feet.

"Here you have Ser Lawrence," Collin said. Lawrence had long black hair and dark blue eyes. He seemed the strongest of all the knights, and had a heavy two handed sword slung across his back. "He is Lord Haren's brother, and once stood Commander of the Honor Guard of Cobra Palace before joining the Honorable Academy and gaining his knighthood."

"And how are you at the melee?" Clique asked him.

"Melee are too dangerous." Ser Lawrence grinned. Clique raised his eyebrow at a momentary loss for words, and the knight laughed.

"Ser Lawrence is widely known for killing a man with his first blow," Ser Ringley said, as he gave Lawrence a stern look and killed the laughter.

"I too have that problem." Clique patted his scythe.

"Axe killed two men with one cut," Harold boasted.

"Is that true?" Clique looked to Axe Treefort.

"It's true," Axe said. He had been silently watching from the back, and even now spoke softly. "There wasn't much to it. The man's neck just didn't stop the swing, and the other man got in the way."

It was clear to Collin that Clique was studying Axe. Collin allowed his gaze to linger for a moment before speaking up. "There stands Axe Treefort. And here, our final Huntsman is my good squire, your cousin Samuel." Collin motioned towards young Sam, who also stood quietly off to the side.

Clique nodded politely to him. "Cousin."

"Cousin." Sam smiled.

"That is all of us, Lord Commander," Collin said. "And we *eleven* are at your disposal."

Clique stood to attention before them. "Then to your horses, Huntsmen!"

It was less than an hour later that the twelve Royal Huntsmen crested the top of Hawk Hill, where Clique reared his white destrier, and called on them to stop. All eleven halted their horses to join Clique in taking pause to admire the view. White clouds in a peaceful blue sky hung over the black and grey heights of Stormbreaker Stronghold and its adjoining city. Davik had ordered the gates open to any who would seek shelter during the summit. And so folk from across the entire region were making their way into the city in fear of the approaching armies. Davik had assured them that no harm would come to their holdings, but even Collin knew it was impossible to guarantee that. The best they could do was provide the people shelter, and pray it did not come to war. And if it did, all they could do was hope that the fighting stayed outside the city walls, if not for out of Midgard altogether.

"It was night when I arrived," Clique explained to his men, but they all had understood.

"It is an impressive castle!" Collin turned his horse back to the Cloak Road. "Now let us see if we can bring it honors! Hyah!" Collin rode off, and his Huntsmen followed after him.

CLIQUE

Clique stretched out his legs by the campfire and groaned with contentment. The meals prepared by his cousin Sam outdid any he'd had while on the road before. Clique winced at the memory of the rations his father's knights had served while escorting him to his uncle. *I ate better in the ship's cabin,* he had once thought while tasting Ser Walthaus' poorly cooked mash of beans and burnt chicken, *but at least I have real wine.* Each night with them he'd drank himself to quiet sleep. Such would not be possible with the Huntsmen. It was the second night of their range, and if the first was to be any indication, he had expected hours of song and jest. His head pounded all the second day's ride, and he worried about whether his fortitude would allow him to keep pace for a second night of drinking. But instead of laughter and mirth, that second night was met with a queer silence that had overtaken them. Clique thought it to be nothing more than a reflection of his own desires for some peace, and relished the sounds of the forest instead of men's voices. *One thing about the Devilkin I do not miss is the quiet.*

Their days had been filled with lessons and histories of the Royal Huntsmen and their exploits. They spoke with all manner of people heading to the castle and took in local gossip. They walked their horses along road, and other times they rode through the forest and discussed the tactics bandits might use against them in such terrain. Still, there was no sign nor tale of trouble save for the wide reaching unrest that the populace had at the arrival of the armies. What was meant to be a triumphant event for peace was met with skepticism and fear by the people whose lands were being crossed by thousands of foreign troops. *I would be scared too if I were them.* Clique empathized with their plight. *They may not be our enemy, but if peace is shattered, it will be our fields they fight and die in.*

Clique knew that Midgard's eighteen governorships had their own standing military, but no orders had been given to rally their troops. Instead Davik and his father had seen to it that all mercenaries and standing military men were to retreat to their castles. Only sworn knights of the Academy were permitted to wander in small groups to ensure that peace was kept. Even so, they were instructed to keep their distance from the Cloak and Wind roads, unlike the Royal Huntsmen who had made their camp right in the middle of the Cloak itself. It would have been both clever and folly for any bandits to prey on travelers in that lapse of security a day before the army arrived. Anyone coming down the Cloak would pass right by their fire, and it was right there in the middle of the road that Harold Wood laid down with his ear pressed to the stone. At first Clique thought he might be listening for something, but it had been nearly twenty minutes, and Clique figured he'd fallen asleep. Clique's thoughts returned to the governorship's defenses, and his gaze fell upon Lord Chase who was pensively sipping on a silver cup of wine.

"Lord Chase," Clique whispered, and drew his attention.

"Yes?" He turned to face Clique and set his wine down.

"How many men defend the city and stronghold together?" Clique asked him.

"Near eight hundred, but we could put them all ahorse if need be," Chase told him. "Ser Grissel commands the City Watch with five hundred men beneath him. They stand about fifty knights, two hundred family men, and the rest trained guardsmen. Ser Flynn commands the Castle Guard. His are a hundred knights and the rest a motley mix of two hundred men. The House Guard is captained by Jack Havensword, but numbers only thirty. No knights for them. Just men who can be trusted."

Clique went over the numbers and people in his mind, and for a while the Huntsmen sat again in silence. It was clear to Clique every man was thinking the same thing. *Would it be enough should it come to war?* Some had expressed their concerns that the standing armies of Midgard were not also summoned to protect the Realm, but Davik had apparently been quite stern on the matter. He did not want to give any incitement of mistrust towards the peace, no matter how small, and was even welcoming armies of greater number than seen in a millennia with open arms. No doubt each and every one of them hoped it was not blind folly. Stormbreaker Stronghold might be nigh but indestructible, but the city and the vast expanse of undefended countryside could easily be pillaged and sacked. Somehow the fate of Midgard had been intertwined with the fate of war between the East and West. Clique had not yet been told what dastardly plot his uncle and father had cooked up, but he prayed that they knew what they were doing. *The Realm could have fought itself to destruction, and still Midgard would have stood. But now, one false move by my uncle, and his ambitions will have brought doom to our civilization and our House.*

"Does anyone else hear that?" Harold bolted up and looked around.

Clique listened and thought he heard horses riding in the distance. "Riders?"

Collin clapped his hands together and smiled. "It's a volia."

Clique felt both fear and hunger course through him, and his mouth watered with the thought. Volia were great reptilian beasts that lumbered about on four powerful legs, and consumed all vegetation in their wake. With their scaled hides, strong stature, aggressive nature, insatiable hunger, and delicious meat, they were both scourge and delicacy across all of Eldaria. Here in Midgard, which was fully surrounded by wall or sea, the only volia that still remained roamed alone or in small groups rather than in great herds, and were much smaller than those found elsewhere in the world. It wasn't that they were protected as a game species and not hunted to extinction, it was simply that the volia bred quickly, and were difficult to catch or trap, let alone kill. In fact, it was standard courtesy in Midgard that a caught and killed adult volia was not only worth a fine amount in coin for its meat and hide, but came with it one honor from the Academy. Such a prize was highly sought after, as an honor could change a man's life either socially, politically, or even economically. Honor could be physically traded or sold at high value, and its possession brought with it not just wealth, but respect and influence.

"It's over there," Axe pointed.

Everyone looked, but Clique couldn't see anything but darkness. "How can you tell?"

"I see it," Axe said. "It appears to be resting, for it has come to a stop a hundred fifty meters in that direction."

"A fine claim, but no one could see that far!" Clique laughed, and looked for agreement from his men. "He has to be making a guess."

"Oh, he can see it alright," Ser Montgomery said.

"That's impossible," Clique protested. "It's too dark."

Ser Lawrence nodded. "The man could sex an eagle in flight."

"Spot its balls or not, he means," Ser Montgomery chuckled. "I've seen him do it."

Lord Haren waved the feat off. "He might sex one, but I could fell that eagle with one arrow, and that's the better trick."

"Axe is a poor shot?" Clique inquired, curious about the man's keen vision.

"It's not that..." Collin explained. "Axe is a wonder at anything he sets his mind to."

"Thing is he won't use a bow of any kind," Montgomery said.

"Well why not?" Clique looked to Axe, who was still gazing at where the volia might be. Axe turned to face him, and for some queer reason, Clique's blood chilled when the firelight caught Axe's blue eyes, and hinted at some inner flame.

"Because I might miss," Axe answered with ice in his tone.

"Every man misses," Clique chided him.

"It's not that," Collin answered for him. "Axe will do nothing that might put an innocent's life in danger. He trusts only what he can touch."

Clique was astonished. *The man was a peasant vigilante that now aspires to the Virtues?* Axe seemed an enigma to him. *Who can see distance in the dark, and has the strength of ten men...* Ser Thomas interrupted his thoughts when he picked up his spear and patted Clique on the shoulder.

"Alright. Let's go, Lord Commander," Ser Thomas said.

Clique stood. "All of us?"

Thomas laughed. "No."

Five minutes later Clique found himself flanked by Ser Thomas and Collin, with Axe guiding them through the dark forest. Axe stopped and motioned for them to quietly approach. It was found in a small glade lit only by the dim shadows of the Silver Star that filtered down through the tree canopy. The volia was much larger than Clique expected. Its body was a dozen feet long and as thick as a big wagon, with a terrible tail that extended another ten feet. Its neck was strangely plated with grey skin, and it had three horns upon its head. The thing lay on its stomach and rumbled with every heaving breath. *It is asleep, just as Axe had seen.*

"It's huge!" Clique whispered as quietly as he could manage. "It's the King of all volia."

"No," Collin whispered with a strange sobriety. "It is a kavolia."

"What the hell is a kavolia?" Ser Thomas whispered too loudly. The beast rumbled but did not awake, and Collin pushed the boy with disdain.

"They are volia's elder cousins," Collin whispered.

"I've never seen one," Ser Thomas quietly jested.

"I should think not," Collin told him. "They are beasts of Fenria, and are almost never seen in the Realm."

"Well how did it get here?" Ser Thomas asked.

Collin shrugged. "Either it's always been here, and there's a few of them lingering still, or someone smuggled it here, somehow. I can't imagine it swam the bay, and it didn't just walk through the wall all by itself, unnoticed."

"Maybe it was brought as a baby," Axe mused, and everyone looked to him. "What?"

"No, you're probably right," Collin whispered. "Such a creature would grow fast, and get away from its handlers."

"I may be Lord Commander," Clique said, "but Collin, what do you think we should do with it?"

Collin grinned. "Kill it, of course. There's no capturing that thing, and it can't be left wandering so close to the road with a King on his way." Collin rubbed his hands together. "This is the perfect opportunity for you to get your honors Clique. Ser Thomas and I will stand at the ready."

"And I?" Clique asked him.

"And you will kill the thing where it rests." Collin gave him a glorious smile, while young Ser Thomas frowned and kicked his foot in disappointment. "No need to worry. Get your first blows in, and Axe will put it down. Finish with a ceremonial stroke, and the honor will be yours."

"Axe..." Clique whispered to him. "Your axe blades, could they pierce such a hide?" He'd heard the man had great strength, but still the type of weapon seemed inappropriate against such a creature, and Axe seemed to agree with him.

"You are correct," Axe agreed, and Ser Thomas gave yet another look of disappointment as Axe took from the boy his iron spear. "This will serve much better."

"Alright." Clique fastened his scythe blade to its pole. "Let's do this Axe."

Clique inched into the glade, and with every lesson of his training put to use, quietly crept upon the sleeping behemoth. He maneuvered around its body and came alongside the thing's bulging neck. Axe readied himself nearby, and with a final deep breath, Clique raised his black steel high in the air, and swung it down upon the creature's body. The blade cut deep into the creature's hide, but he found it had more resistance than he'd expected. *Its very skin is stronger than armor,* he thought to himself as he pried the scythe out and came down for a second cut that pierced deep into its neck. The beast groaned and opened its eyes. Clique jumped back, prepared for it to lash out, but instead the kavolia wailed in great pain, and fell helplessly back to its stomach. Its tongue lagged out of its mouth, and it seemed a pitiable thing. Axe lifted the spear as if to ready his killing stroke, but Clique held him off.

"Wait..." Clique walked up to the beast and gently approached its face. The kavolia's eyes looked deep into Clique's, and he saw the emotion that laid within, and felt the waves of its passing. The thing was dying, and the pain of his scythe was nothing compared to whatever was plaguing it. Clique waved Collin and Ser Thomas closer, and they confusedly approached.

"What's the matter? Why did you not kill it?" Ser Thomas immediately inquired.

"It's sick," Clique said with a sigh. *What sad turn of fate. Not only is there no honor to be had, but this magnificent creature is reaching a dismal end without seizing any glory of its own.* "I think it's dying."

Clique's scythe had drawn some blood, but considering the thing's size, the wounds seemed fairly superficial. Clique wondered if he even might have been able to kill the thing at all if it was healthy, or if he would have solely relied upon Axe. *Collin would not have risked my life with a creature so dangerous if he did not truly believe Axe could fell the best.* Clique's eyes passed over Axe with renewed curiosity when the man spoke again.

"Clique's right," Axe said. "The reptile is near death."

Clique sighed and stepped back. "Well then... Put it out of its misery, Axe."

Axe had everyone step back as he walked up to the kavolia's face. He paused for a moment with the spear raised, then with his palm on the butt of the spear, plunged the steel spearhead between the thing's eyes. The spear traveled a good three feet deep before sticking firm, and with a low groan the creature's last life passed from its mouth. Axe went to remove the spear but Ser Thomas stopped him.

"Leave it," Thomas said. "I have others." They all took a moment to mourn its passing, and Ser Thomas inaudibly whispered some style of prayer. It was only a few moments later that Clique caught whiff of the stench.

"What is that vile..." Clique rubbed at his nose. "Did it shit itself?"

Collin stepped closer to what they had thought was blood that leaked from the kavolia's neck. Ser Thomas pulled a torch from his pack and lit it aflame with a strike of flint on steel. When he held the torch up it covered the glade with its fiery glow, and all of them, save for Axe, balked at the sight of it. The blood was black and festered with some odious wild-growth of congealed black bile tentacles. They gave off a noxious smell, and still quivered with some parasitic form of life.

They all leaned close, but not too close, to examine the stuff in silence. Collin poked at it with a stick, and Clique dry heaved at the terrible odor. All except Axe jumped back in fright when the flesh around the spear burst with a loud pop. A hideous black ichor spurt from the wound, and black seeds lingered in the air, held aloft on strands of dark silk in the light breeze.

Clique did not like the look of the stuff, and it was clear that Collin did not either. "Fetch the Huntsmen," Collin turned to Ser Thomas, "and burn it."

Clique watched as the Huntsmen gathered lumber and kindling, and it was not long before the beast and its ill sickness was being consumed by a great fire. The canopy's edge became singed from the heat and Clique questioned if the fire might spread, but Harold cast his doubts aside. The ranger explained that recent rains had wet the ground, and the trees that surrounded the glade did not burn easily. It was lumber from across the Cloak that they'd gathered to burn, and he had the right of it as the fires did not spread.

Clique's steel scythe was laid into the fire to cleanse the blade of whatever sickness infected the kavolia's blood. Three small jars of the kavolia's black bile were carefully collected and sealed at Clique's command. *Some should be sent to Starcrown and Starspire for study, and some for my uncle to inspect. I have never seen such a malady, though I have also never seen such a creature that bore it.* Clique felt the waves of something more sinister afoot. His thoughts on the subject were wrenched from him when Harold Wood reentered the glade with dread on his face.

"Lord Commander! Lord Collin!" Wood cried in alarm. "You'd better come take a look at this."

Clique, Collin, and Ser Ringley followed Harold ten minutes walk to the East. They all wanted him to explain himself, but the man refused, and said it was a sight meant to be seen. In time the thick forest opened up to a wide clearing. There the grassy plains would lead to the tall cliffs of the Eastern shore. The Silver Star had since risen and now bathed the open fields with its light. Harold walked them up the hill that barred their view of the plains. Clique paused to look at the Silver Star.

"What brought you this way, Harold?" Collin asked.

"I don't know," he admitted. "The forest just didn't feel right. I wanted to get a better look."

Harold, Collin, and Ser Ringley reached the top of the hill first, while Clique lagged behind. As Clique still climbed, Ser Ringley raised his hands to his head in shock. "Dear Goddess!" he cried.

"Ma'at save us," Harold said.

"What?" Clique groaned. "What do you see?"

Clique reached the top of the hill, and as he caught his breath, he cursed underneath it. A great herd of near fifty kavolia lay dead and scattered across the plains. They died where they fell, and now festered with the strange shadowy growth. The Silver Star's radiance cast its light upon the foul plumes of black seeds that drifted up into the winds and blew East in a dark cloud. "The plague spreads," Ser Ringley muttered with a chill.

"It was no lost baby kavolia that we found, but one of this herd." Collin sighed. "They must have swam the channel and come a great distance before finally giving out to..." His words froze.

"We're in luck the wind takes the plague out to sea," Wood

pointed out the obvious.

"Something drove these animals to our lands," Ser Ringley said. "And whether or not they fled Fenria or the far East, they have brought with them this sickness."

"They cannot be left to fester," Collin spoke stern. "We must take advantage of the winds while they still blow away from the forest, and burn them all."

"It is no small task!" Ser Ringley objected. "The grass will not burn easily, and the lumber will have to be felled from across the Cloak and drug."

"And still I trust you will get it done!" Collin commanded him. "Use the horses for the lumber, but be wary not to get them too close. Keep your hands gloved, your mouths covered, and stay upwind of the plague's vapors."

"You mean to report back to Lord Gracious?" Ringley asked.

"Yes, and I'm taking Axe, Ser Thomas, and our Lord Commander back with me."

"Axe should stay here," Ringley suggested. "With him it will take less time."

"I must leave immediately, and I will not ride without Axe," Collin told him. "Stay as long as it takes, Ser Ringley, and see to it every last trace of this plague is burned."

"But what about the summit?" Ringley complained. "I'm to sit Honor Guard."

"I need you here to lead our men!" Collin answered him. "I'll not have it said our best knight sat on his arse while Midgard rotted. I will sit your seat if necessary. Ser Thomas is too young."

"Aye. It will be done." Ser Ringley nodded.

"Will you be telling the Kings?" Harold asked.

"That is for Lord Gracious to decide." Collin turned and started back. Clique gave a silent look to Harold and Ser Ringley, before following after Collin.

They returned to break news and camp, and soon Collin, Axe, Ser Thomas, and Clique had left their Huntsmen behind and ridden South towards Stormbreaker Stronghold. They rode all night and day, and in that time spoke little. Each of them were lost in thought about their circumstance. *Where did the kavolia come from?* Clique pondered. *What is the sickness? Will it spread?* His dreams brought him no solace nor answers, and they broke camp early to ensure their quick return. Early that afternoon, they saw in the distance a carriage stopped by the side of the road. While it was still a purple and blue speck on the horizon, Axe drew one of his weapons.

"Four bandits with swords have killed two riders and a guard," Axe said. "The carriage flies a Draven flag, and there is a woman in distress."

Clique now knew better than to question the veracity of Axe's claims, and all drew weapons and rode their horses to a gallop. Three men scattered when they saw the Huntsmen riding them down. Ser Thomas chased after one, while Axe and Collin rode after two others into the forest. Clique dismounted next to the wagon and readied his long scythe. The door to the carriage was shut, but he could hear the struggled grunts of a man over the soft whimpers of a woman. Clique's hands held the scythe close, and with his foot, pulled the door open. Within the carriage a revolting brown haired bandit was atop a young girl, no older than twenty, with a knife pressed to her throat. Her clothes had been cut and torn from her body, and he was having his way with her. Clique's scythe was not meant for such close quarters, and he knew he would need to draw the man out. Their eyes met and the man stopped his thrusting.

"What the fook?" The man muttered in alarm.

"Step out peaceful and you won't be harmed," Clique told him, as they heard the death screams of the other bandits. The girl had hate and tears in her emerald eyes, and her long black hair was a knotted mess where he grabbed her. The man stood and twisted her lovely locks until she was helpless to him. His knife remained held by her throat.

"Get the fook back or she's dead," the man told him, and Clique obliged. When the bandit and the girl had emerged from the carriage, the other Huntsmen were returning. The bandit wore soiled leathers with blood stains on his breeches, while she stood with her pale ivory skin naked to the wind. Viscous crimson blood spilled from her womanhood and ran down her thigh. The man demanded they keep their distance, and with a wave of his hand, Clique kept them all away.

"Everything's going to be alright. Just relax," Clique told him, but his eyes were on the girl. "Just tell me what you want."

"What I want?" The man's eyes fell on Collin, who sat on his horse across the Cloak, then turned back to Clique with his scythe blade held high. "I want you to get back on your horse, and for you and your men to get the fook out of here."

"That's not going to happen," Clique said.

"Well if it don't," the man held the knife close against her neck, "I'll slit her throat."

"How about if we give you a horse, and you ride out of here instead." Clique took a step back.

"I'll be taking her with me," he said, "to make sure you don't follow."

"Sure. That's fine. Whatever it takes to keep her safe." Clique smiled through his teeth.

The man started walking her towards Clique's horse, but Clique stopped him. "No, no."

"What the fook do you mean no?"

"My horse is dear to me." Clique grinned. "I've had her since a foal." Clique glanced over his shoulder. "Hey, Collin! Dismount your horse and walk it over here! He wants to take it."

"Aye my lord!" Collin said as he got off his horse.

"Fook that! Tell him to stay back!" The bandit pointed at Collin.

"You tell him. He'll listen to you." Clique smiled again.

As the bandit shouted to Collin and bid him to reluctantly stop, Clique gained the attention of the girl with his eyes. "Jump," he mouthed sweetly to her.

"What?" she whispered.

"Jump," he mouthed silently again.

She half shrugged in confusion. "What?" she whispered.

"Jump!" he yelled. The Bandit's head turned confused and the lady jumped into the air. Her feet only rose barely a foot from the ground, but it was all Clique needed. His scythe spun low lightning quick, swept under the girl's lifted heels, and severed the bandit's legs at the ankle. The man fell backwards, and Clique stepped in with a second stroke. The scythe loosed the bandit's head from his neck, and as his corpse fell flat, the head rolled beneath the carriage and out of sight.

Collin and Ser Thomas hooted in triumph at the victory, while Axe calmly put his bloodied axes away. Clique tossed his scythe aside and threw his robe over the girl's naked body. "My lady," he told her, and helped her to her feet.

"Are you one of Robert's sons?" she asked him quietly as she took his hand and stood.

"Yes. I'm Clique, his first born." Clique smiled honestly this time. "Have we met before?"

"No, I do not believe so." She smiled. The remaining Huntsmen approached her.

"Who are you, my lady?" Collin asked.

"I am Alana Toril, King Harloque's niece." She stood tall when she said the words. Clique marveled at how brave she was, to compose herself with such dignity and grace after a horror that might have driven a lesser girl to helpless babble. "And I am ill to inform you that I am most displeased with your lack of security along the road."

Clique could have laughed, and he detected a thin smile passing her plump purple painted lips. Collin knelt before her. "I am sorry, my lady. The fault is mine."

"And who are you?" she asked him.

"I am Collin O'Brien, and..." Collin threw Clique a look, who nodded to him. "I'm Lord Commander of the Royal Huntsmen. We are responsible for not clearing out the last of those cretins."

"Do not take it to heart, Lord Collin." She smiled down at him. "If not for your Huntsmen it would have been far worse." She looked at the dead guardsman with sadness in her eyes. "My men may have fallen, but they have been avenged. No seed was spilled. A bastard will not be born from this day, and I am safe to sing the song."

Collin stood. "You are most practical, Lady Toril. I trust this will not reflect negatively on the peace summit. But I must ask... Why are you not with the wagon train of the army?"

"I am not here for the summit. I am here for your uncle," she told Clique.

"What business have you with Lord Gracious, my lady, that must be spoken before the peace?" Collin asked her directly.

"Those words are for Davik alone," she said.

"Can you ride," Clique asked, "or should we ready the carriage?"

"I'll ride with you, Clique." She smiled. "On that fine horse of yours."

"As you wish, Lady Toril." Clique smiled back.

"Please. Call me Alana." He helped her onto the horse.

"What of the others?" Clique asked Axe quietly.

"All dead," Axe told him, and Clique was satisfied.

"Ser Thomas." Clique looked to the young knight. "Fetch all the bodies and load the carriage with them. Treat Alana's men with the honor. Clear all trace of what happened here, then ride the carriage for the Stronghold. I'll not have the King's outriders see this mess."

Ser Thomas remained behind while Collin, Axe, and Clique and Alana rode South along the Cloak. By midnight they were safely within the walls of the stronghold. Clique commanded Collin to inform Lord Gracious of their return, and to have them wait in the solar, while he told Axe to more effectively seal the three samples of the black ichor before presenting them to Lord Gracious. While they left to perform their duty, Clique escorted Alana into the inner castle. There he handed her off to one of Keira's bed servants so she could bathe and change. Clique waited patiently until an hour later she emerged refreshed, and looked a proper lady again in a green gown that paired with her eyes. *She's so beautiful,* he thought to himself as he made small talk and brought her to the solar. Clique found himself somewhat smitten with the girl, and idly wondered if after the peace they might make a suitable match. *I shall have to inquire my uncle upon the matter. Her beauty, bravery, and high birth make her a tempting prospect that my father might agree to.*

They entered the solar through the Silver Tower's entrance, and were met by Davik and Collin at the table. Davik rose and hugged Alana in his arms. "Alana, my poor child. I was furious when I heard what had befallen you."

"It's alright Davik." She kissed him on his cheek. "Your brave nephew saved my life, if not my virginity." Davik's face bore the fury in his heart, but Alana soothed him with her hand upon his cheek. She turned to Clique and smiled. "You are ever in my family's debt Lord Clique." She curtsied.

"You will have honors pinned for this, nephew," Davik told him.

Clique waved off the comment. "None are needed. It is my only regret that we had not arrived sooner." Davik motioned for everyone to sit. He took the head of the long table, while Collin sat to his left, and Alana to his right. Clique pulled her chair like a gentleman, and sat down beside her.

Davik's servant, a young man with brown hair and black eyes, lingered in the shadows by the Silver door. "Boy!" Davik called after him. "Boy!"

He took a few steps forward and bowed nervously. "Yes, my lord? It's Kendrick, my lord."

"Fetch a few bottles of wine!" Davik commanded him. "This should be a celebration!"

"Don't you think that's a little macabre?" Alana asked.

"Nonsense!" He slapped his hand on the table. "Any day where I *almost* lost someone I loved, but *didn't*, is a day meant to be celebrated!" Davik patted her hand. "I would never have forgiven myself if I lost you."

"How do you know each other?" Clique asked his uncle.

"Her mother and I were once very much in love." Davik's eyes became distant. "But those days have long passed, and so has Lady Toril. You know you look more like her every time I see you."

"You flatter me, Davik." She blushed.

"She would have been so proud to see the courageous woman you've grown to become." Davik glanced over his shoulder. "Where is that damned wine?"

"Lord Collin." Clique rubbed his hands together and carefully phrased his words. "Have you told my uncle of the Huntsmen's task?"

"Yes, I've heard it, damn you," Davik said. "Where is that peasant knight of yours anyway?" His words were pointed at Collin.

"He'll be here shortly. He set off to make sure the samples were more properly secured." Collin looked uneasy and Alana picked up on it.

"What kind of samples?" she asked Collin, who didn't know how to respond.

"They found some sick animals along the Cloak," Davik told her. "We're sending out samples of their blood to be studied."

"I was right. You *have* grown macabre, Davik." Alana giggled.

"It is all to prevent the illness from spreading," Davik explained. "I'll not have my people sick. A good lord will do anything to ensure the lives of his people." He smiled his best smarmy smile. "And I hope a good King will do the same, as what costs more lives than bloodshed?"

"Hear, hear!" Collin rapped on the table.

Kendrick entered with a rolling tray of goblets and wine bottles. Axe followed beside him and came to attention. "Lord Gracious." Axe held a large wooden box in his hand. "All three specimens have been contained separately in this crate."

Davik was doubly thrilled at both deliveries, and waved his wine boy to pour while he addressed Axe. "Excellent. Please, set it down over there, and come join us. You'll drink with us, won't you?"

Axe smiled. "Oh, yes my lord. I've grown quite fond of good wine." Axe set the crate down as instructed and took the seat next to Collin. "I will not drink anything with even the smallest hint of sour. I prefer my wine sweet and savory, and alongside red meat."

Davik grinned. "I like a man who knows his tastes." The boy filled four silver goblets with light red wine from a decanter, and placed each for Collin, Clique, Axe, and Alana. A gold chalice was served to Davik, and Kendrick filled it with a dark purple vintage from a bottle he held in his hand. "Let's see if this is sour or not." Davik grabbed Alana's cup and took a sip of the light red. "No, no.

This will not do, not for my guests!" He took the goblet for his own, then grabbed an empty goblet from the cart. "Here! Try some of this!" Davik reached for the purple wine bottle Kendrick had in his hands, but the boy recoiled. "Give that here!" Davik told him.

"My lord, it's your personal stock," he protested. "You told me it was for you alone."

"I know what I told you, you damn boy." Davik gripped his golden chalice of purple wine the boy had just poured, then emptied Axe's wine onto the floor. He filled Axe's cup and Alana's new silver goblet with the purple wine from his chalice. "There! Try that! I bought four cases of it off a ship out of Tussus for a thousand doubloons." He forced the silver goblets of the stuff into Alana and Axe's hands, then took his stolen silver goblet of the light red for his own. "You'll try that and tell me if it's sweet enough for you."

Alana and Axe moved to take a sip, but Davik stopped them. "Ah, ah, ah!" Davik protested. "We need a proper toast!" Collin raised his goblet, and Clique followed suit.

"To my dear friend Alana!" Davik toasted. "I thank the Goddess she is alright. And to my Huntsmen, who brought her back to me."

"Hear, hear!" Collin cheered, and they all drank from their goblets, Davik, Clique, and Collin of the light red, and Axe and Alana of the purple. Kendrick nervously set the wine bottle on the tray, and bent with a rag to clean the spilt wine from the floor.

"This is sweet wine indeed, and the finest I've ever had." Axe smiled as he drank every last drop of it. "Thank you for the tasting, Lord Gracious." Clique could not help but notice Collin's smug smile, and wondered if Axe's etiquette was in part tutored by Collin. *How else would a peasant learn to drink with lords and ladies?*

"Yes, it's quite good. And *so* expensive." Alana took a few more sips, and set her drink down. "I always knew you had exquisite taste."

"After the summit, you should visit our cellar." Davik gulped his wine thirstily. "I've collected vintages from across all of Eldaria."

"That sounds splendid," she agreed.

"In the meanwhile you must see Keira and the children." Davik set his goblet down. "But first... We should take care of business. I was told you had some urgent news to tell me."

"Yes..." She took a sip of the thick purple wine, and looked around suspiciously. "But it is meant for your ears alone."

"Kendrick!" Davik shouted.

"Yes, my lord!" He hopped to attention from the floor.

"That will be all," Davik dismissed him, and the boy quickly made his way from the solar. "Whatever you have to say can be said before my nephew and my Huntsmen. I trust their counsel, and I trust your secret will be kept." Davik threw a look to Axe and Collin, who both had stern looks of agreement.

Alana cleared her throat and pulled at her collar. "It is not news I bring, but a message."

Clique noticed a bead of sweat drip down her face. *Such a brave girl, and she seems nervous. This message must be of dark import.*

"It was entrusted to me by one of Jacynth Irvalis' spiders." The words came hard for Alana, and she took a few more sips of wine to steady herself.

"Who's that?" Clique asked Davik.

"He is Alexander Warne's wizard." Davik gritted his teeth. "And no friend of this House."

Clique knew that Alexander sat the head of the Warne family, which was one of the three Great Houses of the Eastern Kingdom. He'd also known there was some animosity between them and Midgard, but knew nothing of the specifics. *It must be some O'Brien matter. Otherwise what would Midgard care of events in the Realm that had nothing to do with the summit?*

Alana seemed to be distracted, and her gaze had become distant. "My lady?" Clique placed his hand over hers. She was sweating, and her skin felt cool and clammy to the touch. "It's alright. You can tell us." He smiled. "What was the message?"

"It's... It's fifty words," she explained. "They're a jumble of nonsense. I've written them down in a hidden note, but I have them memorized as well." She took a napkin and wiped her brow. The wine had given her cheeks a red flush. "Should I get the original? Or should you get some paper?"

Axe spoke first. "My lady!" He said the words louder than Clique had ever heard him speak, and everyone's eyes drew to his attention. "I will remember them for Lord Gracious. Speak the words."

Davik seemed unsure, but Collin assured him with a silent nod.

Alana took a sip of her wine. "Does the labeled wisdom fork the pulp? An obstruction..." She pulled at her collar again, and coughed. "Romances the initiate inventor... the march..." She coughed again, but this time blood spit from her mouth onto her hand. "Talks around..."

"Alana," Clique said as she coughed in a fit. Her eyes went wide when she saw the blood.

"What? I'm..." Her nose bled and her eyes were watered. She looked to Davik with horror in her eyes. "Davik?" Her hand reached out for him and she knocked her silver goblet off the table. The purple wine stained her green gown alongside the blood, and the goblet clanked to the floor.

Davik shouted for a priest and went to her side. Collin rushed over and brought her water. Clique took a step back and watched the events unfold with his own horror. *I felt no waves.* He shuddered with the thought. *How can that be?* In that moment he rued returning before his training was complete. *I could have ignored Marcus, but I chose to obey my father.*

Alana had fainted to the floor, and was being cradled in Davik's arms. She coughed, and gurgled, and was unable to speak save for a few whimpers of, "Davik," and what was probably her mother's name. Davik whispered soothing words in her ear and stroked her lovely hair. By the time an old woman in white robes had come to her side, it was too late. The fire faded from Alana Toril's emerald eyes, and her hand fell limp at her side. Davik let out a moan of despair, and buried his head into her neck. Clique was stricken speechless at the sight of his uncle's sobs, and Collin had taken to crying as well.

Clique turned to one of the nearby House Guards and took him aside. "Fetch Sheriff Baldric immediately." The man ran off with purpose. Clique looked back to the sad scene, and the puzzle clicked into solution in his mind. *If the wine was poisoned, then it was meant for my uncle. But what about Axe?* He looked at the man with his usual curiosity. *I fear I am as confounded about him as ever. Perhaps his fortitude is so great it had no effect on him. Alana, no matter how strong her will, was but a small girl.* A fury began to overtake Clique such as one he'd never felt. *Someone has meant to kill my lord uncle, and has murdered my future bride to be!* Clique felt his fingers digging into his palms. He stomped his way over to Axe, and grabbed the man by the arm. "Axe. Answer me true." He spoke the words quietly, but his voice was stern. "Is it possible the wine was poisoned, and you, who also drank from it, are simply immune?"

Axe glanced down at his arm where Clique held it, then shrugged nonchalantly. "It is possible."

Clique released him. "Fetch the wine boy Kendrick."

Axe nodded with understanding and left. Clique knelt beside his uncle and placed his hand across Davik's back. "I'm sorry, uncle, but you must know." Davik raised his head and wiped the tears from his face. "I believe your wine was poisoned."

"But Axe..." Davik meekly protested.

"Has the constitution of no mortal man." Davik steadied himself. "The venom was meant for you, uncle. Alana has given her life that you may yet live." He watched as Davik's melancholy transformed into a ferocious rage. The Sheriff Baldric Vehement entered the solar flanked by five House Guardsmen.

"Sheriff!" Davik did not rise, but still held the poor girl close to his chest as he spoke. "Has the man who raped the butcher's wife been hanged yet?"

"No, my lord." The Sheriff had come to attention and looked down at his lord with all the solemnity he could muster. "That cretin was rotting for tomorrow, first of the Rat's Moon."

"Bring him here at once." Davik released Alana's corpse to the priestess who had been unsuccessfully tending to her. "His day has come."

The Sheriff set three of his men to the task with a nod, and approached. "My lord, the outriders for the armies have arrived." The Red Star was rising over the horizon, and its morning light shone through the stained glass windows of the Southern Wall. The colors gave Baldric's dark stature an eerie motley. "King of West and East make camp by nightfall, and demand summit the following morning."

Davik cursed under his breath. "See to it no word of what has happened here reaches the delegations. I will not have them think there is danger."

"And what *has* happened here?" Baldric queried.

Clique answered for his uncle. "Lady Alana Toril drank my uncle's wine instead of him, and has died for it. We are not certain the wine is the thing, but mean to find out. Ahh, here is the boy who served it." Axe entered with two guards dragging Kendrick in.

Davik stormed over to him, and for a moment Clique thought he might draw his dagger and kill the poor boy on the spot. But instead Davik paused inches from Kendrick's face and leered at him with hate in his eyes. "You served me poison wine."

Kendrick's fear from being brought by the guards transformed into mortal terror. "I didn't do it, my lord! I didn't!" Kendrick squealed. "I just poured the wine! I didn't know it was poisoned!"

"You didn't give me the bottle when I asked!" Davik screamed at him. "Is that because you knew it was death, and wanted only me as your target?"

"No! No, my lord!" Kendrick was in tears. "I swear it! All I did was pour!"

"Where did you get the bottle?" Clique asked him.

"It was all there in the Silver kitchen, my lord," Kendrick whimpered. "Go ask Kelly and them. I filled the decanter with wine from the barrel, and took Lord Gracious' personal stock from the shelf."

Collin finished whatever prayer he was muttering over Alana's body, and made his way over to where everyone crowded around unlucky Kendrick. "How many bottles were there?" Clique asked him. "Just the one, or a group?"

"Just the one, my lord," Kendrick said. "Which I thought was odd, since there were three left last night. I just thought his lordship had a great thirst while I slept."

"Sheriff!" Davik wiped away tears that still clung to his red eyes. "Throw this idiot in the dungeon to be questioned later." The wine boy was dragged away by two guards while he protested fiercely of his innocence. "I want the poisoner found, Sheriff."

Baldric frowned. "The matter will be investigated thoroughly, and at once, my lord." He took another two guards with him and left for the kitchen.

"We only heard seventeen of the note's fifty," Axe said. "Is it enough to have meaning?"

"No." Davik sighed. "They must all be taken together to decipher."

"What if it was a warning that you were to be assassinated?" Clique suggested. "The message might contain the killer's name."

"She said she had it written down," Davik answered. "Collin, I want you to find that note."

"It may have been hidden in her carriage, or have been found by the bandits," Collin said. "Ser Thomas has stowed both carriage and corpse in private stables."

"Go now, and have the lad assist you," Davik commanded him.

"Check her old clothes, and in the room she changed," Clique suggested. "Keira's bed servant may have seen her hide it, or would at least know where she had access to."

"I will." Collin nodded. He left as two guards brought in an ugly fat man that smelled of shit and piss. He hadn't shaved in weeks and his skin was pale. Loose skin flapped from whatever weight he'd shed in the dungeon.

Davik gave Clique a cold stare, and Clique understood the thick of it. He filled a silver goblet with the rare purple vintage, straight from the bottle, and approached the prisoner. "It must have been a long time since you had wine, yes?" Clique asked him. "You must be parched."

The man smiled hesitantly. "Yes, m'lord."

"Here you are." Clique offered the goblet to him. "Have a drink."

The prisoner's eyes fell upon the priestess where she burned incense and muttered prayers over Alana's dead body. He saw the spilled wine on her dress and the goblet beside her corpse. His hand paused and did not take the goblet.

"Hold a sword to his neck," Clique commanded, and a guard

obliged. The man tried to struggle away but two guards held him firm. The long steel tip of a sword was held against the side of his neck. "Draw a little blood..." The man eyed the steel as it kissed his neck, and a small trickle of blood licked back. Clique offered the goblet to him once more. "Drink it. I insist."

The man took the goblet and hesitantly drank the contents. "All of it, now," Clique told him. "There you go." They all watched with bated breath, and Clique found himself strangely satisfied when the man bled from his nose and collapsed to his death. *I was right about the wine,* he told himself. *And Axe as well.*

Davik lifted one of the fine wooden chairs and raised it over his head. With an angry cry he brought it down into the stone ground and smashed the thing to bits. Everyone watched as he destroyed a second chair in his rage, then collapsed into a crying heap next to Alana's body. *He loved her like a daughter,* Clique realized, and he wondered if she may have even been his. "I want every last one of those wine bottles checked for poison, then cast from the tower and into the sea!" Davik commanded them through his tears. "I trust what remains in the poisoned bottle is enough to test its origin."

"Yes," Clique told him. "It will be easily done."

"See what you can uncover, nephew," Davik said. "Then see yourself to my study when the Red Star has set this evening." Lady Keira entered the solar in a huff and ran to Davik's side.

"Yes, uncle. I will." Clique turned away from the sad sight. "Axe."

"Yes, Lord Commander?" Axe came to attention.

"You're with me." Clique left and Axe followed.

HAVIK

"This must not be done!" Narvis shouted. Her outburst caught everyone's attention, for she was a person who spoke little, and when she did, did so quietly. "If any of you have reason to trust me, then hear me now, and trust my words. Look around you!" She spread her arms apart and made motion to the shadow behind her, then circled about and pointed to the lightning above, the smoke and flames of the fissures in the distance, and to the Sea of Heavens that loomed overhead like a ghastly storm. "This place is not to be trifled! I have come on this mad quest because I too have lust in my heart. *Some* lust for riches. *Others* for power and glory. *I* have come because I lust to see the world! This place is sacred to me... and to the people I call brother, sister, master..."

Brackens and Flint had managed to find themselves beside one another. Havik saw Brackens ask something quietly, and Flint tapped the sheaths on his belt. Jaxon, Nimmet, and Horoway were taken by Narvis' speech and had come from the wagons to hear her. Brownbeard listened intently, as did Kevin and Jhev, who were shocked to see her acting this way.

"I told you not to go, m'lord!" Narvis cried. "We had no right to disrupt the Mother's wound! It must be returned. I beg of you!

Please! Give me the thing, and I will take it back to the shadow myself."

Tears were in her eyes, and the truth of her terror unsettled him. *She truly fears the thing.* Havik felt like retching. "Narvis." He took three long steps towards her and stood tall. "What did you mean when you said it has no color?"

"You... You would think I'm mad."

"Too late for that!" Brackens hooted.

"If you are to give me counsel, then speak up and give it!" Havik yelled. "I have no use for men or women in my service that give me half truths and riddles. If you don't wish to serve me, then say so and be done with it." Even as Havik spoke the words he was unsure if he was being too hard with her. *How firm a hand is too firm when grooming a woman for council?* Still, he knew she was stronger than she revealed.

"I can see them," Narvis finally admitted. She seemed relieved, as if it were some great secret that had weighed upon her soul.

Havik was unfazed. "Everyone can see colors."

"No..." she whispered. "The colors of magic."

"Is this some trick you learned when you took the black?" Havik inquired.

"No, m'lord. They... They only ever took me in *because* I had the sight."

"Were you born with it?" Havik asked.

"I..."

"Well should I open it or not?" Brackens complained.

"Quiet!" Havik shouted. He saw that Flint had already begun fidgeting with the thing, his knife scraping on its shell, but Havik didn't care, and was, in part, just trying to calm her down.

"You were saying," Havik said softly.

"Years ago, my father, he..." Narvis started, "well, he made me..."

"I know the story," he said, and calmly approached her. *To walk the plank is a cruel fate.*

"When they pulled me from the sea I was half dead, and half mad. It was days before I knew where I was, or even *who* I was. They said I had terrible nightmares. The things they said I screamed in the night. It gives me terrors." He put his hand on her shoulder in consolation. "When my wits returned I had the sight."

"What is it like?" Havik asked. *Her eyes are a most curious shade of green.*

"Auras of light and color that surround all things," she said, her eyes shimmering as she spoke. "Stone, and fire. Water. The sky. They all have their own color that glitters in waves around them. Living things, like birds, and trees. Their colors are mixtures of the eight, and they glisten golden by day, and glimmer silver by night. It's people that have the most spectacular colors of all!" She smiled gloriously then. "Their bodies shine pink and sparkly when in love, and glow fierce red and melt with black when hate is in their hearts." Her smile left her. "My sight lets me know the truth of a man's soul..." she whispered cautiously. "A grievous thing to know in a world of masks and masquerade."

Havik found his amorous thoughts leave him as quickly as they'd come. "That dirt there. That black rust, there. You see their colors?"

"Yes," she replied.

"That horse. That wagon. That damned star up above. Colors? All of them?"

"Yes." Narvis sighed.

"And when you look at the nut?" Havik knew the answer, but a part of him wanted to hear her say it again. "What color then?"

"It has no color," she whispered. Havik felt as if she were still holding something back.

"But what does that *mean*?" he shouted, quite frustrated. "What do you *see*?" He didn't wait for her response. He turned away and strut fast up to Flint and Brackens who were toying with the nut. Havik grabbed it from Flint's hands and rushed back to Narvis. Her fear was showing on her face again. When she calmed her demeanor had changed to one of sadness, but as he approached her with the nut in hand, her green eyes shone the color of horror. She cried again, and a soft moan whimpered from her lips. Everyone else in the camp might well have been scared shitless, but for Havik, it didn't matter what they thought, or felt. *What I think is all that matters. I am the one with the choice.*

Fool! You've already doomed them all!

"What do you see?" Havik found himself shouting. He shook the nut in front of her face but she turned away, almost as if she were terrified just to see the thing. Havik grabbed her by the arm and tried to force her. She struggled against him.

"No!" she cried out. "Please!"

"Look at it!" His hand gripped tighter but still she refused. He balled his fist and backhanded her across the face. She grabbed at her cheek and stared with the color of hate in her eyes. "What do you see? Tell me!"

"Nothing! Damn you!" she surrendered. "I see nothing!" She ceased her crying and stood tall.

"What do you mean nothing? No colors?" Havik asked.

"No! I mean I cannot even see it! When it is covered all I see is cloth. But when it is there, for all to see, and I look upon it, it is not black. It is not empty of color. It is a hole! A hole in the world, that distorts all around it like some terrible lens. A cracked mirror is what that is. Empty and dark, and I fear if I should get too close I might tumble inside and lose myself forever." She looked at him, her eyes a nameless color. "And when a man holds it bare in his hands." Narvis backed away from him, where Havik held the thing in his bare hands that very moment. "His is the very color of death."

No one spoke those few seconds.

Narvis straightened her hair and gained her composure. "Even if you will not heed my words, and wish to take it as a trophy, do so, but never open it. I do not know that thing, and it is terrible to behold. Consider my words carefully, m'lord. The risk is too great."

Havik had nothing to consider. He had already made his choice. He tossed the nut to Brackens, who caught it cheerfully.

"Flint!" Havik spoke forcefully.

"Yes, m'lord?" Flint answered, surprised he was addressed directly.

"Those knives will never do... Fetch the sledge hammer," he commanded.

"Yes, m'lord!" Flint chirped, and with that he rushed off to the wagon.

Narvis was horrified, and a small part of Havik was glad that she was afraid. *Let her fear her colors.* He smiled. *There is no magic. Only Scientos.* Brownbeard and Kevin approached him then, while the others crowded round.

"Why not heed her words?" Brownbeard asked. "If she suggests we take it back unopened, then let us do that."

Havik shook his head. "And what? Leave the glory to my uncle and father? And worse yet, should they open it themselves, with great pomp and circumstance, and it turn to poison cloud that kill them both? What then? Give the House to my young cousins and take great stain upon my honor?" Havik half laughed. "She is correct in one thing. The risk is too great."

Brackens had laid a tarp on the ground so that pieces of the shell would be easily collected. He delicately placed the nut upon the tarp's center and patted it gingerly with a smile.

"No, Brownbeard," Havik said. "We'll open the thing here. Now."

He watched Flint approach with the hammer in hand. "And see what color the meat has in store for us."

"No!" Narvis shrieked. It was kind fate that Havik stood unbalanced in that moment, for when he turned at the screech, he stumbled. The blade struck high, and put gash upon chin and cheek rather than sweetly slit his throat. *She meant to kill me!* His mind raced as he fell back to the ground, and he felt hot blood trickle down his neck and soil his tunic.

Brackens was upon her first. *Good Donner Brackens,* Havik thought, as the man drew a knife from his belt and stepped between Havik and the mad woman. Their blades parried knife on knife, until Narvis' miracle of somersaults and kicks resulted in Brackens head over heels a few feet away, with Brownbeard doubled over, his hands grasping at his injured groin.

Kevin drew his longsword and lunged at her. She jumped back, and drew a second blade from her robe. For half a moment they stood still, gauging one other. Horoway and Jaxon rushed in, their own knife blades drawn. Havik stood, and meant to give command, but found himself cradling his cheek instead. *It hurts something fierce,* he pondered at the sight of his own blood. When he looked up again, the woman had moved five feet, and Kevin was on his back, with his longsword lost.

Jaxon slashed at her wildly, but took a kick to the chest and fell back to the ground. Horoway was luckier, and managed to step round her leg and cut deeply into her thigh with steel. She grunted in pain and fell to her back, but as she did so swept out Horoway's legs and dropped him as well. He made move against her with his knife, but seconds later her blade was in his heart, and Horoway sounded a guttural groan as his life left him.

That was when the sledge hammer clipped her shoulder, which broke her arm and sent blade from hand. Flint stood over her, his hammer in motion for the coup de grace.

"Enough!" Havik bellowed. Flint halted his attack. Tears were in Narvis' eyes from the pain of it. Blood pooled from her leg wound. The other men stood round her and she yielded the second blade.

Havik walker closer and looked down at Horoway's corpse. "It needn't have come to this..."

"Do not open it," was all she could say.

"Restrain her," Havik said. Brackens spit as he grabbed a piece of rope, and with Jaxon's assistance, tied her hands behind her back. She gave a hideous cry as they took hold of her, but Brackens was unmoved by her sobs and tied her all the same.

"We should kill the bitch!" Nimmet protested. "She murdered poor Horoway."

"She's hurt, my lord," Brownbeard said. "She'll die if we do nothing."

"Tend to her then," Havik allowed. Nimmet grumbled.

Brownbeard set to the task. Havik could no longer stand to look upon her, so he turned away. *Her fear has overcome her,* he thought as he stepped over Horoway. *By the time we've returned to the Realm she will have come to reason.* Havik had already forgiven her momentary weakness, and as for the subsequent death of the sailor, did not think it need tarnish her bright future as a priestess. *Best keep Brownbeard with her til the ship, lest one of Horoway's mates finish the deed.* Havik considered giving direct order that if she were harmed, he'd lay inquisition upon the man that did it, til he'd confessed *all* the sins of his mortal life. It's what his uncle would have done in his position. *That can wait,* Havik thought. *I've a nut to crack for now.*

"Flint!" Havik bellowed.

"Yes, m'lord!" Flint yelped as he came up beside him.

"Why don't you put that hammer to use," Havik quipped. And at that, Flint smiled.

It was all everyone could do not to watch in bated breath. Havik held a bloody cloth to his cheek, and wondered whether Narvis would away from the sacrilegious act, or whether she, like all of them, would be driven by her base curiosity to gaze in awe at the spectacle. He didn't care enough to find out. Flint readied his stance and took a few practice swings.

"Go ahead. Do your worst," Havik commanded, and Flint obeyed.

With a heaving raise of the heavy hammer, and a mighty down stroke, the steel struck its mark. With a weighted thump, the shell sunk halfway down into the dirt. It was uncracked, and had been driven down like a stake.

Narvis whimpered unheeded protests while the heavy iron anvil was brought from the wagon and placed upon the spot where the nut once sat. Brackens used a clamp to fasten the nut to the iron, and this time, they were prepared to see the thing split. Once more Flint's aim was true, and the hammer squarely hit the nut's crown. A resounding boom not unlike a heavy flash of thunder clapped out, and all at once a fell wind swept dirt and ash to the air. A shrill ringing noise reverberated from the iron and steel, and it pained their ears to hear it.

As the dust settled, they saw the foul black shell had split in twain, and two equal halves of it had fallen upon the cloth. The core of the shell was egg white, with black shell encrusting its outer edges. There upon the anvil, no longer in clamps, sat a clump of pale white moss. No one spoke as Havik gingerly approached the anvil and examined the lump close up. *Not moss, but sea foam like in its consistency,* Havik thought as he rubbed the stuff betwixt his fingers. After a moment of consideration he plunged his hand inside, and pulled from within its depths a white bean no larger than an apple.

The thing was delicately curved and irregular in shape. It was slick with slime to the touch and difficult to hold. Havik thought it smelled of morning dew on grass, but upon second whiff he found it fragrantly sweet. He licked his lips and tasted honey. *Not a bean...* Havik concluded. *A seed...*

When at last he looked up, Havik saw all eyes upon him. Narvis' mouth hung open at the sight of it, and Brownbeard had tears in his eyes. *Are they thinking what I'm thinking?*

"And what color is this, my lady?" he finally asked.

Narvis' eyes were a display of wonder. "*All* colors..."

"You spoke of a giant tree, wizard?" Havik chortled.

"Not just any tree, my lord," Brownbeard cried out, "the world tree! The tree of life that first was planted in the times before the Doom. When the Gate of Heavens opened and the Goddess made Eldaria her home, she planted this tree."

"That is a lie!" Narvis shouted.

Brownbeard was aghast. "It is no such thing."

"The masters say the tree was here even before the Goddess," she said.

"That's absurd," Brownbeard proclaimed, "the texts say–"

"Your books are wrong! When the world was young, a girl came to this place. She was thirsty and tired, and sat beneath the tree. She drank from the waters that pooled by its roots, and slept in the shade of its branches."

"What shade?" Brackens quipped. "The Dead Star's aura–"

"Was not there," Brownbeard interrupted. "The tree stood before the Doom."

Narvis solemnly continued. "By the light of the Silver Star she dreamed, and in her dream the tree became a beautiful man. There, beside the stream of life, he came in the night, and made love to her. When she awoke she was pregnant with child."

"So what you're saying is," Brackens laughed, "she dreamed she fucked Eldaria's cock!"

Kevin laughed and Brownbeard frowned. Narvis nodded to Havik's surprise. "Yes," she said, "and the child she bore became the Goddess."

"Blasphemy!" Brownbeard shouted. "The Goddess is no child of a mortal woman! Sage Dioratemus in his scripture wrote, *'And as the Gate of Heaven tore a hole above the world, a sea of stars that never shone upon the sky unfurled. The Goddess made her home beneath the sky she held so dear, and left the children of the stars forever free of fear. And she was not of mortal kin, and lived forever young. Where men would die, she would live on, her song forever sung.'* " Brownbeard took a breath. "His words are clear... The Goddess made her home here *after* the Gate opened. Would you deny it?"

"M'lord..." Havik thought he heard Flint say, but his eyes were upon Narvis.

Narvis was unshaken. "I can speak scrolls too. *Isfet, his heart black, his reign finished, cursed Ma'at a hex of vengeance. Mortal once, so mortal shall you be again. And Isfet closed the Gate, and doomed the world.*" She smiled sweetly.

Brownbeard's anger flared. "You speak a *cursed* tongue!" He rose in a huff, and his face flushed. "I will not suffer this woman's heresy!"

"And *I* will not suffer this pointless debate!" Havik shouted. "Enough!" He gazed fiercely at Narvis, then Brownbeard in turn. "Eldaria's cock. This tree. You both admit it once existed?" They both nodded. "Could this not be its *seed?*"

"M'lord?" Flint whispered under his breath, but Havik paid him no mind.

Havik held the white seed aloft before them. "Could this seed not be planted?" They must have thought the words before he said them, but even so, it was only after he spoke that their anger faded and Narvis and Brownbeard alike held wonder in their eyes.

"Well, my lord," Brownbeard began, "it looks... and smells fresh enough to me."

Havik looked to Narvis, and her eyes rose to met his. "It's growing even now," she said.

"Do you mean to plant it here?" Brownbeard asked immediately.

"M'lord?" Flint asked again.

Havik shook his head and paced about the ground. "Here? In this wasteland? No, of course not."

"If it truly is the world tree's seed then it is a holy relic!" Brownbeard proclaimed. "It must be brought to the Academy," he continued, "where they will see it safely to Starcrown Cathedral for the High Priests to decide what to do with it."

Havik looked to Narvis, but she was speechless at the sight of the thing. "If this seed will grow a tree that all the world will covet, then I will see it grow on Davenport land, behind Davenport walls." He smiled innocently at Brownbeard. "Let the Priests pilgrimage."

"Your uncle will prize this above all else!" Jhev announced. "Should we not bring it to him at once?"

Havik grinned a wicked grin. *My friend knows my mind.* "Yes, Captain. My uncle will surely–"

"M'lord?" Flint queried once more.

"What!" Havik roared as he turned to face him. "What is it?" But when he expected to meet Flint's gaze and hear his words, he saw instead that Flint was bone white. *Fear has taken him.* Flint was pointing down at the ground and his knees quivered. Havik's eyes followed Flint's gaze, and came to the two half shells of the cracked nut beside the anvil. A queer black ichor had pooled beside each shell. The pieces were no longer black on the outside, and were now as egg white without as they were within. Small spilling stains of a rancorous dark bile still dripped from the shell pieces, and where it fell to the cloth, it puddled about like spilled mercury. As Havik speculated over the strange substance, a quiet passed over the group. Jaxon and Nimmet had been seeing Horoway's body to the wagon, but upon sight of the stuff, dropped his corpse into the dirt with a fright.

"What..." Havik thought he managed to sound aloud, "is that?"

"The shell..." Jhev muttered. "It was... It had..."

"I think what our dear Captain is trying to say, m'lord," said Brackens, "is the nut wasn't black at all, but just had this shit all over it."

"It looks like ink," Kevin Gracious said. Havik just then noticed Kevin stood beside him, with his longsword recovered and in his sheath.

"It looks expensive, I think." Brackens smirked. "Shall I fetch a few jars?" He looked to Havik for his command, and Havik was just about to give it when the choice was removed from his concern.

All at once the two pools of Stygian fluid sent forth tendrils like a living thing and pulled two halves to one. The small juicy pond of the wicked stuff gathered together into some cancerous bubbling concoction. Flint fainted from shock of it, the hardened sailor that he was, and Kevin pulled his sword.

"Dear Goddess!" Brownbeard gasped.

"What *is* that thing?" Jhev queried.

Jaxon and Nimmet stood terrified whilst Narvis strained to see.

Brackens thought fast, and in one swoop covered the horror with the other half of the cloth tarp. "I don't like the look of it, m'lord," he said, and Havik nodded silently. "May be best if we leave it be."

Havik struggled to show no fear before his men, and stepped over the hidden puddle. He casually came to a knee alongside the nut shell, and tapped his fingers against it. *It feels like glass. Why should it feel like glass?* he pondered. "This is odd. Brownbeard, feel this."

Brownbeard held his breath and approached. He knelt beside Havik and brushed his fingers across the polished ivory of the shell, and when he did so twisted his mouth in surprise. With a thought, he rapped his knuckles against the shell. It made a strange hollow sound. "It is white glass, my lord."

"That makes no sense." Jhev sighed, no doubt feeling lost in the mysteries of archaeology.

"Glass?" Brackens howled. "No way it's glass, m'lord. It took a full hit of the hammer and cracked in two. Glass would shatter."

"If I may?" Brownbeard took the shell and was about to throw it upon the ground as if to shatter it, when Havik stopped him.

"Idiot! Brackens. Get the other half of the shell," Havik commanded, and Brackens retrieved it. Havik still held the white seed close to his chest. He watched as Brackens fit the two pieces of the shell entirely together into a small, perfectly shaped, white sphere. It was only slightly larger than the seed itself. Brackens and Brownbeard were horrified by it, but Jhev looked as if he did not understand.

"What is so unusual?" Jhev remarked. "Glass or not, yes, it cracked cleanly."

"But it's so much smaller!" Brackens hollered. "Look!"

It really is smaller, Havik thought. *How much of that bile was on there? And why had it melted so suddenly after having been split asunder?* The question burned at his mind. Havik was a man of Scientos. He truly believed there was a logical explanation for the mystery before him. His mind whirred with the skills he had been honing his entire life. Havik had come to understand that the essence of what allowed the Davenport House to rise to power, was the secret of advanced reasoning and logic. "In a world where magic is dead," his uncle had once lectured to a six year old Havik, "all men stand as equals. And yet the only thing which distinguishes us, from the beasts, is our ability to reason. Money, land, and power all come at a price. But your mind is one weapon that is free, and you had best learn to use it!" Havik treasured those early years when Lord Hubert Davenport first introduced him to Scientos. It was then that his puzzling games began. His own father preferred swords in the courtyard, but his uncle was a brilliant strategist, and insisted all Davenport children train their minds foremost.

"Do my Ancient eyes give advantage to Davenport reasoning uncle?" Havik once asked after he deciphered a particularly rousing riddle posed to him. He recalled his uncle stared at him, quiet for some time, before he gave a brief wicked smile and suggested they move on to the next puzzle to solve.

Concentrate, he said to himself. *Think. The woman sees colors. The seed was rainbow and the nut black abyss. The seed is alive, and was kept in egg white foam like a yolk. The shell is glass. Man made. Ancients most like. They stored the seed in a jar. But the outside...* Havik glanced back to the tarp, and half stepped away as he looked down. The stuff was still hidden beneath the cloth. *It was hard like a carapace and difficult to shell. It cracked as a solid thing, and soon turned to liquid. What chemistry causes such a feat?* he asked, but he seemed to already know the answer. *It pulled itself together, but that could have been magnetics.* He found himself sweating. *Why did it melt? Was it the salt? The Dead Star's aura? No, it did not melt until cracked.* The thought crept up on him. *It chose to melt.* The fear was full upon him now, and Havik did not fight against it. He almost lost the contents of his stomach, but pressed forward in his puzzling. Havik knew from his logic games that if you removed whatever could not be true, then whatever remained, however impossible it might seem, must be allowed for as the truth. *It's alive. It chose to be hard, and it chose to be a liquid.*

But why? Why did it choose to melt once cracked?

The others had begun to chatter amongst themselves with their questions and concerns. *Concentrate.* Havik strained to shut them out. *Let me put aside for a moment the religious implications of all colors, and no colors. The tree grew here, and here where it grew was found the seed. It is reasonable to assume the seed is of the tree. It was protected in glass for preservation, and found covered by some living thing. It is possible that blackness grew upon the glass over the years, but what if it was already there when the Ancients first placed the shell upon its salty altar? But if so, why would they not simply remove it? Did they place it there on purpose? What if it could not be removed? If I had my holy seed relic set upon by a foul growth that would not burn or cut, I would certainly not smash it for fear of shattering the glass inside. What then could I do to protect my object? I'd place it someplace safe of course, until I could figure out what was to be done with the thing. And where to put it? Why, in a pit of salt to preserve it and ward off hexes.* Havik seemed satisfied with his conclusion, but his fear pulsed within his heart again and he took it a level further. *It was surrounded by a wall.* He remembered the standing steel towers and the wall's broken remains. *All that black rust... At one point it was inside an iron castle. The treasured relic had a growth they could not remove, and at the heart of the shadow it was buried, for longer than the castle itself stood. And so, after so many years passed that the castle rusted, the carapace sat in salt and withered. But why would it melt once broken? Why would it choose to melt?* Havik arrived upon a conclusion that made his consciousness twist with a convulsion of horror. *Because it could not, previously, get inside the glass.*

Fool! You should have listened to her, and now they're all dead!

"My lord, you're bleeding," Brownbeard said.

Havik's sweat beaded over his mouth, but when he wiped his

sleeve he found he had bled from the nose. He swore under his breath. "We'll put the seed back in the glass for storage."

Havik gingerly handed the seed to Brackens, who seemed well in agreement to this. "Aye!"

Havik walked up to the anvil and once again examined the white sea foam moss that spilled when the nut cracked. He ran it once more between his fingers, pooled some in his palm, and raised the spongy mix to his nose and sniffed, but it had no aroma. Without warning he felt a queer burning along his face, and he realized some of the foam had blown off onto his cheek where his fresh wound still bled. Havik swore, raised his sleeve, and wiped away the foam and blood.

"My lord, your wound!" Brownbeard cried out.

"What now, damn it?" Havik protested. "I know, I'm bleeding. I can feel it better than you!"

"No my lord! It's gone! The wound on your face! It's healed!" Brownbeard shouted.

"Quiet, will you! My head is pounding!" Havik rubbed at his cheek and felt the open scar where his would-be priestess had sliced him chin to cheek. But the wizardly jester was right. It was no longer there. In giddy amazement he rubbed his face. "Dear Goddess! You're right! It's all healed!"

Impossible but true, Havik reflected. *This small bit of foam and its healing wonder may be more valuable than seed and metal together. I wonder if the foam nourished the seed, or the seed the foam.*

"That's incredible! I see it as well!" remarked Jhev in astonishment.

What kind of healing powers might this plant have? Havik wondered.

Kevin stepped close and looked. "It's healed. It's true!"

Havik thought Narvis was either too humbled or cautious to speak, and he suspected some part of her wanted to use the foam to heal her painful wounds, no matter how sacrilegious it might be to her.

What Havik did not expect was Nimmet to speak.

"M'lord!" he shouted as he rushed up alongside Havik at the anvil. "Let me scoop this foam into Horoway's heart and revive him!" But before Havik could protest, Nimmet had already begun to reach down towards the foam with outstretched palm.

Havik could not help himself. With the back of his hand, he slapped Nimmet across the face with such force that it brought him to the ground. "You presume too much, sailor!" he shouted, angry with him. "This prize is far too precious to be wasted on the likes of him." Nimmet had hate in his eyes just then. Havik saw the color of it. *I should be more cautious with these small folk so far from the Realms.* "Moreover! I will not risk the Dead Gods' wraths. Steal from that nightly caravan and you take from the Heart-Eater's dinner plate. They may plunder *your* soul instead to balance their wagons." Jaxon and Kevin made the sign of the Goddess. *That should appease them.*

Nimmet humbly rose to his feet, and nodded. "Yes, m'lord." Fear replaced hate. *Good.*

"Even so, I will not have one of our wizards die on the journey back." Havik addressed Brownbeard. "Come take some for the girl."

"Yes, my lord." Brownbeard nodded to him, and took a small bit of the foam onto his fingers. Narvis did not object when Brownbeard set to healing her wounds with the strange stuff.

Havik turned to Brackens. "The seed is in the jar?"

"Yes, m'lord," Brackens answered.

"Bring it here," Havik said, "I mean to put the foam inside for keeping."

Brackens parted the sphere and revealed the seed within. As Havik had his hands full with precious foam, his mind was aswarm with delusions of grandeur on the miracles that might be performed with such a, dare he think it, *magic* power in his hands. *In my uncle's hands... And if he should live forever by the magic of some plant...* Neither Havik, nor Brackens, who also had his hands full, heard the scream until it was too late. Narvis let loose a shrill shriek that made Havik's hair stand on end. He saw Jaxon fumbling with a dagger, and Brownbeard standing aghast with horror at some spectacle behind Havik's back. He turned to find the ebony sludge had pooled up through the cloth, and now reached itself up from its puddle, rising into the air as if some ghostly amorphous hand composed of the vile ink. Almost by instinct, Havik took what remained of the foam into his pants pockets.

"Protect the seed!" Narvis cried out in desperate terror. But the glass was unwieldy, and Brackens was ill prepared for such a start. Foam had been sopped on top of the seed, but not so much as to fully submerge the thing. As Brackens raised the half shell to cover the other, the blob of malignant ooze loosed spurts of black goo from its mass like a bow would an arrow. Some shot wide and fell upon the ground, where the droplets slithered towards their mother. Some landed upon the white sea foam, and it hissed horrifically and dissipated like shadows at star-rise. But no one save for Brackens and Havik saw that some of the Stygian fluid fell upon the seed itself, and seeped into it, where it muddied the delicate white of the seed with spirals of black like ink upon milk. Narvis sounded a foul screech that pained Havik to hear it, and by the time Brackens had closed the shell once more, the seed itself had turned as black as tar.

Havik had little time to ponder the mystical significance of the seed being corrupted by the monstrosity, for the wicked abomination still stood before them. Brackens, Havik, and all others backed away from the thing, save for Kevin, who swung at it with his blade. The sword sliced through as if it were porridge, which slowed the swing and covered the blade with its drippings. As the fluid crept up to the hilt, Kevin tossed aside his longsword in alarm and backed away. Narvis sobbed hysterically.

"We should leave," was all Jhev could say.

Havik nodded. "Ready the wagons! We're going. Now." Jhev, Jaxon and Nimmet rushed to the wagons, while Brownbeard grabbed the overwrought woman and dragged her away kicking and babbling incoherently. Kevin scurried off to ready the horses, while Havik continued to take steps away from the evil substance. Brackens remained at Havik's side with the sphere in hand.

"What about the... thing?" Brackens inquired.

"We leave it," Havik said.

"The anvil as well, m'lord?" he asked.

"We are done with mining. Let it rust."

"Shall we leave him as well?" Brackens quipped, and their eyes turned to Flint. That poor sailor who had fainted straightaway, still lay unconscious not three feet from the villainous creature that rose from the cloth in arrogant defiance of the laws of nature. *Curse him,* Havik thought. *I'll not risk getting near that thing.*

"Flint!" Havik yelled. "Flint!" And Brackens got the gist of it. Together they hooted and hollered in attempt to wake him from his state. It seemed as if he were beginning to respond. His hand rose, reached for his head, and he moaned in pain. *He must be hurt.* "Flint! Get up!" Flint grabbed at the cloths covering his nose and mouth, and removed them to take in a deep breath of air. The nebulous demon seemed to take notice of Flint's movements. Whether by sight, or feeling, or sound, the fiendish thing returned to a flat puddle and snaked its way towards Flint. The cloth it left behind was tattered with holes.

"Flint! Look out!" Brackens screamed, but it was to no avail. As Flint looked around in his daze, the blackness crept upon him, and trailed along his chest.

"Dear Goddess," Havik muttered, as Flint swatted at the puddle making its way towards his face. He cursed and cried out in alarm, though perhaps that was folly, for when his mouth gaped wide in fright, the obsidian horror gushed its way in. It parted his lips and spilled over his tongue, until the whole sum of it was swallowed in one great heaving gulp. Havik's stomach wrenched, and he bent over his knees as if to vomit, but nothing came. He saw Brackens' urine spilling from his breeches to the dry ground of the Barrens. Brackens turned, just then, and ran. He stopped to look back after he'd gone some distance.

"M'lord!" Brackens shouted. "Are you coming?"

"Wrap the sphere well and place it in the wagon!" Havik shouted. "The one Narvis is *not* bound in! Leave at once and lead the wagons East towards the gate!"

"What about you m'lord?" Brackens was anxious ridden. "You can't mean to stay here!"

"I do not plan to!" Havik grinned. "Have Kevin and Jaxon bring me my horse! And my sword!"

Brackens ran off post haste, while Havik cautiously approached Flint. *The obsidian horror has corrupted my seed, turned my priestess mad, and taken my man. Perhaps if I shove this foam down Flint's throat it might cure him of his affliction.* Havik had witnessed with his own eyes the ooze splash upon the foam and fizzle away as if disenchanted. *Magic or chemistry, the foam is the thing.* By now Flint's body had finished its cacophony of seizures and laid still and lifeless. *Maybe he is simply dead, and it nests within his chest, growing like a parasite.* Havik stepped closer to Flint and looked for signs of breathing. *Or perhaps it lies in wait like a snake in its lair.*

The thought did not please him. Havik stood there, frozen in indecision. He considered whether he should rush in and feed Flint the foam while the opportunity still presented itself, or give in to his cautious nature, and wait for his squire and his sword. *Do not hesitate!* his uncle screamed in his ear, but his doubt had already cost him the chance. All at once Flint rose, as if a shade from his grave, and stood with his arms hanging loosely from his shoulders. His neck was limp, and he held a vacant gaze upon the floor.

"Flint?" Havik felt the fear pulse through him.

The man let loose a guttural groan that held no hint of voice or reason.

A man possessed, Havik thought, as he heard the clop clopping of hooves in the distance.

AXE

The dank dungeon hall held some of the stranger and more unpleasant smells that Axe had ever experienced. Somehow, beyond the rotting of molds and bodily fluids, the air tasted of salt and rusty corrosion. The upper dungeons held nearly fifty prisoners, all taken in as a result of recent unrest in the city. Here in the lower dungeons it was darker, and Clique and the gaoler each carried torches. For a brief while Axe considered what it would be like not to see. Whether by lack of star or flame, or simply by closing their eyes, Axe knew men could turn the world to darkness. When Axe closed his eyes, he only lost four percent of the spectrum of light that made up his visual input. *It is a wonder that normal men can see at all.*

Axe had known well by now that all his senses were heightened to extents no other man could achieve, but the poison that killed Alana, and only made Axe drunk, yielded a revelation of its own. *Even my blood is immune to mortal weaknesses.* That thought had made him question whether he was even mortal at all. *Am I the son of some god, the immortal deities that people seem to pray to?* Only the gods in their legends held the secrets of immortality. *Or am I something not of antiquity, but of novelty? If I am not a descendent, then perhaps I am unique?* Axe had toyed with the question a trillion times. *Instead of a mother, do I have a creator? Or have I done this to myself? Or has someone done this to me?*

Axe knew the answers might never be solved, and his inquisitions into places like Treefort, or the symbols he remembered, had yielded nothing. The best any wizard or priest could tell him, was that it was likely a foreign place, though Collin suspected his powers may have something to do with the djinn. Axe noticed Collin and Keira displayed a sense of reverence to those particular deities that were frozen asleep in ice that never melts. Except for the Dravens, the other Eastern Houses, and particularly the citizens of Midgard, seemed to have a disdain for strict worship of the djinn, and instead believed in the Goddess, and an ideology they called Scientos. Scientos seemed to Axe nothing more than an extension of logic, and he became confused whenever he tried to understand how people could take things on faith, or believe in the unproven, like the Goddess, while they simultaneously revered logic and the need for proof. Even so, Axe wondered if his own very existence was proof that Scientos could create gods, or if he himself were proof that deities were real, and that they had borne children. Either way, Axe considered himself an enigma that when solved, might crystallize the theological disputes of mortal men. In the meanwhile, he planned to diligently serve as a Huntsman. He would remember in his actions the family that took him in and shaped what he considered his childhood, and he would bring honor to House of Gracious that gave him such a high position. *If I am to give myself my own purpose, let me live as a Royal Huntsman,* he had told himself. *Midgard is my home now, and in the service of Lord Davik Gracious I will protect it... Above all else, that means protecting him.*

As they descended the final stairs Axe heard a man and a woman's voices coming from the hallway below, but when the gaoler opened the sturdy wooden door they fell silent. "Here they are, m'lords," the grizzly jailer said as they approached the two cells at the end of the hall. This hallway had been lit by torches set in sconces, and they were the only two prisoners on the level. In one sat Kendrick, the wine boy, on a pile of hay, and in the other sat Kelly, the fair faced kitchen servant.

"Your name is Kelly, is that correct?" Clique asked her.

"Yes, m'lord," she said.

"Tell us what you told the Sheriff," Clique commanded her.

She came up to the iron bars and wrapped her hands around them. "All I did was fetch the bottle from the cellar. I saw the shelf was empty when I woke to prepare breakfast, so I went down there to get it for m'lord's waking. It was the last bottle in the crate, and I didn't think to open another." She started crying. "I didn't even know he was awake in the solar until I'd already returned with it, and started boiling water."

"And who entered the kitchen after you fetched it?" Clique asked.

"No one except Kendrick," she said. "Please, you can't think we had anything to do with it."

"I believe you, poor girl," Clique told her with a sigh.

"Then tell the Sheriff. Please, you can't let him hang us! We didn't do nothing wrong." She grabbed at his wrist while she begged. Clique pulled away from her.

"It is not up to me," he told her. She continued to plead, while Clique led Axe out of earshot. "What do you think?" Clique asked him.

"Two things, Lord Commander," Axe said.

"Clique. Just Clique." He smiled.

"Two things, Clique." Axe smiled in return. "Firstly that the next logical step is to find whoever is responsible for guarding the wine cellar."

"I'm sure that's where the Sheriff is now," Clique agreed. "And second?"

"Someone's hiding fourteen meters that way." Axe motioned down a nearby hall. "She was talking to a man before we came in, and it wasn't Kendrick. Shall we go find out?" Axe patted his axe.

"Yes." Clique nodded. "Let's."

Axe wielded both his axes and led with Clique lagging behind. Clique was not only mortal, but also had no weapon other than a simple dagger, so they both silently agreed Axe would take point. Though Axe went nowhere without his weapons at his side, he took note that men of high birth, such as Clique, often left their primary weapon of choice behind, and chose to walk the castle halls with nothing but a dagger. The irony was not lost on Axe, as he noted that a man who could not be killed had even less need for a weapon than a mortal. Even so, Axe chose to see it that his nature gave him a responsibility to always be prepared to uphold justice, and protect all mortal men as his morality dictated. For now, that meant serving as a Huntsman, and protecting the peace of Midgard.

The young guard they found lurking in the shadows claimed his name was Daniel, and that Kelly was his betrothed. "I know a thing or two about honor," he'd proclaimed, "and my beloved is innocent of these charges." He had apparently been born the fourth son of a lesser Midgard House, and was apprenticed to be a blacksmith. On his sixteenth year he had met the girl, and though she was not noble, she lived in the castle and was ever out of reach to him. Three years ago he bought out his apprenticeship and joined the guard. Interestingly enough, this was his first week as a member of the House Guard. Clique seemed surprised when he volunteered that bit of information.

"You say this is your first week?" Clique made the man repeat.

"Yes. I only just started yesterday, truth be told," Daniel said, "but I hope you don't think *I* had anything to do with it!"

"Jack Havensword is your Commander, yes?" Clique asked.

"Well, yes. He's our Captain. But I haven't met him yet," Daniel answered.

"Are there many new members to the House Guard?" Clique asked again.

"About twenty altogether." Daniel nodded. "All hand picked by Havensword on orders of the Sheriff to bolster the guard during the summit."

"If you were hand picked by him," Clique queried, "then how is it that you've never met the man?"

"I didn't say *I* was hand picked. One of the old guards died. Hibbeld I think it was. Lord Gracious demanded the House Guard be exactly fifty men, so the Sheriff gave me the honor of it."

"How is it he chose you?" Clique asked.

"It was just by chance," Daniel told them. "I alone guarded the door when the Sheriff received word from the priest that Hibbeld died. He was writing a letter and just looked up, and said, 'Dan right? How would you like to join the House Guard?' How could I refuse?" Daniel pleaded with them. "And to be honest with you, my lords, most of that time's been spent with Kelly. Hasn't been much to guard before the summit starts. It can't have been her. It just can't."

Clique warned the man not to do anything foolish, and promised he'd ensure the girl was not hanged. He thanked Clique profusely, and was told to return to his post, and not see Kelly until later that evening. Daniel begrudgingly agreed, and left the dungeons. "So did you believe his story?" Axe asked Clique once they were alone.

Clique dismissed the question. "It's not him I'm worried about. It's these twenty men of Havensword's."

"What's so unusual about that?" Axe asked. "It was Gracious and the Sheriff's own orders."

"New men taken into the guard, that I can understand." Clique frowned. "But it begs the question, *where* is their Captain?"

"Perhaps the Sheriff knows. You can ask him right now, he's coming this way."

Moments later Sheriff Baldric entered through the wooden doors flanked by his own small retinue of guards. They came to a stop beside Axe and Clique in the hall. "What have you found Sheriff?" Clique asked him.

"Grim news, I'm afraid." The Sheriff shook his head. "We discovered which men were responsible for guarding the wine cellar during the time the crate must have been tampered with."

"And what do they have to say for themselves?" Clique asked.

"Little and less." Baldric sighed. "For both men have conveniently gone missing."

"They must not be allowed to escape!" Clique told him.

"They haven't left the castle grounds. Of that I can assure you," Baldric said. "I have my men looking now. They will be found."

"Sheriff..." Clique patted him on the shoulder. "Where is Jack Havensword? I hear he has not yet taken command of his new recruits."

"Jack's not taken command?" Baldric seemed genuinely surprised. "That's not like him."

"You'd best have your men look for him too. I fear he may have come across the conspirator and met an ill fate." Clique yawned. "For now I'm going to get some rest. Send me word once you have made further progress."

"Yes, Lord Gracious." Baldric and his guards continued towards the prison cells.

"Axe, I want you to get some rest too," Clique said.

"I'm not tired." Axe stood to attention. "I will continue the investigation."

"Neither of us has slept since the road, and we must be fresh for tonight, as well as tomorrow." Clique and Axe started their ascent out of the dungeon.

"I will be fine without sleep. I–"

"You're under the impression it was a request." Clique interrupted him. "Bathe yourself and change into clean clothes, then sleep. I'll come for you when you're needed."

"Yes, Lord Commander."

Clique left him when they exited the dungeon, and Axe took the long walk back to his room. He had taken one of the unused chambers above the Royal Huntsmen's gathering hall. In some elder day it was used as a lock room for armor and weapons, so it had no windows, and a solitary heavy iron banded door. For Axe, it was perfect. He emptied it, cleaned it, and had servants furnish it like a normal bed chamber. Whenever he took that heavy oak bar and fastened the door shut from the inside, Axe felt a contentment like no other. *The world of men is a place of endless sensory input,* he thought that first night he spent in his room. *I understand a man's need for privacy.* Such a secluded and secured room was the closest Axe might get to darkness while in a place as crowded as Stormbreaker. He could see just fine at the higher frequencies of light, and through the thick stone walls he could often hear the sounds of the nearby stable. He could even feel the vibrations of people walking down distant halls, and that seemed to bother him the most. His ingenuity had led him to construct a bed that rested on springs, and in doing so lessened his sensations even more, and brought him closer to that feeling of complete peace which he sought after.

Axe's thoughts were for his bed as he passed through the halls of the stronghold, but fear and suspicion were in the eyes of the guards that past him. *They will search for the assassin, while I prepare for diplomacy.* He laughed to himself. *I become closer to a lord each day.* He looked down at his clothing and saw the reason for Clique's order to bathe. Brown blood stains were the predominant color on his garments, and his armor was damaged from where the bandit's mace had hit him. *He didn't even have enough strength to wound me.* Axe sighed. *If fame of my strength were more well known, he might have surrendered at the sight of me, and would yet live.*

Axe took no pleasure in killing men, and it was primarily the blood and gore of the killing that had given him a distaste for it. He secretly wished he had some manner of combat that could fell a man and leave no trace of blood. Save for snapping a man's neck, which is altogether risky and difficult in open battle, Axe's strength made bloodshed not just a certainty, but supplied it in excess. Samuel Gracious had vomited the first time he saw Axe kill a man. Axe meant for his attack to disarm the man, but his opponent ducked at the wrong time, and the attack severed his torso at the shoulders. The font of blood that erupted drenched Axe in the stuff and made for a gruesome spectacle. Axe soaked in water all that night to remove the feeling of it that lingered on his skin. *Perhaps death is meant to be uncomfortable,* Axe had mused that night in the bath, *and a good life is one cleanly lived.*

When Axe entered the Huntsmen's gathering hall he was met by two servants. He bid them to prepare hot water for a bath, and to fetch him a hot meal. It was not long before Axe was clean, fed, and locked away in his chamber. He chose the finest suit he owned, one for which he'd saved and purchased expressly for times of diplomatic engagement. He carefully laid it out on the table beside his bed. *I had thought my first meeting with Lord Gracious was going quite well until we drank poison.* Axe sighed at the memory. *Though now I realize my bloodied rags must have been impolite... Still, it was the blood of the bandits we saved Alana Toril from. Perhaps he saw it as a badge of honor for the rescue.* Axe climbed into his bed amidst a chorus of squeaky springs, and when he found his comfort they fell silent. *I hope he does not bear me any ill will that she died and I did not. I must prove to him my strengths are his. As a Huntsman I serve him... He will come to use me... He will...*

Axe closed his eyes and felt his higher processes shut down. His dream was the same as it always was. He dreamed of the near perfect stillness of his bed chamber, and there, at the lower left of his vision, was the green square. It shone with neon splendor but gave off no light, and it blinked with repeated regularity. Blink. Blink. Blink. His dream ever awaited further input... Further commands...

Axe woke to the sound of knocking against his chamber door. He opened it to have one of his servants instruct him that Clique was waiting below. Axe dressed himself in his suit, fastened his two axes upon his belt, and descended to meet his Lord Commander. Clique was dressed in his finest as well, and carried only his dagger in noble fashion. "Clique," Axe said as he approached, "what word is there of the investigation?"

Clique rose and by the frown on his face the result was clear enough. "Havensword and the two guards are still missing, and two armies are at our doorstep. Come, my uncle awaits us." They entered the Red Tower by way of the third gate, and came to a stop outside of Davik's study. Two members of the House Guard flanked the door in their black armor, with black shield and short sword. They came to attention as Clique and Axe walked up. "Is he alone?" Clique asked. They both nodded, and Clique opened the door and pushed his way in. Axe followed and the guards closed the door behind them.

The room was circular with a conical ceiling thirteen meters high. Three stories of bookshelves with multilevel walkways surrounded the walls of his study. Davik sat across from them at a grandiose desk that was masterfully sculpted from a single block of wood. Oak veins were brought out by its stain, and as Axe entered he found himself admiring its craftsmanship. *If I had access to an equally large piece of wood, I could replicate such a piece of furniture.* Axe was confident in his woodworking skills from his days on the farm, but had also taken on a number of odd tasks since his time at the Stronghold and had learned much. He had even reached the point where he was expanding upon the knowledge he'd learned, and experimenting with novel inventions of his own design. His bed of coils was only one such device, and he had many other ideas in mind. *Perhaps I could make him a wondrous chair to match the desk, or a bed frame for a bed of coils?*

Davik fastidiously scrawled away at a letter. Sheets of paper scattered the surface of his desk. Axe found his gaze pass over the paperwork. They were a good ten meters away from Davik when he looked up and smiled. "Ah, nephew. Good." He hastily gathered all the papers together in a pile and turned them upside down upon his desk.

"There's still no word of the assassin, uncle." Clique sighed.

"Yes, yes, I know. Baldric has kept me informed." Davik stood up. "But I am undeterred, and we must move forward as planned. Axe, is there something I can do for you?"

Axe was taken aback by the question. "My lord, I thought I was to join you in discussions for the summit?"

Davik rubbed his hands together. "No. I'm afraid what I have to say is meant for my nephew's ears alone." He glanced down at the overturned paperwork on his desk. "Everything here is confidential and must remain secret, even to the Royal Huntsmen."

"Yes, my lord." Axe nodded.

"So I'm here as your nephew, and not Lord Commander?" Clique asked.

"Yes, that's correct." Davik motioned for Clique to sit. "That will be all Huntsman."

Axe turned to leave and made it halfway to the door before he stopped. *If I leave, I am lying to my lord by remaining silent.* Axe considered his predicament. His advanced sight had already processed all the written information in the papers on his desk. Its contents had been laid completely bare to Axe, and though he did not directly think of it or logically assimilate the information as it was private to his lord, he still had access to it none the less. *By confronting him with my knowledge, perhaps I can demonstrate my worth, and prove my leal honesty in his service.* Axe turned, and walked back towards the desk.

Davik and Clique seemed quite surprised at his return. "Yes?" Davik asked him. "What is it?"

Axe stopped and bowed his head. "Lord Gracious, you must know that I, Axe Treefort, am both your honorable Huntsman, as well as a leal servant to the Gracious House. I will follow your every command, and those of my Lord Commander."

Clique bore a curious smile, but Davik was simply confused. "Yes, and what of it, Axe?"

"You have commanded me to leave because the contents of those letters are private," Axe told him. "But I must inform you that in the time I have spent in this room, I have managed to read all of the letters. Quite inadvertently, my lord, but I have read them none the less."

Clique's mouth gaped open, stunned, but Davik laughed in disbelief. "You can't expect me to actually believe this. That's impossible!"

Clique snickered and shook his head to his uncle. "Axe is a savant at the impossible."

"No one could have read these letters that fast from that far." Davik slapped his hand on top of them. "They were all upside down, and stacked one on top of the other." His eyes squinted. "If you truly know their contents, then it is of some treachery or deceit, and I could have you hanged as a spy."

Axe remained firm. "I swear to you my lord, it is no trick, but my eyes alone. If you were to write a new letter, I could stand across the room with my eyes closed, and tell you what you wrote as the letters appeared as ink on paper."

"Uncle." Clique sat up and spoke with solemnity. "Axe Treefort is an honorable man. In what little time I have spent with the Huntsmen, I have learned they all respect him and his virtuous nature. None speak more highly of him than Ser Ringley and Lord O'Brien. If Axe says he read your letters, and will serve our House loyally, then I believe him, and I vouch for him. Let him sit counsel in our matters. I would feel the better for it. Axe Treefort is a man we should count lucky to call our own."

Davik considered his nephew's words carefully before nodding in agreement. "Very well. Take a seat Axe." Once Axe found himself in the chair beside Clique, Davik sat as well. "Now... Axe... As only Clique is left unawares, why don't you inform him of their contents." He smiled.

"It is quite a sum of information, my lord," Axe explained.

Davik leaned forward. "Paraphrase."

Axe accessed his memory and reviewed the words in his mind. When he was done processing what the words meant, he found that he no longer had the same opinion of Davik Gracious as he had going in. *He is diabolical,* Axe thought. *Such would not be the acts of an honorable man. Is there still honor here to be gained? Should I still service House Gracious?* The cascade of concerns that flooded Axe in those moments made his stomach turn, and strange unpleasant emotions rose up from the pit of him. *I need time to consider this. In the meanwhile I will serve obediently,* he decided.

"Clique. Your uncle means to have a man murder Melinda Draven, King Harloque Draven's wife, Lady Keira's aunt, in her sleep." Clique did not bat an eyelash, and remained unmoved by the revelation. "He has half a dozen variations of the plot all with the same result. The Queen of the East will die, and evidence shall be planted to make it seem a failed attempt by the West to kill the King." Davik was astonished by Axe's recitation of the plan.

"I figured it would be something like this, uncle." Clique scratched at his chin. "And I'm sure there is a body, and a cover story to prove the claims once the deed is done?"

"There are three–" Axe started.

Davik cut him off. "It's all taken care of, Clique. Except for the man who does the deed."

"You want *me* to do it, then?" Clique shifted in his chair. "Is that it?"

"Everything is accounted for, but all rides on the task itself." Davik smiled. "In the seven years of our planning, Robert and I have had time to build a history so deep to the plot that no wizard will doubt the truth of it. But we have always known that all our plans, and all our schemes, would hinge on one crucial detail. We needed the perfect man for the job. Someone on the inside whose presence at a summit would not be questioned. Someone who would not be seen, and not be heard, and would not fail." Clique grunted with some realization. "Yes, Clique. This is what your father had in mind when he sent you to the Devils Guild. This has been your purpose."

"But it was *my* idea to join," Clique protested.

Davik laughed. "Yes, and I remember the night you first posed it to Robert. We had been worrying for weeks over the dangers of war coming on too soon. We had the beginnings of the plan, but no one in mind capable of carrying it out. I wasn't even Lord of Stormbreaker yet. But then you came in, with your heart set on secret knowledge and training with the devils. It was your idea as much as ours. The Gracious House would have its assassin, and Midgard would have its salvation."

"But how will war serve to protect Midgard?" Clique asked.

"It wouldn't." Davik gave a devilish grin. "War would destroy Midgard."

"I don't understand," Clique confessed. "You can't mean to purposefully bring about Midgard's destruction for some other gain?" he asked Davik with fear in his eyes. *What could be more valuable than a realm?* Axe pondered.

"No." Davik laughed and thrust his fist into the air. "I mean for Midgard to become more powerful than ever! We are at the cusp of history, nephew, and you shall be its harbinger."

"But if I kill the Queen, and it's blamed on the other kingdom, it will mean war!"

"Oh, yes," Davik agreed. "War would be an outright inevitability. All but impossible to prevent. Even my grandiose diplomacy would be helpless to prevent it from coming to blows between Kingdoms."

"But if war will destroy us–"

"Oh, most certainly." Davik laughed.

"Then why start the war?" Clique asked, dumbfounded.

"If I may answer." Axe raised his finger and got their attention. "Clique, your uncle means to stop the war once they have taken the field, by providing new evidence."

"What evidence is that?" Clique seemed desperate to know.

"Evidence," Davik smirked, "that the assassination was nothing more than a Gulgari plot, seven years in the making, to destabilize the Realm!"

At that moment a great gust of wind blew open one of windows. The rusted metal flap which held it fastened shut broke off with a twang and went clinking across the study floor. The wind picked up loose papers and tossed them about the chamber before dying down to a light breeze. It was still before starset, and warm red light shone through the window into the room.

"What interest would the Gulgari have in the Realm?" Clique asked.

"Over four hundred million doubloons worth of interest." Davik rubbed his hands together. "And if it came to open fighting, the banks of the merchant cities would be readily available to lend both East and West the coin to finance their war. In fact, such plans have been put into motion for years. There are Gulgari out there, even now, who truly believe their plot to be real, and for the better part of a decade their agents have been fanning the flames of war. Fortunately the paper trail will lead back to them, and serve to fortify claims of their deception." Davik poured some light red wine from a nearby decanter and filled a cup with it. He took a few sips and set it down while they pondered the information.

"You mean to direct the war South into the Central Sea?" Clique smiled now.

Davik nodded between sips. "Yes."

"And have the Realm invade the merchant cities?" Clique asked.

"Yes," Davik answered.

"And in doing so will expand the worth of Gracious holds ten fold." Clique laughed.

"More to the point." Davik raised his goblet. "It will solidify and endear Midgard's desire for peace forever in the hearts of both Kingdoms, and ensure our tender alliances for generations to come."

"It's diabolical," Axe admitted, and Davik laughed.

"Sheriff Vehement has all of the details you'll need to know," Davik told Clique. "From what you must wear, to how the deed must be done. I trust your father and I were correct to entrust this great responsibility into your hands, Clique."

"Yes, uncle." Clique nodded. "I will not fail our House."

"Good... Good." Davik seemed appeased. "Axe, since you are aware of our little scheme, I will have you kept close during the summit. I mean for you to sit Honor Guard for the Huntsmen."

"That task was assigned to Ser Ringley," Axe mentioned.

"Actually, it was reassigned to Collin," Clique told them. "He will be disappointed."

"I mean for him to sit as well," Davik explained. "As Lord Commander of the Huntsmen. *You* will sit counsel."

"What about Baldric?" Clique snickered. "He'll be most disappointed."

"He will be no such thing," Davik snapped at him. "The assassination attempt has left him with more important matters to attend to. Neither of us believe it to have anything to do with our plans, or even the summit. We have been too thorough in every regard. It was either a personal vendetta, or the assassin was tapped to prevent me from coming to learn whatever message sweet Alana died trying to deliver." Davik took a sad sip from his goblet. "Collin has yet to turn up any note, and has retired to prepare for tomorrow. I fear without directly confronting Irvalis I'll not know the meaning of it, and it is doubtful he is here for the summit."

"What about Alexander Warne?" Clique asked. "Will he be riding with the Eastern army?"

"Undoubtedly." Davik sighed.

"I could arrange to speak with him privately," Clique suggested.

"No," Davik said. "Under no circumstances will I risk secret communication with either side. I will not have some minor matter derailing our plans with hints of suspicion or rumors of favoritism."

"But what of Alana's father, and family?" Clique asked carefully, and Axe knew they tread on thin ground when it came to Davik's emotions regarding Alana. "Surely they must be told what fate befell her."

"Yes... Yes." Davik stood and looked wistfully out the window while he walked to it. "After a full day of what will no doubt be trying and tense negotiations, I will break the sad news to Harloque over dinner. It will be his duty to pass the news to her father. Even so, Harloque will be fraught with sadness, as Alana was well loved by all who knew her. I will not have him thinking heated thoughts before diplomacy has had its chance."

"But you will have him thinking heated thoughts before bed the night his wife is killed."

"The summit may last many days." Davik looked out over the sea whose waters were set aflame by the light of the setting Red Star. The waves were troubled with winds from the East, and dark clouds loomed on the fiery horizon. "It will not be until negotiations have yielded successful result, and a formal declaration is drawn up, that you will make your move, dear nephew." Davik finished his wine in one long gulp, then cast the goblet out the open window. It tumbled out into the wind and was heard clattering against the stone of the Stronghold before crashing into the rough waves below. "The day will come where it is decided that on the morrow, in front those who speak for each of the six Great Houses, a peace will be signed between Kings. Then, and only then, will that be the night to act. When true peace is in the Realm's grasp, we will wrench it away from them and flip the coin of fate." Davik pulled the window's shutters closed, and fastened it with a bit of rope. "After the Sheriff coaches you on what must be done, we must never speak, or dare even think, of the plot until it is completed. Do you both understand?"

"Yes, uncle." Clique nodded.

"Yes, Lord Gracious," Axe said, "I understand."

"Does Keira know all this?" Clique asked.

"No! Of course not. Queen Melinda is her aunt. She must *never* know the truth of it. Only you, your father, Axe, myself, and Sheriff Vehement know... That will be all nephew," Davik said. "Go find Baldric at once, and take careful note of all he tells you. It is to be the crux of it."

"As you command." Clique exited and Axe followed suit.

Davik stopped him with a word. "Axe." Axe turned back and the door shut behind him.

"Yes, my lord?" Axe asked.

"Come here and try this wine." Davik took an unusually curved bottle of green liquid and poured half the contents into a silver cup. "I picked it especially for you."

Axe happily approached him. "Thank you, my lord. I do love a good wine."

Davik handed him the chalice with a pleasant smile. "Go ahead. Drink it all."

"None for you my lord?" Axe asked as he took the cup in his hand.

"That vintage is not to my liking." Davik watched him with curiosity as Axe took his first sip.

"It has an odd tang, my lord," Axe said. "An intriguing flavor."

Davik was amused. "Drink all of it, Axe."

"If you insist." Axe drank the full contents of the cup and set it down on the table with a cough and a heavy breath. "Wow!" He wiped some from his lips, and burped. "It has quite a kick!" Axe giggled. "Wherever did you come across such a vintage?"

Davik was bewildered. He studied Axe with his eyes. "It came to me from the monks of Ghostwyck across the Eastern mountains."

"I take it that's a long ways away," Axe marveled. "It must have been expensive."

"Yes." Davik nodded. "Very much so."

"I know most wines are made from grapes," Axe admitted, "and others still from fruits and grains. What was this fine drink made from? It is a marvel of taste to be sure."

"It is no wine, but the pure venom of the manticore," Davik said, "and you drank enough to kill a thousand men. Maybe ten thousand if you poisoned a water supply."

Axe considered his words. "Why?"

"I had to be sure." Davik patted him on the shoulder. "And now we both know."

So my lord knows the enigma of me. Axe felt... happy. *Will he help me find my home?* "But what does it mean?" Axe asked him.

"I don't know, Axe... I don't know." Davik took the empty cup and tossed it into the trash. "But we will come to learn the truth of it," Davik patted him on the shoulder, and pinned a golden honor upon Axe's suit breast, "together."

"Amy." Keira shifted in her seat. "Come feel this."

Amy, her beautiful healer, bed servant, and midwife, knelt nearby and placed her hand on Keira's plump stomach. "His little lord is restless." She frowned. "It's from all this excitement."

"Could you get me some more of that tea?" Keira asked her. "The flowery one."

"Yes, my lady." Amy went for the door, but paused when she opened it. "My lady, there are some knights approaching." She came back to her side. "It's time now. I'll have the tea brought to the solar for you."

"Best bring some for everyone then." Keira sighed. "I do not wish for anyone to take offense that only I am drinking tea."

Keira had been carefully coached by her husband each night for well over half a year on how to act during the summit. "This is not a social engagement, Keira," he'd told her one of those first nights so long ago. "We are not to play the part of friend, or ally, or represent ourselves and our own interests. We are to be but neutral arbiters, meant only to see the negotiations through to a successful peace."

"So, in other words," she tried to understand, "when I speak with Melinda, I am not to think of her as an aunt, but as a stranger who stands equal to everyone else in the room."

"Yes, darling." He'd looked at her proudly in that moment, and she relished it. "Exactly."

"But what do you mean we don't represent ourselves?"

"In there, it won't matter that you are O'Brien, or even Gracious," he'd explained. "We won't even be speaking for Midgard. What's best for us is meaningless. We are to observe, and help mediate a peaceful process that will lead to an accord. If there is a concern that regards Midgard that the Kings need to address, it will fall to our counsel."

Keira loved how patient and kind Davik had always been to her. She thought that he was the smartest man alive, and though she was confident in herself in all things, somehow she always felt a fool around him. He would often say something brilliant to her, in his all too charismatic way, and when pressed for a response she couldn't help but giggle and blush. But while he might grow wroth and lose his temper at a thousand men for a thousand reasons, never once in their near four years together had he raised his voice to her, or treated her unkindly. The way he carefully and methodically taught her the finer arts of diplomacy stoked her passions to ravenous extents. After that third night, a few weeks of their lessons comprised mostly of making love by the fire in his study. *This child will be borne of peace,* she had mused when the familiar signs of her pregnancy revealed themselves. *It will be a son.*

"Are you sure I should serve everyone the jasmine, my lady?" Amy frowned as she helped Keira to her feet. "It may not be to their liking."

"No, I suppose you're right." Keira considered a moment. "Bring out the cinnamon first." Keira was never really a tea drinker, but she found that it helped settle the unborn son she carried. *He is a warrior, this one,* she'd come to learn as her date approached. *He can't wait to escape his mother.* "Bring out the jasmine a little while after everyone else has been served." Keira made her way to the door and smiled when she saw Ser Grissel and two of his knights enter her waiting room.

"Lady Keira, your radiance is a splendor to behold today." Grissel took her hand and kissed it as he knelt. Keira loved how gallant and noble he was, and not just with her, but with the entirety of the life he'd lived. Grissel Chanspire was a knight in a long line of knights, and fought for Keira's grandfather at the Battle of the Bridge so many years ago. After months of siege and too much bloodshed, Rickard Gracious, her husband's father, and Ser Grissel fought a duel of honor to determine the fate of the war. He was the O'Brien's champion, and had slain Rickard's first born son, Davik's brother Harold, in the course of the siege. Rickard defeated Grissel in combat with swords, and though Grissel did not yield, Rickard spared his life. In exchange he demanded Grissel's service, and the famous knight swore fealty to the Gracious banner. In near forty years of service his hair had greyed and his skin wrinkled, but he still held the same fire and grace as he did when he was younger.

Keira was too young to have known him, but her mother would speak of him often with great affection. Four years before Keira and Davik had even met, even though the man had killed Davik's older brother, Ser Grissel was promoted by Davik to Commander of Stormbreaker City's Watch. In a city of over fifty thousand, he commanded half a thousand men, and had gained great honor and privilege befitting of his rank. The slayer of Davik's brother had become head of his city's defense, and Keira loved Davik for it. In the early process of their courtship, before anything had been settled, she learned of how he had promoted Ser Grissel and treated him with kindness. *It was his father's honor that brought Grissel to change banners,* she had told herself that night, *but it was Davik's kindness and virtuous nature that saw his father's faith in the man through.* Keira was never certain, but she liked to believe it was that night when she first fell in love with Davik, and her world ever since had been a whirlwind of everything she could've ever wished for. She had her perfect love, and a perfect life. She had perfect children, and would soon have yet another child she knew in her heart was a son. *All that is good in my life I owe to Davik. He has healed the wounds of my people, and I will stand by his side to sew the seeds of peace for our children, and all children, for generations to come.* Never had she loved Davik as much as she did then, and never before had she been more resolute to make him proud. *I will be the perfect diplomat,* she swore. *I will be my husband's perfect wife.*

"Thank you, Ser," Keira told him. "Have they arrived?"

"Yes, my lady," Ser Grissel said. "The Dravens from the Red Gate, and the Tarnells from the Silver. I'm to escort you to the solar, where Davik awaits."

"Mommy!" Little Keira ran into the room followed by fifteen year old Mary and two unfamiliar House Guards, one of which walked hand in hand with Charles in his precious little suit. *These must be some of the new men that Davik was talking about.*

Keira cradled her daughter and knelt next to her. "What's the matter, Keira? You know that I'll be back later to sing to you."

"I"m sorry, Keira." Her younger cousin Mary sighed. "She refused to listen unless she got to see you one last time. I figured since you hadn't gone in yet..."

"It's alright, Mary." Keira stared into her daughter's sparkling eyes. "What is it, baby?"

"I have to tell you a secret..." she said. Keira leaned close and she whispered in her ear. "I miss Alana." Keira's heart broke when she heard the words. It was never meant for the children to know, but they had woken and followed her into the solar to bear witness to the poor girl's corpse. Charles understood more than little Keira did, and he cried for her. Davik had taken Keira aside and told her that the children must not meet the diplomats until the second day. It was critical that Alana's poisoning remain secret lest it interfere with the first day, which was to be the most delicate. Davik planned to break the news over dinner. The children might let it slip, and so they were to be kept hidden away from summit until the morrow.

"Oh, Keira." She hugged her close, wiped tears from her own eyes, and kissed her daughter on the forehead. "I miss her too, sweetling. But mommy has to go. Please keep your brother company for me, alright?" With a few more hugs and kisses she surrendered her children to Mary and the two guards, took her gallant knight by the arm, and walked to the solar.

The next hour of her life was a mindless blur of posturing, introductions, and small talk. There was her husband, and Davik's nephew Clique, her own cousin Collin, and his Huntsman Axe. Each King arrived with their Queen and a number of men in tow. Ser Grissel and his guards left to escort all but six remaining dignitaries out of the Inner Castle. King Harloque Draven, the King of the East, was a tall and shrewd man in his fifties with skin as white as virgin snow. He was albino, and his pale skin matched his white silky hair, while his eyes were an icy blue. Even so, he was quite handsome. *The Dravens have always had a distinct look, but Harloque has his own charisma to match it.*

His wife and Queen was Keira's cousin Melinda O'Brien. It was never meant for her to be Queen by marriage, but Dameon's wife was barren and a child would not quicken in her womb. He died without even siring a bastard, and control of the Kingdom passed to his younger brother. By then Melinda and Harloque had already been married ten years and had four children. *There are plenty of heirs now,* Keira thought, *and never before have the O'Brien's had so much influence in the Realm.* Her mind turned on the thought. *Or so much to lose.* Melinda had long since gone grey, and she and her husband made a pretty old pair in their purple and blue garments. Keira had chosen plain black with only hints of grey as her wardrobe for the duration of the summit. Each dress was carefully designed to play down her distracting beauty while allowing her to be comfortable. Diplomatic tasks would be difficult with her little lord tumbling within her and her back always hurting, but she hoped the tea would soothe her nerves. *I will not let my discomfort jeopardize the peace. Whether the summit lasts one week or two, I will grit my teeth and bear it. But if it goes three weeks,* she laughed to herself, *I might break water at the table. And that, would not be proper etiquette for a diplomat.*

The Honor Guard for the East was Ser Tarbeld Draven, King Harloque's distant cousin. While one of the five most respected knights in the Realm, he was the only one who swore fealty to a kingdom. The other four, who had each amassed over one hundred honor in their lives, were in the upper echelons of the Honorable Academy, and had a higher calling to all the Realm of men, and not any one of its Kingdoms. The fine knight wore chain mail under his white tunic, and he carried two swords. One a white longsword with the sigil of House Draven on its hilt, and the other the Ancient blade that men called Shadow. Keira did not care much for blades, but she smiled all the same when she saw Collin's eyes linger on Shadow's blackwood hilt as if it were a bare breasted whore. Ser Tarbeld may have been old enough that he fought and won the Battle of Baypeak over forty years ago during the height of the war, but he still could have cut through every person in that room. With that blade Shadow in his skilled hands, none would stand his equal except one man, and he was the one who worried her.

The Honor Guard of the West that eyed Ser Tarbeld with wary

suspicion in his eyes was Ser Laurence Brae. He was, without doubt, the finest swordsman known to man. His Ancient forged longsword was Starsinger, and with it he'd carved a hundred victories across the Pirate Isles and the Starset Coast before taking his place as Honor Guard to the King. Typical of a Brae, he had blue eyes and fine silvery hair though not a day past thirty five. He complimented himself with silver armor and a blue tunic. If Ser Laurence saw fit to kill them all in a frenzy of madness, if not for Ser Tarbeld, he would easily succeed. "Starsinger is the more well known blade," Collin had told her earlier that day while they discussed his sword collection. "With it a dozen Kingdoms were fought for and won, while Shadow has not seen blood spilled in a score of generations." Collin explained that when Ser Tarbeld became Honor Guard near twenty years ago and gained privilege to wear any sword he wished, he chose the blade Shadow from the Draven's most guarded reliquary. Since then he wore two swords, and in all that time had never once drawn Shadow. An unbroken black wax seal on the Ancient blade's hilt marked the truth of it. Keira hoped that she would never see its naked blade. *Even the act of unsheathing it will bring with it fame and import.* Keira shuddered with the thought. *That sword must not see the light of day, and I will do everything within my power to see its shadow uncast.*

But... Should it ever come to blows between these two, I am not sure my Collin is capable of standing them apart. Keira's eyes fell to Axe Treefort, who was dressed in no doubt the finest black suit in his possession, and carried two simple steel axes on his belt. Her memory returned to the sad tale of the family he'd lost, and she hoped that he was a wise choice to sit in place of Ser Ringley. *I do not know why our master knight and loyal Huntsman Ser Ringley is not here, but I hope that Collin's faith in Axe to replace him is well spent.* Keira did not truly believe it would come to blows, but she had been warned that such a thing was known to happen in prior peace talks. Even so, they were all permitted to carry their weapons with them, and even the Kings had daggers. *Should one be unsheathed in a fit of anger, it may fall to Axe to see it does not come to violence where our words for peace have failed.*

Ser Laurence's sister, Vivian Brae Tarnell, and Queen of the West, was a magnificently toxic old woman in her fat gown of red and silver silk. Unlike the scattered and isolated politics of messengers and diplomats between the Houses of the East, in the West politics were a game that was played almost exclusively at court. The climate was much warmer in the West, and the towns and villages there sprawled out over vast distances instead of being huddled together behind sturdy walls and tall chimneys. Grand villas and estates controlled by the King hosted year round courts where the upper tiers of business and politics were carried out. Keira counted herself fortunate that she never had to travel West for her duties as Davik's wife, and hoped that should peace be declared, she would not have to travel to support it. In truth, the West frightened her, and she still harbored old grudges in her heart from friends and loved ones lost against Western enemies. But she was a Gracious now, and beyond that, an arbiter of peace. O'Brien discomfort and discrimination needed to be cast aside. Even so, she could not help but marvel at how slick and slippery a cretin that Vivian was, especially compared to Keira's cousin, who was a good O'Brien woman despite her Draven inflated ego.

Vivian's blue eyed husband was William Tarnell and King of the West. His classically handsome but wrinkled face sported an equally handsome grey beard to match his Brae wife's long silver hair. A Brae's hair remained silver, even in old age, and never took the dull grey that other bloodlines were cursed with. *Would that my red would never fade,* Keira wished. Her husband Davik had taken to keeping his hair black with dyes, and knew when the time came she would enjoy that luxury as well, but no false color could ever match the perfect red of her hair and how it looked when starlight shone through it.

I wonder if they use dyes in their hair in the Western courts, Keira thought to herself after all eleven of them had taken their seats at the table in the solar. For some time there was discussion of their journey, the magnificence of Stormbreaker, the beautiful artwork, the magnificent clock, the delicious tea, how handsome a couple Davik and Keira made. The triteness of it all made Keira want to vomit into her teacup, but she remembered her training, kept her smile and her tone, and gave no hint of disinterest. Eventually only the men were talking, and the conversation had turned to direct negotiation. Keira understood the importance and implications of every word spoken or look given, but still her mind could not help but drift to thoughts of the little lord inside her, and what his name might be. Davik did not share the same whimsical fascination with daydreaming names for the children, and had plainly suggested their daughter be named Keira. She wondered if it was because he was indecisive or if he truly believed what he said when he explained there was no name more beautiful, and that he wanted it for his daughter. Somehow even his flaws, when expressed with his marvelously charismatic demeanor, always swooned her. He had such a tight grip on her heart that if he asked her to fly she would figure out a way to please him. *Maybe I'll name my little lord Davik after my husband.* She made the final decision of it. *A younger brother just like his father.* It was perfect. *Little Davik.* She giggled in delight.

King William, Ser Tarbeld, and King Harloque all stood with their attention on a large map that had been unfurled across the table. For a good half hour they had been in a heated discussion over trade rights along the Dagger River and neither side seemed willing to budge. Ser Tarbeld had long since raised his voice, and William had no difficulty in shouting back. Their faces were red with their wroth, and all the while Davik smiled his dashing smile and rubbed his hands together with expectation. Her giggle drew a pause in their argument and William gave her a bewildered look. "Lady Keira, whatever do you find so amusing?"

Keira's heart raced. She knew she could not admit to being lost in thought and not paying attention. She also would not yield her power by explaining it away as her baby kicking. *I am not here as myself, I am here as arbiter of peace.* Keira sat upright in her chair and tried to look as serious as possible. "I was thinking of the irony of it, gentlemen." She smiled at each of the men in turn. "Isn't it better that the only red in this battle is in the blush of your puffed cheeks, rather than the red of blood on the battlefield?"

For a moment all was silent, until both Ser Laurence and King William broke in with hearty laughter. Harloque himself chuckled, and Keira's men, Clique, Collin, Davik, and Axe laughed as well. "You are right, my lady!" King William pointed out. "It is indeed better."

"Hear, hear!" Collin rapped on the table, and Axe and Clique stomped their feet along in Huntsmen fashion.

After that the negotiations seemed to go much smoother. Davik would convince one side to take concessions, and be aggressive in other matters. With masterful precision he avoided potential pitfalls and still managed to drive the discussion towards the important issues. "Why mention a specific lord's name or House and invoke a myriad of history, when you could focus on what really matters?" Davik had once explained to her. "The people. The resources. The money. That's what they really care about. They have just been blinded by too many years of ingrained thought patterns. The key to any successful negotiation is detachment. Since the egos of the

Kings are far too great to allow for such detachment, it is our job as the arbiters to provide that perspective for them." Keira did not fully understand what he meant, but understood what it meant to be blinded by thought. *My grandfather would be rolling in his grave if he knew I now shared tea with Tarnell and Brae alike.* Keira had no idea what her husband was thinking about, but whatever it was, he seemed quite pleased with himself. She knew his face so well that she could tell when his smile was a mask, or if his solemnity masked a smile. In this case he was nigh but euphoric, and each time their eyes connected she sensed he was as proud of her as he was of himself.

All through the day it was much of the same. Occasionally each person present needed to take their leave to relieve themselves. Where the Kings went their Honor Guard followed, and Keira's own House Guard followed everyone everywhere. A few select servants handled their refreshments, and Amy was never far from the solar ready to attend to Keira's needs. Early in the day it had been raining, and as the afternoon progressed a storm fell upon the castle. The Commander of each of the King's armies interrupted the summit and requested permission that they be allowed to move their armies up against the walls of the Stronghold and the City to shield themselves from the storm. The matter might have been cause for concern if unrest had been fostered that day, but the negotiations seemed to be going well. Davik gave his consent, whereupon the Kings informed their Commanders that peace was beginning to take shape. And, as such, their armies should orient themselves accordingly with peace in mind. Keira noticed that Collin seemed quite unsettled by the notion of the armies taking shelter by the walls, and assumed it had something to do with battle strategy. She'd overheard talk of how they'd kept their troops far apart for tactical reasons, and worried anew at whether the concessions of the West were some vile scheme to catch the Eastern army unawares. *You can't trust a Tarnell,* she told herself, and immediately cringed at the thought. *I would make a poor diplomat if I sat in Harloque's place.*

Dinner consisted of several courses of soups and fish and pastas. All were prepared by three of the finest chefs in Midgard who had been acquired for the duration of the summit. Conversation was polite and consisted more of trivialities than anything of any importance. Clique seemed to drive the conversation with tales of the South as Davik grew quiet. His mood darkened and turned somber by the end of dinner, and Keira braced herself for the news he needed to break. Davik played with his wine goblet, and as one of the servants asked if everyone was ready for desserts, Sheriff Baldric entered and whispered something in Davik's ear. *What does he want?* Keira asked herself. Secretly she was quite pleased that Clique would be taking over some of the roles previously filled by Baldric Vehement, such as sitting counsel at this very summit. She could have danced for joy when she discovered she would not be sitting beside the Sheriff for weeks on end after all. Clique was handsome, polite, and more than that he was family. Keira saw little of her family since she'd moved to Midgard, and Davik's own family rarely visited. It was always up to Davik and Keira to take the trip to Cliffwatch or elsewhere to see them, and Keira was always unhappy with it, especially considering that since their marriage began she was more often than not with child. She was overjoyed when she heard Davik's nephew would be coming to live with them, and with what little time she'd spent with Clique, had come to think highly of the man. He was quite like both Davik and Robert in his ways, but somehow there was the hint of something greater in Clique. She saw in him the qualities of her husband without the flaws of his ambition and smarm. Somehow she expected great things to come from Clique, and wondered if Davik and Robert had felt the same.

Baldric left and Davik gained the attention of his guests with a few loud coughs. Keira sipped her tea, averted her gaze, and played with her hair. She did everything she could not to think about Davik's words or to soak in the reactions of others at the table. She was fragile enough as it was, and if she gave in to her grief over the loss of dear Alana, the tears might over come her. *That poor girl suffered so much. No! I must not think of it. I will be strong for Davik.* Keira took it badly enough when she found Alana poisoned on the solar floor, but when she heard that Alana was raped on the road she lost her stomach. *After the summit, when I have a moment alone with Clique,* she had told herself later that night, *I must thank him for rescuing her. If he had not, then both she, and my husband, would be dead.*

Harloque took it well enough, though Melinda was brought to sobs. Even Ser Tarbeld wept at the news. The girl was largely unknown to the West, but King William gave his most heart felt condolences, and Vivian walked round the table to hug Melinda close and comfort her. It was a grand gesture that was not lost on anyone, although Keira couldn't help but see it as the false act of a conniving viper. Even so, Melinda was pleased by her display, and the two Queens cried together. When the wave of emotion had passed, and some cakes and sweet wines were brought out for dessert to lighten the mood, Davik stunned them with his words. Keira found herself doubting her ears. *Is this really necessary?* It seemed that Sheriff Baldric was bringing the two servants responsible for the death of Alana Toril up from the dungeon and into the solar. Davik wanted King Harloque and his wife to see them with their own eyes.

The Sheriff soon entered with two guards from the dungeon who led the prisoners behind them in shackles. Both the girl Kelly, and the boy Kendrick, had their mouths bound with cloth, and their hands bound by iron. They were cleanly dressed and not unkempt nor foul smelling, but were a sad sight to behold none the less. Davik explained how they took no part in the plot directly, but were both instrumental in handling the poison and delivering it from cellar to goblet. Unfortunately the two guards responsible for protecting the wine cellar were missing, and there was no further lead on who the culprit that planted the poison wine might be. Davik made a point of assuring everyone that all the food and drink served during their stay at Stormbreaker was being tasted, and though the investigation was still ongoing, the immediate danger had passed. To further compound the matter, Davik placed the lives of the two prisoners in the hands of Queen Melinda and King Draven. It was their family by marriage who was lost to them, and Davik had decided it would be them who would determine the prisoner's punishments. He assured them that neither had any knowledge of the intrigue, but their ineptitude and inability to notice the ruse had cost sweet Alana her life. Keira's heart was pounding in her chest and her throat clenched. Clique seemed disgusted by the whole scene and exited the room through the Silver door. Collin was displeased, and even Axe seemed on edge.

For a while no one spoke. Melinda and her husband whispered in hushed tones. When they turned to face Davik, Melinda straightened with such gravity that Keira's breath froze. *No, please...* She cried inside. *They're just children.*

"We will ever be so grateful Davik," King Harloque said, "to your valiant nephew Clique and his Huntsmen in rescuing Alana in her hour of need." Melinda stifled a sob and even Harloque wiped a tear from his cheek. "And we hold you to no blame for her death, Lord Gracious. There are men in this world who have done their best to prevent this summit from taking place... Men who will continue to fight to see this fragile peace shattered." Harloque took his goblet of sweet wine and called for a toast. "My darling niece Alana was as much a victim of this war, as any knight or peasant who ever fell upon the battlefield." He raised his goblet into the air and everyone reciprocated the gesture. Keira raised her teacup. "Let us do our best to see that her death, is the very last death this war will ever see. To Alana Toril! And to peace!"

Everyone sipped their cups and agreed with the toast, though Keira keenly noted that Collin did not give the Huntsmen cheer and call for the stamping of their boots. It all seemed so macabre, and she hoped that the next words out of the pale man's mouth were not the ones she feared he'd speak. *Dravens are so prideful and breezy with death. It is no wonder their ancestors are said to be born from monsters.* She thought of the primordial terrors that inhabited the darkest, deepest shadows of that Ancient castle the Dravens took for their own when they settled in the Realm. She knew it was nothing more than an old wives tale, but still she counted her blessings that it was her sister who married to Aztoz, that cursed castle of legend, and she to Stormbreaker Stronghold, a fortress of wealth and majesty. *Though I may not wear a crown, I have gotten the sweeter deal.* She laughed inside about her comparison to her cousin, and felt sorry for her at the same time. But that empathy turned bitter in her mouth with Melinda's next words. "And in Alana's memory, we would like to wipe the slate clean of those who have done her wrong," the Queen said. "Until the true perpetrator of this crime has been found, these two shall have to suffice."

Davik had ice in his veins as he nodded to her. "So... To be clear. How shall we proceed?" Davik smiled ever so slightly, and Keira knew he was not altogether pleased. "My dungeons can hold prisoners for years."

"Kill them," King Harloque said, "here, now, in front of us." Harloque unsheathed his Kingly dagger. The clock struck seven and it played its tune. Ser Laurence's hand went to his hilt and Ser Tarbeld's hand drew to his own in response. Harloque tossed the dagger onto Davik's dessert plate. "With this."

Keira thought she heard an objection, but it was muffled, and must have been Kendrick's voice. Everyone seemed to be reacting to the command with their own surprise, but Keira felt carved of stone. She kept her eyes fixed on Davik, and hoped he would deny them, but knew he would never refuse. *It is not his choice to make, but damn him for offering.* Still, Keira in her heart knew he had the right of it. He couldn't look incompetent for not finding the assassin, and Dravens were too proud not to have something given to them. Davik picked up the dagger. "As you wish." The clock finished its song and began to chime its loud bell for each of its seven hours. *Ding!* Davik wiped cake from the dagger's blade and handed it to the Sheriff. *Ding!* "Do the girl first," Davik told him.

"No," King Harloque pronounced. *Ding!* "It was *your* life Alana saved. *You* will see it done."

"As you wish," Davik said politely. He took the dagger from the Sheriff and stepped behind Kelly, the beautiful young kitchen servant who had served faithfully in the castle for years. She was on her knees in tears. *Ding!* Davik knelt beside her and readied the killing cut.

"Stand her up," Melinda commanded. "I want to see." *Ding!* Keira hated her cousin just then. *She relishes death like a Draven, though perhaps she just plays the good Queen for her King, and plays up her conviction to appear strong to the West.* Keira sighed. *Either way I do not like her for it.*

Davik whispered something into Kelly's ear. *Ding!* Kelly stood and closed her eyes. *Even now he comforts the girl.* Keira loved Davik so much in that moment. *He has such heart, unlike these vicious Kings.* Davik pressed the cold steel against Kelly's neck, and held his breath in preparation for the killing stroke.

Ding!

Before Davik drew the blade across her throat, the North entrance to the solar pushed open, and a dozen House Guardsmen entered dressed in their black armors. Davik removed the dagger from Kelly's neck and turned his attention to the men. "What is the meaning of this interruption?" his voice boomed. Kelly's eyes opened and she seemed relieved for her stay of execution.

The men did not stop their march, and Keira eyed the red hooded man who led the guards. *Who is that?* she wondered, before her eyes fell upon the crossbows that all save the hooded man carried. *Twang!* Before any could react, the men raised their crossbows and released their bolts. The three jail guards that had entered with Sheriff Baldric were slain by the volley. Sheriff Baldric drew his sword and stood in front of Davik, while the two House Guards that stood in the corners took arrows to the face and fell in bloody heaps. Ser Laurence and Ser Tarbeld were the first to act. Laurence drew his blade and was making his way across the room while Tarbeld stood and cast his chair aside. His hand fell upon the hilt of Shadow, and the hooded man spoke. "Don't!" he shouted. Four of the guards raised their crossbows to the Queen's heads. "Or they die." Everyone stood down, and within seconds the men had taken the room. Ser Tarbeld and Ser Laurence retreated next to their Kings.

"Who are you?" King William Tarnell slapped his hands on the table. "I demand to know what's going on here!" *I know some of these men,* Keira thought. *They are Havensword's new guards.* Her world fell out beneath her. *Some of them were with the children!*

The wails of men dying in the distance was heard, followed by a loud thunder of stone upon stone. The solar reverberated for a moment, and two smaller and more distant thunderclaps followed. "What was that?" Harloque asked. "What just happened? What did we just hear?"

The hooded man approached the table with a slow walk. Keira's eyes were watery with emotion from Kelly's brush with death, and she did not know if it was some trick of the light, but the man seemed to have a blue glow about him. It was as if some thing inside his robe had pulsed with a blue luminescence of its own, then faded away to nothing. She wiped her eyes and squinted at him, but the color was gone. "Davik can answer that for you," he said.

"It was..." Davik's words caught in his throat. "It was the sound of the three Gates of the inner castle being sealed shut."

"If you mean to disrupt the peace, it is too late!" Harloque lied. "We have already signed accords and the war has ended."

"Is this your doing Davik?" William demanded. "You must be mad to take us hostage with our armies at your doorstep!"

Several of the guards circled the room and closed the two back entrances to the solar. "Relax, my Kings." The hooded man laughed. "Davik is just as much hostage as you."

"Harloque is right!" William shook his fist at him. "There is nothing you can do that will prevent the peace from going forward. You are too late!"

The hooded man's laughter was so loud and shrill that it gave Keira chills. "I don't give a fook about your peace!" He giggled with some manic madness. "Kill each other! Fook each other! I don't care! Your peace summit holds no interest to me."

"Then why have you taken us hostage?" Harloque asked. "What is this?"

"This..." He removed his hood and flashed a devilish smile. He was a pale skinned man in his late thirties, and had jet black hair in thick dreadlocks. His eyes were purple with flakes of silver and gold. He brought his hand up to rub his chin, and Keira's eyes fell upon his fine silver ring with a golden octopus sigil. "... is a robbery."

CLIQUE

Clique tightened his hand around Daniel's mouth and listened with his ear to the door. He only managed to make out a few words before the heavy door pushed its final inches shut. Clique heard the inner irons being fastened across, and knew the way was barred. "You almost got us killed." Clique released the guardsman and pushed him against the wall. "The next time I say be quiet, you better follow your command."

"What's happening in there?" Daniel seemed more confused than frightened. "I don't understand."

It was only minutes earlier that the wine boy Kendrick and the serving girl Kelly had been paraded into the solar. Clique had recognized Daniel, the House Guardsman, by the Silver door, and felt the waves of his death approaching. Daniel's veins bulged and his heart rate accelerated. His fingers twitched against his sword's hilt. Daniel's emotion was boiling to the surface in his eyes, and Clique would not allow his folly to take place. Clique pushed Daniel out of the solar and into the hallway, and mostly shut the Silver door behind them. "I know what you're thinking, Daniel," Clique had told him, "but you must not do it."

"I could go in and protest," Daniel pleaded. "I could make my case to the Kings and Queens and swear for her life upon my honor."

"That's very virtuous of you, Daniel," Clique comforted him. "And what then? Do you really think they'd let her go based on your confession of love?" Clique sighed. "The Dravens would see you as part of the plot, and hang you right alongside her. Is that what you want?" Clique stared at him. "Is that what *she* would have wanted?"

The poor boy was love stricken, and when they heard the command that she have her throat slit, it was all Clique could do to hold him back. *I will knock him unconscious if need be, but he should be the one to tend her corpse.* Clique thought it noble of himself to keep Daniel from interfering, and the boy had broken to sobs by the time the enemy entered the solar. Clique covered his mouth and near smothered the boy to keep him quiet. Clique had managed to sneak one quick look into the solar, and was fortunate he was not noticed before the door was shut to them. "Men have taken the summit hostage," Clique told Daniel straight to his face. He was confused and Clique shook him. "Do you understand what I'm telling you, boy? I have need of you. Get a hold of your senses."

"Our lord is held hostage in his solar," Daniel said.

"Yes. And they are dressed as men of the House Guard." Daniel did not like the sound of that.

"That's impossible. Our own guard wouldn't..." Daniel paused. "Havensword."

"That's right, Daniel." Clique caught his breath and took a step back. "Your Captain has betrayed us."

"The extra twenty men," Daniel said with wide eyes, "it must be."

"Maybe ten in there right now." Clique's eye twitched. "The rest are at the gates, and will most like be sweeping the castle. I need you to find guards that aren't Havensword's men, and warn them. Can you do that?"

"Yes, Lord Commander." Daniel drew his short sword and readied his shield. "What about you?"

Clique smiled. "I mean to find my squire." He drew his dagger and led Daniel to where the hallway split in two directions. "Avoid the gates. If you see any of the new men, feign ignorance, but do not hesitate to strike the first blow. They"ll kill you should they get the chance."

Daniel took the right passage while Clique headed left. His only weapon was a dagger, and his first thoughts were on making it back to his bed chamber. One of the towers in the Silver had been afforded to Clique, and its uppermost level held both his suite and quarters for his squire and servant. The tower was tall, and there were many such empty halls and towers that circulated the upper levels of the inner castle. *It is unlikely they will ever even climb my tower. And likelier still that my squire and servant are waiting there for me with hot bath and wine, unaware of the dangers lurking the halls below.* By the shaking of the shutters and the wailing of wind it was clear the thunderstorm raging outside was growing worse. *The sound of thunder will have muffled the closing of the gates. It may be that the lower castle are as unaware as my squire. I must find a way to warn them.*

He took a roundabout way back to his tower and kept to the side paths that clung against the outer wall. *Those who built this castle must have been mad.* The upper castle boasted near forty towers in its heights, but most of them were unused, and Clique wondered in that moment what Stormbreaker must have been like nearly a millennia ago when hundreds of lords called it their home. *There were more people back then.* The thought was as cold as the drafts that filled the empty rooms Clique snuck through. *Has the Realm's wars taken so many lives from Midgard,* he wondered, *or has man expanded his Realm to the point where our numbers have grown thin?* Neither explanation seemed the truth of it. Midgard remained mostly neutral in the war, and its borders had remained constant. A colder thought entered his mind. *Maybe we nobles are the dying breed. Even now the highest nobility in all the Realms of Men have their lives in the hands of mercenaries.*

His reflections were cut short when he heard the whimpering of a woman from a nearby room. Torch light within cast three people's long shadows across the dark chamber of white cloth covered furniture. Clique pressed his back to the wall and peered sweetly into the room. It seemed to be some kind of pantry. There were tables and wall to wall shelves, all filled with food stuffs, dishes, and innumerable kitchen supplies. His brunette maid servant, whose name he could not now recall, had her arms pinned to the wall by a House Guardsman who was unfastening his breeches. A second guard stood watch by the main entrance and looked out into the hall. They neither saw nor heard Clique as he crept from the dark room, silent as a shadow, and slit the throat of the man accosting the girl. Her whimpers fell silent as the blood sprayed across her face, and when the other guard turned, he saw Clique running headlong at him. He was too slow in drawing his sword, and soon found Clique upon him with his dagger in hand. Clique stabbed his wrist, and his sword went clanking onto the stone floor.

Before Clique could pull the dagger out, the man bashed him across the side of the face with his shield. Clique fell to the floor with blood leaking from a gash across his temple. Clique was not altogether helpless, however, and from the ground kicked out the man's feet and brought him to his back. Clique leapt atop him and throttled him by the throat. He had oily matted brown hair and the look of a Gulgari. Upon his lower neck was a green and black tattooed tentacle that hinted at a larger pattern hidden by his black leather armor. Clique squeezed his thumbs into his throat and tightened his grip trying to choke the man's life from him, but Clique was still weakened by his voyage, and the man was the stronger of the two. He wrestled Clique off and threw him into the wall. Shelves and dishes clattered everywhere in a storm of breaking glass.

The man pulled the dagger from his wrist, grunted at the wound, and sheathed the blade on his belt. He switched his shield to his bloodied right hand, and cracked the knuckles of his left fist. The veins of his thick muscular neck bulged and bled, and his face was flush with fury. Clique's hand gripped a glass pitcher and he tossed it at the guard's face. His aim was true, but the man was ready, and batted it away with his shield. The guard's short sword was at his feet, and when he knelt to retrieve it Clique knew he could not hesitate. He took a jagged wedge of broken glass and lunged at the man. The guard raised his shield and readied the sword, but where he expected Clique to strike high, Clique instead feigned a high strike, stopped short, and sweep kicked the man's feet out from under him. When he fell to his back Clique jammed the wedge of glass into his good wrist. His grip on the sword weakened, and Clique wrested it from his fingers, took it for his own, and took a swing at the man. His opponent was no slouch, and recovered his stance quickly. Clique's sword stroke missed, and they found themselves staring each other down, Clique with the short sword, and the man with a shield and bloodied hands.

Clique made a few wild attacks to keep him at bay, but each was deflected by his shield. They both took notice of the girl at the same time. She must have been hiding behind one of the tables, but she now stood prone a few feet away. Her face and chest were stained with the dead guard's blood. The guard's eyes came back to his, and Clique knew the man's mind. *He means to take her, and use her as hostage to throw down my weapon.* The thought passed through his head like lightning, and when the man made move towards her,

Clique pressed the attack. But the guard's shield-work was superior. He deflected Clique's blows and easily evaded him. Clique thought he'd lost the girl to his capture, but she surprised them both by producing a small sack of flour from behind her back. She opened it up to his face and the powdery explosion blinded them both. It was all the distraction Clique needed, and soon the man's neck was parted by steel, and he fell lifeless beside them. Clique tossed the weapon aside, recovered his princely dagger, and helped the girl to her feet. "That was very brave of you," he told her. She looked up at him with her fearful eyes.

"Lord Clique..." She hugged him, and he cradled the fear from her.

"Come on." He took her by the arm. "Let's get you back to the tower." Clique shut the side entrance to the pantry, then scouted out the door to the hall. Confident it was empty and that no one was coming, he led her out, shut the door behind them, and they quietly made their way to his tower's entrance. It was an inconspicuous silver pine door at a junction where the outer hall met at an angle. Once inside they climbed the scores of steps that led to the top. Their ascent took them past five levels of empty chambers suitable for housing and feeding a compliment of fifty men. *Perhaps once this debacle is sorted out, I'll make use of these quarters and claim myself a compliment of mercenaries of my own.* Clique hated Havensword in that moment, though he'd never even met the man. *Whether by betrayal or incompetence, if he has cost the life of my uncle or his wife, I will inquire upon him for eternity.*

The storm shutters over the windows at each level of the tower rattled with the frenzy of the winds outside. An ill timed thunderclap startled the poor girl and she nearly jumped out of her skin and fell. But Clique gallantly caught her, and his own broad smile brought one to her face. When they reached the top of the tower and opened the door to the suite, they were met by the smell of roast chicken. "Is that you Felicity?" Clique's squire Janson asked as he turned to face them. His goblet of mead dropped from his hands when he saw them, and he rushed to their sides. It took Clique all of five minutes to explain everything that had transpired. Janson had already been in Stormbreaker for two years before being taken up as a squire, and knew the halls in ways Clique did not. He instructed Janson to arm and armor himself, and while Felicity washed, Clique and his squire prepared for battle. Clique put on the clothes he'd worn on the boat, and donned his old faded black leather doublet, while Janson wore brown leathers and took up a longsword. Felicity tended to Clique's wounded temple.

"Be valiant Lord Clique," she said. "I know you will not fail to rescue our lord and lady."

"I want you to stay here and hide," Clique told her.

"I can fit in the wardrobe, m'lord."

"Good. Good. Sleep in there if you must. Do not come out for anyone, you understand? They are pretending to be guards. Wait only for someone you know well."

Felicity kissed Clique's cheek and rushed off to hide, while Clique fastened the scythe blade onto his iron banded pole, and grinned. "It's about time we had you blooded Janson."

"What's the plan, Lord Commander?" Janson asked as they descended the tower. The boy was sixteen years old with brown hair and dark eyes. Clique couldn't remember his family name, but it was some minor House that was loyal and nearby. Janson was appointed to him by his uncle the first night Clique arrived, but they had barely shared a word in all that time.

Clique paused to examine Janson's brown armor, and inspiration came to him. "I have an idea."

They made their way to the pantry, wherein Clique instructed his squire to change into the black House Guard armors of the men he'd killed. It was a loose fit, but Janson played the part well. Blood and flour were wiped away and from a distance it would suit Clique's purpose. They exited into the hall and crept towards the large spiral stairwell that descended to where the Silver Gate would be found. Two guardsman had taken watch near the stairs, and Janson and Clique spied them from the shadows. "Do it exactly as I told you."

"Yes, Lord Commander," Janson said.

Moments later Clique was hiding with his back to stone. He couldn't see the guards from the doorway he was crouched in, but he could see Janson. "Hey! You two! Quick!" Janson waved their attention from down the hall. "One of the knights is escaping! We have to stop him!" Clique heard their footsteps as the guards chased towards his trusty squire. As instructed, the lad turned his back on them, and waved them to follow. "This way! Hurry!" Janson hooted.

By the time the two guards passed the doorway, it no longer mattered whether they believed in the ruse or not. Clique emerged with his black steel scythe held high and swung the heavy blade with quiet ferocity. It sliced through armor and bone with ease, and since the man was caught mid run, his upper and lower body tumbled a few yards forward before coming to a stop in a bloody mess. Clique rushed for the second guard and prepared for his swing, but Janson had moves of his own. He saw the young boy stop and spin back to face the man, and in one smooth manner drew his longsword and mauled his face. The guard fell, and Janson took no hesitation in serving the coupe de grace that put him to death. "Nicely done, Janson!" Clique congratulated him.

The boy wiped the blood from his weapon and sheathed it. "It's true then, my lord?"

Clique caught his breath. "What?"

"The Devils Guild." Janson motioned to the severed corpse. "You joined it."

The boy is smart, as much as he is talented with the blade. "Was that really the first man you've killed?"

"The very first," Janson admitted, "save for the rope."

"The rope?"

"I've lynched a man or two for my father, my lord," Janson told him, "back when—"

"Later," Clique interrupted him. "Be quiet, and follow me." *There's too much blood to hide signs of this fight.* Clique relinquished the possibility of covering his tracks, and prayed that they would go unnoticed amidst whatever true goal these cretins had in mind. When they began to descend the spiral stairwell, they saw the flickering red luminescence of torchlight rising below. Clique stopped and listened, and Janson held his breath. "Two men," Clique whispered.

"Should we take them in similar fashion?" Janson asked, but was met by another of Clique's wide smiles. "Another idea?"

Janson followed Clique back up the steps, and gathered the two halves of dead guard's corpse. They waited near the top of the stairwell, and when the two unfamiliar men in House Guard armors were in reach, Clique and Janson tossed the pieces of the dead man. Entrails and blood showered upon them, and the guard with the torch dropped it. As the falling and fading light cast terrible shadows upon their bloodied attackers, Clique knew the two guards were both taken unaware and effectively horrified by the act. Clique drew the scythe from his back and used their fear and surprise to his advantage. In seconds the man's head was cut from his body and tumbled down the stairwell. Janson was not so masterful, and when he drew his longsword and made for an attack, stumbled on the bloody steps and slipped to his backside. The living guard turned tail and made a hasty retreat down the stairs.

"Don't let him escape!" Clique stepped over the gore and chased after him. The man was too far ahead, and in a desperate attempt Clique flung his scythe. It took a cut from the man's arm, but otherwise fell away to no great success. *He must not warn the others.* Clique briefly considered leaping down at him, but that risked breaking his own neck. All at once he remembered the dagger on his belt, and with a silent prayer to his master's red eyed gods, cast the dagger overhand. It struck the man at the base of his skull just as he reached the doorway, and he stumbled out into the hall and fell dead. Clique dove out after his body. To his left, the hall curved left again and led to supply rooms. To his right, about eighty feet away, the hall opened to a wide chamber where the Silver Gate of stone stood guarded by two men. As luck would have it, they did not see him, and Clique pulled the corpse into the stairway unnoticed.

Janson knelt beside him, and Clique explained their predicament. "We could pull the same trick," Janson suggested, but Clique shook it off.

"No," Clique said, "if we make for the gate we risk alerting the rest of them."

"So what?" Janson smiled. "You're Devils Guild. You could kill them all."

Clique sighed. "Think, Janson. Think. All they need do is use their prisoners against us, and leverage our surrender... Plus they have crossbows."

"What then? Surely there are allies in the lower castle who work even now towards our rescue." Janson frowned when Clique denied his words again.

"No. It's unlikely anyone knows what's happened." Clique sat against the wall and took a few deep breaths. "Think about it. If they have men on the inside, they might have men outside as well. The closing of the gates can be explained away long enough for them to accomplish whatever they came here to do. Our only chance is by somehow alerting those below sooner, rather than later."

"How?" Janson asked him point blank. "We're three hundred feet above the shore, and there's a storm outside. How could we send a message?"

Clique grinned, and Janson was not pleased with what the smile meant. "*We* will be the message."

"How's that now?" Janson pulled at his collar, and Clique told him his plan.

They covered their backs in the black cloaks of the men they'd slain in the stairwell, and with purpose in their steps, walked out into the hall, and turned left. They moved at a normal pace and Clique knew Janson was tempted to look behind them to see if they'd drawn notice. "Don't look," Clique reminded him, "and don't run either." Soon they turned the corner and gained access to the supply room. Janson rummaged for the rope he'd sworn he could find as Clique guarded the hall. They were both relieved to discover their passing had gone unheeded, and no one had come after them.

"That should be enough." Clique eyed the four bundles of silk rope his squire had uncovered. "Well done. Now take some and follow." They took the rope coils under their arms, and made their way across the castle, far from the Silver Gate. Near the Southern side they entered a dark and untraveled hall, and chose the furthest room for their task. It was a dusty bed chamber that mustn't have seen use in a generation. Janson closed the door and locked it shut. Clique approached the windows. The wood and iron storm shutters were fastened closed by rusty hooks that took some prying with his dagger to release. The shutters creaked with age, and when finally opened, a burst of fresh salty air filled the room and kicked up the layers of dust. "I was right!" Clique exclaimed against the wind. He leaned out and looked down. "The wind's coming from the sea, but the gusts won't be so bad here. Look!" Clique showed Janson how the curved walls of the nearby tower shielded this hall's chamber windows from the brunt of the wind. "This should be a breeze!" Clique laughed. In truth he feared for his life, but he would neither besmirch his image in the eyes of his squire, nor frighten the boy from the task. "We'll be fine, you'll see."

They tied the rope coils together at the ends and fastened it into one long piece. "If there's any danger to us, it won't be in these knots," Clique explained. "The more weight pressed upon them, the tighter their grip will be." He tied one end of the rope against the heaviest furniture, and fastened it to second piece for good measure. The other end he tossed out the window, and they watched it unfurl and come to a stop at the ground so many feet below.

"I'll go first my lord," Janson was quick to say, but Clique grabbed him by his collar and pulled him back.

"First, we will not being climbing in our armors." Clique removed his doublet, and made the boy do the same.

"And our weapons?" Janson asked.

"Leave them. We'll need them when we return." Clique smiled, and Janson nodded solemnly.

"A wise plan," his squire agreed. Janson, once out of his armors, again prepared to climb out the window, but Clique stopped him once more. He was quick to protest, but Clique took some pieces of rope he'd cut, and showed the boy how to tie them round his shoe. They'd help with slowing their descent and would make a difficult task far easier. Janson went first and Clique climbed out shortly after. Both he and his squire dug their boots into the rope as Clique instructed, and within a minute they reached the muddy ground. The sound of the waves crashing against the shore was deafening so close to the shoals, and when their boots were unbound, Clique led them along the edge of the wall, and away from the water.

It was only a few hundred feet before they turned round an angle, and saw the tents of a vast army huddled against the wall of the Stronghold where it met the city's Southern gates. The rain was coming in a torrential downpour and no pit fires were lit, but many of the tents had lanterns within and it gave the encampment a ghostly appearance. Clique and Janson made it not ten feet from the camp's edge before being stopped by guards. Clique could tell by the sigils on their armor that they were sworn to the West. At first Clique and Janson were considered spies, and the guards demanded their surrender, but when Clique announced himself with conviction and demanded they take him to the Commander of the army, they were believed and obeyed.

The sheer size of the camp was staggering, and neither Janson nor Clique had ever seen so many people gathered in a single place. The rains and their numbers had made the once green fields a muddy mess, and by the time they reached the outside of the Commander's tent, much of the blood that covered their face and hands had been washed away. The tent was silver and green and had a compliment of knights guarding its entrance. After a minute of waiting they were bid to enter the tent, and found the warmth and shelter from the elements therein most inviting. The tent was split into two sections, with a finely decorated waiting room and a separate main quarters. The floor was covered in wood and rushes to protect from the mud, and Clique could hear hushed words being spoken from the inner room. The guards who brought them left, and two knights stepped out from the inner tent. They eyed Clique and his squire suspiciously before allowing them to enter.

Two men greeted them inside. The first Clique recognized by name and title only, as he knew Lord Walter Brae was commanding the Western army, and around that man's neck was the amulet of command. He was in his fifties, with the silver hair and blue eyes of the Brae. He was the proper Lord of The Obsidian Towers, and sat the head of the Great House Brae, sworn to the King of the West. Even at this late hour his look befit a Commander. He wore a silver doublet and had a Kingly short sword at his side. The second man was a wiry fellow in silver robes with blonde hair and amber eyes. "Lord Brae." Clique gave a short bow, and Janson did the same. "I am Clique Gracious, Lord Commander of the Royal Huntsmen, and nephew to Davik Gracious."

"Yes." Walter stepped out from behind the table. It had been hastily covered in a long piece of fabric, and a map's edge hinted at military plans not meant prying eyes. "But why have you come to us in the middle of the night in such fashion?" It was clear he meant the blood that stained their clothes from top to bottom.

Clique frowned and gathered himself. "I come bearing ill news." He spent the next ten minutes explaining all that had happened. He highlighted that a peace had been reached and the summit was going smoothly, and carefully outlined how Jack Havensword had betrayed them, and orchestrated a coup within the House Guard that took them completely unawares. By the time he had finished his story the unnamed lord had been taken by fury, and demanded that their army be allowed main entrance to the Stronghold to take the matter in their own hands. Walter had remained silent and stood still as stone while he heard the tale. As the lord complained, Walter filled a goblet with wine and drank the entirety of its contents. He poured a second and thrust it into the lord's hands.

"Drink this and calm yourself," Walter told the man. "Lord Commander, you were wise to come to me directly. It would be disastrous if knowledge of the situation spread. The peace would be jeopardized."

"I agree," Clique said, "but we must take action quickly."

"Do you have any idea what they want?" Walter asked him.

"No. But they have the nobility of the Realm at their disposal, and must not be allowed to accomplish their goals."

"This is some Gracious or Draven trick!" the lord complained. "A coup in their House Guard? You can't mean to believe these lies! Sire, we should take Davik's nephew hostage, and announce ourselves to Stormbreaker Stronghold immediately. He is second in line to rule over Midgard, and will make a valuable hostage for exchange."

Walter seemed to consider the words and Clique found himself angered. "Who are you, to question my honor?" Clique asked him.

"I am Frederick Brae, Chancellor to the King, and I have more honor than you." Frederick turned to his Commander. "My lord, Clique was trained by Devilkin, and is a member of the Devils Guild. Lies are his lifeblood. You cannot trust him."

Janson could not stand for his lord to be slandered. "Lord Clique risked his life to warn you!" Janson shook his fist at him. "How dare you question his actions! You should be thankful of his training, or you wouldn't even know that your precious King was in danger! You should judge a man by his actions not by his past! You should–"

Clique patted his squire and calmed the man down. "Janson. Janson. Janson, that's enough." His squire bit his tongue and ceased his rant. Frederick was taken aback and seemed ready to complain further, but Walter silenced them all with his hand.

"How would you have us proceed, Lord Clique?" Walter asked him.

"Involve too many men and we'd be noticed." Clique rubbed his hands together. "You have all the best and brightest soldiers, mercenaries, and knights that the Western Realm can muster at your disposal." Clique smiled confidently. "Give me four of your best men, and my squire and I will lead them back into the castle from where we made our escape. With such a small but elite compliment,

I believe we can take them by surprise, and free our Kings from the inside."

Chancellor Frederick complained that if not a trap, the plan was at least madness. He begged Walter to take Clique hostage, and advised him to send as many men as they could muster to take Stormbreaker Stronghold from the inside, using Clique's escape route for the invasion. "Then, even if our King and Queen are lost to us, and it turns out to have been some Gracious trick," the Chancellor explained, "we will have taken over the heart of Midgard, and secured a defensible position in case it comes to war. What was once impossible has been laid bare by Clique's rope, and we must take hold of this advantage."

Clique briefly feared whether he'd just handed over his family castle to an invading army, but he felt no waves and the Aspects seemed at peace. While the Chancellor was as wily and slick as a serpent, Walter had the proud and confident airs of military nobility, and was unswayed by the Chancellor's protests. He agreed to Clique's strategy and orders were issued. Within half an hour four select knights had joined them in the Commander's tent. Each wore black leather armor, black cloaks, and carried short sword and black shield in the fashion of the House Guard as instructed by Clique. Two had crossbows as well, and they all had a number of concealed knives both large and small. Together they seemed a small arsenal, though only their sword was mainly visible. They were introduced as Ser Jonathan, a pale fellow with dark hair and darker eyes, Ser Jackson and Ser Dugen, two blonde haired blue eyed Tarnell knights, and Ser Dustin, whom Clique recognized by way of fame. His hair was grey with age, and he had a patch over his left eye that barely hid the scar from where Dameon Draven had removed it in battle so many years ago. Clique explained the situation to them and noted the time. It was precisely seven that the solar was taken, and the

Commander's clock now showed nine fourteen. Walter commanded Ser Dustin to lead the mercenaries, but to follow Clique's orders, and soon the six of them were off.

It was half an hour later that Clique, Janson, the four knights, and the two Royal Guardsman they'd met outside the Commander's tent, had made their way up the ropes and secured the chamber. The two guards were ordered by Ser Dustin to defend the rope room against all intruders. It was wise to ensure that their escape route, and path for potential reinforcements, was kept safe. Clique carefully made a point of explaining to the six Westerners that he had an inside man in the House Guard named Daniel. He described the man to the best of his ability, and told Ser Dustin and his mercenaries to try not to kill anyone fitting his name and description in their murderous assault on the House Guard. As Clique and Janson equipped their armor they came to the decision to split up. After discussing the layout of the castle, Dustin and his three men planned to secure the Silver Gate, while Clique and Janson would return directly to the Silver Door and spy out the solar. If their assault on the gate created an alarm, then it would also serve as useful distraction for Clique to attack the solar, should they be able to gain entrance.

Axe is in there. And at the very least, he will hear me at the door, and provide my entrance at the opportune time. With his scythe readied and his squire at his side, he split from the group of Western mercenaries led by the one eyed knight, and followed after his squire. *That is*, Clique thought coldly, *if Axe has not already killed them all.*

"Flint?" Havik asked once again. Flint's ear twitched and his head tilted. *He heard me.* "Flint!" Havik shouted at the top of his lungs. It was then that Flint's head spun most unnaturally to gaze back at him. His body followed suit in a queer manner, and he stiffly lurched into a stance that left Havik feeling uneasy. *It is as if his body is foreign to him.* Flint's eyes looked upon Havik's. They were utterly black, with no mortal white visible, alien and vacant and devoid of light. *No color.* Havik was afraid. *It is the obsidian horror that moves him.* The thought played at his sanity, which had, until now, been carefully wrought with logic and Scientos. "Flint..." Havik whispered.

Flint's mouth fell open, and where Havik expected a groan stained with death as before, instead he witnessed Flint speak a single word. "Heeeellllllllloooo..." The word was uttered in a long and drawn out fashion. The tones of his voice resounded with aberrant bass and tinkled with peculiar chimes of high pitched resonance. "Eldarian..." Flint spoke that word quicker. It was only then that Havik realized both words were spoken in Ancient, a language that was queer to read and queerer to speak in civilized times, but was none the less part of his uncle's training. His mind reeled with possibilities and explanations. Havik certainly knew that Flint spoke no Ancient, so it was easy for Havik to discern that it was the fell thing speaking in Flint's place. *He called me Eldarian,* Havik emphasized in his puzzling. *That word could stand to mean human, as all men are of Eldaria, but why not just say human then? Ancient has many words for mankind and the other folk in the South who are neither man nor beast...* Havik was consumed by the ludicrous nature of his final conclusion. *It could also mean this... intelligence... is foreign even to Eldaria.* Havik looked deep into Flint's unfamiliar eyes. *Could it have come through the Gate of Heavens, and not be of this world at all?*

Ever since he'd entered the Barrens, so much had happened to Havik outside the realm of normal rational expectation that he was beginning to struggle with his sanity. While his understanding of Scientos structured his perception of the world, Havik also believed in the Goddess. That belief was taken on faith, though what little he had of it, and it didn't require of him the tangible evidence that Scientos demanded. "Magic is dead," he would often say when dismissing the outlandish beliefs of the religious devout. But in truth he never believed it existed at all, and Havik *chose* to believe that all of myth and legend was based solely on the Scientos of the Ancients.

It was that solitary belief which fueled his desire, along with the rest of the Davenports, to better themselves above all mankind, and reclaim the power lost when Doom came and the Ancients fell. "In so doing, we Davenports will elevate all of humanity to its former glories, and our mark on civilization will be immortalized," his uncle had once explained to him while giving lecture on how Scientos was the key to their House's future. Havik found it strange, but in that moment he seemed to remember Lord Kefka present at the time of that particular lesson. Havik had run in on them pouring over scrolls together. He was only twelve at the time, still learning the arts of Inquisition, and his interruption of Hubert's private meeting earned him two weeks of organizing the library and a lengthy lecture on Scientos and their House's future. Even so, ponderings on the importance of Scientos were all well and good, but not especially useful when confronted with things not meant for man to see. But Havik had Ancient eyes, and he would not lose himself so easily to a shattered paradigm of reality. *I am dealing with magic,* he concluded, *so I must think like a wizard.*

Havik hurriedly tried to recall all he had come to know of myth and legend, the wild beliefs of gods and goddesses, of magic trees, and magic gates, and millions of tiny stars instead of the three real ones in the sky. With it still fresh in his mind, he found himself mulling over the brief argument that Brownbeard had with Narvis earlier. *Something about the Goddess coming through, or not coming through, the Gate. There was the magic tree. We've got that... But what, or who, is this... alien?* Havik felt as if he were almost upon it. The answer to his riddle was right there for the taking. *Two gods were mentioned, and one magic tree. Eldaria has her cock, the Goddess was born, and...* Havik felt fear in that moment as he never had before. *It is no mortal thing.* His blood drained from his face and his skin paled white with horror. Havik knew that to the devout the Goddess had a name. They called her Ma'at, and she was the Goddess of truth, justice, and above all else, *Order.* He knew the Goddess Ma'at had a mirrored twin across the mirrored Gateway of Heaven. Thoth he was called, and he was the god of magic, but he had no power here in Eldaria. When the Gate closed, Thoth remained on the other side. This all men knew. Only one other god, apart from Ma'at, remained in Eldaria after the Doom. *The dark one.* Havik couldn't bring himself to believe it to be so, but found himself thinking the word all the same. Two gods. One the Goddess of Order. The other the God of... *Chaos.*

Havik felt himself teetering on the brink "Are you..." he asked in Ancient, *"Isfet?"*

Flint's mouth yawned impossibly wide, and his throat made an unkind gurgling sound. Black bile spilled from his open mouth, rank with the wretched ink of the Stygian thing inside his body. Once the foul stuff fell to the floor it scampered back onto Flint's boot and scurried into his clothing. Havik was disgusted, but even that paled to the unnameable feeling of what he could only assume was pure fear, fear at the thought that Flint was about to say *yes.* Instead the gurgle repeated and grew louder. A hideous smile blossomed upon Flint's face, and Havik realized that whoever spoke for Flint, was laughing at him.

"No," the creature finally managed to say in the Ancient tongue. "The Lord of Chaos is trapped within his temporal prison. *Never* has the Gate swung open, and *never* will it close." And the thing laughed again, longer this time, and rife with pleasure.

"Are..." Havik started to ask, half relieved, and half confused by its answer. Havik prepared himself for the realization that the being possessing Flint, which was neither man nor beast nor djinn, might really be a god. *"Are you a god?"* he finally found the words to say.

"I am..."

If not Isfet then which? "Then... Who are you?"

Havik stood with bated breath for Flint's answer, awash with peculiar fears and preposterous notions. The thing raised its hand loosely up at him, and seemed to softly mutter a word. Havik's Davenport curiosity was full upon him, and he found himself slowly inching forward to better hear what the antediluvian entity, which stood before him performing the impossible, was trying to say.

"I... am..." the thing started to moan in guttural Ancient, when the clop clopping of hooves came suddenly to his side, Jaxon shouted beside him.

"Look out, m'lord!" Jaxon cried as he rode past Flint on horseback.

"No!" Havik shouted too late. Jaxon struck his sword across Flint's chest in the passing, and the blade cut a swath through flesh and bone. With it came a splattering of blood and gore. The torso ought to have fallen, and Flint ought to have collapsed from the force of the blow, but where magic is concerned, Havik concluded, things might take unforeseen twists. Instead of the expected result, Flint's feet stood firm, and the horrific black tendrils of the primordial abomination that lurked within held the body together. Blood and flesh spilled freely. What remained was anathema to behold.

Jaxon rode round in a circle to attack again, while Havik heard Kevin roar, "My lord, your sword!" and when Havik turned to his beckoning, he found the sword in air. His hand caught the hilt, and he brought the longsword to his side. Kevin unhorsed beside him.

Flint's eyes were on Havik's, the holes that they were. His mouth dripped bile and blood. "You will pay for your transgressions!" the god croaked in the language of the Ancients.

Do not hesitate! his uncle urged him on, and this time Havik would listen. He thrust his sword out, lunged forward, and drove the tip of his blade through Flint's chest to the hilt. The thing snarled. "No blade can defeat me!" Flint's mouth gaped wide as it laughed.

Havik grinned just then. His off hand was cupped and laden with foam, and while the accursed devil laughed, Havik rammed his hand into Flint's mouth and shoved the foam down his throat. When Havik pulled his hand away the being screeched in such fashion that glass might have broken all around. It was a terrible high pitched whine that drove Kevin to his knees and drew blood from Havik's ears. The horses reared in terror. Smoke and mist rose in toxic clouds from Flint's mouth. It grasped at its throat and gurgled venom. Havik lifted his boot to the thing's chest, and with both hands on hilt, loosed the sword from the corpse. The body kicked away and fell to the ground.

"No blade," Havik declared.

While his words were in Ancient, and he knew that Kevin did not understand, the triumph seemed fine in his squire's eyes. Havik savored his victory for a few long breaths, but Jaxon had not heard his sweet words and would not be so easily appeased. The hardened sailor, and fellow ranger of the gate, leapt from his horse with blade in hand. Havik made no move to stop him as Jaxon struck his steel down across Flint's neck, and severed head from body. Much blood had already been spilled, so when Jaxon kicked Flint's head away, little seeped from neck or skull. Steam still rose from Flint's body in rushes, and there was none of the black bile to behold.

Jaxon wiped his blade clean with a snarl and a spit. "Flint's curse is lifted. His soul will pass. Look at how he steams of cleansing."

Kevin was smiling. "Lord Davenport used the stuff that healed his wound," he remarked. "I saw you, my lord!" Kevin turned to Jaxon with excitement upon his face. "He took it from his pocket, and stuffed it down Flint's gullet! Twas that which cured the curse, and not your sword."

Jaxon sheathed his blade. "It does not matter how they die, little one. Just as long as the killing is done." Jaxon spit once more. "I saw what it was, and I saw it go inside him. This task is half finished."

Kevin seemed confused. "What do you mean to do?"

"Burn him," Jaxon answered, as he retrieved lamp oil from his horse pack.

Havik felt himself speechless until he was overcome by a sudden fit of laughter. Kevin and Jaxon looked at him queerly as if he'd gone mad.

"Something funny, my lord? Or are you just happy to see the

thing slain?" Kevin asked.

"I'm recalling something Flint said to me," Havik giggled. "He said, 'Men have no magic, and men can't be gods.' "

"I don't follow, my lord," said Kevin.

Havik held his breath. "It said it was a god."

Jaxon spit. "Foul magic and lies. Some devil in the rust, perchance, but no god."

Havik felt the fear pulse through him once more. "I am not so sure." *Gods are gods because they are not mortal. But can a god kill a god? Could the spillings of Eldaria's cock and its myriad of colors fill that hole of darkness?* The analogy seemed reasonable, but Havik would not be so easily satisfied. *I need Narvis.* "Kevin!" he spoke firm. "Fetch Narvis and bring her here. I mean to know what colors she can see."

Havik expected Kevin to hop to his duties, but the boy paused in apprehension. "Narvis has been put to rest, my lord. A potion to cease her screaming."

"Hmm..." Havik watched Jaxon uncork a bottle of lamp oil. "No, Jaxon. That's too little oil. We've no tinder to waste, and the flesh is too wet to burn so easily."

Jaxon wasn't pleased. "We can't leave the body to rot. I would see that demon burn."

Havik nodded. "As would I."

"Then what would you have us do?" Jaxon asked. "The nearest wood is days away."

"We'll drag the body by horse to fissure. While the wagons go East, we will go South, and set poor Flint to a pool of molten rock. Such an end will leave no ash of him."

"But that's a day's ride in the wrong direction," Jaxon protested.

"And will be more days still on the returning!" Havik answered in kind. "I do not mean to cross the fire lands. The others will wait for us with the wagons at the gate."

"And supposing while we drag him, the thing emerges from Flint," Jaxon went on, "and it climbs up the rope behind us unawares."

"Why not just sling the body over its own horse?" asked Kevin.

"And have a demon horse to answer for? I think not." Jaxon laughed.

Havik had an answer that would appease them. "Jhev and Nimmet will take the wagons, Brackens the garrons, and Brownbeard to watch over Narvis. You two will ride with me. We'll take three garrons. Jaxon you'll pull the dead man behind you, and Kevin, you'll ride with him. Backwards. Keep a mindful watch, and should the thing climb up the rope... Cut it."

They meant to argue the point further but Havik would hear no word of it. Commands were given, and soon the three of them parted company with the wagon train and began their day's ride South. Flint's corpse was wrapped in the cloth canvas, head included, and it dragged behind them lagging in the dirt. They pushed the horses to the brink of exhaustion, and only then made camp. After they rubbed their three mounts down, and watered and fed them, they ate meager meals and spoke little. They slept in shifts, each in turn keeping a careful eye on their dead companion. They did not linger long, and soon set off on their grim task. So as not to run Jaxon's horse ragged, that morning they dragged the corpse behind Kevin's mount.

During the journey Havik took long hours to ruminate over all that had happened. He was consumed by the question of what god the creature could have been, if not for the Goddess or the dark one. *I can claim to be a god, and that does not make it so,* he repeated to himself, as if that were to comfort him after what he'd seen. *God or no, and dead or no, it will be gone to the depths when put to Eldaria's blood. But what of the seed?* He had seen with his eyes the bile turn to steam upon the foam not once, but twice. First was the splatter of the ooze upon shell, the second when he'd forced it down Flint's throat. *But what of the seed?* Havik's logic game had culminated with the notion that whether still cursed or not, the seed would remain protected and inert inside the foam, and inside that glass sphere. He would enjoy the requisite conversation leading up to his dramatic presentation of the thing to his uncle and father. *That will be a lecture for the ages, and I shall be the one giving it,* he fantasized. No doubt his uncle would take his time in consulting scrolls, and priests, and wizards, and using all the resources of the Davenport House and name to his advantage. *If the seed is corrupted, I dare not imagine what kind of fell tree it would grow. But surely the consciousness of he that is known as, 'I am,' will be lost to the fire. If the foam can give life, then why should the tree not heal itself as a body heals a cut?* he asked himself. *But can a mind heal madness?* Still, he was unsure about the seed, and wondered then whether his uncle would indeed bother with consulting anyone at all, and simply not just plant the damned thing and see what happened. *Maybe even on someone else's land. At the Barrows perhaps, or...*

Havik's fantasy was interrupted by Jaxon's words. "Look there, m'lord!" he cried.

Havik looked up from his saddle and focused his eyes to the purple distance whereupon he spied the rising plumage of a smoking fissure. Havik smiled. "Goddess be praised. The sooner this is done, the better."

Kevin twisted his neck as he strained to see, but Jaxon elbowed him in the back. "Keep your eyes on Flint!" he said, and Kevin obeyed.

It was a short ride to the abyss but it seemed far longer to the three of them. Their sense of foreboding anticipation to toss Flint into the flames reached its pinnacle when they were within fifty yards of the place. The horses would go no further, for fear of the heat and smoke, and they were forced to dismount. *We will need to go right up to its edge to toss the man.* Havik reflected. The dust and sand laden ground typical of the Barrens gave way to ash and sulphur here at the borders of the fire lands. They were a cruel pox upon the Barrens, and star metal that fell to that place was unreachable. Jagged scars cut the landscape in fractal patterns, and to tread across them would be entering a labyrinth of smoke and flame with no end. Shallow inch deep rifts in the ground spattered every solid patch of dirt, and they released noxious fumes that made breathing a hazard. Fortunately their party had been accustomed to using cloths and ointment to improve the quality of air, and Havik hoped they would not have to hold breath long when set to task.

Havik stepped off his horse, fastened his sword to his belt, and took a long sip from his canteen. Jaxon and Kevin were equally weary from the journey. Kevin stretched uncomfortably while Jaxon drove a long stake into the foul ground and tied up their mounts. "We'll take him to that ridge there," Havik pointed. "See how it glows. Eldaria's blood is below. That jut of land overhangs it, and we'll toss him over into the fire."

Jaxon approached the corpse and with a slice of his dagger cut the rope from its bundle.

Kevin was not so sure. "All three of us my lord? You should stay here. This is a squire's task."

Havik laughed at him. "I'll not have my glory taken from me. I am not afraid."

Kevin stood fast. "Your glory has already been won. I'll not return to the Realm, and tell of my noble lord who fell to smoke and flame after felling himself a demon. Let *me* do the deed, and you command from the rear as a King would his army."

Perhaps he's right, Havik considered briefly, but before he could make his choice Jaxon gave out a shout of confoundment, and Havik and Kevin quickly came upon his side.

"What is it?" Havik asked, but as he said the words he saw for himself. Jaxon had rolled the sack over and revealed a most heinous sight indeed. Tens of thousands of small puncture wounds littered the bottom of the thick cloth canvas that wrapped Flint's body. One might assume it was the result of sharp ground along the path, but the look of it was familiar somehow.

Kevin stuttered his words. "My lord. Holes of the same kind were left when the puddle..."

"Ah, yes," Havik stopped him. *This does not bode well.* "Whether the thing is in the body or not, it does not change our task. We must burn him at once."

"While you wait here, my lord? No!" Kevin complained, and he looked around, nervously. "It... It may be out there." Havik grew annoyed at his squire's warnings.

"I will either burn the body or wait here," he grumbled, "but I will not get on my horse and flee, as you would have me do. So which way would you have your lord? Burnt or bedeviled?"

Kevin Gracious was at a loss for words, and Havik did not care. Jaxon had already begun to drag the corpse towards the fissure, and he would not be shown up by a sailor. Havik pushed past his young squire and lifted Flint's corpse by the other end. "Stay and watch the horses!" he commanded. "I don't mean to walk to the gate from here." And with that Jaxon and Havik set off.

The heat grew spiteful hot when they came to the smoking grounds, but they needed to press much further to reach the ledge. With grunts and moans of exasperation, the two of them carried Flint's dead weight across the treacherous earth. They'd gotten no further than fifty feet into the fire lands when Havik began to cough.

All at once the searing heat of the foul place and its noxious air took its toll. Havik's world spun. He dropped Flint's body and came to his knees. Each cough was labored with pain as his lungs gasped for relief, only to be refilled by scorching hot vapors. For a moment all was black, until Havik felt himself awakened and refreshed by cool water that spilled over his face and into his mouth. "There now. Take a drink, my lord," Kevin said to him.

Havik sat up and drained the offered canteen of its elixir. "What happened?"

"You passed out for near ten minutes," Kevin told him. "Your mask was bone dry. When's the last time you applied Brownbeard's paste?" Havik shrugged with uncertainty. "Here, put this on. I've wet it for you."

Havik took the mask and fastened it over his nose and mouth. The odor of shit and vinegar was overpowering, and Havik knew his squire had applied it quite liberally. "Go back to the horses, Kevin."

"Are you sure–" Havik stopped his squire before he had the chance to complain further.

"Yes. I'm alright. I'm fine now. Thank you." Havik stood, regained his composure, and thrust the empty canteen back into his squire's hands. "Jaxon and I shall complete this task. See to the horses. This won't take long."

Kevin begrudgingly left them behind, and with a heave of exertion, Havik and Jaxon again picked up Flint's corpse, and headed deeper into the fire lands. Several times the caked ash gave way beneath their boots, and they'd plunge down to the knee in hot ash. Once Jaxon's leg rose aflame and he dropped the body as he stamped it out in alarm. At last they reached the narrow precipice that overlooked the gaping maw of the fissure. It ran lengthwise below them, and the depths of it bore the infernal red hue of molten lava. They set the body down with a huff of exertion. Jaxon drank from his wineskin and emptied half the contents into his open mouth, and the rest spilled over his head and hair with relief. Havik took five willful steps towards where the ground met open air. He firmly planted his feet, then leaned cautiously over the edge in an effort to peer over. The drop was no farther than a hundred feet. The rock rose to an outcropping here, just as he thought it would, and the lava was directly beneath them. Unable to resist his baser urges, Havik gathered phlegm in his throat, then spit over the cliff. He watched it fall with precision and disappear to an inaudible explosion of vapor somewhere in that hellish sea.

Havik turned away from the ledge, ready to perform the deed and leave that place, yet he got no further than a single step before freezing in unrestrainable dread. The obsidian horror rose from the ground behind Jaxon, who was cluelessly refreshing himself with the contents of a second wineskin. Havik raised his finger in terror, but when he opened his mouth, sulfurous air poured in, and he found himself coughing.

"Lookout! Jaxon! Behind you!" Havik pitifully attempted sounding to no avail. The breath seared at him, and he had no waters to quench it.

Jaxon caught eye of Havik's pointed hand and he shrugged with his hands in confusion. Havik coughed and hurriedly pointed over Jaxon's shoulder, and the message took. In realized panic Jaxon turned to face the unknown. There, behind him, the dark one that is not the dark one was waiting. Without warning or hesitation it leapt into Jaxon's mouth and was consumed by him. Havik cried out, enraged. "No!" *Do not hesitate.* He said the words to himself this time, and it was not his uncle's voice.

Havik charged forward and tackled Jaxon to the ground. He was felled easily, and soon began to violently seize in a fit of madness. Havik steadied himself and came to his knees. He grabbed at Jaxon's collar, forced the butt of his wineskin through his teeth, then pried his mouth open. Havik reached into his pocket and pulled out some, but not all, of the remaining magic foam he had within. When took it in his hand and force fed it to Jaxon, the man's seizing intensified and Havik was thrown to the wayside. Jaxon let forth a horrific screech and foul steam poured from his mouth. For the smallest moment, Havik even believed that he had saved Jaxon's life, but the sweet of it turned bitter as Jaxon's eyes turned black then detonated in puffs of creamy smog. *He is dead, or like to be.*

Jaxon fell still and Havik saw his chance. He lunged forward once more, grabbed at Jaxon's corpse, and dragged him towards the ledge. The heat was unbearable, and Havik smelled, even above the shit and vinegar of his ointment, the odor of burning human hair. He felt like retching and his back hurt something fierce from when he'd fallen, but still he pressed on. The weight was nearly too much for him, and soon he was on his side, digging his feet into the ground as he tried to pry himself and Jaxon those final feet closer to the cliff. Soon he felt ash and rock give way, and a blazing heat overcame his shoulder. Havik stole a glimpse at the fiery chasm below. *No god or devil can survive that drop.*

Havik summoned his remaining strength and stood. He took hold of Jaxon's ankles and struggled as he pulled the corpse horizontal to the ledge. He knelt alongside the dead man's chest, then dug his boots into the ash for leverage. As he placed his hands on Jaxon and pushed with all his might, the obsidian horror emerged from Jaxon's mouth and poured over Havik's coat and tunic. Havik became unhinged. He stood as if a man on fire and pulled at his clothes. He stripped bare to his skin, and tossed his shirts down onto the floor before him. The vile entity of amorphous black ink clung to his vestments and left none upon Havik's person. He moaned in relief and fear. Jaxon's body teetered for a moment, then with a rustle of loose ash and rock, tipped from the cliff face, and fell to the blazes.

Havik backed away from the thing and fell as he tripped over Flint's bundled corpse. The obsidian horror slowly slithered towards him, and Havik continued to back away, now scrambling on his backside with eyes on the terrible organism. The thing followed patiently but relentlessly, and it passed over Flint's corpse and maintained a steady pursuit of its next Eldarian victim. Havik felt his fear crescendo to impossible heights, when the ground gave way behind him, and he almost fell back to plunge into the hell fires himself. He took one final glance over his shoulder at the abyss, then steadied himself, and came to his knees. The thing was upon him now. It puddled before him not three feet away. With snail like precision it began its vertical rise from the inky pool and formed the amorphous blob that it seemed to take before claiming a host. Even there, at that moment of certain inevitable fate, Havik had a choice. *I can be taken by a god, or I can spit in his face and cast myself to the flames.* But Havik did not truly have it in him to kill himself. All Davenports everywhere clung to life most fiercely, and would do anything, even going so far as to betray their own family, to ensure their individual survival. But here, in this unique situation, the Davenport name would live on only in form. *My mind will not be my own,* he considered, *and that seems a fate worse than death.*

Havik removed the cloth that covered his nose. *If I will die, I will not do so smelling shit,* something which he knew was a luxury oft not afforded to those who died in battle. Havik rose to his feet, took a deep fiery breath, and spit at the monstrosity that was growing in size and awe before him. Havik stepped that last precious step backwards and came to a stop where he felt air upon his boot heel. *So this is how Havik Davenport comes to his end.* He could almost laugh. *Fire or fraud.* Havik lifted his left foot and hovered it over the edge. *One simple step and it will be done.* Havik regretted his bones might not be buried with his ancestors, and with his new found belief in gods and magic, he found himself taken by fear. And so he paused, and did not take the final step. *If I melt in flame, will I go to the netherworld? Or will I cease to be?* Even becoming someone else did not seem as terrifying to Havik as ceasing to exist altogether. Succumbing to his instincts and fear, he pressed his foot down, and did not sacrifice himself to the inferno.

"*My* name is Havik Davenport!" he said to it, as it rose to its penultimate heights. "And I..." He paused as a queer thought overtook his dying monologue. *Do not hesitate!* his uncle shouted in his ear, and Havik Davenport smiled. He dug his left hand into his pants pocket and pulled from it all that remained of the magic nut's frothy elixir. The thing reacted as if he meant to throw the suds, for it reared up like a stopped horse and flinched away at the thought of the cleansing white foam assaulting its evil form. But wasting such precious panacea in a desperate attack was not the trick. Havik opened his mouth wide and poured the foam in. He ate it happily, grinning all the while. With the last lavish lick of his palm, Havik gurgled, and laughed, and smiled, and giggled as magic foam dripped from his teeth and frothed on his lips as would a mad dog. "Ha!" he cried triumphantly. "I win!"

The god may have been beaten but it was not dead. It was also not pleased, and it let out a horrendous squawk of godly rage. Havik covered his ears, and before he could gather his wits, the sound stopped as promptly as it had begun. The obsidian horror returned to puddle, then sped off down the path from which they'd come. *It moves with such speed!* Havik marveled as the terror fled from sight. He took some much needed steps away from the precipice and gave a shout of joy. Havik Davenport had never felt so relieved, nor thought so highly of his ingenuity in all his life. But all at once, a single word turned the taste of his celebration from wine to vinegar in his mouth. *Kevin!*

Havik would not leave his noble squire to such a ghastly fate, and so he began to run. He found his strength and vigor restored to him by way of the magic foam, and the pains in his back and legs were gone. He also found he no longer tasted the heat in the air, and the smell of sulfur no longer overcame him. *The foam truly is a marvel... Some yet remains within the sphere,* he reminded himself. The way back seemed much easier to Havik with freedom of breath and no bundle to carry. Even though his chest was bare, no sweat glistened on his skin. It was as if the foam were cooling him from the inside. As he slowed, and carefully rounded weak ground near a small chasm, he wondered whether he should ever bother to come back and finish off Flint's burning. His corpse still remained on that fiery cliff. Havik pushed the thought from his mind. He had more urgent matters to deal with first. *Concentrate on the puzzle at hand. Suppose Kevin is taken, what then? Shall I come to terms with the foul thing? Bargain my services? The seed is what it wants. Or does it already possess the seed, even now? Shall I offer the seed freely? And if not, what then? Cut off Kevin's legs and flee?*

Fool! He's already dead, and your fate is nearly sealed.

He steadied himself on the wider part of the path and again began to run. For want of vision through the thick smoke rising ahead he would not have sight of the horses for a little while. Still, it made Havik feel uneasy that he did not see the thing. *It moves quicker than man as a liquid. Should Kevin be taken, it will only serve to slow it down.* Havik prepared himself for what was to come. He found himself praying to the Goddess that when he passed the smog's curtain wall he would spot Kevin upon horseback. *If he is yet on horse, he could out ride the thing.* Havik held his breath and pushed through the airy pollution. It's when he emerged from the other side that he heard the screaming of the horses. Kevin had fallen onto his back, sword in hand, and was scrambling away from the obsidian horror while taking wild swings with the blade. Havik pressed on with all his legs could give, but it would not be enough. Neither sheer strength of will nor all the want in the world could shorten the distance between Havik and his squire, and the obsidian horror was reaching its penultimate height.

"Kevin!" Havik shouted with all his fury. "Run!"

He knew that Kevin heard him, for the boy dropped his sword, and fled. He took off in a panic towards the Barrens. Leagues and leagues of empty endless terrain. The horror shrunk back down into a puddle and glided after him. Havik thought he heard it shriek, as if it realized Havik's words lost it its easy kill. By the time Havik reached the horses one of them had broken its leg in its frightened struggle to free itself. *I'll not leave this animal to be taken by the god.* Havik adjusted his own sheathed sword, then knelt and recovered Kevin's naked blade. He placed his hand on the wounded garron and calmed it for a moment, then stepped back, and with Kevin's sword, cut across the beast's bare throat. He looked away so he'd not bear witness to the sight. *A sad end for Jaxon and his mount.* Havik said a silent prayer as he mounted his own horse. With the bloodied longsword he cut the rope restraining the two remaining horses free, then tossed the weapon aside to the dirt. He grabbed the reins of the second horse, and soon was off riding towards Kevin, where the obsidian horror was slowly gaining ground.

"Kevin!" Havik yelled. "Get ready!"

The boy looked back at him, the fear plain to see on his face. "What?"

Havik shook his head in frustration. "Your horse! Get ready!"

Havik was upon them. Kevin ran just feet beyond the horror, where it was rising from its puddle even as it chased him. *It will not have him!* Havik swore. His mount fought against him when they passed the horror that was slithering close at hand, but Havik was an experienced rider and the horses were battle trained. Kevin ran nearer to his horse, and with a dextrous test of his athletics, managed to pull himself up onto the garron. Their victory was short lived, for the demon launched a tentacle that leashed Kevin's steed. With incredible speed the monstrosity flowed as liquid up its own tentacle until the thing was upon the back of the horse.

The boy was in a panic. "No! Ahh!" Kevin screamed in mortal terror.

"Kevin!" Havik roared. "Jump to my horse!" He rode himself beside his squire and extended his hand. Kevin glared at the Stygian fluid that rose up before him, then looked back to Havik. He saw the color of cowardice in Kevin's eyes as the boy hesitated and did not grab hold. *The fear has taken him.* "Kevin!" Havik cried, but the young squire had looked back upon the ebony viper, beholden to its hypnotic form.

Havik cursed and grabbed hold of Kevin's collar. With all his might he pulled Kevin as if a sack of sand from one horse to the other. Havik reared his own horse away from Kevin's and came to a stop. The horror, however, had made its move. The thing had attached itself to Kevin's leg and was slithering up his body. Havik pulled at the boy and they both fell to the ground in a heap. Kevin screamed and cursed. He jumped to his feet and swatted at his clothes in fright. Havik tried to rise but he had broken his leg. He grunted in pain, cursed, and spit blood from where he'd bit his tongue in the fall.

"Get your shirt off!" Havik yelled to no avail. The boy twisted helplessly as if set aflame.

Havik watched the dreadful sight as the unholy creation slipped inside Kevin's skin and began its dance of death. Havik felt a queer sensation in his mouth just then, and he realized the foam was

244 | Gregory Mandarano

healing his cut. He tried to rise, and found to his amazement that his leg had completely healed. *The foam's magic!* He hopped on his feet, overtaken by the wonder that had replaced his fear. But when Kevin began to haltingly stand, the fear was again full upon Havik Davenport. Kevin's garron stood nearly fifty yards away, but his own horse was beside him. He mounted his horse and unsheathed his sword, then turned to face Kevin. *Better him remain unharmed. At least he is a boy and not a man.* He waited until Kevin had stood and faced him before sheathing his sword. Kevin smiled grotesquely, and his body gently shifted as the creature inside began to find its center of balance.

Havik felt unsure of himself. *How shall I proceed? Shall I strike a bargain?* Havik forced himself to concentrate in what little time he had. *At the very least, I will see what it has to say.* Havik decided he should take the opportunity to speak first. *Perhaps an apology? No. That will make me look weak. I did best the thing's wits once, and it does not know I have no more of the foam. It may yet fear me. Best use that to my advantage.*

"Who are you?" Havik asked in Ancient, with a strong voice and firm tone.

Kevin steadied himself. He took one graceful step forward and stood tall. *It shows me it has mastered the body. A show of its own strength. It does fear me. And it truly is intelligent.* The boy who once was his squire opened his mouth, and black bile dripped and puddled from his tongue. "I..." the thing said, and it tapped upon the temple of Kevin's head with Kevin's own fingers, "know what *Gracious* knows..." and it grinned the wickedest grin to which Havik had ever bore witness. *That... is the worst of all possible outcomes.* Havik felt as if the bottom had dropped out from beneath him, and the noose of terror was tightening around his neck. *It knows me... It knows my family... It knows the Realm... Dear Goddess, if it had taken me...*

"What do you want?" Havik asked again.

The thing smiled once more, then let loose a horrible wail that whined with such tremor Havik grabbed at his ears and grew dizzy. *His answer or his attack?* Havik thought as his horse bucked. He barely managed to keep himself from falling off. All at once the sound ceased and Kevin began to run. *Not towards me?* Havik was thankful but confused. He felt dizzy and nauseous, and had trouble regaining his wits. *That noise incapacitates. In battle against it, one must muffle one's ears,* he taught himself. Then it hit him. *He runs to the garron.* Havik steadied his horse and reared it to gallop towards Kevin's mount. It was no fair race. The horse was far enough that Havik easily outpaced Kevin and reached the garron with time to spare. He came to a halt and took the second horse by the reins. "Hyah!" he shouted as he commanded the horses to start the ride and moved to a trot. When he looked back to gain certainty of his victory, he loathed to see that his wits and his haste were all for naught. Kevin raised his hand and sent forth a terrible tentacle of the Stygian fluid from his palm. It wrangled the horse and pulled it back with such force that Havik lost the reins. He came to a stop and turned back to find the creature bucking against the demonic rope.

Do not hesitate! he heard his uncle speak as if he were there. Havik pulled his longsword from his sheath and rode forward. Kevin had stepped up to the garron and was beginning to mount it, when Havik swung wide with his sword. The sharp steel cut true across the steed's neck, and the blood spilled in sheets. Havik reared his horse a few yards away from the creature's death throes, and turned again to face his foe. Havik's blade was held high in the air with the horse's blood dripping from its steel, and any mortal man would have been overcome by the fear of his countenance. Kevin Gracious, however, was no longer a mortal man, and the black tentacles slurped back up into his hands. The boy turned and looked bare into Havik's soul with cold, black, empty eyes. It was a foul look, and might have born the color of hate if there was any to be had. *I do not like its empty stare. Narvis would die of fright,* was all he had time to think before Kevin started to run directly towards Havik.

Dear Goddess! Havik shouted in his mind, as he turned his horse and prodded it to flee. As his horse sped away Kevin launched tentacles again from his palm, and they latched around the mount's side satchel. With a desperate attack, Havik swung at the ebony strand and cut it in twain. The tentacle retreated into Kevin's palm, while some black squirming bile remained on the satchel and his sword. *This foul stuff is relentless! Could it possess two people at once?* The thought horrified him. With no alternative, he threw his sword wildly into Kevin, and managed to topple the boy to the ground. Then, with no time to spare, he pulled his dagger and cut the side satchel from the horse. The bag, its cargo, and the black bile atop it all went tumbling to the ground. Some of the Stygian fluid even managed to grab hold of his dagger, and he was forced to toss that away as well.

Well, there goes the food, Havik grumbled and thought of the hungry days ahead before he reached the wagons. Still, he counted his blessings. *If it took the other satchel, I'd really have had a puzzle on my hands.* Havik knew he still had with him the water and horse rations. Without those he would have been forced to turn back, with the thing between him and the other horses. Even so, as he rode forward and looked behind him, he felt the pangs of a dread that would not retreat. Havik watched as Kevin paused near the satchel with Havik's own longsword in hand. The remaining black bile slithered to his boot and up his leg. *The drop rejoins the bottle.*

Even from the distance, Havik felt Kevin's eyes meet his own, and the fear flowed through him. His fright even pulsed anew when

Kevin soon thereafter began to run. Havik reared at his horse and bid it gallop faster. *The horse had little time to rest. It will not keep this pace for long.* Havik watched over his back as they rode. Kevin would not stop running. He remained in sight as a spot in the distance for a long while. Eventually he couldn't be distinguished from the dark purple landscape of the Barrens, but Havik knew he was there. *He's chasing me. Whilst I am ahorse I will outpace him five to one. Three to one might be safer lest I run my horse ragged. And only that because the ground is hard for a man to walk, and the temperature uncertain. Anywhere else and it would overtake me. Even so, with each three hours of rest to my one of riding, I should not have difficulty making time.* Havik came to a halt and dismounted. He opened the side saddle to fetch water, and he said a silent prayer to the goddess when he found a simple tunic packed in as well. Although the Barrens' weather no longer seemed to bother him since he'd eaten the foam, he felt uncomfortable riding such an inhospitable terrain with no clothes above his waist. He happily put on the shirt and watered his horse. *I have no man to keep me watch, and soft as death it will creep upon me.* His body chilled. *It knows my squire's mind.* He shuddered at the thought. *It knows the path I mean to take, from here, to the gate, to the ship itself.* Havik laughed. *It even knows the ship's crew well, which is far better than I.* He took one last sip before putting away the water, and got back on his horse.

I will have to take an irregular course, just to throw it off my trail, he decided. And with that he adjusted his heading and made for the endless horizon. For three full days he traveled. He slept uneasily the first time he rested, but was confident he'd lost the thing by the end of the second day. Of course Havik could only guess at the passage of days and nights. The Silver Star was not visible here beneath the ridge wall of the Barrens, and the clock they'd been using to tell time was on the wagon with Brownbeard. Havik figured it had been three days, or perhaps four, by the time he saw the wagons in the distance. He was well into the horse rations by then, but he had accounted for a few more days journey, as he did not expect to come across the caravan until the gate. He had thus far staved off hunger by eating some of the oats sopped in water, but he was careful not to eat too much. *I could go on water alone, but my horse cannot,* he had told himself one of those lonely nights when he forced himself to sleep without having any supper. *I won't outpace a god by walking.*

When Havik spotted the wagons in the distance he cursed under his breath. *This bears ill omen. They should be much further than this.* The fear coursed through him as he wondered what horrible fate might have befallen his rangers. *They could have disobeyed me, and meant to wait for us along the path instead of going full to the gate.* The thought pleased him, but Havik had not been feeling particularly lucky as of late. Instead his carefully wrought plans seemed to be collapsing all around him. So too were his servants and squires. His stomach rumbled as he grew closer to the wagons and saw the movement of the horses. *At least they are not all dead, slain by some unknown horror. If the horses are safe then my rangers are safe as well.* Havik found himself yearning for some of Brownbeard's meager rations. Food he once called a sacrifice for glory, he now thought of as a treasure unto itself. *Savory fried sausage and beans over a hot oil lamp. Rum... Hard bread for the grease and hard cheese for the wine.* His mouth watered. *I must be a day ahead of Kevin by now, at least. There'll be time to inform them of the horror. I can ride in the wagon. That pace may be the same as his, so we must make good time while we can. At least I'll have one good sleep. Yes. I'll eat my fill and drink myself to stupor as I tell tale of what chases us. I'll sleep one night soundly while we move, and have one night's drink and rest with no fear. I've come so far. I deserve my night.* Havik had wrestled with whether to give up the drink for the remainder of the journey. He had decided he ought not dull his wits whilst that thing was out there. But he yearned for the drink, and he fought over the risks of rum and wine alike.

His musings of food and drink and a night of dark celebration were soon wrenched from his grasp. He came close enough to the caravan to discover that one of the wagons had lost axle and wheel. It lay nearly flat upon the ground, its right side crushed from broken wood. Havik cursed under his breath at his cruel fates, then prayed to the Goddess for mercy as he approached the camp. The other wagon was settled nearby. A tarp had been pulled over it as a covering, and the drays and garrons were all roped and resting nearby. *No doubt Brownbeard put it up for Narvis, if she's still bound.* The wagons would have been covered once they passed the gates, but here in the Barrens there would be the occasional terrible gust of wind that might rip it asunder. It also served them more easily to fumble about their supplies and load the ore while they were set to the task of mining the stuff. Rain was also no concern in the Barrens, and there were neither animals, insects, or plants. Only lightning haunted them. *They must all be in the wagon, or behind it,* Havik thought, but when he counted three of the garrons were missing.

"Hello! Is anyone there?" Havik cried out. He rued not having a sword in that moment, and he wondered whether he might go fumbling about in the broken wagon to find one. He did not even have a serving knife, for it had been in the satchel he'd discarded from the horse, and his dagger was gone as well. *If Brackens has betrayed me and taken the seed for himself, I will give him the lowest levels of Witchblood's dungeons, and inquire upon him until we are both old and grey.* Havik cursed under his breath, which seemed to be becoming a habit for him since he'd passed through the Demon's Gate. *Three horses gone. Three betrayers? No, it would be*

Brackens with his sailor Nimmet. And Narvis, the wizard, tied as his second prize. He cursed again. *Brownbeard and Jhev I will soon find dead in the wagon. Sailor's Law be damned. Brackens is the first mate, and he had three months to plan his mutiny. I'm sure some of the finer pieces of star metal are gone as well.* Havik counted the drays and saw two of them were missing. *Two drays for cargo. Choice rations and more star metal no doubt.* Havik hated Brackens just then, and all his fear had been overcome by anger and want for revenge. *He's foregone wagons of metal for the glory of bringing the seed straight to O'Brien hands.* Havik's heated emotions dissipated as horror upon foam when Nimmet hopped cheerfully from the back of the wagon.

"M'lord!" Nimmet cried aloud. "Thank the Goddess you're safe!" He rushed forward and came to the side of Havik's horse. "We feared the worst."

Havik was of singular mind. "Is the seed safe?" he asked from atop his tall garron as he looked down upon the sailor he'd only seconds ago thought to be a traitor.

Nimmet nodded solemnly. "Yes, m'lord." He pointed at the broken wagon. "It's packed in tight. We wrapped it with cloth and straw, and buried it deep in the pile of ore. It's not going anywhere." Nimmet frowned, and spit. "And neither are we."

"Five horses are gone. Three garrons and two drays." Havik pointed out.

"Aye, m'lord." Nimmet nodded and told the tale. "The wagon hit some loose rock and broke the axle as you see. Wheel's busted too. With such a heavy load we ain't got the wood to repair it. Jhev was most distraught, and he said we should just leave the wagon behind. 'One wagon o' metal's better than two if it means our lives,' he said. But Brackens wouldn't hear none of it. First mate he may be, but he didn't seem too quick to follow Jhev's command. It finally came to fisticuffs, and Jhev took a black eye and a broken rib or two, but Brackens got the better of him and won the argument. He ordered Jhev and I to remain here and watch both wagons while he went for wood. He meant to take Brownbeard with him and two drays for the lumber that they'd gather past the gate, but Brownbeard didn't trust Narvis back here with the seed. So in the end Brackens ordered Narvis along as well, and she seemed content enough to help. She'd surely abandon them to go back to the ship herself, but knows getting back without her Captain would only mean her hanging. If she wants to live, she has no choice but to play along. She thought Brackens might try to kill her for Horoway's death out there, but Brownbeard pledged he'd protect her if he did, and she believed him. Them wizards stick together they do."

Good Donner Brackens, Havik mused. *He may be a spy, but he's a fellow ranger of the gate as well. And a greedy one at that! Who knew Jhev was so yellow as to abandon a King's random so easily? Brackens knew the truth of the danger, but chose not to leave our cargo behind.* He could have kissed the man just then. *Good Donner Brackens. His greed has given me my night of rest.*

"When did they leave for the gate?" Havik asked him.

"Two and a half days ago, m'lord. It's less than a day's ride to the gate from here, and it ain't much wood we need. They'll be back soon. I'm sure of it."

"Well, it was good for Brackens to try to fix the wagon and save our cargo," Havik said, as he dismounted his horse, "but the situation has changed in a way Donner does not know. I mean to abandon the wagon, and head straightaway for the gate with the one that remains to us."

"But all that star metal!" he protested.

"Yes," Havik said, "but it is not lost. It will sit right there, unmoved, until a second expedition comes to our hidden cove, and uses our map, and takes our path through the Barrens to claim it. We'll have our prize, and you your fair share eventually," Havik told him, though he knew the words were lies. *I will never return to this place,* he said to himself. *It is cursed with devils, and when I sing my tale of this place, it will be shunned for generations.*

"That's true," Nimmet conceded.

"Fetch Jhev. I mean to tell you what happened at the fissure before we unbury the seed."

"Aye, m'lord. I heard the terrible news." Nimmet took off his cap. "I mourned for poor Jaxon all last night I did." He held the cap over his heart with sad eyes. "He was like a brother to me, he was."

AXE

Axe shifted in his seat and waited for Collin to make his move. It had been exactly two hours and forty nine minutes since they were taken hostage when the clock struck seven. Every second was ticked by the clock, and each one echoed in Axe's ears with the urgency of the situation. *The longer I wait to act, the greater the risk,* Axe told himself, but still he did nothing, and said nothing. Within the first five minutes their compliment of guards had been killed, and the bandit leader and his eleven men secured the solar. Every weapon in their possession, including the Ancient blades of Ser Tarbeld and Ser Laurence, had been collected from them and placed in the corner. The sword Shadow was taken by their leader, and a second man took Starsinger. Early on there were moments when Axe believed the knights would suicide themselves into the task of fighting back, but their Kings quieted them.

In that first half hour the women, Queen Draven, Queen Tarnell, Keira Gracious, her servant Amy, and the kitchen girl Kelly were brought to the Northern corner of the room and put to guard by four of the men. Two others encircled the table where the two Kings and their two knights, Lord Gracious, Collin, Sheriff Baldric, Axe, and the wine boy Kendrick were seated. The bandit leader and his men exited into the Red Tower, and amidst protests by Keira, assured her that her children were locked away and would remain safe provided they made no attempt to escape. For a short while everyone spoke in hushed tones and discussed their predicament. All were curious as to what they could possibly rob from Davik's possession, beyond the Ancient swords they'd taken from their knights, but Davik was tight lipped about the subject of his wealth. When they pressed further, Collin deflected their accusations by explaining that Davik was a collector of many rare things, and must have come across something of particular significance to the robbers.

"What they seek must be small," Collin had suggested. "I don't see how they could expect to escape with any significant amount of spoils, let alone escape at all. Where would they go?" With the gates shut, it was agreed the only way out would be through the windows. And yet, there was no ship capable of braving the shores below during a storm, and any escape into the courtyard would be easily noticed by the guards. The only other choices would lead them into the hands of either army, and when that point was made by Ser Laurence, the Kings accused each other of perpetrating the crime, and they and their knights bickered til they were silenced by the guards with threats made against the Queens' lives.

Two hours and four minutes into their capture, the leader and four of his men returned and took Davik and both Kings away into the Red Tower. Before leaving the leader whispered something in a foreign language to the two guards watching over them. It would have been impossible for any normal man to hear, but Axe was no ordinary man. When the door was shut, Axe saw both guards take careful note of the time on the clock. When the two guards approached the four nearest the women to pass on their orders, Axe spoke the words that he'd overheard their leader say. Only the Sheriff understood, and he went white when Axe said them. "It's Gulgari pirate cant," Baldric told them. "He said, if you've not heard word of us by ten, then they've given us no trouble, and the vault has been opened. Tidy up here, then follow the plan... They responded with, 'Yes, Captain.'"

"Captain..." Collin wondered aloud. "Perhaps they *do* have a ship."

"Do you think they mean to free us and make off with the Kings?" Kendrick asked. The look the Sheriff gave the boy could have killed a man with a weak heart. Kendrick gulped.

"No," Ser Tarbeld said. "They mean to kill us all." The old knight glanced to the corner where Melinda and Amy were huddled up on the floor next to Keira who clutched protectively at her pregnant stomach. Vivian sat a meter away from the group crying softly into her arm with Kelly beside her.

"We can't just sit here and do nothing," Ser Laurence complained. "We should act now."

"If we take action, they'll kill the women, and fire bolts against us," Ser Tarbeld whispered.

"If only I had a weapon of some kind," Ser Laurence complained again. "I can't fight six men with a spoon."

"We have two advantages on our side," Collin told them. "We know that the closer it gets to ten, the less likely it is the other six men will return."

"That's true," Sheriff Baldric admitted. "We should make our move close, but not too close, to the hour."

"The other advantage?" Laurence asked. "You said we have two."

"We have Axe." Collin smiled. "I've seen him punch a man dead."

The knights were stricken with disbelief, but the Sheriff admitted he'd heard the same tale from the Huntsmen. "Even if he could kill them quick and easily, he'll be prone to arrow fire," Ser Laurence objected.

"I've taken thirteen arrows and seven crossbow bolts," Axe told them, "and here I sit."

Again the knights thought it was a fanciful boast, but Collin told them the story of how he'd faced down ten men at the same time, and killed all save one to sing the song. Both knights seemed skeptical of Axe, but were willing to use him as arrow fodder in the attempt. "Whatever we do, we must do it quickly, and focus our effort on those guarding the women," Ser Tarbeld said. "We'll all need to act together, and do what we can to ensure their safety."

The plan was plotted in quiet whispers, and when the clock struck nine fifty, Collin began the ruse. "Lord Gracious is a good man!" He declared to Ser Laurence beside him. "How dare you besmirch his honor!"

"Your lord is a cunt," Ser Laurence replied, "and has no honor!"

The guards took notice. Collin stood and charged Ser Laurence. "Brae bastard!" He tackled him backwards in his chair and onto the ground. One of the Queens' guards moved closer with his crossbow raised to get a better look, while the two guards nearest circled round, each with crossbows aimed as well. Collin and Ser Laurence grappled on the ground with their hands clawing at each other's throats. The Sheriff feigned trying to break them up and was knocked aside in the melee.

"Stop that!" A guard shouted, but another contradicted his order.

"Let them kill each other!" the man said. "My bet's on the one with the fancy blue shirt."

Collin and Ser Laurence rose to their feet and cast curses at one another. They exchanged a few careful punches, and circled one another as they waited for the opportune time. The nearest guards were ready for any sign of deceit, and should the battle be a ruse, seemed prepared to kill anyone that tried to overtake them. Axe rose from his chair and inched his way closer to the brawl. Ser Laurence and Collin exchanged a knowing glance, and Collin charged at the knight, who side stepped him, and sent Collin running out of control into the table nearest the women. Glass shattered and metal clanked to the floor as he came to a crashing halt. When Collin fell, Axe made his move. He ran at one of the guards with uncanny speed, and put his closed fist through the man's skull. Axe balked at the feeling of brain upon his fingers, but had no time to concern himself with discomfort. He ran towards the men guarding the women as the corpse was still falling to the floor. Two loosed their crossbows, and two arrows found their way into Axe's chest. One impaled inches through his suit into his ribs, while the other struck him in the gut, and blood spilled from his armor in rushes.

The battle was full on now. He heard the sounds of the Sheriff, Ser Tarbeld, and Ser Laurence as they began their battle versus the two guards remaining nearby. In Axe's sights were the three men standing beside Collin and the women. Two had fired their bows and were drawing their swords, while the third fled to the corner. *Let the others worry about him. I must kill those closest the women first.* Collin rose and saw some spectacle that made him rush past Axe, and left the men guarding the women to him. Axe ran at them headlong. They swung their short swords at Axe, but he didn't care. *Their blades cannot harm me!* He laughed to himself. One glanced a blow against his armor while the other stabbed him in his chest. Axe grabbed the man by his wrist, where the hilt stuck out of his armor, and with his other hand, Axe punched the man's head to ruin. He fell away in a bloody heap, and Axe drew the blade from his own body. When he turned to face the man that remained, Axe felt first an arrow whiff past his side, and second felt the cold steel of the man's sword strike him in his neck. It buried itself two inches through flesh before stopping with a resounding metallic twang. His eyes went wide in astonishment and fear as blood flowed from Axe's neck but left his resolve unchanged. Axe buried the blade of his own sword into the man's heart, and left it there as he dropped dead.

Axe turned round to find his allies were engaged in a bloody fight of their own. Ser Tarbeld had taken some gashes across his arm and chest, but had gained the sword from the fallen guard, and was now readying himself for a duel with another. The Sheriff and Collin were both bloodied, and both grappled with a guard upon the ground. Ser Laurence had taken an arrow to his right shoulder and was on his knees. Nearby the guard with the crossbow had already loosed his arrow and missed, and was now reloading it. Axe rushed at him fearlessly. The man panicked. He dropped his crossbow and drew his sword, but by then it was too late. Axe dove and tackled him to the ground, then ripped his head from his body and tossed the skull aside for it to tumble across the room. When Axe rose to his feet to find another target, he discovered the battle was nearly done. The Sheriff had choked the life from the guard's neck and was only now loosening his grip. Only Ser Tarbeld's man remained, but the knight made short work of him with a few choice deflections of the man's sword with his own, then a swift stroke across his opponent's neck. The guardsman grabbed at his slit throat in terror, then collapsed to die.

Collin gave a hoot of triumph that was cut short by the cries of anguish from the corner. Keira had taken an arrow to her chest and was moaning in pain. "Lady Keira's been injured!" Amy cried. "Please! Someone help her!" Collin and Ser Tarbeld rushed to her side, while Axe approached Ser Laurence and the Sheriff. Kendrick cowered beneath the table, where he'd sought shelter when the fight broke out, and Axe stepped over his head that peeked out from below.

"Sheriff," Axe said as he knelt beside Ser Laurence, "get some wine and a torch for Ser Laurence." Axe saw that Ser Tarbeld was already doing the same for Keira, and thought it equally wise. The Sheriff and Ser Laurence's eyes were glazed with some horror as they looked at him.

"Your neck..." the Sheriff muttered. "Your injuries..."

Axe felt at the loose slabs of flesh where his neck had been severed, and became acutely aware of the volume of blood he'd trailed across the room in his wake. By now no blood was seeping from his wounds, and his veins had gone bone dry. Axe pulled the two arrows from his chest without flinching and tossed them aside. "I will be fine." He glared at the Sheriff. "Now get what I asked for!" Baldric did not complain, and set off with purpose. Ser Laurence seemed woozy and his heart beat fluctuated unsteadily. "Ser Laurence." Axe gently laid him down on his back. "Is this the only wound?" He had an arrow sticking out from his right shoulder, and the knight nodded to him. Axe broke the arrow's shaft, unstrapped his armor, and carefully revealed the wound. The arrowhead had struck bone, and no arteries were severed. *It will be easy enough to remove it.* Axe gave Ser Laurence a strip of cloth to bite, and when the Sheriff handed Axe a bottle of wine, he dumped half its contents over the arrow and pulled it from the shoulder. Ser Laurence moaned in pain and ground his teeth into the cloth. *The wound is not bad,* Axe thought, *but his pulse is weak.* Axe examined the metal head of the arrow, and frowned when he saw remains of a viscous blue liquid upon the silver steel.

"It is poisoned," Axe said. He handed the arrowhead to the Sheriff and made attempt to suck the venom from the wound, but it did not help. Within a short handful of seconds Ser Laurence's heart stopped and his gaze became a cold stare. Axe spit the blood and poison from his mouth, closed Ser Laurence's eyes, and drank the other half of the wine.

"How is it you're not dead?" Baldric asked Axe as he wiped his mouth clean.

Axe patted him softly on the shoulder. "Ask Lord Gracious... after I rescue him."

Axe stood and looked to the corner where everyone had fallen silent. Amy cried at Collin's side, where Keira was held lifeless in his arms. Ser Tarbeld had lowered his head, and Kelly and the Queens were in shock. *I will kill whoever is responsible for this,* Axe swore as he saw his lord's wife dead at Collin's side. Axe heard a muffled voice from behind the Silver Door. *Is that Clique?* He approached it and unfastened the heavy wooden bar that locked it shut. The Sheriff drew a sword and came to his side. When the door opened, and Clique and Janson entered with weapons readied, Baldric let loose an audible sigh of relief. *Ding!* The clock struck ten and sounded its song. Clique was moved to tears when he saw what happened to Keira, and took a few moments to recover himself while the Sheriff explained all that had happened.

"Janson," Clique said as he wiped the tears from his eyes, "lead the women to the rope. Sheriff, go with them and take Ser Tarbeld and that boy with you." Janson set off.

"What's happened Lord Clique?" Baldric asked.

"My squire will explain," Clique said. "Go! Now!"

When Queen Vivian passed her brother's corpse, she fell to his side in grief, and madly protested being taken away from him, but she was ushered away by the Sheriff all the same. Soon only Axe and Clique remained, with Collin still grieving over Keira's body. They walked up to him, and Clique knelt beside the man. "Lord Commander," Clique whispered, "I'm sorry your lady is gone." Clique placed his hand on Collin's shoulder. "But now is not the time to mourn."

"Her child..." Collin whispered. "With her last breath she begged

I save her baby." He cradled Keira's face with his palm and stroked her red hair. "I told her I would. I promised her. But even if I took my blade and tore the unborn lord from her belly, it would have done no good." Collin sniffled and wiped mucus and tears from his face. "The poison would have killed the baby first." Clique looked to Axe, who nodded in the affirmative. *The child's heart no longer beats.*

"Keira has two other children," Clique said, "and they need you." The words struck Collin like a sword to the chest. His hands clenched into fists and he stood up.

"He said it was a robbery, Clique." Collin turned to face him.

"He?" Clique asked.

"The pirate Captain." Collin grit his teeth. "He took them through the Red Door and spoke of a vault. Do you know where the vault is?"

"I always knew Stormbreaker had a hidden vault." Collin frowned. "But its location is a closely guarded secret. It must be somewhere in the Red Tower."

"The door is locked from the inside," Axe told them, "but I could break it."

"No," Collin said, "the sound would alert the guards and put the lives of the Kings and children at risk."

"Is there another way into the tower?" Clique asked. "You know the Stronghold better than I."

"No." Collin sighed. "With the East Gate closed that door is the only way in."

"What about from the outside?" Clique motioned to the window. "Janson and I escaped by rope where the wind did not accost us. Could that be done to cross to the tower?"

"No." Collin lowered his head in defeat.

"No, what?" Clique pushed him. "No there is no path, or no it cannot be done?"

"It can't be done. It's impossible," Collin said. "Even if you could scale thirty feet of sheer stone to the roof, and once there scale another hundred to the nearest tower window, it would not matter." Collin wiped more tears from his eyes. "The wind here makes up the last line of defense for the castle. No mortal man could..." His voice trailed off, and Clique and Collin shared a look then turned to Axe. *No mortal man could...* Axe repeated the words to himself.

"But I can," Axe said. "I'm strong enough. Give me rope, and a grappling hook, and I won't fall." Axe saw the glimmer of hope returning to Collin's eyes.

Clique ran off to procure the equipment necessary for Axe's climb, while Collin explained the path he should take. He was to climb and enter the tower where the children's bedchamber was located, and rescue them first. Only after they were secured would he make his way back to the solar to let Clique and Collin in. Axe armed himself with a few throwing daggers taken from the fallen guards, and retrieved his axes from the corner. When Clique arrived Axe fastened the grappling hook and rope to the end of an arrow, and readied it in a crossbow. They briefly admired the stained glass window, before Collin gave a nod, and Axe pushed a section through and collapsed it. As the heavy pained glass fell away to the dark depths below, the wind rushed in with a fury. Axe crept to the edge, steadied himself, and fired the crossbow. The hook launched over the vaulted roof and struck its mark when it became ensnared upon a stone gargoyle that peered ominously out to sea.

"Good luck," Collin told him, and with that Axe took hold of the rope and started his ascent. Wind and rain washed over him, and foot by foot he climbed until he reached the top. There the storm was no longer barred by walls, and Axe felt the full brunt of it against him. The gusts blew at over forty meters per second, and Axe clung safely against the stone while he gathered up the rope and marked out his path. The crossbow was tied to the end of the rope, just as he'd instructed, and he readied it for another launch. With the rope coiled on his belt, and the crossbow slung across his black, Axe crawled on his hands and knees along the vaulted stone. He dug his fingers into every hold he could find, and went until he could go no further. Twenty meters below was another angled roof, and each side of it gave way to a hundred meter drop. Ten meters of open air stood between him and the wall of the tower he'd need to ascend. He took his aim at a barred windowsill and fired the crossbow. It took two failed attempts before he managed to ensnare the hook on the ledge. He pulled with enough force to mimic his weight, plus fifty percent, and once confident that it would hold him, he secured the bow to the end once more, wrapped the rope round his hands, and swung across the gap.

The wind caught him in mid air and for a moment it seemed like Axe was flying. It was the single most exhilarating feeling Axe had experienced in his life. With his feet out he landed against the tower wall and steadied himself. Gusts of rain whipped over him with such force that the droplets damaged his ocular nerves and weakened his vision. Axe imagined that for a normal man it would have been impossible to see, let alone hold on. Even with his great strength Axe was having trouble climbing. The winds were strong and the rope was slick. He dare not raise the coefficient of friction too much lest he squeeze too hard and sever the rope. He would climb a few meters well enough, then the wind would pick up in a gust, and blow him down further than he'd climbed. He thought he'd come upon a good method of climbing in the tempest, when the wind blew with such ferocity that his hands slipped altogether. He slid down the rope and in slowing himself down ripped the flesh from his palms down to the bone. His feet crashed into the crossbow that hung at the rope's end, which cracked in two and went careening into the depths.

His hands gripped round the knot at the end of the rope, and his body and legs dangled freely into the night sky.

Axe looked down. It was a hundred plus meter drop into jagged rocky shallows. Waves fifteen meters in height pummeled the shores with enough force to shatter a man to shreds. *This is the strongest storm Midgard has seen since I awoke in the woods,* Axe calmly mused as he waited for a break in the wind to continue his climb. *For months the land was beset by such drought that crops were dying and people were starving. Now the rains are so plentiful it will bring all the rivers to flood.* The wind softened and Axe climbed. Each time a gust came he held on with all his might and waited it out before ascending any further. *Perhaps it is true what men say,* Axe wondered. *The weather is broken, and the seasons change without reason or rhyme. But still...*

Axe looked to the sky, and with his inhuman vision scanned the horizons. His view was limited with so many towers around him, but the heart of the storm seemed to lurk somewhere over the sea, and the tides were rising at a terrible pace. *If it rises much higher it will flood out the armies and force them to break camp in the storm to seek higher ground. The Eastern army to the North of the city would have an easy time of it, but the Western army to the South of the city would be flooded to ruin, and many would die.* Axe knew the walls of the city and stronghold were high enough to protect the entire population inside. He also knew Ser Grissel. The man was an O'Brien before he lost the Battle of the Bridge to a Gracious and was sworn to change his fealty. Even so, while he was a good Gracious man, and had been honored and promoted to his prestigious position as Commander of the City Watch, his blood was thick with loyalty to his former House. He would sooner die than open the gates and risk the city for Westerners, no matter how many lives might be saved. *With the inner castle sealed, there is no one in all of Midgard that holds higher command than Ser Grissel.*

Axe wondered if the Westerners knew the danger of the abnormally rising tide, and thought that if he were a godly man he might pray to the Goddess that they did, or that the waters would not swell any more than they already had. *If the tide floods them out, their only chance would be a coup by the watch against Ser Grissel's orders to keep the gates closed.* Axe knew those odds were closer to zero than they might like. Axe made further calculations while climbing that last five meters, and he stumbled across a realization that intrigued him. *Such an unusual storm has occurred at the same time as the summit, with armies camped nearby, thus creating the potential for danger. And it also coincides with an attack by a pirate Captain and his crew. The odds for such events to overlap are impossibly remote.* Axe had learned that the overwhelming majority of the time, the actions of every person and event in the world could be logically predicted if they were subjected to analysis. Aberrant events that went against prediction were exceedingly rare, and an aberration of such a magnitude that it put the lives of a hundred thousand men in jeopardy was nigh but impossible to consider. *There are only two possibilities,* Axe thought as he reached the window and prepared to open the shutters. *Either someone is somehow causing the tide to rise, or the Westerners are simply unlucky, and have fallen victim to a most unfortunate and unlikely fate.*

Axe pushed on the storm shutters until the latch that held them shut broke. He climbed into the spiral tower and took a moment to recover himself. The palms of his hands had been ripped to shreds, and the bone below his flesh shone silver beneath the red of his clotted blood. *My bones are metal.* He had suspected they were, but now knew the truth of it. He did not give himself time to further speculate on his many mysteries. He cut some fabric from the woolen curtain that hung over the window, and with it bound both palms and the unsightly gash round his neck. When finished he silently made his way up the steps. He passed several levels of abandoned chambers until he reached the top. Lantern light shone from underneath the wooden door, and a rope had been tied round its handles, preventing the door from being opened from the inside. Axe unwound the knot and crept in, where he found the two children, Keira and Charles, safely asleep together in bed. He searched the room before examining the children closer. They reeked of wine, and it seemed their captors had drugged them to settle them down. *Better than killing them.* Axe smiled. *Perhaps they are not entirely monsters, but even so, their actions have caused the death of my lord's lady, and I will see them dead lest an order stays my killing hand.* Axe left the children to sleep undisturbed in the chamber, and bound the door once more with rope. *Best not have them wandering off should they awaken while danger still lurks in the halls.*

The chamber at the bottom of the steps showed no sign of men, and the halls of the Red Tower, which itself contained a score of towers, seemed dark and unused. Axe heard voices and movement in the direction that led back towards the solar, and he crept along the shadows as he made his way closer. Soon he came across the remains of a battle that had been recently fought. Seven men dressed in House Guard uniforms were dead, and it would be up to the Sheriff to determine who fought bravely and who turned traitor. The hall from there led into a lit chamber where two men guarded the solar door. As Axe crept forward, a hallway appeared to his right that was not visible until he stood directly beside it. By some trick of design the wall had been built on levers, and some secret passageway had been opened. Intrigued, Axe slipped into the opening. A wide vaulted stone tunnel extended thirty meters and opened into a much larger room. There on their knees sat the two

Kings and Lord Davik. Their hands were bound behind their backs with their mouths gagged, while a man with a drawn sword stood guard over them. *This must be the vault,* Axe thought as he backed away and exited the tunnel. *Best gather my allies before making the final assault.*

Axe crept along the wall, silent as a shadow, until he reached the edge of the chamber. The Red Door had been barred by a metal plank, and two guardsmen paced impatiently. *The vault room is not far from here, and if either should scream, my presence will be noted and the hostages put at further risk.* Axe drew both his axes and measured their weight in his hands. *I will have to throw them,* he decided. *I will be sure to tell Clique if I miss.*

Axe turned the corner in a rush, and neither guard had any warning of his attack until the axes were mid flight. The first embedded itself in the side of the man's skull and killed him instantly. The second struck the other in his chest and dropped him to the floor. In seconds Axe was atop him, and before the man could scream, Axe had him by the throat and broke his neck. It was not long after that Clique, Collin, and Axe had been quietly reunited, and song of the vault room had been sung. Clique convinced Axe and Collin to clothe themselves in the armor of the House Guardsmen that had just been slain. When all were dressed in their blacks, they approached the secret tunnel. "Walk quickly and quietly behind me," Axe whispered. "When I reach the man with his sword, I'll kill him with as little sound as possible. I heard the voices of two other men in the vault, though I cannot be sure of how many more there are."

" Axe, when the guard is dead," Clique told him, "use your body to shield Lord Gracious and the Kings from any further attack." The remark seemed to anger Collin, whose face flushed and heart rate accelerated.

When they walked the length of the tunnel Lord Gracious turned his head and spied them. Axe drew Davik's gaze and witnessed his demeanor transform from one of defeat, to hope, then back to feigned defeat. Davik averted his eyes and remained calm, in spite of the adrenaline Axe knew had hit his system. Clique and Collin remained back, while Axe entered the chamber first. He casually approached the guard whose eyes were fixed on the Eastern wall. The room itself was about twenty meters long by ten meters wide, and was made of the same black and grey stone as the rest of the stronghold. Its East wall, however, was cast of solid steel, and had a three meter diameter circular doorway that had opened in a six piece spiral. *The vault's entrance has been opened.* Axe saw the glow of lanterns coming from within, and by play of the shadows knew there were two men inside. The guard turned as Axe approached him, but Axe's calm demeanor and black armor confused the man enough to keep him silent that final second. Axe punched him dead, and cradled his body softly to the floor.

"My Kings. My lord," Axe whispered. "How many are in there?" Axe waved Collin and Clique into the chamber while he freed the prisoners and took away their gags.

"Three," King Harloque Draven whispered. "Just the three."

Collin came to his lord's side and helped him to his feet. "My lord..." Axe saw the tears welling in Collin's eyes.

"My children?" Davik asked. "Are–"

"They are safe in their beds," Axe told him. "I have seen to that."

Axe heard someone walking the secret tunnel. Axe bid them quiet and hid against the wall. When the man came through, Axe grabbed him and covered his mouth. He was prepared to snap his neck when Clique recognized the boy as Janson, his squire, and stayed Axe's hand. "My lords," Janson whispered, "we've taken back the castle."

"Janson," Clique commanded the boy, "take Lord Davik and the Kings to safety."

"Lord Davik..." Collin's words were choked. "There's something you must know."

"There's no time." Davik had fear in his eyes. "You have to stop Davenport."

"Davenport?" Collin asked.

"Hektor Davenport," Davik said. "You can't let him escape with our treasure."

"Uncle." Clique smiled. "You heard my squire, the castle is taken. If he is in the vault, then our men will flush him out."

"No." Davik grabbed his nephew. "The vault has a secret exit known to him. That is how he means to leave. You have to stop him."

"Don't worry uncle." Clique walked him towards the tunnel. "I will catch this thief."

"What treasure?" Axe asked, but his question went unheeded. *Collin must have the right of it,* Axe mused. *This Hektor Davenport seeks after something small and rare.*

"Janson." Clique stopped his squire before their party entered the tunnel. "Daniel... Did you find him?"

"I do not know." Janson sighed. "He may be amongst the dead. Ser Jackson died in battle, and Ser Dugen is gravely injured."

Janson led the two Kings and Davik away through the tunnel. Axe, Clique, and Collin readied themselves. Collin wiped tears from his eyes and Clique patted his ally's shoulder. "Better you did not bear the burden of telling him. If you wish to go with him, I understand. Axe and I will take it from here."

"No." Collin straightened himself. "Let's do this... for Keira."

"Wait," Axe said, and Clique and Collin looked incredulously into his eyes. "I'll be back."

Axe fled down the secret hall. "Axe. Where are you going?" Clique whispered after him.

Axe stopped the royal procession before they entered the hall. "King Tarnell. Lord Davik," Axe got their attention and they turned to face him. "The Western army is in danger. The flood waters rise impossibly high, and if the city gates are not opened to them immediately, I fear many lives will be lost."

"I will see it done," Davik told him.

King William grasped Axe's shoulder and the look he gave Axe spoke volumes. With a nod, Axe turned and made his way back to Clique and Collin. Axe wielded his axes, Collin a short sword, and Clique his scythe. They started for the vault's entrance and saw the grand spiral staircase that descended from the main chamber within. "Axe," Clique whispered, "Collin and I will take care of these two. Find Davenport and stop him."

"Yes, Lord Commander," Axe said. "Be careful. One of them has Starsinger."

The three of them crept into the vault in silence and shadow. The vault room was larger than Stormbreaker's inner solar, and contained a great wealth of chests and cluttered bookshelves. Collin crept after a man in a red cloak who rummaged through scrolls by the North wall. Clique crept South where the man who held Starsinger was set to work filling a small chest with select items he'd gathered in a pile. Axe followed his orders and made his way East down the grand staircase. It descended clockwise below the level of the vault room, and circled wide round a pit fifteen meters across whose bottom was a hundred meters below. Every five meters of the descent the steps opened to another level of vault chambers. Axe calculated there were twenty two levels to the vault, and each seemed to be filled with the dusty wealth of the scores of lords that ruled Stormbreaker before Davik.

Axe leaned out over the railing of the staircase and saw the light of a lantern halfway down the pit. Axe circled round and spied

Hektor Davenport making his way down the steps. Axe measured the weight of the axe in his right hand, steadied himself for the attack, took aim, and threw. The axe flew with strength and precision the dozens of meters necessary to reach its target. Whether his throw was ineffective, his calculations were off, or Hektor had gotten lucky and slowed his descent after the axe had left Axe's hand, it did not matter. The blade missed by inches and sailed past Davenport's face before clanking harmlessly away upon the stone floor. The pirate Captain came to the railing, looked up, and immediately made eye contact with Axe. *I stand in pitch darkness, but his gaze finds my eyes none the less.* The thought and its meaning had no time to linger in Axe's mind. An explosion rocked the vault chamber above, and the bursting flames illuminated the stairwell. At that moment Axe had no doubt that Davenport could clearly see him, and when he broke his gaze, the man began to run.

Axe hesitated. He glanced over his shoulder and up the stairwell at the fires burning above, then looked back down below at Davenport who was making his hasty descent. *Clique gave me a command,* Axe said to himself, *but Hektor can wait.* He turned and made his way back up the steps as quick as his feet could carry him. *I will not leave them to die.*

When Axe reached the chamber he found the South side of the room was split by a small inferno of fire. Most was the red flame of burning books, scrolls, rugs, and chests, but some was a green fire that blazed white hot in three scatter patterns from where the glass receptacles which carried the fire oil must have shattered. Collin had taken no injury, and stood nearby over the corpse of the man he'd been tasked to kill. Collin's armor was slashed in a few places, and the dead man held a dagger that dripped with the same venom that had done in Ser Laurence and Keira. Through the flames Axe saw Clique had not been so lucky. He had taken terrible burns to the left side of his body and face, and Axe immediately knew no healing would ever repair that scorched flesh. The long curved blade of his black steel scythe had been cut in two, and he held the weapon up in a defensive position with his left arm hanging limp at his side. Across from him the robber stood unhurt, and he held Starsinger aloft as he readied himself for another assault. It was clear that Collin had no means of braving the blistering heat to come to his Lord Commander's aid, and had only just finished his own mortal combat. Axe, however, was not Collin, and suspected his flesh would miraculously regrow as he slept whether burned to a charred crisp or cut and torn from his body as had happened so many times before.

Axe switched his one remaining axe to his right hand, and leaped through the flames. His clothes and hair were set afire and his skin sizzled and burned. The man was taken aback by Axe's approach, but was not taken unawares. He raised Starsinger in counterstrike, and with a last split decision, Axe hesitated his attack and raised his weapon to deflect the bite of the Ancient steel sword. *My flesh may regenerate, but that blade will sever my limb, silver bone or not.* Still, Axe suspected that his bones were Ancient steel themselves, and considered that while the blade might yet do him no harm, he was not about to risk it. Axe ducked and caught the sword with his axe blade. Starsinger cut through the steel as if it were butter, and while his weapon was cut in twain, he remained uninjured. Fortunately, the man did not know that Axe needed no weapon to kill, and with a quick punch plunged his fist into the man's chest and tore the heart from his rib cage. The shower of blood doused the flames that had covered Axe's body, and as the man fell to his back, he briefly witnessed the horror of his vital organ being tossed aside by Axe into the fire. Starsinger dropped away unheeded and Axe came to Clique's side.

"Axe..." Clique took a knee and kept himself propped with his scythe pole. "You came back."

"I could not leave a fellow Royal Huntsman behind." Axe placed his hand on Clique's shoulder, as seemed to be proper fashion, and analyzed the man's wounds. It was a miracle he was still conscious.

"What about Davenport?" Clique asked. The flames were spreading and growing worse.

"Don't worry." Axe tore the dead man's cloak from his body and wrapped it round Clique. "Collin and I will capture him." Axe took Clique into his arms and lifted him up. "But first, let's get you out of here."

Axe pulled the hood over Clique's face, and prepared himself for a quick leap through the flames where on the other side waited Collin, ready to help douse him of caught fire. Before Axe took the plunge, a great wind kicked up in a vortex around them. The flames flickered against the storm of it, and for a moment Axe thought the roof had caved in somewhere and wind was blowing from outside the castle. All at once the flames were put out, even those in the lanterns, and the room was cast into relative darkness. The windstorm ceased and the air fell still. Clique struggled in Axe's arms and he put his Lord Commander down, who stood with his own strength. For a few seconds they did not speak, and when at last Axe was about to suggest that Collin take Clique to safety while he went after Davenport, a curious thing occurred that violated Axe's understanding of the laws of nature.

A luminescent energy bubbled in the vacant air a meter from the three of them. It was a fractal bubble not twenty centimeters across and it pulsed with a soft blue light. Axe thought he might be the only one seeing it, but the energy shone across the entirety of the spectrum that Axe was capable of seeing. When Collin and Clique turned to the spectacle, eyes wide with wonderment, he knew it was a shared vision. Space itself seemed to warp around the bubble, and dust in the air rose against gravity in spiral wisps. They watched in silence as the bubble popped and showered them in a mist of wet blue radiance. It did not float away lost into the room, but instead was absorbed equally into all three of their bodies. Axe felt it course through his flesh with a luxuriously pleasant tingling sensation. With uncanny speed, the cells of his body regenerated, and within seconds all of the wounds he'd suffered were healed.

Clique gasped in pleasure as the energy surged through him and transformed his burnt flesh into fresh perfect skin. He laughed in astonishment and marveled over his magical regeneration, then ran his fingers over smooth skin that he must have thought he would never feel again. *It must be a horrible thing to be crippled or disfigured. And to be cured of such a fate, equal in emotional magnitude.* Axe's thoughts were lifted from him when he felt a pull that tugged at every cell in his body. Whereas before the energy's presence was pressure against him, now it was a force that grasped at some unknown thing deep within his being and wrenched it out of him. The same thing occurred to Collin and Clique, and for each of them, in one great heave, a wave of energy emerged from their chests and coalesced into three crystals that hovered in the air before them.

Each crystal was twenty centimeters in length and was impossibly rounded with millions of perfect facets. They were only four centimeters in diameter and were thin and marvelous to behold. The crystals were double terminated, and came to slender tips at both ends. The one that emerged from Axe was a blazing red, while Clique's shone a golden yellow, and Collin's a dark brown. When Axe thought the situation could not turn any stranger, in each of their crystals they saw a vision. In Clique's golden crystal they saw his reflection transform into a reproduction of the events of his day, but backwards. First was the duel with the man that left him burned, next the events in the solar, then his journey through the tower. Collin and Axe's crystal showed similar visions but of their own lives in reverse. The speed of the telling increased, and over the course of a handful of seconds it told of days, then weeks, in backwards clarity.

Collin and Clique seemed uninterested in their own history, and both turned their attention to Axe's crystal. Soon it showed the events of Hopsdale, then the farm, and then the woods. They all watched with bated breath to learn the truth of Axe's history. While their own crystals showed their childhood, the red crystal showed Axe laying in the woods, and next, him sitting on a table with the familiar old man beside him. The crystal showed Axe nude and muscular. In reverse time, Axe laid down on a silver table beside the old man, and a metal and glass box rose from the bed and enclosed him. With a release of steam, it opened, and revealed Axe's true form. His flesh was entirely gone, and he was naught but a silvery metal endoskeleton with reinforced limbs, hydraulics for internal muscles, a plated chest, and a silver skull with two monstrous glowing red eyes. Though comprised of nothing but metallic bone, Axe sat up, and his mouth opened and closed as if speaking. Collin, Clique, and Axe gave a collective gasp when they saw in the vision a dozen similar metal skeletons hanging from a rack by the wall.

They were similarly startled when the blue energy that had entered them moments earlier was present in the vision. The energy exited in spirals from out of Axe's eyes, and the red light within them faded to a lifeless black. In Clique and Collin's vision they saw the moments after their birth, with umbilical cords still attached from mother to child. The blue energy rose up from their eyes in spirals before they witnessed their own first breaths and were placed back inside their mother's womb. Each crystal pulsed with a bright colored flash, and next they saw visions of themselves as men.

Clique wore golden magnificent armors and Kingly robes. He ran across a snowy mountain top and leapt into the open air. Lightning shot from his hands and he rode it across the sky. Two poles of frozen lightning with curved golden blades hung from his back. On the grounds below, the shadows suggested a gathering army, and with swings of his golden scythes, Clique sent streaks of lightning cascading down upon them. Smoke and flame erupted in the wake of his assault. Collin wore armor made of brown stone, and impossibly carried a sword five times the height of him. He ran through a barren field and came upon a cliff where far below an army of shadows had gathered. Collin raised his arms, and all around him the cliff collapsed and sent itself careening in avalanche. The mountain fell to the destruction of the army, and beneath Collin a solitary column of stone remained. It was all that connected him cleanly to the ground hundreds of meters below. Axe wore a plain red robe and carried no weapon. He stood atop a hill gazing down at the gathering of shadows. His hands were raised and above him a vast orb of fire, as if a small Red Star, had gathered in the sky. *Is it something between the flame and the dirt that casts the army of shadows?* Axe asked himself, but there was no answer to be had.

Collin's earthen crystal showed a winged shadow that overtook him. Collin looked to the sky, where a long silvery black reptilian behemoth snaked down from the winds and came upon him. Axe's fiery crystal showed a similar shadow. From the skies above an ice blue reptile with millions of crystalline scales approached. Clique's golden crystal portrayed an equally terrifying shadow, only his enormous reptile was dark blue and shimmered with the wetness of the ocean. All three were similar to volia, and had four legs, two eyes, and clawed teeth, but they appeared of some terrible antiquity, had Cyclopean wings that caught the air and gave them flight, and their size put even the kavolia to shame. All together their three monsters consumed their bodies whole, and the visions dissipated away, lost amidst the crystal's natural glow.

Without warning the crystals jolted towards their recipients, and each one embedded themselves in their right palms. The crystals impaled the bone at the base of the hand, and burrowed deep. Each of their crystals were soon inside their forearms, but there was no pain. Axe rolled up the cloth of his shirt and saw that one side of his red crystal remained visible above the skin. It had attached itself on the inside of his arm, between elbow and wrist. It flared with a crimson light, and the crystal communicated with him in his mind. It wasn't a voice, or even a vision. It was as if a memory, or a knowledge that one moment was unknown and the next seemed as natural as walking. In that instant Axe knew the truth of it. Within a sphere of twenty meters around the crystal, Axe could control the element of Fire. His own weapons could blaze with red heat, and he could accelerate a flame from the smallest kindling ember to a roaring inferno. *I am...* The crystal spoke its only words. *Fire.*

COLLIN

"I am... Earth." Collin said the words aloud as he stared into the light of the brown crystal in his arm. Somehow he knew that around him bubbled a sphere of influence that merged his mind with the element. With but a thought, Collin made a portion of the stone floor gather itself like wet clay and form a misshapen boulder beside them. Clique made his golden crystal shine so bright that it blinded Collin, and they all were fascinated by its brilliance. What Collin found most curious, was that both Axe and Clique seemed to glow with a light blue aura. It was similar to the energy that had encompassed them, but now seemed as if it were a part of them somehow. Some object nearby glowed with a blue aura as well. Collin approached it. *Starsinger...* He knelt down and retrieved the Ancient blade from where it had fallen. *Poor Starsinger,* Collin spoke to sword in his mind, *your master has been murdered without you in his hand.* He wiped the blood from its shimmering blue blade. *I will help you avenge Ser Laurence.* He took the sheath from the dead thief's belt, tied it round his waist, and sheathed the Ancient weapon.

"What just happened?" Axe asked.

"We'll have time to ponder the significance of this later. For now," Clique pulled down his sleeve, and picked up his damaged scythe, "we have a thief to catch."

"Davenport!" Collin made the word a curse. *Lady Keira will have her killer in the grave, and I will wield the sword that puts him in it.*

The three of them descended the grand staircase and came to the balcony that overlooked the pit. Axe let his crystal shine and their way was lit by a crimson glow far brighter than any torch or lantern. "I saw him heading to the bottom," Axe told them. "Davenport saw me in total darkness."

"How?" Collin asked. "Is he a man of steel, like you?" Collin knew that Axe possessed a magical sight that allowed him to see great distances in the dark, but never before had such a feat been accomplished by normal men. Of course, Collin now knew that it was not magic which allowed Axe to see as he did. Inside he was a man of steel with red eyes, and somehow that strange skeleton was put inside his body by the old man in white. It was clearly this metal construct that gave him his great power, and it was the work of the old man, whether sorcerer of magic or Scientos, that removed his bones and replaced them with metal. *There were other skeletons... Somewhere out there, this old man may be giving more people his bones of steel this very minute.* The thought did not please him. *We will have to find this... Treefort.*

"I believe that he is in possession of a crystal similar to ours," Axe explained.

"What makes you say that?" Clique asked, and at that Axe turned off his light. The room fell to pitch darkness, but Collin's own body, Axe, and Clique all glowed in the dark with their new found blue aura. "Wait... I know this."

Collin knew it too. "Yes," Collin said. *How do I know this?* "We can *see* magic, and... We *are* magic." *The crystal knows... so I know...*

"He must have seen the magic of your skeleton!" Clique puzzled out. "But what's this Davenport doing with a crystal?"

"What are *we* doing with crystals?" Collin asked. None of them had a very good answer.

Axe climbed up onto the balcony and looked as if he were going to jump. "I think I can make it," he said, but after a moment climbed down. "On second thought, I'd better not chance it."

Axe reignited his red light and the three of them made their descent down the long spiral stairs. One level had dozens of prison cells, a few of which contained skeletons. Another level was a crypt with stone tombs, and others were cluttered with old furniture, chests, and the random assorted items of the forgotten storage of ages past. "We'll have to explore the vault later," Collin said as they ran.

"Indeed," Clique answered. "Some of the things I've seen have glowed with energy."

"You mean there are constructs of magic in this vault?" Axe asked. "But I thought that before me... before us... magic did not exist."

"There was magic before the Doom," Clique said. "Before the djinn froze and before the weather broke."

"Starsinger is magic." Collin laughed. "It glows, and that means the Ancients had magic."

"But have you ever heard of crystals before?" Axe asked.

"Never," Clique answered.

"Nor have I," Collin admitted. "But crystals *are* magic, and if Davenport has a crystal, then there must have been *some* magic still left in the world, and some of it has found its way to us. You yourself were made magic by that man, Axe."

"Unless it was Scientos," Clique suggested. "There has been no magic since the Doom."

"But if it *was* magic," Axe pressed, "then this Davenport may know something of where I came from."

"It will be amongst the many things that I inquire upon him." Clique had venom in his tone, and though it was dishonorable to do so, Collin relished the thought of inflicting pain upon the man. *I will make him pay for what he has done to my lady.*

"How deep is this damned vault?" Collin complained after fifteen minutes of the run. "It would have been faster to just get the rope."

"Over a hundred meters. The height of the castle," Axe said as he recovered his thrown axe, "but the width and number of steps make it seem much further."

Collin stopped them and caught his breath. "Come on, Collin!" Clique turned back. "We need to hurry."

"Hold on." Collin smiled. He stretched out his right hand and focused on the floor with his mind. The stone rippled outward with his command, and a few seconds later a hole opened up in the floor wide enough to fit through. Collin lowered himself down and made the fifteen foot drop. He tumbled to his hands and knees. Axe and Clique followed suit.

"Wow." Clique was astonished. "You did that?"

"Yes... Somehow, I just tell the stone to move in my head, and what I *will* it to do... It *does*." Collin made another hole. "Watch." This time he gathered stone up from the stair level below, and in seconds raised it to a platform. Collin stepped onto it, and the thing lowered himself gently to the ground. Collin stepped aside, but Axe, and Clique dropped through without waiting for it to rise again.

Clique laughed. "My uncle will be furious we ruined his staircase."

Collin shared the chuckle, relieved at the first bit of mirth since... "I can fix it after we kill Davenport." Collin opened the next hole.

"You mean capture him," Clique clarified.

"Yeah." Collin dropped down and they followed. "That's what I meant."

"He has answers to questions that *must* be asked." Clique sighed. "We have to take him alive."

"I understand," Collin said.

Clique grabbed his shoulder. "Promise me." Collin nodded.

"It is a rare day when the assassin lectures the Huntsman on taking prisoners," Collin told him, and meant to turn away, but Clique stopped him.

"Say the words." Clique stared with his black eyes.

"We take him alive," Collin said, "but when the time comes that he must die, I swing Ser Laurence's blade."

"Agreed." Clique released him.

They did not speak until they descended the seven levels that remained to them through Collin's seven magically constructed holes in the stone. The lowest level of the vault was largest of all, and at one time must have held a vast wealth of gold. Eight immense vault rooms were accessed by eight hallways that surrounded the octagonal chamber. Golden coins thinly scattered every hallway and every chamber, as if left behind after great stores of them were removed. By the amount of dust in the halls it was clear there had been no treasure hoard here in years. The coins glinted magnificently off the light of Axe's Fire crystal, and for a moment Collin was taken aback by the beauty of it. Axe disrupted Collin's fantasy of a sea of glittering gold when he drew their attention against a ninth darkened hallway. Axe tightened his beam of light in such a fashion that it seemed a spotlight, and all within was burning bright while all without was shadow. "He went that way," Axe declared.

The hall was made of black stone, a different brick altogether than that which was used to construct Stormbreaker's walls. The tunnel went on for forty feet before descending down a flight of steps that leveled out somewhere below. Clique stopped at the top of the stairs and ran his hand across the wall. "This is onyx, and is a stone not found in the Realm," Clique told them.

"It must have been quarried somewhere else and shipped here," Collin said. "What of it?"

"It is insanely expensive," Clique marveled. "This hallway alone would fill the vault with gold itself. Collin, cut me a piece of it. I wish to have it appraised."

Collin reached out with his mind, but the stone did not move. *Why isn't it working?* he asked himself, as he focused his thoughts and tried again. Still the stone did not move. "I can't." Collin sighed after the third attempt. "It is not stone. I cannot change the shape of metal either. Perhaps it is a gem, or crystal?"

Clique groaned with dissatisfaction but said nothing. He made his way down the steps, and Collin and Axe followed. The hallway opened into a cube shaped room maybe fifty feet across. It was all made of the same onyx, and the red light of Axe's crystal reflected off its highly polished surface and filled the room with a ruby radiance. Eight onyx pillars rose round a stepped altar twenty feet high. Collin ascended the steps and looked around.

"Do you smell that?" Axe asked, but they did not. "The air smells like the sea. There must be another exit. I'll go find it." Axe left their sides to encircle the room.

"What is this place?" Collin wondered.

"If not built by Octavian Greyson," Clique mused, "it must have been made by Ancients."

"This might be the secret of Stormbreaker," Collin suggested.

"What are you talking about?" Clique seemed excited at the prospect.

"Clique, I've served your uncle for four years, and in that time learned that Octavian built this place to hide a secret. This room... It must be it." *But why keep a room secret, other than to hide something secretly in it?* "Well... Every Great Castle in the Realm has been built around the frozen djinn. The Barrows itself has three," Collin said. "And while everyone considers Stormbreaker Stronghold a Great Castle, it is the only one not to have any djinn at all."

"That's because Octavian chose to forge his empire in the wild lands. He founded Midgard not on ruins, but on freedom," Clique explained. "Cliffwatch has no djinn either."

"Cliffwatch is no Great Castle. Only those built over a millennia ago can claim a djinn. Rumors place other djinn outside the Realm, but none have been claimed by stone and steel."

"So *this* is what makes Stormbreaker Stronghold so Great?" Clique laughed. "I always knew there were secrets here, but I thought it was a treasure room, and not a *treasured room.*"

"Perhaps this altar held the treasure which Davenport's stolen," Collin said, "but the room itself is a marvel to be sure.*"

"I found something!" Axe cried out from the corner. Clique and Collin rushed to where Axe was on his knees examining the floor. "This ground was disturbed." Axe stood and rubbed his hands against the wall. "Lord Gracious said there'd be..." Kathunk! The wall pushed inward from invisible seams and slid aside. "... a secret exit." Axe smiled.

"Nicely done, Axe!" Collin congratulated him with a pat on his back and pushed his way forward into the tunnel. A salty humid wind rushed over them, and they knew it led outside. The onyx of the chamber immediately gave way to a crudely carved tunnel in solid stone just wide enough to fit a man. Collin widened it unintentionally as he walked. He simply wished it was wider and the stone around him obeyed. *I need to be careful,* Collin realized. *It is too easy for a half willed thought to bring someone unintentional harm.* Clique had no idea that Collin used his magic unintentionally, and he praised him for his incredible new found powers.

They emerged from the tunnel onto a cliff that overlooked the sea. An old path not three feet wide cut to the right and led to the shores below. The way was treacherous with uneven ground and no place to grab hold of, save for the wall. The storm raged on with symphonies of thunder and violent streaks of lightning, and the rain came down in wicked sheets. In moments Collin was soaked to his bone. As luck would have it the wind blew straight against the cliff, and its gusts pushed them flat against the wall, rather than blowing them with its terrible ferocity to the tempest of waves below. Collin's mind dizzied with the thought of the deadly drop, and he summoned his focus to widen the path and make handholds against the cliff face. After a few hundred feet the crude trail rounded a bend and revealed a secret port. The Southern wall of the Stronghold created a ceiling over a stone dock and hid view of it from above. A second wall extended across the water and hid the enclave from the sea. Some sort of small boat was roped to the dock, but it sat low in the water and may have been sunk. "Look!" Clique pointed along the cliff and Collin saw him.

"Davenport!" Collin shouted. The man clung to the cliff face and was nearing the easy ground of the docks. When he heard Collin's cry he turned to face them. His way was lit by a magical blue light, and he was bathed in an aura of energy similar to their own.

"I was right." Axe smiled.

"Your mastery over earth has bested him Collin," Clique boasted. "We've outpaced him on this difficult terrain."

"Davenport!" Collin shouted again and ran after him. The earth rose up to meet Collin's stride. *You are mine!* Davenport hurried but stumbled against rocks and nearly fell the thirty feet into the deadly swells. He clung to the wall and locked eyes with Collin. Far behind him a group of men had exited the boat and were making their way across the docks with lanterns and swords. Davenport gave one look to the waters below, then glanced back up at Collin, and let go.

"No! Collin!" Clique yelled. "Don't let him fall!"

Collin reached out with his mind and tried to bring the earth to meet him, but the man was not yet in range of his sphere of influence, and he fell helpless into the raging water. Collin stopped and cursed as Clique and Axe caught up to him. "Do you think he's dead?" Clique asked. "He may have the treasure."

"No, Lord Commander." Axe tightened his belt round his waist. "The timing of the storm... The flood that would have murdered an army." Clique had confusion in his eyes. "Don't you get it?" Axe took a deep breath. "He's *Water*." Axe leapt from the cliff and dove into the waters below. He disappeared beneath the frothy waves as an arrow whizzed by their heads and ricocheted off the wall.

Collin drew Starsinger from his sheath and charged down the path. The stone rose to his command and he quickly reached the port. Two men with swords approached nearest to him on the docks, while two others with bows stood atop the boat. It's then that Collin noticed the waters had stopped their waves, and were beset by unnatural calm even though the wind still blew with a fury. An arrow whipped past Collin unheeded, and the first of the men met Collin's sword with steel on steel. Collin wielded Starsinger in his right hand, and it effortlessly sliced through the man's blade, then took off his other arm at the elbow. The man fell back in pain, while Collin sidestepped the second man's sword and brought the Ancient blade against his leather armor. The sword was light and well balanced, and it cut through leather, flesh, and bone, then flesh and leather again, as if cutting through thick soup. All parted across the blade's edge, and the man collapsed with his insides spilling everywhere. Starsinger's third strike was a clean stab to the center of the one armed thief's chest, but the result was not as expected. Beyond just piercing him through and through, he felt an elemental energy surge from his hand and channel through the sword. In a fractal circle from where the blade had struck, the man's armor and clothing turned brittle and rotted away to dust in seconds.

The curiosity of the power he'd just exhibited left his concern when an arrow struck him in the thigh. He felt the jolt, and a stab of pain, and for a moment thought he'd been crippled. But when he knelt and wrenched it from his flesh, he saw it had barely hurt him. His skin and muscle had been toughened somehow, and he saw wisps of brown elemental energy evaporating from the blood that clotted his wound. Collin tossed the arrow aside and looked up to take stock of his attackers whose bows were aimed at him, when Clique burst onto the docks and came between him and their sights. Clique's scythe was gone, and he raised his unarmed hands and screamed. To Collin and Clique's amazement, a great bolt of yellow lightning arced from the skies and struck the top of the boat. In an explosion of force and electricity, both men flew from the impact and trailed smoke behind them into the water. Collin rose to his feet, sheathed Starsinger, and stood beside Clique. The two men floated atop the still waters, both charred and lifeless.

"I am..." Clique caught his breath. "Lightning." The expenditure of his power tired him.

"Wow..." Collin could barely process the magnitude of the events that had unfolded.

"How could someone ever defend against lightning?" Clique wondered aloud.

"There he is!" Collin pointed beneath the water where Davenport swam several meters below. Clique raised his hand and forced down another bolt of lightning, but it didn't penetrate the water's surface and dissipated harmlessly away. "He's making for the boat!"

Collin raced across the docks and Clique followed. They jumped the two foot gap onto the roof of the vessel and stopped at the closed hatch. Clique grabbed at it, and tried to turn the metal wheel, but it remained stuck. "It's locked from the inside. Can you force it open?"

Collin tried, but it was to no effect. "No. It's metal and the boat's wood." Without warning the boat lurched, and a great rumbling sound came from below. Wisps of black smoke bubbled from the side of the vessel and rose from the water in a noxious cloud. The wind dissipated the harsh fumes, but it was enough to draw their curiosity. The boat shook again and it brought them to their knees. *The rot!* Collin drew Starsinger and struck the blade against the hatch. The steel on iron drew sparks sure enough, and Collin felt the energy surge through him once more. When he pulled Starsinger away for a second strike, they saw the iron hatch decay and wither.

"It rusted..." Clique was impressed. Axe emerged from the water and climbed onto the docks, when the boat jolted forward and began to move as if unfurled sails had caught the wind.

"Axe! Jump!" Collin reached out with his mind, and as Axe ran, he extended the dock ledge to give Axe better reach. The man of steel leaped. He tumbled against the edge of the boat, dug his axe into the wood, and easily pulled himself up.

"Hit it again, Collin," Clique told him. Collin raised Starsinger, and with it struck the hatch three more times. Each strike of the blade decayed the rusting metal further until it collapsed into the hull of the vessel and shattered on the floor. Davenport and a Gulgari sailor with wire framed glasses looked up at them through the hole. Davenport raised his hands and his red sleeves slipped back. The sapphire crystal attached to his right forearm ignited with a brilliant light, and it seemed as if he were about to summon some unknown power. Collin readied Starsinger defensively in expectation of Davenport's magical assault, when from the heavens a thunderbolt came down and struck Davenport in his face. The flash blinded Collin, and the force of the strike knocked him to his back. When he stood the battle was over. The sailor was a charred crisp, and Davenport was lying still with no color in his crystal.

Before either of them could celebrate the victory, auras of energy, like weak cinders being stoked to brilliance, radiated from their bodies in the color of their crystals. Even Davenport had a blue aura. The blood and bodies on the docks, and the corpses of the dead men in the sea and boat, all took a violet glow of their own, and soon the whole of the carnage left behind by Collin and the dead men were effervescent with lavender light. The energy seemed to swell, then all at once gathered together as if carried by the wind. It swirled and coalesced around Clique, Axe, Davenport, and Collin. Their bodies drew in the violet energy where it soon was absorbed by their crystals. When the moment passed their crystals had grown dark, the energy was gone, and Collin could no longer see the docks as they faded into distance and darkness. The three of them shared a curious look before entering the boat to get out of the torrential wind and rain.

The interior of the cabin was a spectacle of levers and buttons lit by a number of small lanterns. Glass windows gave sight of the way ahead, and it seemed the vessel was designed to travel underwater. "What was that?" Collin asked. He could not seem to draw any coherent thoughts together, and was a mess of adrenaline. Waves shook the boat left and right, but the deck did not yaw as a boat that rode above the water, and it remained level and flat despite the rough vibrations. Rain and sea water splashed through the open hole, but not enough to be of sinking concern.

"I believe I can answer that question," Axe said. "We absorbed the life essence of the dead."

"What the hell is that supposed to mean?" Collin asked.

"All I can say is my crystal is vibrating at a higher frequency than it was before." Axe pulled up his sleeve. "And we all saw the light exit the dead and enter us."

Clique knelt beside Davenport and checked his pulse. "He's alive."

"Good. You made me a promise Clique," Collin told him.

"And I intend to keep it." Clique looked at him. "*After* he has served his purpose."

"Can you make sense of the controls of this boat?" Collin asked Axe, who was already examining the central console. "How is it moving?"

"It seems to have some kind of internal propulsion," Axe told him. "It is not altogether unlike some of the new designs circulating the library. Give me a few minutes." Axe left the console and descended down a ladder into a lower cabin.

Clique removed Shadow from Davenport's belt, and took the sword for his own. "Don't unsheathe it," Collin said, but the look Clique gave him made him feel stupid for pointing out the obvious. Collin took a moment to marvel at its sheath and hilt, and wished he could see its blade. *It still hasn't been drawn,* Collin thought as he saw the unbroken seal of black wax where Shadow's hilt met its sheath. *Ser Tarbeld will be relieved to know.* But when Collin removed his eyes from the sword, Clique seemed as if he'd seen a ghost. "What's the matter?"

Clique had Davenport's hand in his own, and was staring at the ring on his finger. It was a gold octopus with seven tentacles, the eighth in its mouth, on a silver band. Clique pulled the ring from his finger, pocketed it, and sung Collin the song that Wodkins sang, and how the man still lurked in a dungeon cell at Cliffwatch. "There may yet be a trial," Clique explained, "to appease the masses for the loss of their lady. I'll make sure Wodkins confesses against him."

"If he's the same man. The ring may be signet for some order, perhaps consisting of seven or eight men?"

Clique cast his question aside and went further through Davenport's belongings. They both gasped when he drew from his inner pocket a purple silk bag that glowed blue with magic. "The treasure?" Collin gulped. Clique untied the bag and slid it open to reveal its contents. Inside was a single tiny glass bottle. The thin vial was opaque white glass, and was plugged by a tiny cork stopper sealed with red wax. The wax bore the emblem of an *L* and *G* with sword above and shield below. The vial pulsed with a magic energy and emitted a blue aura that glowed brighter than the lights of himself and his fellow crystal bearers. "Its magic is blinding!" Collin was awestruck and leaned closer. "L... G..."

Clique raised the vial close to their eyes. "The Lord of the Grey."

"It has been sealed a millennia!" Collin's mirth turned solemn just as quickly. "Do you mean to open it?"

For a moment Clique considered the notion. "Yes." Collin's heart raced with anticipation, but Clique slipped it back in its silk bag, and stashed it in his armor. "But not here."

Axe climbed up from below and manned the console. "Have you found anything Axe?" Collin asked him.

"Yes, my lord." Axe pulled levers and spun wheels. "The boat's furnace is heating water, and the steam spins a curved oar for propulsion. I can control its spin and the rudder from here." The boat slowed and rose higher in the water. Through the cockpit windows the murky blue of the sea broke way to the violent skies of the thunderstorm, where flashes of lightning illuminated a massive wooden ship. It was larger than any ship Collin had seen before, and had seven masts, three of which were much taller than the others. Its sails were furled but were clearly green canvas. "The side of its hull reads, 'The Green Algae.' "

"What about its flag?" Clique asked as their boat steadily approached it. "Can you see its flag?"

"It is a white skull on black with crossed bones below," Axe said. Clique's face went pale.

"Can you pilot this vessel, Axe?" Clique asked.

"Yes, Lord Commander." Axe nodded.

"Turn us around then, and bring us back to port." Clique sat down in a nearby chair and caught his breath. "Collin, find some rope and tie up our prisoner."

Collin set to the task and roughly bound Davenport's hands behind his back. "Do you recognize the ship's colors? A skull and bones..."

"It is called the *Jolly Roger*," Clique told them.

"And it means pirates?" Collin asked. "And Davenport was their Captain?"

"Yes, and no," Clique answered. "I heard speak of it twice. First from my masters before I departed, and once again from my father's man Marcus, who got the tale from the ship's crew. Pirates started flying the Jolly Roger two years ago, and since then they've gotten organized. The masters called it a demon's sigil, and said it was as old as Doom. Also... They told me to fear any man that commanded under its power. Every demon has a heart, but this Davenport is not it. The true bearer of the emblem would be no man, but Devilkin, and the Jolly Roger is a Devilkin god even the red-eyed gods abhor. Rumor has it the pirates rally past the Emerald Isles up by Port VanWook. Davenport may have been Captain of the Green Algae, but by the Jolly Roger, and this ring, is part of something greater."

"Shouldn't we apprehend them?" Collin asked.

"Did you see the size of that ship?" Clique laughed. "Granted, if we gathered a team of mercenaries and used this submersible boat to assault them in secret, it could be done. With our crystals, our

Ancient steel, hell, with even just Axe alone, we could probably take the entire ship. But it would be unwise to strike without knowing our enemy. Let them flee upon morning without their Captain." Clique cracked the knuckles in his hands. "We have more important things to discuss with our very special friend here." Clique kicked Davenport in his side.

The next few hours were a blur of activity. Axe docked their boat back at its hidden slip, magically cooled the furnace so it wouldn't burn down while they were gone, and carried their prisoner back up the height of the vault. Its inner entrance was occupied by Janson, and four knights, who informed them that while the vault door could not be shut, as the key had gone missing, the secret entrance was now being guarded by the Sheriff's most trusted men. Clique ordered Janson to secure the secret port and its boat with a compliment of guards. When they exited the tunnel, and passed the men that blocked off the hall, they found the castle aswarm with people. Castle guards, servants, and knights of all banners walked the halls. The solar was overflowing with Western nobility, and when the three of them entered with their prisoner slung over Axe's shoulder, they were met with a roar of applause. King Tarnell's army had been rescued from the floods just in time thanks to Axe's warning, and while the soldiers and common men crowded the city, those of higher status were offered stay in the Stronghold. There were dignitaries and knights from the Eastern Realm present as well, and all intermingled in shared celebration. Everyone sang their names and gave them heroes praise.

Clique whispered private command to Sheriff Baldric Vehement, whose eyes went wide with astonishment, then firm with purpose. He led a dozen guards and a company of knights off to place Davenport in heavy chains and under heavier guard. Clique and Collin shared a look. Collin suspected that the Sheriff must have been told of Davenport's magic crystal, and instructed to keep knowledge of it hidden from even the men that guarded him. They knew they needed private conference with Lord Gracious to discuss their magic, but first, Collin, Clique, and Axe were forced by etiquette to mingle with the crowd. They hid their crystals beneath their sleeves, and when Clique brandished Shadow and offered it to Ser Tarbeld, a hush fell over everyone. "It has not been drawn," Clique assured him.

When Clique relinquished the Ancient weapon to the knights possession, Ser Tarbeld pulled the sword from its sheath to a chorus of gasps. Its wax seal snapped to pieces, and he held the black blade aloft. To Collin the weapon glowed blue and seemed a miraculous nebula of color, but he knew the spectacle was not visible to everyone.

"Clique Gracious. Collin O'Brien. Axe Treefort." Ser Tarbeld looked to each of them. "Kneel." The three of them did as he bid. "I, Ser Tarbeld Draven, Commander of the Honor Guard to King Harloque," he tapped the flat of the blade gently upon their shoulders, "hereby dub each of you, 'The King Saviors,' and name you Heroes of the Realm."

Ser Tarbeld sheathed Shadow, and the three of them rose to shouts of, "Long live the King Saviors!" and thunderous applause.

It was not long before the three of them managed to satisfy proper courtesy. Their ragged and battle worn appearances gave excuse for Axe, Collin, and Clique to slip from the solar and set to more important matters. Axe was sent to see to Davenport's imprisonment and wait, while Collin and Clique found their way to Davik. The chapel room dedicated to the Goddess had only been set up for Keira in anticipation of when she first moved to Stormbreaker. Even though Davik, like much of Midgard, believed in Scientos, he knew his wife would require a place to pray as there were no djinn. While the old gods had no place in Midgard, belief in the Goddess was a welcome faith, and Keira did not care where she prayed as long as it was a godly place. Davik had the chapel constructed of white painted wood with red and silver patina. It was one of Keira's favorite places in the castle, and now she was a corpse upon its altar with Davik in tears beside her.

Two guardsmen in full plate armor came to attention and blocked the way with poleaxes when Clique and Collin approached. Clique managed to convince his uncle to let him enter, and he bid Collin to wait outside. Clique shut the heavy wooden doors behind him while Collin remained. *King William will be wanting Starsinger back,* Collin thought. *I should seek his audience and present it, along with my request to use it for Davenport's execution.* Collin would have returned it earlier, as Clique had relinquished Shadow, but Ser Laurence was dead, and he would not entrust his blade to anyone save his sister Queen Vivian, or the King himself, both of whom were not there. *Let them rest after such a harrowing experience. I will call upon them tomorrow.*

Although the guards were inflamed with resolve to stalwartly protect Lord Gracious after the shameful events of the day, when Collin caught them both sneaking looks at Starsinger, he could not help himself but to unsheathe it and show them the blade. Smears of dried blood still dirtied its steel, and Collin wondered if he should clean it first, or present it as it was. He told the guards of how he recovered it from one of the thieves, and cut through a man's sword, *and* his arm, in a single swing. "It was only two men that I slew with Starsinger," Collin explained, "but after wielding it, I can rightly say that Ser Laurence owed much of his unmatched victories to the miracle of this steel." Collin sighed. "And when Davenport robbed him of his blade, so too did he rob him of his life." He hung his head low and sheathed the Ancient sword. "Ser Laurence deserved to die with Starsinger in hand, but if not for his sacrifice, it may have been more than Lady Keira that died this day." The guards had tears in their eyes. "At least it can be said that he died a knight undefeated. That is something... To Ser Laurence!"

"To Ser Laurence!" The guards cheered.

The doors opened, and Clique allowed Collin entry into the chapel before shutting them behind him. Davik had cried his eyes raw, and when Collin entered Davik stood and faced him. "Show it to me," Davik commanded him.

Collin looked to Clique for permission, who gave it with a nod. Collin raised up his sleeve and showed him the brown crystal. He brightened its glow for his lord, then dimmed it. "Show him the trick," Clique said.

Collin pointed at the second empty stone altar, and with his mind and will alone, moved and reshaped the stone into a chair he created beside Keira. Davik wept salty tears again, and Collin guided him to sit down. "Extraordinary," Davik gasped. "So yours is Earth, and yours Lightning. And Axe, and the thief..."

"Fire for our brave Huntsman," Clique said. Collin threw him a look at the comment. *Did he tell Lord Gracious of Axe's bones?* "And Davenport's is Water."

"Each are of the eight colors," Davik explained. "I will have my wizards find the relevant texts, but I would expect there to be four more of these crystals. One of Air, Ice, Light, and Darkness."

"What are they, and why would we have gotten them?" Clique asked. "It doesn't make any sense, uncle. What could it all mean?"

"The only thing we can say for certain is that magic has returned. It may be that the djinn are awakening." Davik stood. "Somehow it has come to pass that we control four of these crystals, but we also control something even more important."

"What's that?" Collin asked.

"Knowledge of their existence." Davik frowned. "Only you three, Davenport, Sheriff Baldric, and myself know, is that correct?"

"Yes, uncle." Clique nodded.

"No one else can know. Not yet." Davik paced. "Most especially not while we have armies at our doorstep. The pirates will know their lord of Water has been captured, and will flee to tell the tale. But they know nothing of the others."

"What should we do with Davenport?" Clique asked. "Shall we have a trial?"

"What? A trial?" Davik scoffed. "Learn everything you can from the man, then slit his throat, and hack off his arm at the elbow for the crystal."

"I want to do it," Collin said, "with Starsinger."

" I don't care how it happens! Just see that he's killed for what he's done..." Davik paused and wiped his face. "First Alana and now Keira..." His eyes had fire in them. "I want every man that played part in both plots hunted down and inquired upon! Is that understood?"

Clique and Collin nodded. "What about Davenport's family?" Clique asked. "They need to be contacted at once."

"I'll send my ravens soon enough, nephew, and deliver Hubert Davenport Hektor's bones. Both Kings will run him ragged if he played any part, but politics are no longer your concern... I will not have a man touched by magic rot in court as Chancellor. You will remain as Lord Commander of the Huntsmen. For now, see to Davenport, then bring me his Water. Now go, and leave me to mourn my wife."

Collin saluted him and turned to leave, but Clique had more to say. "Uncle. There's one more thing."

"Yes?" Davik was not surprised.

"The treasure..." Clique started.

Davik brought his hand to his forehead. "I thought you captured him before he stole it! Please tell me it's not lost to us."

Clique produced the silk bag and took out the vial. "Is this it?"

Davik sat back in his chair. "Oh, thank the Heavens it is safe."

"What is it?" Clique asked. "It glows as if magic."

"To be honest with you, no one knows." Davik shrugged. "The heads of House for Midgard have always known of its existence, and have kept it safe all these years. All I know is that the Lord of the Grey had sworn to protect it, and Stormbreaker Stronghold was built for that purpose. You saw the room of the Ancients, did you not?"

They nodded. "What is that place?" Clique asked.

"I'm afraid that secret is lost to me as well." Davik shrugged to their disappointment. "But while this castle may be young, that chamber is as old as Doom, and just as forgotten."

"The Doom is not forgotten," Collin added. "All men have heard song of it."

"Oh, is that so, Collin? And do these men know *why* it happened, or *who* or *what* was involved?" Davik sighed. "Maybe some answers can be found in the guarded tomes of Starspire and Starcrown, but unless you plan on traveling there, and directly revealing yourselves as bearers of arcane crystals, and thus privy to their holiest scrolls, that knowledge will remain lost even to us."

"There were a great number of old books in the vault. Maybe one of them–" Clique spoke, but Davik interrupted.

"Yes, yes. Good thinking, nephew. I'll have my wizards search for anything of value." Davik dismissed them. "Now go, and inquire upon our guest. Find out *everything* he knows about our treasure and these crystals. I don't care what it takes. Get it done! And don't come back to me until he's dead."

Havik had become familiar with the presence of absolute horror, so he was only half taken aback by the wrenching of his gut. *How can he know this? Unless...* Havik felt nausea and fear and madness all at once. He began to laugh just then, his sanity leaving him in waves of realization.

"M'lord?" Nimmet asked, quite confused by Havik's fits of the giggles.

"You said you cried for Jaxon, Nimmet?" he stuttered between breaths of laughter.

"Yes. A cruel fate to burn to death. I don't find it quite so amusing, m'lord," he said, growing somewhat angered by his lordship's lack of courtesy over his close friend's demise.

"And how, pray tell..." *Yes, pray tell, pray tell.* "... did you come by this information, exactly?"

Nimmet did not have time to respond. Jhev emerged from the hooded wagon and called out. "Havik! Is that you I hear?" he asked, as he stepped into view.

Kevin exited the tent behind Jhev. He had a long dagger in his hand with a hunk of sausage on the end of it. "My lord!" Kevin cried happily. "I am relieved to see you safe! We feared the worst when you did not return quickly behind me!" Kevin walked alongside Jhev, his dagger brandished menacingly.

So this is how he wishes to play it. Havik's mind raced. *What a viciously clever creature this obsidian horror is. Perhaps it truly is a god... Or maybe one of the djinn... They'd call themselves gods sure enough.* He found himself considering the possibility of the thing's divinity. *Maybe not quite all of them are frozen.* Havik dreaded the thought, even more so than the presence of some unnamed dark god. *If a djinni yet lives, then there will come to be men that worship the foul thing,* he thought, and Havik knew that a living djinni breathes magic into its followers. *Would those who worship the thing become necromancers of ungodly black magic? Would those who worship the magic tree gain healing magic? Or will the tree be cursed and bestow evil upon the hearts of those who kneel to it?* Havik was not pleased. *I have had enough of magic. Let me have my star metal and be done with it.*

"Kevin!" he found himself saying over a forced smile. "It is good to see you." *Yes. I can play this game as well.* Havik gave him a sly look, but Kevin gave no hint of inner acknowledgment.

"You look ragged tired," Kevin said, sadly.

He acts as if Kevin through and through. Even the way he carries himself and speaks his voice. Havik was frightened by the perfection of its mimicry. *No. This is no mimicry. It is as if he has become him, altogether.* "I lost my way but it seems I found it again," Havik lied. "How is it that you came upon the camp so fast?"

"I was thick with urgency, my lord. Ever since I lost you in the Barrens, I knew it all the more important to reach the camp and summon help." Kevin came to a stop next to Jhev when they reached where Havik and Nimmet were standing. Kevin's dagger dripped grease to the floor. His counterfeit squire took a bite from it, and spoke as he chewed. "I would never let them leave without you."

"How kind of you." Havik smiled through his teeth. "I must remember to thank my uncle for appointing me such a leal squire."

Kevin smiled wide as he chewed. Bits of fatty flesh spilled from his mouth and dripped to the floor. "Hubert Davenport, the Lord of Witchblood Stronghold. How we all love him so. He is as if a second father to me."

He openly mocks me with his intimate knowledge of my House. "So tell me." Havik patted Kevin on the shoulder. "How did you make it here before me without a horse?"

Kevin sighed sadly. "I rode the poor creature half to death." He took another bite of sausage. "It finally gave way to exhaustion, and I had to put her down. As luck would have it, that was just a small ways from where the wagon broke."

Nimmet pouted. "A sad story, but good you're here to sing it."

Jhev nodded. "So the demon's truly dead, then, Havik?"

Havik was unsure of how he might respond. Though Jhev and Nimmet looked to him for an answer, he paused and stood quite still. His gaze was fixed upon Kevin's eyes. *He must be able to pull the blackness deep within, and hide from sight. Another godly trick.* "It's quite the story to tell." Havik smiled. "Kevin, be a good squire and go cook me up some breakfast. And fetch the three of us some wine, will you? Nimmet and Jhev and I have much to discuss." *I'll speak with my men alone, and inform them while it cannot spin its lies.*

Before Kevin could speak, Nimmet waved his arms in protest. "No need to exert yourself, little man. You've both had a rough few days. I know where the wine is, and I'll help you break your fast quite well m'lord."

"No," Havik answered firmly.

They were all surprised by his response. "No, m'lord?" Nimmet queried.

"No," Havik answered again. "It is my squire's task." He grinned devilishly at Kevin. *If he makes his move now, I'll pull Nimmet's knife and set it to purpose.* Havik steadied himself, but Kevin complained instead.

"Oh, *please*, my lord? I'm *so* tired, and am only now just having my first good meal in days," Kevin whined.

"Oh, just let him rest, Havik. No need to break the boy." Jhev smiled at him.

Havik capitulated. *No need to force it just yet.* "Very well. Nimmet, fetch me wine, cheese, and a sharp blade to cut it."

"As you say," Nimmet smirked, "and I'll put some stew on the kettle for you as well."

"If you insist," Havik said, and with that Nimmet rushed off. "So tell me, Kevin..." Havik scratched at his chin. "Actually, I'm quite famished. Might I take that dagger of yours and have a bite of that sausage?" Havik looked upon Kevin with pleading eyes, but the squire shook his head and pouted sadly in return.

"Best not my lord. I've had a queer cough since the fire land," he frowned, and faked a cough. "I may have a flush upon me, and I'd not mean to worsen your health."

Havik laughed. "I am not afraid." He held out his hand. "Give it here."

Jhev patted Havik's back and gave out a hearty bellow. "Ha, ha! Of course! Havik Davenport is afraid of nothing! But still, can you not marvel at your squire's lealty? Best appease him, lad. This one aches for a knightship no doubt, upon return to the Realm.

"Yes," Havik lowered his hand and grinned unpleasantly, "*upon return to the Realm.*"

"Well, let's not just stand about." Jhev motioned for them to relax, and sat himself down on the ground. Kevin sat close alongside Jhev. Havik followed suit and sat directly across the two of them.

Nimmet exited the wagon with a plate of cheese and empty

goblets in one hand, and a bottle of wine in the other. Havik took note it was one of the finer vintages. They'd brought some with them for celebrating once they'd left the Barrens with wagons of precious star metal. "We're short a few men," Nimmet said sadly, "so I thought we'd have a drink of the good stuff to their passings."

Kevin said a prayer to the Goddess while Nimmet set the plate down, straightened the goblets, and handed Havik the knife from his belt. Havik took the weapon straight away, cut himself a piece of cheese, and ate it while he rubbed his thumb across the blade till it drew blood. *Sharp enough to kill with ease, if need be. But what then?* Havik pondered as he enjoyed the sweetness of the cheese. *If I only took his ankles, would he crawl in pursuit, or would he leave Kevin to rot and take another man?* Havik was not so sure. Nimmet unstopped the cork, poured the wine, and soon they toasted in remembrance of Jaxon, Horoway, and Flint. *And poor Kevin Gracious as well.*

"So, you were saying of the demon's end?" Jhev inquired.

Havik rubbed at his chin and played with the knife. "Let Kevin tell the tale again, and I shall sing my song when he is done." He smiled sweetly at Kevin.

"It is just as I told them earlier, my lord." Kevin swallowed his sausage and stabbed a piece of cheese. "When we reached the fire lands you and Jaxon went to bring Flint to his fiery grave, but you fell to the choke of the sulfur and passed out. We carried you to safety, and I continued on with Jaxon in your place. It was at the fissure, where we meant to put Flint to the fire, that the foul thing came out of his corpse. Jaxon struggled with it, and when the wicked thing was upon him, he nobly threw himself to the fires, taking himself and thing down with him to hell." Kevin raised his goblet high. "To Jaxon's bravery!"

"To Jaxon!" Jhev and Nimmet repeated, and the three of them

sipped from their goblets.

Havik rubbed his finger along the edge of his own goblet. *A fine song, this thing sings. And what might it do if I were to call him out for what he is?*

Kevin went on. "It was when I returned that I found Havik in a state of madness. He spoke strange things and looked through me, as if he were dreaming or lost to delirium. I thought him taken with a terrible sickness, and when I found some of the nut's healing foam in his pockets... Well, I fed him a handful. It seemed to calm him down, too. So I secured him in his saddle, and we set out on our horses."

"That's some quick thinking lad!" Jhev exclaimed, and he patted Kevin proudly.

Kevin smiled. "A windstorm came upon us. I lost one of the horses and most of our supplies. In the storm I lost Havik as well. His illness had not completely left him, and I feared him for dead, lost in the Barrens. I am quite glad you recovered, my lord."

"Aye, we all are," Jhev said, "and all thanks to you and your bravery. Good enough for a knightship, yes?" Jhev raised his eyebrows to Havik.

"It's knight*hood*." Havik took a sip from his goblet. "Kind of you to return with my sword and not your own, Kevin. How is it that you lost yours again?" Havik asked.

Nimmet seemed perplexed. "How'd you know he had your sword, m'lord? It's still in the wagon."

Havik had blundered, and Kevin grinned, but Havik would not let the game end so easily. "Only wishful thinking," he recovered. "My sword is precious to me, and I did not mean to leave it behind."

"Look out lads!" Jhev jested. "I think the foam has given our noble lord the magic sight!"

"That would be a sight indeed!" joked Kevin. "Our noble lord who says magic is dead, being magic himself. Flint would be rolling in his grave at the jest of it."

If he'd ever have a grave, and not simply cook forever on his fiery cliff.

The three of them laughed, and clinked goblets, and drank their wine. Havik chewed at a piece of cheese and squeezed at his goblet, anything he could do to keep himself from leaping across and strangling Kevin where he sat.

"So," Nimmet began, "our lord tells me he means for us to abandon the broken wagon."

"See!" Jhev hollered, "I knew my lord's mind all along! Better to have *half* the cargo than *none* at all." The three of them laughed. Havik chewed his lip. "Still... We've both waited this long, and it's quite a lot of metal to leave behind. If the threat is truly dead, as you say my lord, why not simply wait for our rangers and make the repair?"

"Yes... Why mean to leave the wagon, my lord?" Kevin asked.

You know why, Havik told Kevin in his mind, *because when I told Nimmet, I thought you were still chasing us. Little did I know you had already arrived, and planted your lies in the minds of my followers... What game are you truly playing?* Havik stared into Kevin's false eyes. *Do you wish to visit the Realm? Once there you could possess anyone you wanted... Are you waiting for your chance at the seed? Or are you just toying with me, as a cat would play with a mouse?* Havik came upon the answer to his puzzle. *No... It still fears me, and the foam I might use against it..*

Havik set his goblet down with gusto, and stood. He sheathed his cheese blade in his belt, and shook his head. "I will *not* be second guessed by my men, *or* my squire!"

Kevin seemed taken aback. "I was only asking... I did not mean to—"

"I know what you meant!" Havik shouted.

Nimmet and Jhev rose as well, surprised by Havik's ill temper. "Settle down, Havik," Jhev whispered as he took him aside.

Havik was angered by the ruse, and his blood ran hot. "You'll address me as *my lord!*"

"Then settle down, *my lord*," Jhev smiled. "The demon's danger has passed. You are only weary from your struggle, and tired. Kevin's a good lad. When our rangers return you can take stock of our situation with fresh mind." Kevin nodded disarmingly, grateful for Jhev coming to his defense.

Careful now, Havik. One false move and I'll find my men dead, and my cargo lost, as I flee from a puddle across the Northern wastes.

Fool! Your men are dead already, and soon you will be joining them...

Nimmet nodded in agreement. "Aye, m'lord. And it'll do us no good to leave here now, only to come across Brackens with his lumber. We'd have to turn round when we could have just waited."

Havik smiled. "You're supposing I'd mean to come back to fix the wagon."

Jhev was disappointed. "Well why in blazes wouldn't we?" he complained. "If they already got the lumber, it won't take but a few hours to fix the damned thing. And what's a few more hours in the Barrens? We've been here three damned weeks as it is."

"We don't know when Brackens might return," Havik said, "or if he's even coming at all."

Nimmet smiled. "Why not just send a scout, m'lord? I'll ride ahead and find them. If Brackens ain't by the gate, I'll return. It won't take more than two days. And if I come with no word of him, then we count them as lost, and leave with one wagon."

It is sound advice. My mind and Nimmet's would be as one, if not for this god that lurks amongst us. No matter what, I cannot let it get back to the ship. Let the thing swim to the Realm. He smiled, and nodded to Nimmet. "Wise words, sailor." Nimmet was about to fetch his things, when Havik stopped him. "But my mind is on the seed. Whether or not our rangers return, the ore must still be removed from the broken wagon. Whether for it to be fixed, or for it to be redistributed, there's work to be done." The three of them groaned at the thought of the manual labor. "Nimmet. Kevin. I want you to take down the cover and bring the wagons side by side. And clear out all that nonsense. If we're only to take one wagon, I'll not have goblets and crates of wine using up space better served for star metal."

"But the wine?" Nimmet protested.

"Put it in your pack then! Just see to it the work is begun," Havik commanded.

"Aye, m'lord. I think I'll do just that." Nimmet smiled as he grabbed the remaining bottle of wine and walked off to the wagon.

"Me too my lord? But my breakfast?" Kevin whined.

"You can break your fast later." *If he is to play my squire then let him do as he is told, and we shall see how long it is that he refuses to make himself known to us.* "Now be a good lad and hop to it. If you're to gain a knighthood then you'd best be quick about it. I'll have no complaints from a man who's just a squire and nothing more." *I wonder how hard I ought press?*

Kevin flicked a piece of cheese from his dagger and sheathed it in his belt. "Yes, my lord." He turned and went to help Nimmet with the wagon.

Jhev knelt to gather the goblets and cheese and looked up at him. "What's the matter, Havik? With such great victories won I'd expect you in better cheer." Jhev stood with the plate of refreshments in his hands, and frowned. "We have seen terrible things, and lost men, it's true. But look at what we've gained. Your plan has succeeded beyond our wildest hopes. Even one wagon will be a good prize. Why don't we–"

"Jhev," Havik stopped him. Though Havik's eyes were ever on Kevin, he took Jhev by the arm and spoke sweetly in his ear. "Kevin is a man possessed."

Jhev's eyes came wide with shock. "What?" He spoke too loudly for Havik to abide.

"Quiet, you fool. Do you want for him to hear?" *Jhev and I must be of one mind.* While Nimmet and Kevin brought the wagon around, Havik told Jhev the truth of what had occurred, and of how Kevin was now beguiling them with his lies.

As the words sunk in, Jhev became wroth with fury for the deception. "We must thrust the foam upon him, Havik. And force the devil into the open."

"Perhaps," Havik whispered. "But once out of Kevin, what then? It can become any one of us, and we are all at risk... Narvis is the key. She can see colors, and while its ichor may lurk deep within the heart of a man, I'm certain she'll be able to see it, and root it out."

"And if not?" Jhev asked.

"Then I fear it may come to no other alternative," Havik said with ice in his veins.

"What do you mean?" Jhev's fear sparkled in his eyes.

"The thing must be allowed neither seed nor passage to the Realm... I ate the foam, so I know it is not within me."

"Then we could all eat it," Jhev remarked, thinking the puzzle solved.

"I fear the creature kills the man if it's inside him when the foam's consumed." Havik remembered Jaxon's eyes bursting from his skull. The thought sickened him.

"But it doesn't enter a man if he's eaten it already?" Jhev asked.

"It seems not to. As I said, given the chance it passed me up because of the stuff."

"So Nimmet and I will eat some," Jhev answered, "and then we will know the traitor."

"The only foam that remains to us is with the seed. I do not mean to gather it in the thing's presence. Besides..." Havik sighed. "There's not much left, and it doesn't seem to kill the thing, only anger it and kill the man. Whatever foam we have must stay with the seed to keep it safe." *And hopefully restore the seed from its corruption,* Havik thought, but he didn't want to further frighten his Captain with mention of the seed being cursed as well. *Only Brackens knows of the seed's affliction. I wonder what he's told Brownbeard? If a good spy, he's told him nothing.*

"Then what is your alternative, my lord?" Jhev asked, afraid of what the answer might be.

"I mean to separate us into two parties, and have whom I believe to be the thing, whether through Narvis' eyes or not, go with Brackens to repair the wagon and fetch it. *We* would reach the ship first. Then all that's left is to sing a sad song to the men."

"And order us to set sail, leaving Brackens and the thing behind." Jhev smirked.

"Aye. A fell fate, but one in the service of the Realm's greater good." *And the greater fortune of my House,* Havik thought. *One wagon of metal, the seed, and our lives.*

"But wouldn't it protest at being separated from us?"

Havik nodded coldly. "Therefore the ruse must trick everyone, man and god alike." Havik sighed. "We'd have to leave them *all* behind, Jhev. Kevin, you see, is a student of the Litany of Honors. If the thing is of that mind, then whether bearing the memories of Flint and Jaxon or not, the thing won't expect a noble lord to betray his own men."

"Especially not his wizards," Jhev said, understanding.

"Still," Havik mused aloud, "it could slip from Kevin's shell at any time. We'd find Kevin dead, and you possessed." Jhev did not like those words. *Would he die if it left him?*

"Then I must take the foam sometime *before* the ruse, my lord," Jhev said. "A fine plan then. All that remains is for us to gather foam without risking seed within." Doubt seemed to creep over Jhev once more. "But if it finds out I've consumed the seed's magic, won't it suspect our ploy?"

Havik sighed. "If it comes to that–"

"My lord!" Kevin's shout interrupted them. Havik turned to where Kevin and Nimmet had set the wagons side by side and were unfastening the canvas cover. Kevin pointed to the distance, and Havik's heart both rose and sunk together. "The rangers are returning!"

Havik looked and saw it was true. Five horses were approaching their camp from the distance. "Jhev, do not speak of this. Treat Kevin no differently. Mark my words carefully. I mean to consult with Narvis, first, before making any decision in the matter."

Jhev nodded. "I won't stand none too close to Kevin, neither."

Havik mounted his garron and rode towards his returning men. He had only just departed when he saw Kevin mount Nimmet's garron and ride out to follow. *He is relentless,* Havik thought as Kevin approached. *Perhaps it wants a moment alone to gloat or make parley. We are ten minutes from the rangers at least.* Havik slowed his horse, and in that moment regretted not gathering his sword before riding out to meet them. Havik drew some small comfort in knowing that Kevin and himself were armed with naught but a knife and a dagger. *Unless he retains skill as well as memory.* Havik shuddered at the possibility that Kevin might now wield his blade as proficiently as the dead sailor Flint. *Though Narvis did best nearly all of them... Might even be she's the best fighter among us, and is all the more important for it.* When a crueler deduction passed his mind's eye, Havik again felt the fear course through him. *She could be the one it wants!* He swore under his breath. *Each of us are but men. Flint had the right of it. Men have no magic. But this girl... She could see colors, and that makes her more than just a man. Her strange black order took her in because of it. They told her she was special...* Havik made his choice. *She must be made to eat the foam before being exposed to Kevin. If taking her is its plot, then somewhere between uncovering the seed, and giving the girl her meal, it will make its move. The obsidian horror will soon reveal itself.* Havik smiled. *And if she can see it first then all the better.*

Havik reared his horse and turned to face Kevin. "Halt!" he commanded.

Kevin stopped abruptly with a look of confusion upon his face. "What's the matter, my lord? Your squire should be beside you when you ride."

Havik smiled. "Yes, my *squire* should be! Perchance you'll spill out of him any time soon, and give him chance to do so?"

Kevin seemed truly perplexed by the question. "My lord?" he queried uncertainly.

"Come now!" Havik laughed. "No one can hear us! There's no need to play it coy. If we are to speak then let us speak."

"Play coy my lord? I do not catch your meaning," Kevin said. "We *are* speaking..."

Havik quickly grew frustrated. "Do you think that I've forgotten when you possessed my squire in the fire lands? Or perhaps you believe me weak willed enough to believe your lies? No. My leal squire is dead, and you are but his shadow! Now tell me... What do you want from us?"

"My lord..." Kevin had tears in his eyes. "You're frightening me."

Havik saw that Nimmet and Jhev had grown concerned and were heading their way. The returning rangers were drawing near as well.

"I have had enough of your game!" Havik roared. "I *know* what you are! I *saw* you take each of one of them in kind, and Kevin last. Do not pretend to have left him. No mortal man can walk such distance and outpace me on a horse!"

"I told you, my lord," Kevin whined. "I had my horse, and it died towards the end."

"Your lies are empty!" Havik proclaimed. "I *killed* the other horses!"

Kevin gasped, as if coming to a grim realization. "It's the flush, my lord! You must have never truly recovered from your sickness! You only need rest. Three days alone in the Barrens would weaken any man. It's just your mind playing tricks on you!"

"Why must you lie to me, if no one is to bear witness? Tell me true, or I will bathe you in the foam you love so much! Who are you?"

"I'm Kevin Gracious!" he cried.

"Stop lying to me!" Havik's anger flared.

"I'm not lying! I swear by the Four Halos of Virtue I am your leal squire, and Lord Robert of Cliffwatch is my father!"

Could he truly be my squire? Havik considered during the boy's fine performance. *No. Of course not. He plays me for a fool!* Havik became enraged, if he was not before.

"I am no fool to believe your lies when I know the truth of it! You may have a squire's brain but I am a *Davenport*! I will not be so easily toyed with!" Havik reined his horse and rode closer. "This is your last chance, before I force it from you! Who are you?"

"By the Litany and all that is sacred," Kevin cried, "by the fooking Goddess herself, I am my lord father's fifth true born son!"

Taken by his rage, Havik roared as if he were a lion himself, and leapt from his garron to tackle his young squire to the ground. They collapsed in a heap with Havik on top. He grabbed Kevin's chest by the coat and bashed him against the ground in a fury. Kevin was helplessly in shock, with Havik shouting incoherently upon him in his wrath. By the time he'd received his fourth or fifth pounding against the rocky dirt, Kevin's feigned lealty to his lord had seen its end. He summoned his strength and threw Havik aside. Havik charged again, but a well timed punch by Kevin hooked Havik's jaw and sent him falling backwards.

"Nimmet! Jhev!" Kevin shouted over his shoulder. "Help! Help! His lordship's lost his mind!"

Havik was at his wits end. He spit blood, grabbed a fistful of sand, and rose to his feet. When Kevin looked back he threw the dirt in his eyes. As Kevin raised his hands to his face, Havik tackled him to the ground once more and set about pummeling with all the might he could muster. They rolled about grappling with hate in their eyes until Nimmet and Jhev were upon them. Nimmet grabbed Kevin and pulled him away from the tussle, while Jhev came to Havik's aid and helped him to his feet.

"What the hell's gotten into you two?" Nimmet demanded.

Havik pulled the knife from his belt and brandished it before him. "Get away from him Nimmet!"

Kevin pulled out his dagger in response, but Nimmet pushed him aside and got between them. "Stop this! M'lord! This boy's done us no wrong."

Jhev stood beside Havik with ice in his veins. "This *boy* is the demon, Nimmet."

Nimmet turned to face Kevin with horror in his eyes. "No, that cannot be!"

"He has been feeding you lies and falsehoods!" Havik shook the knife's point at Kevin as he spoke. "I saw the foul thing enter him with mine own eyes. He said he came here on a horse that died? I *killed* both the horses myself!"

Kevin looked at their accusing faces and tossed his dagger aside. "I came on a horse! I *told* you! How would I have made it otherwise?"

"On your demon legs you cur! I nearly rode my horse to death trying to outpace you!" Havik glanced over at the fallen dagger. "Jhev, pick up that dagger. Nimmet, go get some rope."

"This is madness, m'lord!" Nimmet complained. "When the thing took Flint it made a voiceless monstrosity. This boy here is Kevin Gracious true and true!" Nimmet kept himself between Kevin and Havik as Jhev recovered the weapon and brandished it himself. "He only just ten minutes ago reminded me of three doubloons I owe him," Nimmet explained. "What kind of demon's going to keep tabs on his gambling debts?"

"A *clever* one," Havik answered. "And you're wrong on one count." His voice grew cold. "Flint was not voiceless when he rose a man dead. He spoke in the Ancient tongue, and claimed he was a god." Nimmet and Jhev did not like the sound of that. The blade in Jhev's hand shook with his fear, and even Nimmet turned towards Kevin with a fright and backed three steps away.

Kevin Gracious was afraid. Blood and sweat glistened on his face by the light of the Dead Star. His freshly changed and clean kept attire was now a mess, and so was his well groomed hair. *If not for the fact he is a demon, that might have been the first real fight the boy's ever been in.* Havik grinned at the thought. *Still, he did last three seconds against Narvis... Concentrate... The boy is dead and the obsidian horror speaks in his place.*

Fool! They're all dead, and soon you will be too.

"Please... Please, sirs," Kevin pleaded, "his lordship is mistaken. I saw the demon fall with Jaxon into the pit."

"Ha! Will you never end this charade?" Havik laughed aloud and gestured at Kevin with his knife. "Can you believe this thing? It *knows* the game is up, but *still* it presses on with its fabrications. Give it up! I know the truth! You're not," Havik pointed, "fooling anyone!"

"I'm not lying!" Kevin begged with his hands. "You must have dreamed it different my lord. You were burning with fever. It plays tricks with a man's mind." He looked to Jhev and Nimmet. "I did everything I could to help him! I swear it! The foam must have made him grow even madder! How was I to know? It's not my fault! It's not!"

Nimmet seemed to be catching onto the fact it was one man's word against another, because he scratched at his chin and looked to Havik. "M'lord. Would you mind if I might ask *it...* and *you* a few questions?" Havik glanced over his shoulder at the returning rangers. They were still a ways away. "You know...to get a fair appraisal of the situation... as it were."

Havik nodded and gestured again with his knife to the affirmative. *Let them talk. I would hear everything this demon has to say. It is more clever than I thought, but no Davenport will give up a game of wits so easily.*

"So... Kevin." Nimmet smiled halfheartedly. "You say you saw Jaxon and the demon fall from the cliff?"

"That's... That's right," Kevin said cautiously.

"Now did you actually *see* them hit the fire," Nimmet asked, "or did you *just* see them fall over the edge?"

"There's no way they survived," Kevin declared.

"So which is it?" Nimmet pressed on. "Did you see them burn or didn't you?"

"No, alright! I only saw them fall off the cliff," he surrendered. "I just assumed... They burned! They had to! No man could..."

"No man," Nimmet said, "but a demon? We all saw it... what it could do..."

"But... But if it survived then..." Fear took hold of Kevin's face. "What if it... It could have..." And Kevin gave Havik a look of mortal dread. *I do not like the color of that look.* "What if the demon took Havik?"

Havik was taken aback by the boldness of the thing, but Nimmet was truly startled. Even Jhev turned to look at Havik with sudden doubt.

"You're not saying... Havik..." Jhev took a few steps back.

"This is insanity!" Havik laughed. "You cannot believe it! By both accounts I ate the foam! By my words *and* his lies I either ate the foam of my own volition or had it given to me!"

Doubt left Jhev as quickly as it had come. "That's true! If he ate the foam, then he cannot be the thing!"

"But what if..." Kevin gazed on with leery eyes. "What if it followed him, and took him later when we were separated?" Jhev certainly did not like the sound of that, and his doubt returned. "The foam kills the man possessed and heals the wounded, it's true. But after a day? Two days? Three days in the Barrens, what then?" Kevin looked to Nimmet and Jhev with his filthy deceitful eyes. "I know I am *not* the thing, and the two of you were here together." Kevin looked back to Havik. "The one who casts the first stone..."

"You can't believe this?" Havik half laughed, half queried.

Nimmet nodded. "He makes a good point m'lord. How are we to know?"

"I am a noble lord and the Commander of our party!" Havik cried aloud, his anger swelling. "It is not yours to know, only to serve and obey!"

"But what if you're not... *you*?" Nimmet asked.

"I am," Havik answered, "and if it comes to it, I will swallow foam to prove it." *But it won't come to that,* Havik thought. *I'll simply use it on him first and be done with it.*

"He must not be made to eat the stuff," Kevin told them.

"Why not?" Nimmet asked.

"Because I am not the demon," Kevin said, "but if *he* is, and we give him the foam, my lord will surely die. We must coax the thing out of him in some other fashion."

Nimmet scratched at his ragged beard. "A *squirely* thing to say."

"Narvis will sort this out." Havik laughed. "Your game of wits is for *nothing*! You want your plans revealed then? This is what *I* think! It means to take over Narvis because of her magic sight. The only people surely *not* taken by the demon are Brackens, Brownbeard, and the woman wizard. She must be protected at all costs. Her *and* the seed. The thing cannot be let on the ship to return to the Realm. *Civilization* would be at stake! Don't you get it? *Everything* is at risk!" *I must be going truly mad to believe such words, but how can it not be so? The thing is a mimic and a self proclaimed god. It could become a King in a day, and ruin the Realm in a year. Although... Flint did say that one djinni alone could lay to waste the works of men. What interest would a god even have in the Realm? No. It is the seed it wants. Why else wait millennia wrapped around it? The girl is its advantage... I must not let her be taken by it.*

The four of them stood in silence while the rangers approached. As they waited, each of them puzzled out the unsettling situation and watched for someone else to make the first move. A dark thought passed through Havik's mind as he stared at Kevin, who was giving him equal appraisal with his mortal eyes. *What if it's already won?* Havik felt his blood freeze. *I saw the seed corrupted. Has its victory been achieved, and this masquerade nothing more than its idea of entertainment to pass the time?* Havik had a sweeter thought. *Or does it play a deeper game? I must not overestimate this thing. However clever it may be, it may yet be vulnerable.* His uncle whispered to him just then. *If you concede the victory, then you have already lost. Either play to win, or worship the damned thing and be done with it. There's a chance the demon makes for a generous master, and it might have a use for you as something beyond host.*

Fool! The game is already finished, and soon it will be you who is lost.

Havik nodded to himself. *My uncle has the right of it. If I am to beat the thing or earn its respect, I must face it to the best of my ability.* But even as he dug down deep to summon his willpower, he knew that he was beginning to slip past the cracks of his sanity. His temper had worn to the point where if the situation turned sour, he might be forced to cut his losses, and prove to everyone, once and for all, that the obsidian horror lurked inside Kevin Gracious and not himself. One final measure to prove that their lord's words were the only truth to be found. *It cannot abide the dead.* Havik's face paled. *What if Kevin was released, and it lurks out there as some undead steed riding the Barrens?* Havik shook his theory aside as madness. *Maybe I really have lost my mind. Why would a god exchange a man for a horse?* Havik felt as if he were about to vomit his cheese and wine. *Kevin did arrive before me... But Kevin's mind is not his own. Perhaps it took the horse with Kevin upon it, then abandoned it for Kevin at the end.* Havik smiled. *That is how it beat me here, and that was Kevin's ploy. A grain of truth hidden in the lie tells the sweetest tale...* Havik sighed. *Or perhaps it simply ran, and I slept out there far longer than I thought.*

Jhev was the one to break their awkward silence. Besides Havik, he was currently the only other man with a weapon. "I'm sorry, Havik. But I can't get it out of my head, and I have to say it." Jhev had a look upon him that made him seem a man at the brink. Sweat ran from his temples, and his eyes were watered with fear and distrust. Jhev turned his eyes to Nimmet and Kevin. "When Havik sung me his song, and said Kevin was the beast, he made plot with me to stop it."

Havik didn't like where this was going. "Jhev! This is madness."

Neither Nimmet nor Kevin would not let him go unheard. "Quiet!" Kevin shouted. "You had your turn *my lord*. Let him speak. I am innocent and I will hear evidence against the accusation. Unless you are afraid?"

Havik's hand clenched around his blade but he made no move. Jhev was eying him suspiciously, and he did not want to come to odds with his Captain, Sailor's Law be damned. Havik simply nodded.

Jhev went on. "He said we couldn't let the thing get back to the Realm, so he meant for me to eat the foam to prove I was clean... then split the party and leave you all behind. The only sure way to escape the thing, and gain both star metal and seed."

Nimmet smiled. "A cunning plan. But I might have done the same thing myself, if I were a fancy noble lord, or a ranger Commander. Which both things I am not. It may have been inhuman of him, but it isn't proof that he's the demon."

Havik smiled. *Nimmet has a bit of logic in him. He seems to be the smartest of the sailors who chose to join us on the range. Perhaps that's why the other three are dead, and he yet remains. It is not the strongest or the fastest that survives, but the one who has honed their mind the sharpest.* Havik stifled a chuckle. *Or maybe he's just lucky. I might find future use for this sailor.*

Fool! Nimmet is dead, and soon you will be joining him.

"No! Don't you get it?" Jhev explained. "He wanted to betray you all, and get everything! It's exactly what the demon would do!"

Havik laughed aloud. "It's exactly what a *Davenport* would do, Jhev! And you know it."

"You meant to leave us!" Kevin shouted. They were all taken unawares as he rushed at Havik in a fit of rage. Demon or not, no one expected young squire's assault. Havik was tackled to the ground and his blade was tossed aside. Kevin was atop him with his hands upon his lord's throat. "You demon!" Kevin croaked.

Havik grabbed at Kevin's face and pressed his thumbs into his eyes. Kevin cried in pain and fell to his back. Havik's scurried along the ground and recovered his weapon. Nimmet tried to restrain Kevin, but was kneed in the groin, and knocked to the ground by Kevin's timely fist. *Kevin's moves, or Flint's?* Havik stood with his blade readied defensively, and Kevin circled round him. Jhev stepped forward with the dagger brandished. "Cease this quarrel at once!"

But both Kevin and Havik were taken by the heat of battle, and they would not abide a man between them. Kevin hungrily eyed his dagger in Jhev's hand, and made a move for it. *I will not let him get that dagger, or I am a dead man.* When Jhev pulled away from Kevin's reach, Havik whacked Jhev's head with the butt of his knife, and knocked him to the ground unconscious.

Havik recovered the dagger, and backed away from Kevin with both his blades in hand. But his squire still pursued him. Kevin feinted an attack left then right, then sidestepped left again. Havik swung at him with the blades, hoping to cut him and deter his attacks, or at the very least force him to reveal his true form. But Kevin was not so willing to be cut. After a few missed volleys, Kevin ducked under the dagger and grabbed hold of Havik's other hand. Havik shifted his weight, meaning to prevent Kevin from grabbing the knife, but it fell to Kevin's trap, and Havik found himself flipped head over heels and onto his back. The dagger flew from his grasp, and the knife was now in both his and Kevin's hands alike.

They rolled over one other, each man struggling to gain control of the knife. They heard shouts in the distance and the clop clopping of hooves on their approach, but all that mattered was the blade. Neither spoke, but instead they grunted and groaned in mortal struggle. Havik once had the point of the knife slowly gaining inches upon Kevin's cold black heart, then soon found Kevin above him, and the blade pressed flat against Havik's throat. *Demon or not, I won't have my death be at the hands of my squire! Curse you uncle, for appointing me my murderer!* As always, he regretted the words after thinking them but did not have time to say a prayer for his sins. Instead he prayed for his life as he struggled against the blade. Perhaps the Goddess herself gave him her blessing in that dark, dark, moment, when he felt the chill of the steel press through his unshaven beard and caress the skin of his neck. Havik spit in Kevin's eye and managed to gain some glorious advantage, for Havik soon ended up with the knife in his possession, and the squire flat on his back. Blood gushed from Kevin's nose where Havik's knee had bashed it in.

Do not hesitate! His uncle screamed in his ear, and it rang with a high pitched tone for some time afterward. Havik seized the moment and fell upon Kevin. His aim found its mark precisely, and the knife plunged deep into Kevin's chest. His squire cried out in anguish, and Havik further pressed his attack. He pulled the knife out from its wound. Blood dripped in hot dollops. When he pinned the boy's chest and arms down with his knees, he held the edge of the knife up to Kevin's throat.

"You've killed me!" Kevin cried.

Havik smiled. *It is no mortal blow, and nothing Brownbeard cannot patch with ease.* Havik trusted his intimate knowledge of the difference between a wound that causes great pain, and one that risks death. Any properly trained Davenport knew the primary tenets of Inquisition, particularly the one that taught pain and life run hand in hand. *A dead man sings no songs... But when I slit Kevin's throat his blood will sing darkness, and we will face a god once more instead of this cursed deception.*

"Who are you?" Havik pressed his face close to Kevin's, and stared deep into his eyes. He hoped to catch glimpse of the true darkness therein, behind the Gracious black.

"My lord... I'm–" Kevin started.

"Careful now... I want the truth this time." Havik's blood ran hot like fire.

Kevin's black eyes, colored with fear and hope together, entreated gently for his life. "My name is Kevin Gracious."

Havik adjusted the knife against Kevin's neck. *There are only two sure ways of finding out if Kevin is the thing, and as both ways mean his death, it should be with steel rather than precious foam.* Havik prepared for the final slice. *But if I'm wrong, and he dies without the demon within, what then? My men will think me mad.* Havik paused, and Kevin was as silent as the reaper. Havik thought he could see the faintest hint of a smile on Kevin's lips. *Is he mocking me? Should I sacrifice a good squire's life on a possibility?* His hesitation cost him part of the opportunity, for as the ringing in his ears died down he heard the clopping of the horses nearby.

"What is the meaning of this?" Brownbeard bellowed in his best battlefield voice. "My lord, are you injured?"

Havik glanced over his shoulder and saw Brackens, and Brownbeard, and even Narvis upon their garrons. Behind them the two drays pulled crudely wheeled sleds laden with lumber and a moose carcass. "Get back!" Havik waved them off. "Get away, all of you! Narvis stay back! Don't come any closer, as your lord I command you!" Kevin laughed madly, and Havik kept the blade at his throat. "Quiet you..."

"What trouble has your squire gotten to, m'lord?" asked Brackens as he pulled his longsword from its sheath. He and the others brought their mounts to a stop a few yards away.

"He's the demon!" Havik shouted. "I saw the foul creature enter his body and wear it as a man would a cloak! Now he's fed his filthy lies to Nimmet and Jhev to make them doubt me!"

"Help! Help, he's gone mad!" Kevin yelped. "It's him! Not me, it's him! He meant to leave us all behind and steal the metal for himself! That's right! Havik's the demon not me!"

"One more word and I'll slit your bloody throat and prove your lies!" Havik told him.

Brownbeard's face went pale. "Havik? The demon?"

Kevin cried. "It's true, I swear it!"

Brackens laughed. "That's *just* what a demon might say!"

It's then that Havik noticed Nimmet slowly approaching him with his hands raised disarmingly. "Easy now... Give me the knife m'lord," Nimmet said.

"Back Nimmet!" Havik eyed him. "Back now!"

Nimmet smiled the sweetest smile, and his tone was sugared water. "If you mean to kill him, kill him now and be done with it. Go on. Cut the boy's throat and we'll see if the horror's inside or not. And if he's not in there, well... Might be that *you're* the one whose throat should be cut next." Those words gave Havik pause, and he found himself listening to Nimmet. "Otherwise... Give me the knife."

"Havik," Jhev whispered, "let the poor boy be. Narvis is here, and now we'll learn what she can see."

Havik seemed a man defeated. Nimmet was upon him, his open palm only inches from the blade. "Easy now, m'lord," Nimmet spoke aloud, "we'll sort out whether Kevin's the demon or not, don't you worry. Just give me the knife."

Havik found himself surrendering. "Alright! We'll discuss this like civilized men!" Havik slowly pulled the blade away from

Kevin's throat. "Just stay back Narvis! And don't take your eyes off Kevin! I've reason to believe the obsidian horror wants to possess you for your magic sight!"

Narvis gasped at the thought of it. "Good Heavens!"

Havik placed the knife in Nimmet's open hand, and let the sailor's fingers slip around its hilt willingly. "You're making the right choice!" Nimmet shouted. And as Nimmet sheathed the blade, and helped Havik to his feet, the man placed his cheek beside Havik's and whispered sweetly in his ear. "Now do you see..."

His words were spoken Ancient, and they chimed in an aberrant resonance. "... how easy it is for a god to set man upon man?" Nimmet smiled.

CLIQUE

Clique played with the dagger in his hand. Hektor Davenport was strung by his wrists with rope and chain. His feet dangled only a few inches from the ground, but that was enough. The dull blue crystal in his arm started to brighten with illumination, and Clique stepped closer. He tapped the tip of the blade against Hektor's chest, and channeled his power through the simple iron dagger. Bolts of lightning arced from its tip and shocked Davenport with a steady flow of electricity. When the blue crystal dulled, Clique stepped back and laughed. "We are far away from the rain and waves here," Clique told him. The man had been taken to the deepest, most secure pit in the dungeons beneath the Stronghold where no one could overhear the inquisition. There were no windows. Apart from the luminescence of Davenport's exposed blue crystal, and the vibrant yellow of the occasional spark, the only light came from a lantern on a stool in the corner. Only Collin, Axe, and Baldric Vehement remained in earshot outside the cell, while the level above was defended by a host of guards. Most importantly, there was no water.

Hektor gasped for breath and his crystal shined blue again, so Clique zapped him until it dulled. "That won't save you now." Clique sighed. The man would not make eye contact, and still refused to speak. It had only been an hour, but Clique was finding that his lightning proved particularly effective in the weakening of the man's resolve. After each electrocution he felt the man's strength draining from him, and the aura of his innate magic grew fainter fainter by the minute. "Nothing will save you except the truth." Davenport raised his eyes to Clique's, and for the first time drew his gaze. Clique thought Hektor about to speak, when the man spit in his face and looked away. Clique smiled. *Such an act of defiance means he is primed.*

"Collin!" Clique cried out, and his fellow King Savior entered. "Cut him loose and tie him to the chair." Collin did as he was commanded. Clique gently drew the point of the blade across Davenport's hand. He was about to press the dagger into the tips of his fingers to claw at the bone, when Axe interrupted, and drew Collin and Clique into the hall for a private word.

Axe shut the door and whispered. "Pain will not make him speak," he explained. "I have analyzed his physical reactions to your magic, Lord Commander, and if that torture has not yet loosened his tongue, no torture will."

The Sheriff snickered. "You are speaking to a Gracious. He knows more about inquisition than the likes of you."

"Yes," Axe agreed. "But still, I have an idea of my own that I'd like to try."

"What makes you think Davenport will respond to you any differently?" Baldric queried.

Axe smiled a secret smile, and seemed about to answer when Clique spoke up. "No, no," Clique said. "Axe *should* make the attempt. A change in strategy might yield fruit. Every Davenport is also a trained inquisitor. An unconventional approach may be just what we need."

The Sheriff seemed swayed by his words. "Very well. Axe, you may proceed." Baldric by rights was in charge of the inquiry as Sheriff of Midgard, and with his permission Axe was quite pleased with himself.

"Do you need to be alone?" Clique asked him.

Axe considered it a moment. "No. On the contrary, I estimate it will be far more effective if you are all present." Axe smiled. "When the time comes, everyone can ask of him whatever they wish."

Axe opened the door and led them inside. The Sheriff shut it behind them, and stood by the door with his hand on the hilt of his longsword. Collin circled behind Davenport, while Clique stood idle nearby and watched. Axe stepped close to their prisoner. "Hektor Davenport." Axe spoke loud and firm less than a foot from the man's face, though Hektor's eyes were fixed in some dark corner of the ceiling. "You do not know me, but I am a member of the Royal Huntsmen. Perhaps you've heard of them?"

Davenport gave no response as Axe rubbed his hand through the man's hair and caressed his scalp. "It's alright. You don't have to speak. First, all you must do is listen... Then I'll make you watch." Axe stepped behind him, massaged his shoulders, and spoke softly. "You already know the questions we have for you. It must seem like all we have for you are questions. But there must be *some* things even *you* want to know." Axe released him and circled the man like a shark stalking its prey. "Go ahead. Ask me anything, and I will give you the answer." Axe stopped in front of him and waited, but, as they expected, did not draw Davenport's gaze. "No? Oh, I'm sure there *must* be some questions you might have for us... Go ahead. Ask... No?" Axe encircled him once more.

"Well, that's a disappointment. One would think you'd at the least be interested in *our* crystals. By now you must have already figured out that Collin only managed to gain his during our pursuit of you. You would have seen Collin had no magic in the solar. But why didn't you reveal your crystal? Why didn't you single me out when you saw I was magic?" Axe stopped in front of him. "Again, more questions for us, and no questions for you." Axe gently pet his head once more. "But what if I told you, that Clique and I gained our crystals at the same time as Collin?" Davenport did not react. "Must I spell it out for you?" Axe took a step back. "I know you saw me as magic when you first entered the solar... *Before* I had my crystal." Axe drew Davenport's gaze, and to their surprise, he spoke.

"You lie." His voice was raspy, but full of conviction. "No man without a crystal is magic."

"Clique." Axe put out his hand, palm up. "Your dagger, please."

Clique handed it to him. "I'll die before I tell you anything," Davenport said defiantly. "Torturing me will get you nothing."

Axe smiled wickedly. "What... this?" He waved the dagger in front of Davenport's eyes. "Oh... Don't worry. This dagger isn't for you." Axe held the blade up to his throat. "It's for me." Axe slit his own neck from left to right, and his blood spilled out in sheets. Davenport's look of determined defiance transformed into one of confusion and terror. Baldric shouted in horror and Collin went pale as snow. Axe pressed the blade deep, and when he reached the end of his neck, dragged the point of the dagger up across his cheek. His flesh split.

"Oh, shit!" Davenport screamed in terror. "Oh, shit!" *Collin and I know the truth of him, but this is an act of insanity!*

Axe continued his slice, and dragged the dagger round his forehead, then down his other cheek and back to his neck. By then a horrific pool of blood had puddled at Axe's feet and the gush of crimson liquid from his neck had dwindled to a few drips. Axe slipped the bloodied dagger in his belt, and stepped even closer to Davenport until their faces were inches apart. Axe brought his hand to his face, and then, in an act of horror that would haunt Clique for the rest of his life, Axe dug his fingertips into his forehead, and tore his face, off.

Sheriff Baldric Vehement doubled over and retched the contents of his stomach onto the cold stone floor. Collin held his breath and seemed faint, while even Clique felt somewhat nauseous. Axe's face flopped from his left hand like a piece of wet leather, and he held it up for everyone to see. His loosened eyeballs fell to the floor with a sodden plop. Where his face used to be was a silver metal skull with large inhuman eyes that glowed with a red light similar to his Fire crystal. Only the teeth in his metal mouth were white. Everything else was silver and red. Though no muscle existed to give the face expression of emotion, the cut of the silvery metal gave his skeletal face such a frightful ghoulish countenance that any man might think him an angry demon upon first glance. Axe chattered his teeth together and spit blood. "Do you have any questions for me *now*, Hektor?" Axe ran his bloody fingertips across Davenport's face. "Or shall I show you what your face looks like as well?" He dangled his own face in front of Hektor's eyes like it were a piece of meat for a dog. "I promise I can do it without slitting your throat."

"What *are* you?" The words barely escaped his lips. Davenport was shocked to the core, and Baldric too was beside himself. Clique waved his hand dismissively, smiled, and nodded casually to the Sheriff in an attempt to play off Axe's brutal revelation as if it were common knowledge and no big deal. The look the Sheriff gave him was worth every hardship Clique had endured in the past day.

"Now, now, Hektor!" The man of steel named Axe Treefort laughed. "That's not how the game is played! Answer all of *our* questions, and then we will answer all of *yours*." Davenport was defeated, and Clique knew it. *He may have been a peasant, but Axe is a brilliant tactician. Collin should receive honors of his own for recognizing the value in bringing such a man to our side.* In that moment Clique thought both of his allies to be the most brilliant and savvy men in the world, while the Sheriff smelt of vomit and was currently the only man in the room without a crystal. *No wonder we have been gifted by the fates themselves. Who better than us to change the course of history?*

"Very well." Hektor broke his terrified stare into Axe's hypnotic red orbs you might call his eyes, and looked down to the floor a broken man. "I'll tell you whatever you want to know."

"What's in the vial?" Clique asked for what might have been the hundredth time. He circled closer to Davenport, but kept his boots well away from Axe's blood. Axe took a few steps back and kept his red eyes fixed on their prisoner.

"The last breath of a djinni." Davenport laughed as they processed his answer. "I nearly lost it when you first asked me that. How could its keepers not even know the truth of their own treasure? It beggars belief."

"Alright. But why steal it? Does it *do* anything?" Clique asked him.

"You really have *no* idea, do you?" Davenport sighed. "Look. Everyone knows that djinn grant wishes. Everyone also knows that people worshiped them to gain their magic. The djinn are frozen, so magic is dead. Or well, it *was* dead." He laughed, and Clique joined him in the laugh and drew closer until Davenport fell silent. "Wishes and magic alike could do anything but bring back the dead."

Clique was astonished. "Are you telling me this vial will grant a wish?"

"No." Davenport laughed. "I'm telling you that vial can bring back the dead."

Collin, who stood behind Davenport, nearly swooned at his words. His face bore the emotional journey of him realizing that if the man spoke true, the vial might bring Lady Keira back to life, as well as her unborn child. They would certainly not use such a precious object on Ser Laurence. Clique chuckled, and Davenport saw his mirth. "How many dead?" Clique asked.

"Just one man..." Davenport said, "or one beast. Might even be it could bring a djinni back to life, that is, if you could get one out of that dead ice first. Might even by that's why they call it dead, and it's the ice that needs the bringing back, not the sleeping djinni inside."

"Is that what you wanted it for, Hektor? To resurrect one of the djinn? Or were you planning on bringing back your grandfather? Don't think that we don't know who you are."

"Come on!" Hektor chided him. "Do you really think a *Davenport* would waste an artifact like that on a person? What one man can do, any man can do. Why bother bringing one back from the dead? And the djinn? All I can tell you is my mastery of Water does nothing to melt their prisons. The stuff isn't magic either, but you can see that glow of theirs deep inside it well enough. Best not go wasting your djinni breath on dead ice. Might be the ice won't melt, and you'd have lost everything on a gamble."

"Do you know who has the Ice crystal?" Axe asked him.

Davenport regarded Axe uneasily and shook his head. "No."

"So what did you want it for then? A pot of gold?" Clique shook his head. "Your family is rich beyond reason. I couldn't imagine you selling it to the highest bidder."

"My family turned their backs on me a long time ago, I'm sad to say." Hektor drew a deep breath and summoned himself. "Hubert cast me out a decade ago for... Well, it's not important. Let's just say I crossed the wrong man and learned the folly of it. My path took me to the Emerald Isles where I fell in with the *Rough Weathers*, a gang of mercenaries from the Realm that sold themselves out to Gulgari for coin. I convinced them to fight for themselves instead, and within seven years I had a fleet of ships. And that's when I met her...

Valencia..." He seemed lost in the fondness of the memory, and Clique rolled his eyes.

"The love interest of your sad tale?" Clique quipped.

"No." Davenport smiled. "She was the woman I murdered to steal her crystal of Water." The way he said those words filled Collin with fury, but Clique waved off whatever foolish action he was about to take. *Interesting!* Clique gasped. *So a crystal can be taken away from someone!* That meant his uncle may get his Water after all. *And if my uncle doesn't want it...* Clique glanced to the Sheriff, who stood listening with a flecks of puke on his chin. Baldric caught Clique's gaze and smiled. Clique nodded politely.

"Who was she?" Clique asked eventually.

"Some whore that acquired it from an old sailor that died in her pretty arms." He laughed. "And before I cut off those pretty little arms she told me everything. The sailor wouldn't tell her *how* he got it, but his ship *The Joking Jester* was sunk two months before. One day the man just rose up out of the sea, the only survivor of the wreck. He went straight to the brothel, and stayed there the rest of his life."

"Why did you kill her?" Collin asked as he stepped round to face Davenport. "You took her crystal. You could have left it at that. Was it to keep the secret of your identity?"

Davenport frowned. "No. I'm not one to avoid the bards. A bit of fame can open many doors."

"Then why?" Collin asked again, no doubt seeking some moral high ground to inwardly justify putting him to death when the time came.

Hektor Davenport sighed. "I'm sad to say, gentlemen, that even though I took the limb, and tore the crystal from its severed flesh, the crystal would not change masters." He smiled. "But once I slit her throat, it became mine willingly."

Clique motioned for Collin to step away, and he obliged. "You *do* realize," Clique told him, "that you have just signed your own death warrant."

"You would have figured it out anyway. Besides," Davenport gave a coy smile, "you could always bring me back to life, *after.*" Everyone except Davenport laughed at the insanity of it. "I could make it worth your while," he added, and that killed the laughter.

"How?" Sheriff Baldric asked, but Clique waved off his question and interrupted.

"Who did you want to bring back to life?" Clique asked again.

"Let me finish my story, and you'll know." Davenport waited for them to fall silent, and he continued. "I did not have the crystal long, before tales of the pirate Captain that commanded the sea itself were sung at every port. With every victory we left a few survivors for the song of my growing power. I had hoped it would draw the very attention I received."

Clique understood. "You wanted someone else with a crystal to seek you out?"

Davenport giggled. "It seems Gracious men are *somewhat* intelligent after all."

Clique ignored the remark. "So who was it?"

"The woman who gave me my ring," Hektor said. "The one you've been so insistent upon. They call her Captain Zephyr, though her true name's Gale. Fitting, as she's the very Wind itself. She was already a pirate when her crystal came to her, but was nothing more than a lacky swabbing the decks. It appeared before her entire crew after she killed a man. Don't know who it was, or why she killed him, but she was blessed by the fates for his death all the same. Every last man of hers saw in the crystal a vision of her whole mortal life, then a prophecy of her killing demons before being eaten by one. I received no such vision. With Water came no insight, only power... You lot must have had them though, yeah? Your whole lives laid bare to the world? Tell me... What was Axe Treefort's past? What did you learn of his amnesia?" The question shocked them. "Don't be so surprised. I've had my spies here long enough to plot my burglary, though I'm sure they've all run for the hills now that I've been captured."

"You've raised more questions than you've answered, Davenport," Clique said. "Tell me all I want to know, and you may yet live." The words drew cutting glances from Baldric and Collin, but Clique ignored them. *His fate is not their decision,* he reminded himself, *nor is it mine.*

"Once she held the power of the crystal, no man could stand against her. Gale rose to the rank of Captain after forcing every last man to bend the knee. Within months she had claimed a veritable fleet of her own ships, and that's when she joined the *Order of Seven*. And later, when she found me... I joined as well."

"There are seven of you I gather?" Clique asked.

Davenport laughed, and Clique found his patience drawing thin. "The others are pirate lords by their own rights. I only ever met one of them. Captain Cask they call him, and his arms are just as wide as them. The Order has no leader, if that's what you're wondering. At least not one that I've met. No one knows who founded the order, but Gale killed one of the seven the night she give me my ring."

"Why do you fly the demon's sigil?" Clique asked.

"The Jolly Roger? I don't know..." Davenport admitted. "But the flag came first, that I *do* know, and it was not for sometime thereafter that the Order of Seven gained its name, *and* its rings. Might even be that once upon a time, there was an *eighth*."

"Why did you want me dead?" Clique asked him.

"Isn't it obvious?" He laughed. "If you killed the Queen, whether war was averted or not, the summit would have been canceled! And then my opportunity would have been lost to me! As the fates would have it, it didn't matter. But the fates can be cruel mistresses, and my plans have been thwarted all the same."

"How could you know all this?" Clique asked.

"I told you," he smiled," I have my spies." Clique looked to Baldric, who shook his head in disbelief. "Don't blame your Sheriff. He's innocent in all of this."

"If you didn't want the Summit canceled..." Clique pressed on, "then why try to poison Lord Gracious?"

"Poison him?" The question came as a shock to Hektor. "Someone tried to poison him?"

Collin stepped forward. "*You* stand accused of it!"

"Well I'm *sorry* to disappoint!" Hektor laughed. "But I'm afraid I had no hand in the matter."

"You lie!" Collin shouted.

"If Davik Gracious died before the summit, then all of my well laid plans would have fallen to ruin!" Hektor shook his head. "The hand that paid the assassin is just as much *my* enemy as he is *yours*."

"We're missing the Captain of the Castle Guard," Clique mentioned.

"Jack Havensword," Davenport said. "I know the man, and I know he's missing."

"Do you?" Clique grinned. *Of course you know him! The man stands accused of placing your men in the castle guard!*

"It was a long time ago that we first met," Davenport explained. "He spent half a year at Witchblood when Alexander Warne and his vicious brood had business with my father. The man squired for Alexander, or one of his brothers, or cousins. He was a devious little shit, just like the Warnes. If he's missing, then there's your traitor."

"Alexander Warne, you say. Was Jacynth Irvalis there as well?" Clique asked.

"Never heard of him, I'm afraid," Davenport said. "But I'm sure Jack Havensword is your man. After all, he was my man as well."

"Havensword..." Clique repeated.

Davenport nodded. "The man was bought too easily by my first mate, and *now* I know why. Betrayal comes easier to a man the second time round. But he *did* follow through. At least that can be said of him."

Clique took a step back and recovered himself. Even Collin seemed satisfied with the truth of Davenport's words. *If he is innocent of Alana Toril's death, then someone else is responsible for Havensword's actions,* Clique wondered. *But who, and why? To avert the peace, or...* Clique shook the thoughts from his head. There would be time to search for the traitorous bastard and inquire upon him soon enough. For now that honor was given to another. "The treasure, Davenport. You still haven't answered my question about the treasure."

"What did I want to bring back to life?" Hektor laughed. "You really are curious about that minor little detail. Very well. It's nothing as groundbreaking as reviving a djinni I suppose, but I thought it was cunning all the same. Eight months ago, not long after I hoisted the Jolly Roger, a fishing vessel sunk while trawling where the reef met dark water. The survivors all sang song of a kraken that rose up out of the deep. It didn't even attack their ship... They were sunk by its passing wake alone. You can *imagine* my enthusiasm when I heard the tale. The creatures of the sea obey my every command, and with a kraken, well, with one of those it wouldn't be *pirate lord* but *Pirate King*! And the Order, and even Gale, would take the knee to me alone. I set my sails for the shores nearby, but no living behemoth was found. The great thing was sickened by some plague and driven to shallow waters, where it beached itself and died... The secret of House Gracious had been known to me from my teachings at

Witchblood. I decided then, over the corpse of the kraken, that with the breath of a djinni I could bring the thing back to life, and have my avatar of the sea. It sits there still, in a great pen of wood I built around it, and covered with as much vinegar as my ships could load. And now, well, here I sit, singing my sad song. You'll be wanting the location of the kraken then? To give to Davik Gracious, your noble lord, and soon to be Lord of Water, his new favorite pet? The map's with my clothes. If you bring it here, I'll show you how to read its secret language." Davenport finished his speech, and soaked himself in the awe struck looks of the men in the room. *No doubt he considers himself the cleverest man alive. A thought which will be remedied shortly.*

Axe interrupted the silence when he broke his fixed gaze on Davenport, and came close to Clique to whisper in his ear. "Lord Commander, Prince Will Tarnell, King William's first born son and heir to the throne of the West approaches. I heard him announce himself to the guards, and by writ and seal he has gained entry past them, against our given orders not to be disturbed." *Wonderful.* Clique made the word a curse in his mind. *Just what we need. Interruptions.*

Clique drew Collin and Baldric close and whispered news of the Prince's approach. "Keep him occupied, and whatever you do, *don't* let him in. We cannot have him see the crystal."

"What about..." Baldric glanced at Axe, "him? He will see..."

Clique considered a moment. "Break the news of his affliction as gently as possible, then Axe will go outside to greet him. Let him *see*. If *that* doesn't send him on his way, then we'll have to take Davenport's arm sooner rather than later." They heard his steps approaching.

The Sheriff slipped outside and shut the door behind him. Collin stood by to make sure it stayed closed. "Trouble outside?" Hektor asked with a mischievous grin.

"None that concerns you," Collin told him.

"Don't take me for a fool," Davenport snickered. "You're trying to keep the crystals a secret, and are finding it increasingly difficult to do so, are you not? Don't bother to deny it. I know how your lord thinks. No one can know of any usable advantage, and soon I will be dead with my crystal stolen. But... If you bring me back to life after Water has been claimed, I will keep your secret safe."

"You are a murderer!" Collin accused him. "Why should we offer you any sort of amnesty?"

"I am no such thing!" Davenport scoffed. "Only a few castle guards were killed, and that couldn't be helped. No more than ten men. My men *were* most of the guards."

"Lady Keira died! Shot by one of your men's arrows," Collin told him. "The poison from the arrow even killed her unborn son."

"I'm sorry," Hektor whispered. "But Keira's blood isn't on my hands. It's on yours."

"Watch yourself, Davenport!" Collin drew his hand to his hilt.

"*You* risked *their* lives, when you brought it to violence," Hektor told him.

"We couldn't sit by and do nothing!" Collin shouted. "If we did nothing, your men would have killed us!" Collin grew angrier. "Don't you deny it! We *heard* you. You said if you weren't back by ten, then they were to tidy up, and follow the plan. You meant for them to kill us."

Davenport sighed. "No... They meant to release you."

Collin laughed. "You can't expect us to believe that."

"It doesn't matter what you believe," Hektor said. "But I'm not a murderer, and if you bring me back to life after you've stolen my Water, I'll make it well worth your while."

"What of the Western army?" Axe asked. "By Water they all

nearly drowned."

"Are they dead? No? Then there is your answer." Davenport spit.

"What could you possibly offer us that's more valuable than Lady Keira's life?" Collin asked.

"The security of the Central Sea! I can lead you to the rest of the Jolly Roger and the Order of Seven," Davenport pleaded. "Without me you'll never find them. I could lead you to Gale! You want another crystal don't you? The very Winds themselves could be yours! Or Gale could be a valuable ally! She is no tyrant, and would gladly sell out the pirates to bring order to the seas with fellow men of crystal."

"I've heard enough," Collin said. He unsheathed Starsinger with great flourish, and approached Davenport with death in his eyes. "Any last words?" Clique stepped well away.

"No! Listen!" Davenport pleaded and struggled with his wrists bound behind his back. "Resurrect me, and I'll take you to where I can get another djinni breath! The treasure of Stormbreaker isn't the only one! I know where! Please! I'll help you bring her back to life!"

Someone tried to open the door but was blocked by Axe, and three loud knocks rattled the door shortly after. "Open up in the name of King Tarnell!" a voice cried.

"Cover him," Clique told Collin. Once Starsinger was placed back in its sheath, Collin wrapped Davenport's crystal with cloth and hid it from prying eyes.

At Clique's command, Axe stepped away from the door and it burst open. In came young Will Tarnell clothed in a motley of red and blue silks. Typical of a Brae, his hair was long and silver, but his eyes were light blue like his father's. "Dear Goddess!" he shouted when he stepped into the room. "You were telling it true, Sheriff! I shouldn't have doubted you." Clique noted that it was not icy fear that gripped Will, but rather a warm fascination and curiosity. The man seemed no older than his mid twenties, and his fingers were covered in gaudy rings of priceless gemstone. A golden dagger hung on his belt, and he carried a tiny golden harp and a silverwood lute across his back. *Is he a Prince or a jester?* Clique wondered. "How is it that my father's savior is a demon?" Will asked them accusingly. "What *are* you, good sir?" he asked Axe.

"*That*, your princeliness, is the question of the hour!" Davenport laughed.

Will did not enjoy Hektor's comment. He took two quick steps to the prisoner and back handed him across the face. Will's rings left gashes across his cheek. Davenport spit blood and a broken tooth. "Speak only when spoken to, sir! Or would you like another?" The strike seemed false to Clique somehow, as if Will were putting on a show of strength to detract from his unease regarding Axe. *I would have done the same thing in his position,* Clique mused. *I do not like this man. He reminds me too much of myself, if I were a royal fool.*

"Prince Will Tarnell." Axe took a step forward and knelt. "The truth of my past is a guarded secret." Axe smartly glanced up at Davenport, then looked back to Will. "If you will accompany Sheriff Baldric and myself outside, and allow them to continue their inquisition, I would be happy to answer any questions you might have of me." *Tactical perfection,* Clique marveled. *He gives him no choice.*

"Very well." Will turned to Clique. "Lord Commander Gracious. I shall await you outside."

Clique smiled politely. "As you wish."

Baldric stood aside and politely motioned for Prince Tarnell to pass him into the hallway, but Will stopped halfway out the door, and looked down. His Princely boots had trodden over Baldric's vomit on the floor, and when he looked up he saw flecks of it on the Sheriff's chin. "I..." The Sheriff started to speak, but Will placed his finger over Baldric's lips and silenced him.

"Your breath is wretched, Sheriff." Will produced a silver flask from his bard-like robes. "Drink this. I insist."

"What is it?" the Sheriff asked. "Wine, or rum?"

"Neither." Will unscrewed the top open and shook his head. "It's only water."

The seemingly innocuous comment drew looks of horror from Baldric, Collin, Axe, and Clique combined, though Axe's horror Clique could only guess at, for his was a cold red metallic stare. Even so, all four of them shouted in warning, but it was too late. The water within the canteen burst forth like an erupting geyser and it showered the room with droplets.

"Collin!" Clique commanded. "*Starsinger* his arm off!" Will was a mess of confusion, while Davenport was crystalline with purpose. Collin drew the Ancient blade once more and approached their prisoner. Though bound, the blue light of Davenport's crystal shined bright enough to illuminate the room with dancing shadows as the rain multiplied and coalesced. Each droplet seemed to give birth to another, and the room was flooding from above as well as below. Rain poured in every direction, drenching them and filling the chamber with such frenzy that the halls outside flooded as well. Collin swung Starsinger down onto Davenport's arm, but water swirled and spiraled around his wrists. When the blade struck, the vortex of water pulled it entirely from Collin's grasp, and flung it across the room to crash against the wall. While its steel did not taste flesh, the rot of Collin's strike disintegrated the rope and chains that bound Davenport, and he rose a freed man. Hektor swept his outstretched palms through the air, and the water responded by gathering into a great wave that blasted across the chamber and pushed Collin and Will against the wall. Prince Tarnell hit his head, and blood spilled freely into the water.

Clique raised his dagger and his golden crystal blazed with fury, when Baldric grabbed him by the arm. "Don't!" Baldric shouted against the rain and waves. "You'll electrocute us all! We have to get the Prince to safety!" The room was flooding impossibly fast, and Davenport backed away into the corner where a wall of water shielded him from them.

"Go!" Clique shouted. "Axe, take them!" Axe protested but Clique refused. "Leave Davenport to me! Go! Hurry!"

Axe patted Clique good luck, scooped Collin and Will up with his arms, and was led by Baldric out through the hall. The water was up to their chests and flooding out the lowest level of the dungeon. "Hektor! There's no way out!" Clique screamed. "Even if you can breathe water, we'll just leave you in here to rot!"

He heard Davenport's laughter amidst the raging tempest, but couldn't make out the words of his taunts. Clique kept his eye on the blue glow of his allies, and waited for them to disappear up the steps and out of the water. Clique took one final deep breath and plunged himself beneath the water's surface. Clique watched as Davenport's protective vortex of water dissipated, and there, as if anchored to the floor with no natural buoyancy, Hektor Davenport brandished Starsinger menacingly in his hands. Davenport lunged forward with the sword, and stabbed through the water at Clique, but when Clique parried the blade with his dagger, he pulsed his lightning through iron, flesh, and Ancient steel alike. The shock sent both weapons hurtling away. Davenport pressed forward and grappled him. Hektor's hands gripped around Clique's throat and tried to squeeze out his life. Clique knew that thanks to his training he could hold his breath for a long time, but Davenport *was* Water, and he would never drown. *Forever is longer than ten minutes.* Clique pressed his hands against Hektor's chest, and summoned all of his will through the Lightning crystal. *If I'm to die, then I'll bring you with me. And if the fates allow it, they shall resurrect me with the djinni's breath instead of Lady Keira.* Clique released the full spectrum of his magic and channeled a massive bolt of lightning into Davenport's chest. After the golden flash, all Clique saw was darkness.

Clique awoke to Axe pressing upon his chest with the flats of his hands. *I was drowned...* he thought, as he hacked up the water from his lungs. "Davenport..." Clique coughed.

Axe shook his horrific head. "I recovered Starsinger, but Davenport is gone." Clique marveled at how, when Axe spoke, his words were perfectly pronounced, even though he had no lips... "One of the cells had cracks in the floor. Veins too small for a man to fit through, but they look to go deep into the ground. He must have turned to water, somehow, and fit through."

"What about–" Clique started, but Axe interrupted him.

"The treasure?" Axe held up the magic vial and handed it to Clique. "I took it from you when I left you with Davenport, in case you should fail."

"Axe Treefort," Clique smiled, "you will be knighted for this."

"Save your sers. I'm a Royal Huntsmen!" Axe helped Clique to his feet. "That's all the title I'll ever need!" Will watched in befuddlement as Clique, Axe, and Collin stamped their feet and hooted.

"What about lands? Will you turn down those?" Clique put his arm round Axe's shoulder.

Axe rubbed his fingers against his nonexistent chin. "I *do* like land."

"What about Davenport?" Will asked, and everyone looked to him.

Clique eyed the two guardsman that stood nearby. Both were staring uneasily at Axe but quickly snapped to attention. "Take Prince Tarnell to safety immediately!"

"Oh no you don't!" Will slapped the guard's hands away. "I *saw* things! Things I won't forget! I demand to know the meaning of all this!"

"I don't have time this! Guards, remove him!" Clique commanded.

The men grabbed for the Prince's sides but he stepped back of his own volition. "Fine! Starsinger." Will pointed at Collin. "It belongs to my House. Give it here."

Collin unhappily removed the sword he'd only just recovered and handed it to the Prince, who snatched it in a huff and stormed off. Baldric and the guardsmen followed. "Collin, could you dig a path for us through the stone, that we might follow Davenport?"

Collin nodded. "Absolutely." Collin and Clique waded into the water, but Axe stopped them.

"We won't catch him by following in his footsteps," Axe said. "We need to cut him off."

"And how would you propose we do that?" Clique asked.

"Simple," Axe told them.

It was not long before the three of them stood over a table in Stormbreaker Stronghold's library. Though terrified by Axe, the scholars and wizards present made short work of their task, and had produced the ancient builder's schematics for Stormbreaker's lowest levels. The foundation sunk deep into the ground, and if Davenport was to make his escape by way of water, it was determined his only course to the sea would lead him through the sewers. There were tunnels that filled and emptied with the tide, and all were accessible by the Southern cove, yet because of the storm would now be flooded and near twenty feet underwater. A young and eager scholar named Peter pointed out that the current would force a man along the sewers, and if he did not wish to rise up back inside the Stronghold, from there would drive him into the cistern. Those tunnels held the fresh water for the city, and from there a thousand exits could be reached to the streets above, where pursuit would be exceedingly difficult. But all this considered, Clique knew that the current would not influence Davenport, as he could breathe water, and would be seeking to return to open sea where he could reach his ship before morning. *Still, it would be unwise not to take every precaution.*

Clique summoned two guardsmen, and placed the pleasantly surprised Peter in charge of organizing men to defend the cisterns. "Look for disturbances in the water," Clique told them. "Use crossbows, and shoot on sight."

"Yes, Lord Gracious!" Peter marched off with the guards in tow.

Clique, Collin, and Axe exited the Stronghold with haste. Axe recovered a rowboat and carried it with him, while Clique and Collin grabbed longswords and short bows from the armory. The flood waters had receded and left the plains a muddy waste. When they exited the gates they followed the paths down to where the rocks met the sea. The worst of the storm had passed, and the rain had dwindled to a light drizzle. Axe set the boat down, and Collin and Clique took off their armors and belts before boarding it.

It was not far from the rocky outcropping of shore where Axe said he saw the tunnel's entrance beneath the pitch black waters. It lay nearly thirty feet below the surface, and if Davenport should pass beneath them, he'd be out of their reach. While he may have already escaped, they decided to wait there for as long as possible, before they would take to the submersible to watch for him by the Green Algae. Axe tipped himself over the edge of the boat and sunk like a stone. Therein he hid by the tunnel and waited for Davenport to emerge. "Watch for my light," Axe had told them. "If you see it shine, then you know he is upon us."

"Kill him, or drive him to the surface," Clique commanded, and Axe swore he would obey. So there Collin and Clique sat in the darkness, listening to the crash of the waves and the blowing of the wind.

"I can't believe we let him escape," Collin complained. "We are such fools not to have killed him when we had the chance."

"Do not blame us." Clique comforted him. "Blame Will Tarnell for allowing water in the presence of the Water-lord, or blame our incompetent guards for obeying a foreign dignitary over my own commands."

"If we do not find him, at least our lordship will be moved with bringing Lady Keira and his child back to life," Collin mused. "Such joyous resurrection will undercut the shame of our failures."

"We haven't failed yet, Collin." Clique looked to the Silver Star that became visible through a break in the storm clouds. The cove and the sea became awash with its pale silvery light. "And I am still not convinced that bringing her back is the right thing to do."

Collin glared at him in the dim silver starlight. "We *must* resurrect her. It is in our power to undo this great wrong. We cannot deny our lord such a blessing."

"It's not right, Collin." Clique kept himself from meeting his gaze. "Answer me this. Why hasn't it been used already? Why has it been kept for so many years in our possession?"

"We know this!" Collin complained, and Clique pressed him to keep his voice down. "The heads of House didn't know what it did."

"They had to know at some point, Collin," Clique whispered. "Elsewise how would the Davenports of Witchblood have known its secret? No, the early House lords, or even Octavian, or the Lord of the Grey himself kept this for a reason. They didn't use it on their dead brothers, or dead mothers, or fathers, or wives. Their dead sons or their dead daughters. They let the dead die, and kept it such a hidden secret that in time its purpose, and even its very nature became forgotten." Clique's eyes met Collin's, and he saw the man was crying. "We *could* bring her back... But at what cost to our future? At what cost to our heritage? Keira has already borne my uncle a daughter *and* a son. His line is secure." Clique placed his hand on Collin's shoulder. "I'm sorry, but I fear that its magic may hold a greater purpose."

"Then what?" Collin pushed his hand away. "We try to bring a djinni back to life?"

"Davenport said that neither magic nor wishes could bring back the dead," Clique said. "But he obviously wasn't the scholar of djinn that he thought he was."

"What do you mean?" Collin had hope in his eyes.

"As a boy I visited the Dravens at Aztoz castle, and heard many a strange legend in that haunted place." Clique strained to remember. "One was of a djinni that healed the sick and brought back the dead." The Silver Star disappeared behind the clouds, and cast the world back into darkness. "I denied the bard's story as false tale, but was overheard by some Draven lord, I can't recall who. He took me aside and told me that not only was it real, but the djinni was once kept inside Aztoz castle's very grounds. The castle, as you may know, is older than any other in the Realm. It was only inherited by men in recorded history after the Doom, and not built by them. But these Dravens claim that in the first century after they took the castle, the frozen djinni of life was dug from its garden, and stolen away."

"So where is it?" Collin asked.

"I don't know, and neither did they," Clique admitted. "Or so he claimed."

Collin shook his head. "So you would gamble Keira and her baby's life on some djinn, that may or may not exist, without us even knowing where it is, or how to find it?"

"It's not really my decision," Clique said. "Is it?" Collin began to speak, but Clique silenced him, and pointed to the shore, where two men were approaching with bows. Collin readied an arrow. "Who goes there?" Clique cried out.

"I"m sorry, my lord!" a boy yelled. "I tried to stop him, but he was quite adamant."

"Janson, is that you?" Clique asked, bemused and angered at the same time.

"And Prince Will Tarnell!" Will exclaimed. "Come now! You didn't think I would stand by and let you recover this fiend by yourselves, now did you?"

A bright red light shone from beneath the water in a vertical column that rose into the sky. It flickered and pulsed for a few seconds, then went dark. "What was *that*?" Will shouted. "*More* sorcery? What *demons* and *devils* do you have in your–"

"Quiet!" Clique commanded. "It means he's here. Be ready." Clique and Collin notched their arrows, and Janson and Will followed suit. Collin pointed and Clique saw it. While his crystal was covered, the shimmering blue aura of Davenport's magical nature betrayed him. And when he emerged from the tunnel, Axe was upon him. Clique watched through the water as his man of steel took hold of Davenport's ankle. It was then that the water become a flurry of bubbles. The boat rocked and an ebullient geyser erupted upon the surface. Will and Janson were flabbergasted by the incident, while Clique and Collin remained unmoved. "Collin," Clique whispered. "Raise up a wall of the sea floor to trap him in."

As Collin's mind focused on the task, Clique studied the water, waiting for Davenport to break surface, or for some sign that Axe had killed him. When the boat shook that first time, Collin fell overboard. The surface of the water was turbulent with froth and foam and Clique couldn't make out what had hit them. When the boat shook again it overturned altogether and thrust Clique into the brine. Once submerged he opened his eyes and beamed a golden glow to light the waters. All around him a vast school of tiny fish swam with devilish purpose. They overtook Collin and passed over him. In their wake Collin's light cloth clothes were tattered and blood from a thousand tiny cuts stained the water. Beneath Collin the ground rose up in slow effort to lift him. *This is Davenport's doing,* Clique knew. *I have to stop him.*

Clique took his breath and swam down through the bubble wall. Therein he saw Axe gripping Davenport's ankle down to the bone. Water steamed and hissed from the fire of Axe's crystal, while Davenport was perpetually keeping Axe at bay with a watery vortex emanating from his crystal. Clique drew his sword and made the attempt, but Davenport deftly knocked the blade aside with a thrust of current. Clique shared a brief look with Axe, who nodded, as if sensing his thoughts. Clique could get no closer to Davenport with his mastery of the waters, so instead he reached out and let Axe take him by the hand. With all the willpower he could muster, Clique channeled a bolt of lightning through Axe's metal frame and into Davenport. Axe released his grips and fell lifelessly away into the water, while Davenport floated listlessly towards the surface.

Clique swam up and gasped for much needed air. The bubbles had stopped, but the swarm of fish seemed to intensify its frenzy. Their passage across the water left a wake of waves and fins as they swarmed towards Clique. Collin had not yet risen from the water, and Clique would not risk electrocuting him as well. He braced himself and readied for the assault. *Collin is a bloodied mess, but he is not dead.* Clique worried as the fish approached. To make matters worse, Davenport had awoken and rose to the surface nearby. His cruel eyes met Clique's. "I have you now!" the master of Water laughed. Clique's rage was cut short, much like Hektor Davenport's victory, when an arrowhead burst from the man's throat, instantly slaying him.

"Yes!" Will shouted in celebration. Clique's eyes met Will, who lowered his bow and pumped his fist. "I got him!" Collin stood on his pillar of stone with his legs thigh deep in water, and his bow was raised at Davenport with an arrow drawn. Collin cursed Will for stealing his kill, and had hate in his eyes.

Clique turned to find the swarm upon him, but as the school of fish passed over, all he felt was the pitter-patter of them brushing against his sides. The fish assaulted Davenport's body in a crazed hysteria of bloodlust. Clique swam for the pillar of rock, but the swarm had finished their meal in seconds, and turned their attention back to Clique. "Collin! Hurry!" Clique cried.

With time to spare, Collin's feet ascended safely above the waves, and Clique channeled his full strength into the waters around him. Lightning came from the sky and struck Clique's hands, and a great burst of golden blue plasma arced through the swarm. Clique's world became darkness. He awoke only moments later in Collin's arms, out of the water, and on the stone ledge that had been created.

"Axe..." Clique groaned. "Is he..." Collin shook his head and pointed. Bathed in his magic blue aura, Axe was visible as he climbed up the reef with the blue crystal of Water gripped safely in his hand. *Yes!* Clique celebrated. *My uncle will gain his magic after all!* Davenport was no more than a mess of chum amidst the thousands of dead fish that floated on the surface. Janson had recovered the boat and rowed out to the stone pillar to retrieve them. The darkness was overbearing, and as the mystery of their crystals had already been revealed, Clique shined his golden crystal and turned night to day. Across the cove he saw Will Tarnell approach where Axe was ascending that final rock to the shore. *The crystal!* "Will! No! Get away from him!" Clique cried out, but it was too late. When Will Tarnell reached down to help Axe up, the Water crystal leapt from Axe's hand. *No!*

COLLIN

Collin shifted uncomfortably in his chair while he waited. Every inch of his body hurt with annoyance. The fish had left so many small cuts and bruises across his body that all he wanted to do was bathe in oatmeal. The priests had given him ointments in the short time they treated him, but it offered no true relief. He refused the potions that would dull his senses, and consigned himself to the discomfort while he waited for Lord Gracious. Beside him sat Clique and Axe, who seemed equally frustrated. Axe had developed a ravenous hunger, and for a full half hour while they sat in Lord Gracious' private solar, all Axe could do was blather on about the different foods he planned to eat once they were dismissed to their rooms. Collin had no such appetite, and twice thought he might vomit from the thought of it. His stomach roiled with the stress of anticipation for his lord's arrival. Clique was tight lipped, and had not given any hint of whether he had come to firm decision on what to do with the treasure. Collin hoped that it would be used for his lady, but at the same time, felt torn. *If we could find this djinni of life and awaken it, perhaps it could bring Keira back.* But that was a big *if*, and Collin was unsure whether Davik would think it worth the risk, or choose to resurrect his wife. *If I were him,* Collin told himself, *I would not hesitate to resurrect my pregnant wife. But I am not the Lord of a House, and I have the luxury of putting my own wants and desires above those of a Realm.*

When Baldric and Davik entered, Collin felt his anticipation crescendo, and he turned to face them. Davik paused and marveled at Axe's face. His look of fascination transformed to a frown, and when he approached the man of steel, Davik placed his hand on Axe's shoulder. "Oh, my poor boy. What have you done to yourself?" He knelt and had fresh tears in his eyes. "You didn't need to do this. I know I said to do whatever it took. But not this." Davik took Axe's hand into his own. "I will have the finest helm–"

Axe politely interrupted him. "My lord... My lord, please. Your compassion honors me, but it is unnecessary."

Davik dismissed the comment. "Nonsense. I can't have my Huntsman disfigured and–"

"My lord," Axe laughed, "it will heal."

"You can't be serious!" Everyone was taken aback. "But your face..."

"Yes. Granted I've never had such a severe injury." Axe scratched the back of his head. "But no, after a good meal and a day's rest I'll be my old self again. I can't explain it either! Whether Scientos or magic, that's just the way I am. I *am* sorry though, my lord, about not covering my face between then and now. I could have had less people see the truth of me."

"It's alright Axe." Davik smiled. "If your face does return as you say it will, then only those few who saw it will ever *truly* believe. Let men have all the more reason to fear the Royal Huntsmen." Axe hooted and stomped his feet, but Clique and Collin were too distressed to join in the revelry. Davik circled around them and sat in his chair. "Baldric has informed me of all that happened." He sighed audibly. "And I am *very* disappointed."

"Uncle," Clique began, but Davik held his hand up and silenced him.

Davik toyed with a quill on his desk. "The fact that the heir to the Western throne possesses a magic crystal cannot be kept secret. Most especially not from the Eastern throne, lest we Midgard be accused of favoritism." Davik set the quill down. "This is a very delicate situation that your incompetence has put me in. There will be a special council tomorrow to properly inform both Kings simultaneously. Be grateful Prince Tarnell has offered to keep silent that long. He plans to tell them of *your* crystals as well. All three. We are lucky Collin is an O'Brien, or the East might have been insulted they hold no crystals by their Houses."

"Will shouldn't have been there," Clique gritted his teeth. "We had no choice."

"Yes. I suppose it couldn't be helped." Davik threw Baldric a venomous glance. "Our Sheriff was careless enough to let Prince Will slip through his fingers. I spoke with Janson. That boy deserves a knighthood. Without even knowing of secrets meant to be kept, he took it upon himself to thwart Will from following you, and when he could not, swore to keep him safe. You will knight him soon, won't you?"

Clique gulped. "Uncle. There's something you must know." Baldric had been informed to keep knowledge of the treasure's purpose secret, so that such vital news could come from family. Now the moment had finally come. Collin held his breath. Davik was devoid of emotion as Clique told him all that they had learned from the inquisition. Davik heard all there was to hear of the pirates, Davenport's plot, the djinni's breath, and of the djinni of life. His face was pale, and his eyes distant. Afterward they sat in silence for near five minutes while their lord poured himself two goblets of wine and drank them both without word. He took an iron poker from the fireplace and stoked the flaming logs within. "Collin." A chill went through his spine as he heard his name.

"Yes, my lord?" he asked.

"What do *you* think we should do with it?" Davik kept his back to them.

"It... It is not my place to decide." Collin squirmed.

"She *was* your cousin." Davik pressed at the fire. "Now answer me."

"My lord... I..." Collin straightened himself. *He didn't ask what I would do,* Collin reminded himself, *he asked what I think we should do. I must act a lord, and not a grief stricken man.* "While it pains me to say. If it was meant for man or woman, it would have been used up centuries ago. We should try for the djinni." Although he was being pragmatic, somehow Collin felt as if he had betrayed Keira just then, and the shame felt real and tangible. "Never before has there been magic such as our crystals. Perhaps it is our fate to awaken the djinn."

"Clique." Davik's voice was cold. "What say you?"

"Uncle." Clique cleared his throat. "We need not decide yet. Davenport's kraken was placed in vinegar for keeping. It may be uncouth, but... Couldn't we..."

"So you think we should wait. Gather more information." Davik set the poker in its rack, and turned to face them. "Is that what you mean?"

Clique sat up. "It's just that the djinn, uncle."

Davik silenced him with a wave. "Axe? Your thoughts?"

"I've never seen a djinni," Axe told him. "I want to try my Fire against the dead ice. And if that doesn't work, I don't see why an Ice crystal would fare any better. Maybe the treasure is meant to bring one back. If it's the djinni of life, well then couldn't that one bring them *all* back?" Axe's red eyes glared at Davik. "So the way I see it, my lord. The question isn't what to do with the treasure. It's whether you *want* these djinn roaming free in the world, or whether you just want your wife." *Wise words,* Collin thought, and everyone seemed impressed at his advice.

"Baldric?" Davik looked to him.

"The kraken could be traded to the Western Realm, now that they have the Water." Baldric was expressionless. "I advise you bring it up in council tomorrow, and forge agreement to carve up the Central Sea between East, West, and Midgard together. Let magic *sleep.* We have our three crystals, and if magic was commonplace, it would be the end of our advantage. Use the treasure and the crystals as leverage to secure the peace, and in so doing you'll strengthen all of Midgard, the Realm, and incite war on the Sea as we had planned to do all along. Only this time, with a kraken, and the waves."

Davik sat down, and even Clique seemed swayed by Baldric's words. *This man frightens me,* Collin realized. *He sees advantage to conquer the world, while we could only think of magic and family.* Collin's blood chilled. *His way would yield the greatest benefit. But is it the right thing to do?*

Davik poured himself a third cup of wine, but never drank from it. He only stared into its murky purple surface as if the answers he sought could be found within. "The kraken..." Davik muttered as he thought. "Magic... The sea..." At last Davik sat up, and pushed the goblet away, as if refusing it. "No."

"No?" Clique was the first to speak.

"I miss Keira." He had tears in his eyes. "I want my wife. None of this was worth it if I don't have her." Davik nodded, as if his own words brought him to make his decision. "To hell with the djinn. Midgard has three crystals, and that is enough. I want my wife, and if it's in my power to resurrect her, then I will seize that chance with both hands and never look back." Davik stood. "I've made my decision. Clique." Davik reached out to Clique with his open palm. "Give me the treasure, and we shall go to the chapel where my love awaits, and see her brought to life."

Clique stiffened. "No."

It was as if Collin blinked, and while one second they were in Davik's solar, the next were in a dungeon cell. Davik and Clique came to a heated argument about the magnitude of the generational responsibility placed on their heads, and Clique refused to allow the treasure, one sealed by the Lord of the Grey himself, to be used on a woman, no matter who she was, or how badly she was missed. He refused direct order from his uncle, and neither man would be swayed by any words. The pride that each of them held was overbearing, and Collin wondered whether it would come to blows, but Clique never once hinted at violence, and Davik outright opposed it. "If you will not obey me, then perhaps you will obey your father!" Davik had shouted so loudly that Collin thought he might faint. Davik ordered a page to send raven to summon Lord Robert, Clique's father to Stormbreaker immediately, then commanded the Sheriff to escort Clique to the dungeons, where he could reflect on his disobedience and await his father's arrival. Clique must have felt the shame of it, but he held onto both his dignity, and the treasure, and agreed to go willingly with the Sheriff. For the briefest of moments Collin thought that he and Axe were kept out of it, but Clique got no further than the door before Davik ordered Axe and Collin to join him. "Perhaps you two can talk some sense into him!" And with that their fate was sealed.

They were given one drab cell in the upper dungeon, but it was roomy, and thanks to Axe, made pleasantly warm. Privilege would not be denied the King Saviors, even though Clique was being punished, and while the priests applied further ointments to Collin's wounds, servants brought feast and wine for them to enjoy. Axe ate enough for ten men and Collin took the respite to get himself quite drunk. Only Clique sat brooding in the corner picking at a bowl of grapes. "Why don't you just give it to him," Collin suggested as he spit out an olive pit. "You said it wasn't your decision anyway."

"Things have changed, Collin." Clique moped. "*We've* changed."

"Yeah." Collin reclined in the chair he'd fashioned from stone and padded with his cloak and straw. "If I wanted to, I could open up the floor right now, and make those iron bars drop in a heartbeat." He laughed. "I'd say that's a pretty big change."

"That's the point, Collin." Clique tossed his fruit bowl aside. "We're more than just men now." He glanced at Axe, who was passed out in the corner covered fully by a blanket. "Just like him. We may not be hard on the inside, but we're something different. And we will be until we die." Clique stood and paced the room with his hands behind his back in the same fashion as Davik. *He's so like his uncle, and yet so very different,* Collin mused. *His uncle may seem cold and calculating, but I know that for all his ambition he's governed by his love, and uses Keira as his moral compass. Clique has no such guiding light in his life...* Collin shuddered. *Come to think of it. Without Keira... neither do I...*

"So what?" Collin asked. "Just because we have magic powers, suddenly we should turn our backs on our obligations and go running off on some grand adventure?"

"Don't be so melodramatic." Clique snickered. "I'm serious."

"So am I!" Collin shouted. "We may be different, but we're still the same people! It doesn't have to change *who* we are."

Clique was frustrated. "That's not what I'm saying Collin! Don't you think I know that! If I wanted to shirk my responsibilities as a member of my House then I wouldn't be in this damned cell!"

"Then what *do* you want?" Collin asked.

"I don't know!" Clique sat and rubbed his face. "If I'm to be a leal

360 | Gregory Mandarano

Gracious lord, then I *must* obey the commands of my uncle. If I disobey him, then I stand against everything I've ever been raised for, everything I've ever believed in. But I'm not *just* a little lord anymore. I'm the master of Lightning, and I can carve out my own fate. We *have* to carve out our own fate, if we're to avoid being eaten by monsters as that false vision prophesied." Clique shook his head. "No, Collin. No. I can't just sit idly by, and let something my family has held onto for a thousand years be wasted because my uncle is too blinded by love to see the folly in it. I won't accept that. I *can't* accept that."

"Well if that's the way you feel, then I stand by you," Collin said. "To hell with our oaths. If you believe, I mean truly believe that it's the *right* thing to do." Collin rose and drunkenly stumbled beside Clique. "Then I've got your back, Clique. You're the Lord Commander of the Royal Huntsmen." He grabbed Clique by the shoulder. "You have me, and a dozen other good men who'll follow you to the world's end if that's what... If that's what..." Collin grabbed the fruit bowl and vomited.

"I may just take you up on that offer Collin," Clique said. "But not just yet."

"So what..." Collin retched a bit more. "What are we going to do?"

"The only thing we *can* do." Clique reclined in his straw bedding. "Wait for my father."

Axe slept full through the second day, and on the morning of the third he awoke completely regenerated. His face appeared exactly as it did before that terrifying incident in a very different dungeon cell. After hearing of Clique's perpetual indecision regarding their fate, Axe, like Collin, the good Huntsman that he was, agreed to follow his Lord Commander no matter what he decided to do. Collin and Clique were relieved to see their friend and ally healed, but once

Collin had seen Axe's true form, he could never quite get it out of his mind. *If my face were removed, one would see a skull of bone just as horrific... Save for what Axe's white robed wizard has done to him, he is no different from I, and is no horror.* He accepted Axe for what he was, a man with a magic skeleton, but the memory of his skull was frightening none the less.

The servants brought them food each day, changed their chamber pots, and provided them with fresh water and wine. But they would give no hint as to the goings on in the castle above. The choicest bit of news they were given, was an answer to questions that Clique posed the jailer. Kendrick, the wine boy, was spared his execution and had been relinquished to the stockades in the city square for public humiliation. Kelly, the servant girl responsible for fetching the poisoned wine, did not fare so well. The guardsman Daniel, who was her betrothed, had been found amongst the dead. He'd died valiantly fighting against the thieves that infiltrated the peace summit. But even the bittersweet glory of his death was tainted when they were told that Kelly had killed herself when she heard of his ill fate. Though she had been pardoned of her crime, after prayers to the memories of Keira and Daniel, threw herself from Stormbreaker's chapel window and onto the jagged shoals below. Clique's heart ached with sadness from tale, and he spent the remainder of the day in sullen silence.

They received no other visitors in that time. In the middle of the third night they were awoken by Axe when he heard footsteps approaching, which was rare for the late hour. They were surprised to discover their visitors were Janson and Ser Ringley, who had recently returned to the Stronghold with the Royal Huntsmen. He told them of how no man was taken sick thanks to Clique's precautions, and in the span of a few short days, they burned every last trace of the plague to ash. At the behest of Lord Chase, they even put all their horses to the fire, just to be sure of it. Clique was distraught at the death of his horse from Cliffwatch, the one that Alana had come to love and made a show of it. But they all knew it was better to be prudent where plagues were concerned.

Janson had shared with Ser Ringley the truth of their magic, the treasure, and their imprisonment, facts which he had learned himself from Baldric. But Ser Ringley could not be prepared for the glory of seeing the three crystals with his own eyes. He openly wept when he saw them, and softly whispered prayers of the litany. Ser Ringley admitted that he loved Lady Keira, and would like nothing more than to see her live again. But his honor would not allow him to stand by and allow his Lord Commander to be imprisoned for the crime of protecting the treasure of his House from the wants of a lord struck by grief. The guards outside had been drugged, and the way for their escape was made clear by his efforts. Collin thought Clique would inform them that he planned on waiting for his father. But whether Clique had come to final decision, or if the pains of living in a dungeon cell had finally gotten to him, Collin was surprised to find that when Janson unlocked the cell to free them, Clique did not oppose.

Their path out from the dungeons and through Stormbreaker was a quick one. Ser Ringley distracted the last of the men that might recognize their passing, and within the hour Collin found himself on horseback with Clique, Axe, and Janson riding beside him. The Silver Star had already set, and the night was as pitch black as it was cool. Collin pulled his black woolen robes tighter around his body. Janson had procured some nondescript clothes for all of them. *Why is it so cold?* Collin cursed the broken weather. Seasons would change abruptly, and no crops were ever safe from the sudden frost, but there had been nearly six months of warm wet weather, and in the three days he'd spent in his cell, a winter had come to Midgard.

Their way wasn't lit, but the palfreys they rode seemed sure of foot and knew where they were going. The mud fields had frozen over, and their horse's hooves made slushy crinkling sounds as they trod along. As always, even though the crystals themselves were covered, a blue misty aura secretly illuminated Collin and his fellow crystal bearers with a magical glow. By its pale ghostly light he watched the mists of their breath swirl and dissipate. Axe's breathing produced a veritable swarm of vapor, and Collin wondered if it was his steel, or his fire, that gave it such volume.

"I assumed you'll be wanting to go to Aztoz," Janson told Collin. "It seems the likeliest of places to start your search for the djinni. Ser Ringley has promised that he will gather the Huntsmen and provide for a ship. Lord Gracious will have you sought after in most every port in Midgard, so we're to cross the wall by the smuggler's way, and meet up with the others at Tanniston." Janson must have sensed Collin's reservations. "No need to worry about the smuggling part. Ser Ringley has–"

"Wait!" Clique interrupted. They reared their horses and turned to find Clique stopped along the path. "We have to go back."

"Back, my lord?" Janson was bewildered. "If you've forgotten something, it's best we leave it."

"What I have forgotten is myself," Clique told them.

"My lord, if we go back now, we will be caught," Janson said. "The guards will be found asleep at their posts by morning, and the ruse will be up."

"Then we've no time to lose." Clique kicked his horse to trot back towards Stormbreaker and his party rode to follow.

"What is it you intend, Lord Commander?" Axe asked. "Are you to confront your father directly and explain your uncle's folly?"

"No," Clique declared. "I intend to bring Keira back to life."

They did not speak as they returned their horses and snuck back into the Stronghold. The way in was easier than the way out, and the guards still slept at their posts. Janson promised to find Ser Ringley to cancel the plans they had made, and he locked the cell door behind them. Clique and Axe fell asleep immediately, but Collin was restless. He couldn't help but feel both relieved and disappointed at the same time. *On the morrow, if the Goddess wills it, my lady will be returned to us.* He tried to find comfort in the thought, whereas he could find no comfort in his bedding, but somehow the thought frightened him. *It is one thing to wake a sleeping djinni, but to bring the dead back to life?* It seemed wrong somehow, and he felt the fear course through him. He thought of Axe, and their crystals, and the magic they'd seen. *There are stranger things in this world than the gift of life.,* he told himself. *My fear is unfounded. It is nothing,* he mused. *It is nothing...*

Sleep came slowly to Collin, and his dreams were beset by terrible shadows that hunted him from every direction. All he felt was fear that night, and as the blackest shadow drew closest, it rose before him in the darkness like a mountainous void meant to consume him. When his fear reached a climax, he awoke.

Axe and Clique were talking with Sheriff Baldric outside the cell. The doors had been opened and three guards stood nearby in a cheery mood. Collin's nightmare had faded from his memory, but he could not shake the feeling of dread that had haunted his dreams. Collin stood and wiped the sleep from his eyes. "What's going on?"

The Sheriff was dressed in finely tailored black embroidered robes, and had his full display of seventeen honors pinned to his chest. He even smelled of perfume. Clique turned to Collin with an expression of boundless good humor. "Brace yourself Collin. This news affects your standing in the Realm as much as it does my own."

Collin was startled, but the bright smile Clique gave him

dissipated his worries. "What is it? Are we to be honored for decision to resurrect Lady Keira?"

Baldric shook his head. "Best you tell Davik that yourselves."

"Then what?" Collin's mind was aswarm with possibilities.

"The revelation of the crystals by Will Tarnell in open council came as an expected shock," Clique said. "The awakening of magic, and its possession by men of both Realms and Midgard together, has helped bring the Kings to common cause. Peace accords have been reached and signed."

"That's wonderful!" Collin cheered. "The summit was a success!"

"There's more," Clique grinned. "It has been said by both Kings, that it should never be forgotten it was Royal Huntsmen of Midgard who became King Saviors, and were graced by magic for their bravery. So the Kings decided that there could only be one proper way to recognize our actions, and in so doing both secure the peace, and pave the way towards a new era for the Realm."

Collin was on edge. "So what is it?" he begged for the answer. "What did they say?"

"It seems we Royal Huntsmen have come into our namesake." Clique placed his hand on Collin's shoulder. "They have named my uncle, Lord Davik, King of the South." Collin was astonished. "Midgard has been declared a Proper Realm, and though we are not a monarchy, whosoever sits head of House and controls Stormbreaker Stronghold, and thus commands the Royal Huntsmen, also sits throne as King of the Southern Realm."

"As second in line to Stormbreaker," Collin said, "that makes you..."

"A prince." Clique smiled. "No doubt it makes for a sweet incentive to obey my uncle's wishes." Clique shook his head.

Baldric grinned. "Fear not. I will tell your uncle that you made your choice before you knew of his coronation, for that is the truth of it."

"Coronation?" Collin asked.

"Yes," Baldric said. "And one which is likely already over thanks to my being summoned down here." The Sheriff grabbed his torch from the sconce and motioned for them to follow. "If you mean to address your uncle publicly we must hurry. Everyone is gathered in the courtyard for the ceremony."

Collin took brief respite to use the chamber pot. He washed his hands, wet his face, and slicked his hair back. He felt dirty and unkempt, but Baldric pressed him to hurry, and there was no time to bathe and change into suitable attire. The clothes they had worn into the prison were stained with blood, so they were resigned to wear the black woolen robes that Janson had given them. "They will think us humble in these robes," Collin posed as they made their way towards the courtyard.

"Better they think us monks, than learn we spent three days in jail," Axe quipped.

"I'm sure they'll *smell* that revelation," Clique suggested.

"Doubtful." Baldric snickered. "Did you really think I would *voluntarily* make myself smell this way? Five minutes amongst all those nobles and you'll come out reeking of roses for a week."

They all laughed. *He does smell like roses,* Collin thought. "Just how open was this council where Will revealed our secrets?"

"The leaders of each Realm and a handful of knights," Baldric explained. "Ser Grissel, Ser Flynn. A few guards."

"Enough that the tale will spread," Clique said. "But best we keep our crystals hidden for now... Baldric." Clique paused and faced the Sheriff. "Is there any news of Jack Havensword?"

Collin stiffened, and Baldric shook his head. "No word as of yet, but he's a wanted man all throughout the Realm. For him, nowhere is safe. He *will* turn up sooner or later. And when he does, he'll be brought here to answer for his crimes."

They walked the remainder in silence, and exited the stronghold by way of the main gate. Dozens of guards in bright full plate stood in rows near the entrance. Baldric paused and spoke briefly with a knight whom Collin did not recognize. Crowding the steps below the gate stood Lord Gracious, the two Kings, their Queens, and a number of other of knights, priests, and wizards. Will Tarnell stood beside his father with his crystal covered. The courtyard was filled with nearly two thousand people. From the banners and spectacle of colors he guessed that every noble from the city was in attendance. Collin spotted the Royal Huntsmen to the side of the steps, and drew Ser Ringley's gaze. Collin pulled down his hood, and the two men exchanged knowing nods.

Collin heard clapping and thought it was from the crowd, but when he turned he saw the castle guards were giving Clique, Axe, and himself, a round of applause. Collin had wondered if word of their crystal had spread, but by their cheers knew that it hadn't. *If they knew of our crystals, their fear of magic, and of us, would not allow so brazen an act as clapping.* He took the cheer as graciously as he could before it died down. *Magic is a thing to be feared,* he told himself. *The world is lucky that men of virtue such as ourselves possess the crystals, but for how long will that be? The Jolly Roger are down to a single crystal, the Huntsmen three, and the West one, but three still remain to be seen. And if Davenport's death has taught me anything, it is that the crystals can change hands, and with it the power to shape the world.* Collin felt a dark cloud overshadowing the mirth of such a joyous day, which was yet to reach its pinnacle with the resurrection of Lady Keira. "One day, we will all be dead," he whispered to Axe and Clique. "But the crystals will remain... The fate of Eldaria will hang in the balance with each generation." Collin's blood chilled, but Axe smiled confidently.

"All the more reason for us to find the other four crystals as quickly as possible,"Axe said. The thought filled Collin with vigor at the promise of a quest, but Clique denied them.

"No," Clique whispered.

"No?" Collin was taken by surprise.

"The others are of lesser concern," Clique said. "It's far more important that we–"

Baldric interrupted them. "I will see that Lady Keira is brought out." He motioned to the knight beside him. "Ser Donovan will escort you to Davik... *his Grace*, when it is time." It was not long before the priest overseeing the ceremony finally placed a thin gold circlet for a crown upon Davik's head. He announced the ritual complete, and bid Lord Davik Gracious of Midgard to rise King Davik Gracious, King of the South.

The roar of the crowd was deafening, and moments later it was time. Ser Donovan led the three of them out through the main gate, and as they descended the steps they drew everyone's attention. King Davik turned and ascended to meet them halfway. "Nephew..." Davik smiled and hugged Clique warmly. "I did not think you would come."

"We were in the dungeon, uncle." Clique frowned. "Or had you forgotten?"

Davik's face turned cold. "Well then. Have you made your choice, or must you speak with Robert? He's here, somewhere."

"That won't be necessary," Clique told him. "I'm sorry for the way I spoke to you. It was wrong of me to be disrespectful, though I will not apologize for taking the time to think. We both know that it was my decision to be made, and my responsibility for what the consequences would be, either way."

"And?" Davik asked. To Collin, it looked like he was on the verge of throttling Clique's neck.

"And..." Clique took Davik by his hand. "Look how many people have come to see you crowned." When Clique removed his hand, Davik held the vial in his palm. "I think it's time you give them proper demonstration for why you are now a King. Something they'll not soon forget."

The look that Davik gave was of a man whose true love was coming back to him. His cheeks blushed and his eyes watered. "Your Grace," Collin said. "Sheriff Baldric has Keira just there." He pointed up the steps. "Shall you make the attempt out here, in the open? And if so, shall you give speech?"

Davik nodded. "Yes, Collin. Yes... Ser Donovan, instruct Baldric to bring my wife just outside the gate." The knight bowed and turned away. "How does it work?" Davik whispered.

Clique shrugged. "I have no idea."

"Open it near her mouth," Axe suggested. "It is called a djinni's *breath*, so I expect she must breathe in the vapors when unsealed."

"Your Grace..." Collin spoke softly. "I must warn you. She has been several days dead."

Davik waved his words short. "I am no stranger to death. Besides... She will not be dead much longer." Collin held his breath.

"Let us hope so," Clique said cautiously.

"People of the Realm!" King Gracious faced the crowd and raised his hand. Everyone hushed and gave him their attention. "*First,* I would draw your attention to the King Saviors!" The crowd erupted into a frenzy of applause and roared with shouts of their names and cries of *long live the King Saviors!* "For their actions!" Davik motioned for Ser Tarbeld who came forward with a silver box. Davik took from it specially crafted medals of honor. Each bore the emblems of both the two Realms and Midgard. Each medal was marked with a sigil representing a full ten honors.

Collin was astounded. "I did not know honors could rank more than one."

"Well now you do!" Ser Tarbeld gave a raucous laugh. "This is just the start of it, lads," he explained as Davik pinned each of them with their prize. "The Honorable Academy will honor you as well. As will Starspire and Starcrown in due time."

Davik faced the crowd once more. "People of Midgard! Noble dignitaries of the West and East! I hereby make this promise to you all! I pledge to dedicate Midgard, the Southern Realm, towards ushering a new age of trade and goodwill between East and West! And so I promise that no man, woman, or child, anywhere in the Realm, will ever go hungry again! I will see to it that grains are shipped from across the Sea, and freely offered to both East and West for as long as necessary until the scars of war are healed!"

Collin was unsure if these promises were negotiated in treaty, but it seemed King Draven and King Tarnell were putting on the show of pleasant surprise. While most everyone wore bright colors in honor of the celebration, Queen Vivian was dressed in black veils as she grieved for the death of her brother Ser Laurence. *Even if there is breath left in the vial, it will not matter,* Collin thought sadly, for the corpse of the valiant knight who had sacrificed his life and met with the same fate as Keira, had been burned. Though he did not know for certain Ser Laurence was ashes, he knew that the Brae embraced the funeral pyre, and held fire to some special esteem, perhaps because of the djinn they possessed. Apart from the Kefkas, the West was not as tempered by the logic of Scientos, and held queer fascination with the djinn beyond just the proper respect and rituals the O'Briens were accustomed to. Even the Dravens valued Scientos, and did not worship the djinn in quite the same bedeviled manner as Western Houses. Collin was struck by the irony that Queen Vivian's son held the Water crystal, and not Axe's Fire. He almost laughed, but remembered his place when he saw the faces of the crowd staring back at him.

Davik continued his speech and everyone fell further under his charm. His words were eloquent, his voice inspiring, and he easily won the hearts and minds of everyone there that day. Right when he had them eating out of his hands, Davik drew their attention to the altar atop the steps, and the mood of the courtyard turned from celebration to sorrow. Davik sung the song of Ser Laurence's sacrifice, and told of Lady Keira's death with his unborn child still inside her. For a moment the sound of a thousand people crying filled the air. Only Davik and those few who knew of the treasure were devoid of sadness. Instead Collin's heart raced as the moment drew near, and he felt as if he might faint. *What if it doesn't work?* A darker thought crept over him. *What if Davenport lied? What if it's something else?*

Collin, Clique, and Axe followed Davik as he ascended the steps to stand beside Keira's body. She was on a wooden altar, and her body had been covered by white silk shrouds, and surrounded by scented herbs and flowers. Even so, the smell of death was overpowering, and Collin found himself holding his breath and discretely breathing through his robes. Davik made no declaration of his intentions to resurrect her, and for all intents and purposes, seemed a King publicly mourning his dead Queen. But when Davik pulled the purple silk bag from his pocket and produced the vial, Collin saw Will Tarnell stiffen and pass whispers to his father. "Are you sure about this?" Clique asked.

Davik turned to face the crowd and held the vial in the air before them. "Behold! The last treasure of the Lord of the Grey!" Then silently, he turned back to his wife, and knelt. He pulled the shroud from her body, ripped the wax seal from the stopper, and uncorked the vial by her mouth as Axe had instructed. The event was seemingly invisible to everyone save for those with crystals.

Whatever was inside the vial that gave it such a vibrant magical blue glow exited the glass and spilled into Keira's body by way of her mouth. Davik was alarmed when nothing came out, and he saw no immediate effect. He worryingly glanced back at the three of them in desperation. The three cold stares and nods to the affirmative that he received set his mind at ease. The djinni's breath coursed its way through Keira's body and coalesced in her womb. It remained there as a vibrant blue light of magic in her belly, and inhabited her unborn child.

When Keira threw back her shroud and sat up, looking as radiant with life and beauty as she ever had before, a collective gasp erupted from the crowd. No one spoke as she removed her veil and freed her lustrous red hair. "Davik? What happened?" An even deeper hush fell over the courtyard.

"You're safe now, my darling." Davik held her hand, but she recoiled in horror.

"The poison, Davik! The baby!" She clutched at her stomach in panic, their audience of thousands all gasped together, but her fear turned way to joy when she felt her child kick inside her. "He kicked... He's alive! He kicked!"

Collin saw the magic blue aura swirling in a vortex within her, and knew that the others could see it as well. "The child will be born magic," he told Davik and Keira. "I can see it."

Davik wept waves of tears and tried to speak, but the words held fast in his throat. He climbed onto the altar and they collapsed into one another's arms, where they cried hysterically from the joy of it. Collin turned and meant to address the crowd, but he found his eyes dripping tears and he could not speak. Axe saw what Collin meant to do, and himself seized the opportunity to address everyone in that glorious moment. He stood tall and spoke loud and clear. "People of Midgard! I give you Lady Keira! Your Queen!"

Never before in the history of the Realm had an announcement drawn such unanimous approval. Everyone cheered with such an upwelling of emotion that people were sobbing and screaming for joy at the same time. Davik and Keira were ushered away by priests, and attendants, and knights, and the high nobility of the O'Brien family followed along as well. Collin made eyes with his father Patrick, who looked back at Collin with pride. Beside him walked his grandfather Ronan, his older brother Liam, their wives, Keira's parents, her brother, and a number of minor nobility Collin did not recognize. All, no doubt, would wish to see the miracle of Keira O'Brien's resurrection for themselves. Collin felt a tap on his right shoulder, and turned to find Keira's beautiful servant Amy beside him. "Amy..." he managed to whisper.

"Collin..." she whispered back, then leaned up and kissed him on the lips. It was completely out of station for her to presume such an act upon nobility, but her lips tasted of cherries and she smelled like Keira's lilac bath water. After a long moment, she stepped back, and left Collin breathless. Without a word she turned and ran off to join the procession of people entering the castle. Collin licked his lips as he watched her go. *I will call upon her tonight,* he thought to himself, and smiled.

The festival of emotions that had swept over the crowd carried over into the celebratory party and feast that filled the courtyard. Hundreds of tables were brought out and set up in every inch of space available, and more food than Collin had ever seen in his life was served to everyone that attended. Collin, Clique, and Axe were swept up by proper etiquette to mingle with the crowds for hours, then eat at a table raised higher than the rest in a place of special honor. The remainder of the Royal Huntsmen were seated by the courtyard entrance to their chambers, along with a great gathering of knights. While Collin had words he wished to share with Ser

Ringley, the opportunity for them to speak privately never presented itself. Collin made jest of the irony of it all, and how in that, their moment of glory, each of them would rather be discussing matters of more importance away from prying eyes and open ears. Every conversation they shared with each passing person held with it mountains of unsaid words, and questions that could not be answered. It was an endless chore of politely smiling and thanking everyone for kind words spoken. Clique and Axe managed to get drawn away by invitations to socialize privately, but Collin remained. By the time Will Tarnell and his father, the King of the West, approached him, Collin found that for the first time since he'd met the man, he welcomed Will's presence. It was almost enough to forgive him for stealing his kill. Almost.

"King William. Prince Will." Collin rose and smiled. "You honor me with your presence."

"You may dispense with the pleasantries, Lord Commander." King William frowned. "King Davik is otherwise occupied, and no doubt will be for some time. I mean to march on the morrow, and as I cannot speak with your King, I have come to lay the burden upon you."

Collin came to attention. "What burden is that, your Grace?"

"He means me," Will snarkily replied. "*I'm* the burden."

"I do not follow," Collin politely answered.

"I'll speak plainly with you, Collin O'Brien," King Tarnell said. "My son is a drunkard, a womanizer, and a lout. He makes a mockery of his high position as heir to the throne, and has shamed me and my House for the last time." He crossed his arms and looked at Will with disdain. "The fates mock me that they have given me an oaf for an heir, one who would rather play with lutes than swords. Now that he is blessed by..." The King glanced around at the watchful eyes of faces in the crowd. "Suffice to say, I will not have the future of our Kingdom rest in the hands of such an impish child."

"I'm sorry to say, your Grace," Collin sighed, "that it cannot be removed until death."

"I don't want to take it *away* from him," the King whispered. "I want you to *train* him."

"Me?" Collin was aghast.

"No, not you, specifically." King William motioned at the Royal Huntsmen who were feasting with the knights and singing lude songs in celebration. "I want him to be a Royal Huntsman. Let him spend his life with people of high honor and integrity. Perhaps their lessons will take root within him. Let him be with others of his..." he glanced at their arms, "... caliber. It is a *burden*, I know. To have someone of his ilk sully the virtue of so noble an order, but he has never taken to squiring." The King put his arm around Collin. "It will be a grand first step in re-imagining the Royal Huntsmen as an order that defends not just Midgard, but *all* of the Proper Realm. Besides..." He smiled wickedly. "There is already one crystal knight in the Huntsmen of *Eastern* blood." He patted Collin on his back. "The crystal of the West should be in the Huntsmen as well. And at least with you lot, he can be watched over. *Properly.*"

I may no longer be Lord Commander, Collin thought, *and yet Lord Commander I remain.*

There was nothing further to say on the matter than for Collin to agree, and introduce Will to Ser Ringley. The news was taken as a shock, and while the Huntsmen had not yet been told of the crystals, Collin knew that such a conversation would have to take place soon. Will was left in Ser Ringley's care, and while he was introduced to their men, Collin left to look for Clique. His search led him to a private chamber nearby the courtyard where some of Robert Gracious' men guarded the door. They announced Collin's presence and he was soon allowed in, where Clique and his father Robert awaited. Clique's crystal was plainly visible, and it filled the air with its golden glow.

"Collin. It is good to see you again," Robert said. "I am so very proud of you and Clique."

"Thank you, my lord," Collin said as he bowed. "You honor us."

"Go ahead Clique, tell him." Robert grinned.

Clique rolled down his sleeve and covered his crystal. "Collin... Your great uncle Mickey O'Brien. Do you know him?"

Collin tried to recall. "Vaguely. He's a wizard, I know that much. I avoided the wizards tower in the Barrows in my childhood, and do not remember having words with the man. Why?"

Clique smiled. "It seems he's dedicated his life to the study of djinn, and my father believes he has knowledge of the whereabouts of the djinni of life."

"I don't *believe* it," Robert corrected him, "I *know* it. My own father Rickard told me as much. He had council with the man in the peace after the Battle of the Bridge."

"What does it matter?" Collin asked. "The treasure has been spent on Lady Keira."

"You forget," Clique said. "Davenport claimed there was another djinn's breath in the world. I mean for us to find it. And when we do, it's best we know where to bring it afterward."

"A sound plan!" Collin cheered. "So it's off to my ancestral home, the Barrows then?"

"Yes..." Clique hesitated, "But I mean for us to kill *two* birds with *one* stone, as it were." He waited no time in explaining further. "My lord father has spoken at length with our King, and has decided that above all else, the most perilous threat facing our Realm is the black plague."

"But Ser Ringley destroyed all traces of it," Collin argued.

"All traces of it in Midgard," Clique added coldly.

"There are rumors of its like being seen in the North," Robert told him. "The Barrows can be reached by ship, and are only six days ride from Astermount, the port city of the North."

Collin understood. "So you mean for us to learn what we can of the djinn, then head to Astermount to investigate rumors of black seed?"

"Not just us." Clique patted Collin on the shoulder. "The Royal Huntsmen, and two companies of men that my father has afforded us."

"Forty heavy horse," Robert added. "Three hundred soldiers, a hundred archers, and sixty knights."

"That is a veritable army!" Collin marveled. "Do we need so many?"

Robert grimaced. "I have heard tale that the wild clans which populate the badlands have grown restless. They've been spotted roaming as far Southwest as Herald's Point."

"But that's along the road between the Barrows and Astermount!" Collin objected.

"And *that* is why you will have an army." Robert laughed. "I'll not have our crystal bearers be overtaken by barbarians."

"I already know the perfect Captain to take us there. We'll need no more than two ships..." Clique looked to his father, who nodded in agreement. "Say your goodbyes quickly, Collin. Then inform our Huntsmen, and fetch your things." Clique grinned. "We depart for Cliffwatch at first light."

Nimmet rested his hands on Havik's shoulders, and he looked upon Havik's face with gentle compassion. "How?" Havik asked softly, at a loss for words. *I have been beaten.* In those moments Havik felt neither fear, nor rage. He felt only humility.

Nimmet took Havik by the arm and led him away from Kevin, whose wounds were now being attended to by Brownbeard. Jhev stood nearby guarding him.

Once out of ear shot, Nimmet stopped and spoke again in Ancient. "One drink from my stream. One night's sleep beneath my branches. One dream." Nimmet ran his hands through Havik's hair as a mother might her child. *My squire... The boy must remember a false dream. I have been unkind to him,* he mused, before disciplining himself to concentrate. It's then that he remembered the reference.

Havik half smiled, pleased for his wise wizard's counsel, but also horrified by the implications of it. "You speak of the Goddess," Havik declared. Nimmet smirked but did not speak. *Tread carefully now, Havik,* he heard his uncle telling him. *You are on treacherous ground, and each word you speak carries with it dire consequence.* "Ma'at's mother drank the stream of life. She slept beneath the world tree. She dreamed. And she gave birth to a god." Havik dared to think he might have puzzled a piece of this thing's true plot from its riddle. "Do you mean to impregnate the girl, and birth kin?" *A race of Stygian gods.* The thought chilled him.

Nimmet raised his head back and laughed with such fervor that it drew attention. Narvis remained some distance away on her garron, and while the others all looked she kept her eyes on Kevin. *That is odd. She obeys my command to be wary of Kevin, and has not seen Nimmet is the fiend.* Havik held his breath as he turned back to face Nimmet.

The creature's mirth sobered, and his smile faded. "Men are not born gods, Eldarian. And those you call gods have only stolen their divinity. The one you call Goddess was once nothing more than a woman. And the one you call Isfet was once nothing more than a man." *Why is it telling me this?* Havik asked himself. *First it plays that mad game of wits and brings me to nearly killing my squire. It goaded me to kill him...* Havik swallowed, thirsting for answers. *But it also tried to talk me down. It gave me a choice... Has this thing been testing me? What does it want? Who is it? What is it? If it will speak, then I will ask my questions and have my answers.*

"Once?" Havik asked, taking hold of the opportunity to question a god.

Nimmet placed his finger upon Havik's mouth. "Predictable." Nimmet's voice echoed with ethereal tones. "All men seek divinity, but leave it to a *Davenport* to seek it so quickly." Havik wondered whether this thing mocked his name because of what it had only just come to learn, or if it had some sinister knowledge of his House from before their paths had crossed.

"M'lord!" Brackens shouted out to them. Nimmet gently removed his finger from Havik's lips. "What's to be done with Kevin? We've got a proper amount of lumber, and some good meat. Shall I set about starting a fire, and readying the wagon for repairs?" Havik was annoyed by the interruption, and before he could wave Brackens off, the first mate continued. "By the way m'lord," Brackens said. "Our apologies for taking so long to return, but I bear troubled news from the gate."

Havik was startled by this and waited impatiently for him to go on. "Well! Out with it!"

"Our way was impeded by some great migration of animals. Packs of elk and caribou, moose, and other queer sorts of large game were carving a path South and West through the forest." Brackens stiffened. "Brownbeard told us it was not uncommon for the animals to move to warmer climates when the cold winds blow, and it was no queer thing but simply a wonder of the North and a blessing to behold. Problem is, m'lord, such game o' plenty brought a number of predators as well. Brownbeard noted the tracks of a great pack of wolves, and we took greater trouble to avoid them catching scent of us."

"Aye!" Havik answered. "So there's wolves in the woods. What's the trouble then?"

"They caught our scent anyway, m'lord," Brackens face paled. "We thought we'd lose them in passing through the gate, but Narvis swears she saw wolves follow us into the Barrens. A mighty queer thing for wolves to do. The gate is afoul with odor, and your wizards said wolves would abhor the place, especially with all the fresh meat to be had out there. But they stalked us all the same." He turned and looked into the empty purple distance. "Might be they're out there right now, m'lord. Coming..."

Havik was unhappy at the thought of wolves, but had better things to concern himself with. *The lies and legends of a self proclaimed god trump a few wolves in the woods.* Still, even amidst the ever descending spiral of madness Havik's mind was taking, he remained a lord and their steadfast ranger Commander. "Everything else can wait!" Havik yelled. "I want you and Narvis to go get the sphere."

"It's under a bit of ore, m'lord!" Brackens answered. "It could take a while."

"Then you'd best get started!" Havik commanded. And with that Brackens and Narvis trotted wide past Kevin, Jhev, and Brownbeard, and rode to the wagon.

Havik turned back to Nimmet. *Let that keep it thinking. Soon, at least, the foam will be close at hand, and the issue of the seed will be forced.* Havik smiled. *It must know by now I have none on me, and yet it still insists to play upon my wits. What does it want? What is it after?*

Nimmet gave a knowing smile that made Havik feel as if his mind were laid bare to the beast. "Your two gods are of the same ilk, Eldarian," it said again in harmonic Ancient words. "Both drank of her spirit and became as brother and sister, daughter and son. Though both drank their fill of her, the man's thirst was not quenched, and he yearned for more."

"Her?" Havik asked, and he regretted the question immediately. *Eldaria.*

"Eldaria," it said.

"Eldaria is just a name we give the planet." Havik grinned. *This thing must respect the fact I speak Ancient. I could hug my uncle for those lessons now. But it may yet underestimate what I truly know.* "Yes," Havik went on. "I am noble born, and I know of worlds beyond the Gate of Heavens. A world is Stone and Fire, Water and Air, but it is no living thing. It is neither a he, nor a she."

Nimmet snickered with such a derisive tone that Havik wondered if his tutelage of the Davenport mysteries or his remembrance of them had erred. *Can a planet be alive?* "You could not be more mistaken..." Nimmet's blue Gulgari eyes sparkled like an ocean on a clear day. "Worlds are gods, and Eldaria is the Mother of all gods that ever will be. Beyond the Gate lay her children." Havik trembled. "And upon her head once sat a crown of eight jewels, and all creation marveled over it, and her for wearing it."

"The eight colors." Havik found himself say the words aloud. He composed himself in sight of the thing. "The eight elements are simply virtues of nature. Wind may be a thing we capture in our sails, but how can it be jewel?"

Nimmet smiled, and the seas became rough in his eyes. "Elements are made of magic, and magic can be frozen." *Like the djinn,* Havik thought. "All mothers have mothers, and it was *she* who bore Eldaria that *crowned* her. All those gods that once were, including the Mother's mother, held hands in willing sacrifice. They gave to their favorite child an empty Castle and her jeweled crown to rule it by." Havik was lost in his words. "So what is a lonely god to do? Why open the Gate to her Castle, of course, and populate her Kingdom."

"How can fire be frozen?" Havik asked, and felt himself a fool for it.

"As crystal," Nimmet said, and his eyes twinkled with the flashes of distant thunder. "The eight jewels were the elements made gem. Through each, Eldaria controlled all elements of creation."

"You said she *once* had her crown." Havik felt strange as the fear coursed through him for the first time in his conversation with the thing, and yet it was not the obsidian horror that made him fear, but the unknown. Still, his feeling of cowardice was heightened by his intrinsic lust for power, and he thought his own eyes must be sparkling too, as he pressed himself on to ask a god about a buried treasure. *Perhaps Kevin was right all along, and I am having a fever dream somewhere as I lay dying.* "The crown. What happened to it?"

Nimmet sighed deeply and looked to the floor. "A long sad tale... Perhaps another time." *He does nothing but toy with me, as if I am some amusement.* Nimmet's eyes met Havik's once more. *This is like some game to him,* Havik thought, and yet he was nothing but hypnotized by the thing's knowledge and presence. *I must know its secrets.*

"Tell me. Please," he begged.

"Eldaria's son was thirsty." Nimmet sung the sad song. "He wished to leave the Castle and drink in the Kingdom, but it was not meant for her chosen heirs to mix with her lesser born children. He grew to despise his Mother, and he desired her crown. Why should the son not rule when he was fit to? So to keep her son from leaving, she set her daughter to guard the Gate to the Castle. The son, enraged by this, threatened to kill his sister if their Mother did not relinquish her crown. When the sister freely offered herself to the sacrifice to protect her Mother, she stepped away from the Gate. The son seized the opportunity gained by his ruse, and closed the Gate to the Castle himself. If he could neither drink the Kingdom nor rule it, then nor could his Mother, for once he closed the Gate even she could not open it. The Mother, in her anger, tore the crown from her head and broke it into eight pieces. If she could not rule, then no one could. But the son was not satisfied. He grabbed each of the eight gems, one by one, and as he had no crown to wear them, he took the gems in hand, and crushed them into a single jewel." Nimmet paused to sip from his wineskin with a queer smile.

Havik heard himself gasp. "What happened next?" He felt a child again, being lectured by his uncle.

"Doom." His smile faded. "And Chaos." Nimmet finished the rest of his wine in two long gulps, and wiped the purple drops from his chin with a gasp for breath. Havik's mind was both awash with questions and yet silent and still. He did not know what to ask or think. Fortunately for him, Nimmet was not yet done pontificating. *Thousands of years in a pit must give even a god a thirst for wine and speech.* Havik stifled a mad chuckle.

Nimmet continued. "The son may have gained the gem, but he did not know the mysteries of the thing. The jewels were not objects to be had, but living beings with their own identities, wants, and even children. They abhorred being forced into a single body when they were of eight minds. So they chose for their one body one mortal form. A chosen hero to come to their aid against the son. And so the hero confronted the god. The magic of the son's gem was useless against its avatar, but the hero's one advantage would not prove to be enough. The hero was slain by the son. As his last dying act, with the minds of the gem in agreement, the hero killed the crystal, and the crystal let itself be killed. The eight Aspects ceased to exist, their immortal lineage come to an end, and the single crystal broke to countless pieces." Nimmet took a breath. "In one moment magic died, and around the broken crystal the universe broke as well. Reality abhors a paradox, and the vacuum of magic and the tear in creation's fabric *must* be contained, or else."

"Or else what?" Havik asked, unable to contain himself.

Nimmet tightened his hands up into balls, then popped them outward with his fingers outstretched. "Poof! The end."

"The end?"

"Of everything, everywhere, everywhen. All confined to the Castle, of course. That is, if the Gate remains *closed*, of course." Nimmet sighed.

"And if it were open?" Havik asked.

"Then the tear would end the Kingdom as well, I'm sad to say. And every man and god within it. But fortunately for everyone, everywhere, everywhen, the pieces of the crystal, and the Lord of Chaos too, both became trapped in eternal prison. How or by who, I cannot say. But it came to be that within a single day of judgment they were separated from all of space and time forever. A dungeon cell in the Castle, if you will, and even that was lost in a hallway millenniums long. So instead of all magic dying..."

"All magic froze," Havik whispered. For the briefest of moments, Havik felt as if some unquantifiable weight was lifted from his shoulders, but Nimmet poured his speech like thick syrup, and gave further performance.

"But, even now, the son, through the bars of his cage, reaches out with his dark influence. His minions seek to open the Gate, and free him."

Havik gasped again. "But wouldn't that destroy everything?"

Nimmet smiled. "Everything and everyone. Even the crystal's frozen children, whom you call the djinn, would cease to be. Only the crystals would remain, as well as whoever possesses them. For around them all reality bends, even if it doesn't exist."

"But the crystals were broken into pieces. How can the son ever possess them?"

"Eternity is a long time for every piece to be found..." Nimmet sighed, and Havik knew the tale was done.

But Havik was not satisfied. The strange history filled with unfamiliar words seemed to leave him with more questions than his logic could account for. All of them hinged on one crucial detail. One question which had remained unanswered. *Who is he?*

"You mean you still do not know who I am?" Nimmet asked. Havik felt the fear crescendo and his blood grew cold. *Did it just respond to a question I gave no voice?*

"Yes. *It* did," Nimmet said. *It can read my thoughts?* "Yes," he said again. "*It* can."

Havik was infuriated, and he spoke aloud this time. "Then why put me through such deceptions with the others? Why pretend?"

Nimmet smiled a most wicked smile. "Because I wanted to see how you think. Yes, it was a test. Why? Because if the son is to gather his minions then why shouldn't I? Your Ancient blood is what I call Eldarian, the first race. Yes, it does give you advantage, and no, I do not know your family's line. Why am I doing all this? Why gather my minions at all? Why toy with a Davenport to see if he could serve me? Who am I? You mean you still do not know?"

Havik spoke aloud. "You said you were a god!"

"I *am* a god," Nimmet declared.

"But who *are* you?"

Nimmet stepped back and threw his arms wide. "You still do not know?"

Nimmet's blue eyed gaze stared deep into Havik's soul and his words were grave.

"I am..."

And at that Nimmet looked up.

Havik's mind crystallized in one great realization as the puzzle was solved. Havik followed Nimmet's gaze into the sky above, and there beyond the broken pieces of the Sea of Heavens the Dead Star sat silently, and watched. *The Dead Star...* And the words it had spoke repeated in his mind. *Worlds are gods.*

Havik's gaze returned to the Gulgari sailor standing before him. The one with the brown hair and blue eyes. The one he thought had a sharp mind. "Are you?"

Nimmet nodded, and smiled. "I am." *Worlds are gods.*

"The Goddess of light!" Havik spoke his realizations aloud. "Ma'at is the daughter! She's the Red Star! Isfet is the Silver Star! And you..." Havik took a step backwards.

"I am," Nimmet said.

"But how can that be?" Havik asked, truly astonished.

"Why do you think men think of their gods as men?" It asked

through Nimmet's mouth. "Because while all worlds are gods, so too are all gods men."

"So what then, is the tree?" Havik asked directly. *If I am to speak to a star, let me rise to the occasion.* Havik immediately rued the thought, as he remembered his thoughts were as if spoken word.

"Think of the tree, as an antenna," Nimmet said.

"And what, pray tell, is an antenna?" Havik inquired.

Nimmet sighed just then, and Havik cursed his godly ignorance. "Think of the tree as a head, upon which shall rest my crown of gems. Well..." Nimmet paused, reading Havik's thoughts. "Let's just say the head won't be planted on Eldaria." And with that Nimmet looked up to the Dead Star, as if he were gazing back at his own reflection through a polished silver mirror. "It is too late for that, now..."

"*Your* crown..." Havik said. "But the crystals are locked away in Isfet's prison! And this still doesn't answer my question! Fine! You are a god! You are the Dead Star above made flesh below before me. But you said Eldaria had only bore herself two chosen heirs, and they are the red and silver worlds in the sky. But who then are you? If all other worlds are the children of the Mother, then are you another one of her sons?"

"No. She's not my mother," Nimmet told him. "I must apologize, I fear I lied about one tiny little thing. Not quite *every* one of the original gods held hands and plunged to death so freely for Eldaria to claim her throne. *One* clawed its way back from the depths of death itself, and when the universe broke in a single place, the Gate cracked, and *one* slipped through. Yes, Havik. Yes. I am to Eldaria as an uncle, and it seems my sister's chosen daughter has led the Kingdom astray. I am back to see things set to proper order. What is my name? Well... As a King requires a crown, one which I do not have, and a noble lord requires a title... My name shall be Prince.

Prince... of... Darkness. Yes, I quite like the sound of that. I could be Prince of Death, as men call me the Dead Star, but I'm not quite dead, now am I? No. My name is Prince, and as for you... As you have *thought* well enough to please me, I shall allow you to be my first servant if you will swear yourself to me. Say the words, and you shall *forever* belong to me, no matter what. And should I ever achieve my crown and the Kingdom is born anew, you will live on, with me, to begin again."

Havik knew better than to even think of the alternative. "Yes, my Prince," Havik said as he made his choice, and knelt. *I will serve my Prince well.*

"M'lord!" Brackens shouted. Havik broke his gaze with Prince and turned to see Donner Brackens waving their attention from the wagon.

"What is it?" Havik yelled.

"It's best you look yourself, m'lord! Come at once to see!" Brackens cried again.

Havik and Prince each shared a mystified expression, and the two of them ran over to find what the commotion was about. Jhev had come as well, though Brownbeard remained with Kevin, where he had put the boy to sleep and was now applying poultice to wound. All around them sat bloodied rags.

"What's happened?" Havik asked.

Narvis sat on the edge of the wagon atop a pile of the silvery speckled ore. Her hands and face were covered by that silvery soot from the handling of the star metal, and it was clear she had been crying from the streaks of clean upon her dirty cheeks. Havik climbed atop the wagon, where Brackens was standing above a hole in the ore pile that had been cleared away.

"At least we know why the wagon broke," Brackens quipped. Havik looked down at the cloth bundle that held the sphere. "Damn thing seems to have taken root, m'lord. I had a look see under the wagon from the other side, and there's a whole damned trunk. Must have been a small one before I left to get lumber, cause I didn't notice it. But it's there *now*, alright! And holding the wagon firm to the ground."

"No!" Prince yelped as he climbed onto the wagon and pushed Havik out of the way. "No! No, no, no, no, no! No!" Prince dropped to his knees and began to grab at the ore and fling the pieces aside to better uncover the cloth.

"Cheer up, Nimmet," Brackens chirped. "We can saw the wagon around it, and put her back together. Don't you worry either m'lord. We've enough lumber to fix it and return with both wagons of the stuff, just as planned."

Nimmet tore at the bundle and pulled out handfuls of straw. There within the glass sphere had shattered into pieces, and where once was a foamy seed there now was a tightly twisted knot of moving black vines. Havik got a sick feeling in his stomach.

"No! This *cannot* be! No!" Prince cried as he tore away the last cloth and beheld the core of writhing branches seething with expectant life. "There is no time to be wasted! We must cut the thing loose before its roots get any deeper! We can't let it take root here!"

And with that, Havik saw his chance. His mind was silent, and his uncle whispered the words, *Do not hesitate,* and Havik obeyed. Without a thought, he took a single step towards Prince, and slipped the cheese blade gently from the man's belt. Then, with the grace of a dancer, Havik knelt behind his Prince, and from left to right, slit his throat.

Red blood and Stygian fluid sprayed from the wound in rhythmic bursts propelled by Prince's heart. Havik's servants stood shocked at the unexpected assassination of the sailor, and were shocked further still when they saw the black liquid seeping from his neck amongst the crimson. When Havik saw the mass of vines greedily consume the spilt gore, only to tremble and flourish with growth from their meal, he also saw further opportunity. Without thought Havik pushed Prince into the pit, where the coiling plant crept over him.

Prince struggled against the embrace of the vines, and with all his strength pulled himself to his feet. For each twirling tendril Prince ripped from his body, others grew anew to strangle at his limbs. His stormy blue eyes looked deep into Havik's with some form of godly terror, and Prince let loose a horrible screech that pained the ears of all who heard it. Havik fell over disoriented, and his hand found a heavy piece of star metal ore. His fingers tightened around it, and with his ears ringing and the blood in his head boiling, Havik stood to his Prince and bashed in his skull. A splash of black fluid sprung from the ruin of Nimmet's head and came to rest upon Jhev's leg. Prince was taken down by the vines. When they consumed him the plant rumbled with a quickening.

Havik believed Jhev to be sounding a horrendous cry of terror as he stared at his leg, whereupon a small bit of Stygian fluid crept up his body. But Havik's ears were deadened to sound. "Take off your damned pants!" he yelled, and Jhev immediately set himself to the task. Brackens stood at the edge of the wagon, and when Havik looked he saw Brackens' eyes elsewhere. Seemingly with inspiration, Brackens leapt from the wagon.

Jhev unbuckled his belt and tugged at his breeches when the wagon began to rise and shift. Havik tumbled from his feet and fell with a painful thump onto the rough ore. Vines grew upward from the pile at an unsettling pace, and the wagon lifted into the air. Havik crawled to Jhev and pulled him from the wagon onto the ground in a tumble. When Havik regained his wits and came to his knees, he saw Jhev's pants were removed, but the liquid was still slithering up the bare skin of his leg. Jhev and Havik's panic were short lived, as

Brackens appeared beside them, and doused the small obsidian horror with salt from his jar. They watched as the fluid sizzled within the salt. It balled together and rolled off his leg as would a solid black marble.

"I had a queer thought, m'lord, and it seems to have paid off," Brackens smiled. Havik's hearing was returning, for to him the words were muffled but audible. "It's the salt from the pit. I saw the jar just over yonder. Nimmet must have unloaded it from the wagon. Since he was the demon, I figured if he meant to get rid of it, it might be of some use to us. Turns out I was right."

Jhev laughed as his panic subsided. "Thank the Goddess! A sound logic if I ever heard it. Right my lord?"

Havik grabbed at his injured head and smirked. "Actually, I told Nimmet to unload it, to make room for star metal." Jhev and Brackens looked to each other in revelation. "Your logic should have been, the thing was solid when in salt, why not be solid by salt again."

"A lucky break then," Brackens quipped, and soon all three were laughing. It's then that they heard the howling of the wolves.

Beside them the wagon had risen near eight feet into the air and chunks of star metal were being tossed every which way. The tree continued its maddened growth with fresh vines from the central mass plunging into the ground and taking root before them. Beyond the swelling tree a pack of wolves was visible in the distance. Havik counted their numbers. *More than a dozen.*

"Brownbeard!" Havik cried out. "Wolves!" He pointed to the distance, and he knew when Brownbeard saw, for the man leapt to his feet in a panic. "Get my squire to horse! Don't let him be taken!"

By the time commands were given, Jhev and Brackens were already to their feet. *What should I do with Prince's frozen form?* Havik wondered, as he looked down upon the marble in the pile of salt, but his choice was interrupted by the obsidian horror's fell screech. *He is relentless!* Havik thought, and he instantly regretted the unspoken words. Prince's body was no longer recognizable as Nimmet when it came into view standing above them on the wagon. It jumped down and took a knee on the ground nearby, before rising up to look upon them. Jhev, Brackens, and Havik all stood petrified in dread of its loathsome form. Flesh, bone, and black bile were entwined as one in the grotesque shape of a man.

If ever, in all his mortal life, Havik Davenport ever truly felt fear, it was in that one moment. Before him stood an angry undead god. Looming behind *him* grew the world tree, which he could only assume was corrupted, as its roots were ash grey, its branches onyx and oak, its vines black, and its budding leaves a wicked purple blemished with black spots. *Dead leaves for a Dead Star.* High in those branches his wagon of priceless star metal teetered on edge. In the distance a pack of large wolves was bearing down upon them, and Brownbeard was dragging his wounded squire to a nearby horse. His only allies beside him to face the foe were a spy for a rival House, and his Captain, who was naked from the waist down and peeing directly onto the cold dirt below. *A fine crew. But where's Narvis?* He regretted verbalizing his thoughts, but he could not help himself. His gaze fell upon the girl who was on the floor unconscious beneath the wagon from which she'd clearly fallen. The wood of the wagon was crackling with stress even then, and bits of silvery star metal dust clouded the air around her and threatened the heavier ore above. Her left leg was bent in a queer direction, and Havik knew that it was broken. Prince's eyes met Havik's for one terrible second, then he turned his abominable form around and ran at Narvis.

"Narvis!" Havik screamed. He pressed his feet into the ash to begin his mad dash to save her. But all at once he kissed dirt as his face planted into the ground when some unknown assailant hit him from behind. Havik had no need to ruminate over who the foe was, for he was uninjured, and when he rolled over he saw the underside of a large wolf leaping over him. *There must be more than one pack!* He cursed his ill fortune and sat up to find Brackens had been knocked over as well. Jhev was standing frozen to his fear. *They ignore us,* he managed to think, as he saw his Prince run past Narvis with the wolves chasing at his heels. One leaped at him, but he swatted it away with a terrible godly strength. The poor creature's ribs were shattered by the force of it, and it tumbled beside the tree. They watched Prince and the wolves turn and exit their view, when a great root rose from the ground beside the injured wolf. In three villainous seconds it grew into the wolf and therein multiplied, for thousands of saplings sprouted from every orifice of the creature. The transformation left a fine mist of vaporized blood in the air. Jhev bent to his knees and vomited.

Do not hesitate! Havik's uncle shouted in his ear, and he made his way towards Narvis. When he reached her he knelt beside her, checked her for breath, and looked up. The sound of splitting wood rained down upon him with silvery dust on its coat tails. With no time to spare, Havik took the girl from under her arms and carried her away as fast he could manage. The wagon collapsed behind them in a blast of sound and fury, and he leaped with her, and fell to the floor. The wood that remained in the branches slowly showered down in pieces, as Havik got up and took stock of the situation once again.

"Brackens!" Havik shouted, and the man's eyes met his. "Come help Narvis!" Havik stood and walked towards Jhev. "Jhev! Jhev!"

Jhev shook out of his terror, bent over, and pulled up his pants. "What?"

"Go get horses and bring them back here! Can you do that?"

"Yes," Jhev resolved, and off he ran.

Havik stopped for a moment and looked down upon the tiny dark marble that sat in the pale white salt. As he palmed at his belt for a vial of some sorts to contain the thing, the ground trembled across the whole of the area. Beneath him and all around, the ground opened up to millions of tiny white and black saplings that grew with incredible rate. *This place will be overrun in minutes!* Havik thought, before he noticed something unusual. No saplings grew round the spilled salt, and when one should chance to touch it, the plant's stalk burned and shriveled to dust. Havik discovered he no longer had the knife, but his clothes had been ripped so he easily managed to tear away a piece of fabric. He gently scooped the black marble in a palm full of salt, wrapped it all up in a wad of cloth, and hurriedly rejoined Brackens and Narvis.

"Quickly Donner!" Havik said. "Pour that salt of yours in a circle round the two of you." Brackens did as he was told. "No, only use half of it. Yes. A full circle. And splash a little here and there for good measure. That's right."

"Why, m'lord?" Brackens queried as he finished, but Havik only took the jar of salt, and thrust the bit of cloth at him.

"Take this," Havik said when he handed him the small wrap. Before Brackens could ask, he answered. "It's a bit of salted horror. Keep it safe, in case I don't return. Wait for the horses, then take her to safety."

Brackens held the cloth close. "What do *you* mean to do m'lord?"

Havik swallowed. "Whatever I can." The man nodded to him. *Good Donner Brackens.* "And Brackens!"

"Yes, m'lord?" he asked.

"I know you are an O'Brien spy." Havik smiled at him. "And I do not care!"

With that Havik held the jar close in both hands, and ran wide round the collapsed wagon. The sinister sapling field spread out nearly twenty yards round the central stalk, and half a score of secondary roots were taking hold now, each growing trees of their of own. As Prince came into view, Havik spied that it was engaged in mortal battle with a dozen wolves. More still loomed in the distance and would be in the encampment soon. Prince had grown half a yard in the few minutes he had been out of sight, and when he lifted one of the wolves over his head and ripped it into halves, somehow the gore that poured from it increased his terrible Princely stature. *Eleven wolves now,* Havik cruelly jested, as he took his fate in hand, and ran towards the devilish entity.

As he approached it one of the nearby wolves turned and growled at him. For a second Havik questioned whether he had come to make a grave error, and that it might have been more timely for him to wait until either the wolves, or the demon known as Prince, were victorious. Either way, the question was removed from his concern when Prince turned and gripped the wolf that eyed him by its throat. He lifted the beast into the air with powerful arms muscled of bone and flesh and corruption. Prince had two mounds of dark bile upon his disfigured face that might have passed for eyes. They gawked at Havik as Prince removed the wolf's spine through its throat, and tossed both body and bone in opposite directions. When the thing opened its mouth and let loose its horrific hateful shriek, Havik screamed to his furious maximum as well, and tossed the contents of the jar into the air. Much of the sacred salt splashed across the thing's chest and face, but most *by the grace of the Goddess* struck true to its mark and fell down the demon's gaping gullet.

Prince grabbed at his own throat and tore vine and flesh from his body, all the while grunting in execrable pain. His form seemed to sizzle and solidify under the burning presence of the salt over his body. The wolves saw themselves no hesitation and were soon upon him. Havik backed away from the grizzly sight as Prince screamed while the pack of wolves tore him to shreds and devoured him. Havik had little time to wonder whether Prince would live on to find a new mortal form, or whether he would become a wolf, or even if perhaps he would be truly dead. As Prince's foul black blood spilt to the ground in sheets, a fell thing occurred that frightened Havik to the bone. All around Prince the saplings that grew rose in such a sudden and furious fashion, that it sent Havik tripping backwards. The monstrous sylvan grove consumed Prince and wolves together in a heaving gulp. The stalks of the plant seemed like a flesh itself as a pulsing sac of leaf and petal formed. The whole mass dripped with a vile purple sap, and all around its hideous pulsing anatomy black flowers bloomed. The petals extended near a foot in width, and their transformation from bud to feral splendor lasted only the time it took for Havik to stand. By the time he had stopped marveling at the sight and was prepared to turn and run in horror, the buds within the blossoms burst, and released a deluge of tiny black seeds that rose up and caught the wind. Havik's fear overtook him, and when he did turn and run, all he could think of was escaping to someplace upwind.

Havik ran until the saplings were no longer underfoot. With a gasp of exhaustion from his mad sprint, he came to a stop and took view of the camp. Doom had befallen it. The other pack of wolves had arrived and set upon the horses in a frightful bloodbath. The second wagon of star metal that had been pulled up alongside the central stalk was nowhere to be seen amongst the brambles of black growth. It was no more than a minute before Jhev rode up alongside Havik. The Captain rode upon his garron, with three other garrons in tow.

"Their packs are laden with food and what metal I could gather," Jhev said proudly.

"What about Brackens and Narvis?" Havik asked, but he already knew the answer.

"Lost in the brambles. I could not see nor reach them."

As Havik mounted his horse, the two of them spied Brownbeard upon one of the drays. Havik's unconscious squire was slung over his saddle and tied to a second dray of his own. Havik and Brackens started towards them, but they stopped when they saw the wolves. Four of the beasts ran out from the budding brush and nipped at the horse's heels. "Brownbeard! Behind you!" The warning was to no avail, as a wolf leapt and tore the throat from the horse, bringing Brownbeard and his mount down to the dirt. Havik cried aloud in frustration as he saw the wolves set upon his beloved jester. They each seemed to grab him from a different limb, and tore his body to shreds in a frenzy of bloodlust. Jhev seemed to half say Brownbeard's name before vomiting the wine he must have downed when he recovered the steeds. Kevin's horse ran terrified from the carnage, and trotted off in the unfortunate direction that led away from Havik and towards another group of wolves.

Havik reared his horse around, and with a shout commanded it forward. Jhev grabbed the reins for the two extra garrons and followed Havik behind him. They had only ridden for a minute before three wolves had gained sight of them and began to make chase. Neither one spoke as they rode the horses to gallop, for the wolves would not be left behind so easily, and they were coming upon their rear with want for blood in their predacious eyes. When the first of their two extra horses fell to the first wolf, Havik rode alongside Jhev and extended his hand.

"Your sword!" Havik shouted. "Give me your sword!"

Jhev unsheathed his blade and held it out hit hilt first. Havik reached to grab hold of it but the distance was too great. As Havik adjusted his horse by the reins and steadied himself for a second attempt at getting the weapon, one of the wolves pawed at Jhev's garron and wounded it. The horse slowed, and bucked, and Jhev fell to the ground.

Havik stopped and dismounted. Jhev had been knocked unconscious, and the wolf had taken down the horse and was in the process of finishing his kill. Havik ran for the lost blade, and when he recovered it turned to his fallen comrade. The third wolf had reached Jhev by that time and sunk his teeth into Jhev's side. The fur of the foul creature was knotted with black seed. Jhev awoke with a startling fright, and Havik lunged forward. He took a wide swing with the bastard sword and cut the wolf across the neck and shoulder. Hot blood dripped from Jhev's wound and the wolf's throat. It backed away from Jhev, snarling, and bared its pink teeth at Havik. He held the point of the sword out and the wolf backed away.

"Jhev, are you alright?" Havik asked, as he stared down the creature.

"Yes... Yes, it's not too deep."

The wolf backed further away from the blade, gave one last growl at Havik, then charged the horse Havik had just dismounted. The horse bucked and began to run, but got no more than ten yards before being brought down and slain by the wolf. Their last remaining horse had run off scared back towards the camp.

Havik and Jhev looked around in a panic as Havik brought his friend to his feet. The wolves that had chased them were sated with the kills of the horses. Two of the mount's had lost their saddlebags in the battle, and the sacks were strewn upon the ground a good distance away from the feeding wolves. One of the sacks was torn, and its spilled silver dust hinted at the star metal held within.

"Grab what you can!" Havik commanded.

Jhev took his bastard sword back and sheathed it, while Havik collected as many sacks as he could carry and strung them over his shoulder. Jhev did the same, with each of their packs containing ample provisions, clothes, and whatever star metal they could manage to carry.

The two of them set off in the direction of the gate, not once breaking the sullen silence that overtook them. Havik tried not to think. For hours their fear kept hold of them as they convinced themselves the wolves were going to be upon them at any minute. But, by the time each of them could press no further, the wolves had still not appeared. Havik and Jhev ate a brief meal, and Jhev drank a full skin of wine from the four he had carried with them.

After a timeless and dreamless sleep, Havik woke to find Jhev had fallen ill in the night. A fever had taken hold of him and he had grown delirious. Havik examined his wounds and suspected his wolf bite was doing poorly. Havik poured bits of rum on it, and did what he could with clean cloth, but he was no healer. They both knew that without Brownbeard or Narvis, his illness would have to remain untreated until they reached the ship. Havik knew that would be a long journey, but he could not risk boiling the wrong root, or using the wrong leaf to bind his wounds. They had none of the healing herbs with them in the packs they had recovered, and their knowledge of the foreign plant life in the North was nonexistent. Havik missed Brownbeard fiercely in that moment, and relived the jester's bitter end once more in his mind. *No, do not think of it. I do not have the luxury of idle thought. I can hide in my cabin and unwind the madness of gods and demons, but first I must reach the ship.*

Fortunately, after Havik did what little could be done to help speed Jhev's recovery, the man still was strong enough of mind and body to walk. So they stood together, and with precious cargo slung over their shoulders, side by side they pressed further on. Havik kept close watch on Jhev, but the man simply drank his wine and marched in sullen silence. It would not be until they reached the entrance of the gate, after two more days of travel, that Jhev had finally seemed near exhaustion. "Just through that gate and we'll be out of the Barrens, Jhev," Havik told him when the opening to the Demon's Gate presented itself. But Jhev's willpower to carry further had almost fully left him by then. His face was pale, his pulse weak, and they were all out of wine. He only managed to muster a limp nod before he pulled his pack tight over his shoulder and pressed on into the tunnel.

Havik stood a moment and looked back the way they'd come. The past two days in the Barrens the wolves had kept their chase, and he woke often in the night to search the horizon for their presence. Each and every time he woke, he saw them. *The wolves are stalking us,* Havik realized, but he could not bring himself to tell his weary Captain. *That will surely drain the last of his conviction to press on.* And each and every time he looked for the wolves, there, looming above them on the horizon, grew the corrupt world tree. Its dreadful countenance must have reached several hundred yards by now, and the royalty of its magnificent branches were crowned with a head of black leaves that sparkled like a Red Starset beneath the light of the Dead Star's purple aura. In the air above the shimmering leaves, clouds of the black seeds were taken by the winds, and rose into the skies above. Even now the dark cloud seemed to be rising over the ridge wall, ever visible against the twinkling backdrop of the endless lightning storm in the skies above the Barrens. Havik took a deep breath.

If I am to sit and ponder the horrors I've witnessed, I'll not have the strength to carry on. Havik looked to his friend who was cautiously making his way into the tunnel. *Leave him to the wolves,* his uncle whispered. *He will only slow you down.*

No, uncle! Havik's inner voice resounded in his head. *I won't leave him.* Havik adjusted his pack and made his way into the Demon's Gate. *He's my friend, uncle. And I won't let him die.*

Fool! He's already dead. And now... so are you...

VANSA

She nervously combed her long black hair, and stared at the clouds in the bright blue sky, as she waited outside the hut. The two warriors that blocked her entrance had their faces painted with green magic sigils. The look of them frightened her, and she made no attempt at casual conversation. When Vansa Ketrien first received her summons by owl, she was surprised to find it told her to come alone. Although she was the princess of her tribe, and by all rights could travel with an escort, she knew it would be unwise to disobey. Her father and his council bid their goodbyes to her, along with the rest of her family and friends. Though the message gave no tangible hint of what was to become of her, they all sensed it would be the last time in a long while that she would be with them. That night she mounted the fastest stag her tribe possessed, and made her way across the plains of Fenria towards Tyr Spar, the home of the Old Mother. The journey had taken several weeks, and now that she had finally reached her destination, she found her sense of nervous anticipation had reached its peak. *I was born for this...*

Vansa, like all other children of the past two generations, had been trained since birth in the ways of life of the Southern Realms. More than just speaking their language or knowing their history, she had carefully learned to alter her speech patterns to reflect which House she wished to impersonate. She was also well versed in minor details, like songs, and the local gossip of East and West together, things no book or scroll could teach. Beyond the ability to pass for a Southerner, she was trained in all manners of subterfuge and tracking, knew the healing arts as well as poison-craft, and could shoot a bow and wield a sword as well as any warrior. And yet, for all her knowledge, some nights she felt she knew nothing of the world, and of what it meant to be living in it.

On those nights she would sneak away into the dark, and when she was far from camp and deep in the wilderness, Vansa would curse Ma'at for forcing the Old Mother's visions upon her. Then she'd fantasize of what her life might be like if she had been born in any other age, or if the Old Mother's prophecies were never foretold. *I would be free to hunt whenever I wished,* she imagined. *Free to sew, and fish, and ride to my heart's content. I could travel the other tribes, and bed whomever I chose.* She would laugh and dance under the light of the Silver Star while deer and squirrels watched. *I would be free!* But Vansa knew they were only delusions of another life. A life that was never meant to be.

It is not a curse, but a responsibility, she came to understand as she grew older and cast aside the day dreams of her youth. *If not for the Old Mother's augury, it would be Doom in our future, rather than salvation.* The Old Mother was the leader of their people, and was a direct descendent of the Great Prognosticator, the Fenrian woman who foretold the Doom so many thousands of years ago. If not for her warnings, then none of her people would have lived. Many disregarded her ramblings as madness, but some listened, and those that did followed her to the Rainbow Caverns to seek shelter. When they emerged a year later to ice and snow, Doom had come to the world, and the face of Eldaria was forever changed. Their people were all dead, but that tiny handful survived, and so their race lived on. If the Old Mother could be believed, a fresh Doom was upon them, and this time, no place in all of Fenria, not even the Rainbow Caverns, would be safe. This time, however, every Fenrian that lived believed in the Prognosticator's descendant's prophecy, and they swore that this time, no Fenrian would be left to die. Their only hope was the Realm, a wicked place where man killed man, and everyone had to fend for themselves to survive. For the people of Fenria, survival meant invasion, integration, or at the very least, passage to lands even further South. Either way it required preparation, and to a Fenrian, that meant the training of all future generations until Doom was avoided.

Even then, at twenty six years of age, she still disappeared into her daydreams as if she were a child. She finally snapped out of her thoughts when the green faced rugged warrior placed his hand upon her shoulder. She jumped out of her skin and slapped him across the face. He touched his cheek with a look of utter shock, and all at once Vansa remembered where she was, and realized she'd forgotten herself. "I'm sorry," she muttered meekly, curtsied, blushed, and giggled uncomfortably.

"It's fine..." He smiled awkwardly. "As I was saying... She's ready for you now."

"Yes! Thank you." She curtsied again. "That's splendid." Vansa sidestepped the man, pushed aside the heavy leather curtain, and entered. After gazing near the Red Star for so long, her night vision was slow to come to her, and she found herself entering a room of abysmal darkness. She hesitated at the entrance as two faint lights came into focus. Between two tiny candles, the Old Mother sat cross-legged on a black carpet. As Vansa's eyes adjusted to the dim light, she was startled to see that the Old Mother was nude. Vansa averted her eyes, took two steps forward, and knelt.

"I have been waiting for you... Vansa Ketrien," the Old Mother whispered in the crackled voice of a woman well over a hundred years old. "All... your... life..." She giggled as if she found her own words hysterical. Vansa gulped. *She is fooking crazy,* she thought in her flawless Southern vernacular.

Vansa stifled her own giggles, and tried to remain serious. "Yes, my lady," Vansa whispered.

"Look at me child," she said.

Vansa raised her head and looked into the Old Mother's eyes. They were purple, and alien, and frightening. The candle's flames reflected in them and brought out the colors of her insanity. In the darkness behind her, Vansa saw the shapes of two other women lurking in the shadows, watching. *The Holy Witches,* Vansa marveled. *Both of them, here...* Her blood chilled as she realized it was no ordinary summons. Each of the witches oversaw tribes at opposite ends of Fenria, and Vansa's own journey was short by comparison. For near a minute the Old Mother silently stared at her, and Vansa found it extremely uncomfortable. "Why are the witches here?" she asked meekly, trying to get the conversation started. The Old Mother was never known for being quick about anything, and was famous for falling asleep while taking visitors. Since it was anathema to leave her presence, or even rise without being given permission, that meant visitors, more often than not, knelt for quite lengthy periods of time. Vansa secretly swore she would try to get set to purpose and dismissed in record time.

"Come now, child." She smiled a toothless grin. "Did you think such a momentous occasion would go unwitnessed?" *What does she mean by that?* Vansa wondered. *Some special task perhaps...*

"I am ready to be given my orders," Vansa said confidently. "I have..." The Old Mother produced a dagger and set it down between them. "... been waiting for today as well..." She eyed the dagger with curiosity and fear. "What would you ask of me?"

"Ask? Mmmm. Yes. Yes. You can ask me anything you like," she croaked.

"Hmm..." *I just did, you old bat.* "Why have I been summoned?" Vansa asked.

"Because it is time! Of course." She rubbed her tired eyes. "Yes... Finally time at last."

Time for what? Vansa said the words in her mind, but knew better than to ask the obvious question. *I can play mad too.* "But how do you *know* it's time?" she whispered.

The Old Mother cackled, as if the question were hilarious. "How does anyone *know* anything?" she asked, and laughed again. By her pause, Vansa realized it was not a rhetorical question. *Riddles? Really! Riddles?* Vansa groaned miserably in her mind. *If I am in store for two days of this, I might use that dagger on myself.* "Go on! Give me the answer!"

"If you sense it, you know it," Vansa said. "If I see the sky is blue, I know it is day. I can taste the salt and know it is salty. I can feel the snow and know it is cold. I can smell the smoke and know there was fire. I can hear the water, and know it is raining." *Does she think I am unschooled? I hope there is a point to all this.*

"Then how did the Great Prognosticator know there would be Doom?" the Old Mother asked.

Of course. A lesson in prophecies. "I don't know," Vansa admitted.

"Why don't you know?" she asked.

"Because..." Vansa wondered what type of answer she expected. "I'm not descended from her?"

The Old Mother cackled. "Of course you aren't!" She laughed, and laughed. "Your eyes are all wrong! And look how small your breasts are!" She pointed at Vansa and chortled grotesquely. *At least they don't sag to the floor you ugly old crone,* she responded silently, in defense of a body Vansa thought was quite spectacular, as a matter of fact. "You are no family of mine, child." The Old Mother's face turned solemn, and the room felt colder. "Why *do* you think prophecy runs in the blood?"

What the fook does she want from me? "If it's not in the blood, then is it something that is taught, like reading and writing and wizardry?" Vansa asked. *There, you mad hag. I have answered your question with a question.*

"No, you stupid child. A thousand times no." The Old Mother shook her head disappointed.

They sat through another minute of silence before it became perfectly clear to Vansa that it was up to her to provide any forward momentum to the conversation. "Am I to travel South to the Realms?"

"No." The Old Mother gave a deep labored sigh.

"Am I to go someplace else then?" Vansa asked.

"No," she said again.

Fook! Vansa was heartbroken. *I am to undergo yet more years of schooling, in Tyr Spar of all places.* The village encampment was set around a small oasis, in the middle of the desert, in the middle of nowhere. Vansa yearned for trees and animals. Here there were only snakes, and insects. "What am I to do then?"

"Nothing, child." The Old Mother frowned.

"What do you mean, nothing?" Vansa asked. *Please don't tell me I have to wait.*

"There's nothing you *can* do," she whispered, "so nothing will you *ever* do again."

Vansa took a deep breath. *This is some kind of test. She's testing my dedication.* Her heart, which for a moment raced with panic, returned to a steady controlled beat. *Ha ha, you crafty wench! You almost had me for a minute.* She drew her face to a smile. "Perhaps you'd like to take this conversation outside, my lady?" Vansa said sweetly. "It is a beautiful day, and the light of the Red Star may bring you some cheer."

"I'm afraid not, my stupid, stupid, child," the Old Mother cackled.

"But, whyever not?" Vansa fluttered her eyelashes.

"Because neither of us will ever leave this hut again." She laughed, and laughed, as Vansa's blood ran cold and sent shivers down her spine. "It has been foreseen!" The Old Mother nearly doubled over from the hilarity of it. All at once Vansa found herself become acutely aware of the three daggers she had on her person. One larger for hunting on her belt, one for eating, and one for rope and leather. *I can handle these three women,* she told herself as she sized them up as potential opponents. *The Holy Witches are not known for fighting. It is those warriors I have to look out for... Unless this is the test.*

"When did you have this vision?" Vansa asked.

"The day I knew that Doom was upon us." The Old Mother stared without blinking.

That's ridiculous. "You're telling me, you prophesied *this* conversation, a decade before I was born?" *What would I have to do with the Doom?*

"Yes, Vansa. I did," she said.

"So then tell me. How did you *know*?" Vansa smiled at her question. "Tell me how you did it."

"I sensed it, of course. You already answered that." The Old Mother smiled. "This, *and* the coming Doom."

"What did you sense, my lady?" Vansa became excited at the thought of receiving an answer never provided to her, or anyone she knew. "What is the Doom?"

The Old Mother burst a tiny vessel of blood in her left eye, and turned the whites pink. Vansa winced. "Come closer, my child," she whispered.

Vansa hesitated, her eyes on the dagger. The Old Mother never blinked nor averted her bird like gaze, and Vansa felt herself naked to her. She summoned her courage and crawled until she sat right across from her, with the silvery dagger half a foot between them. *That is no metal I have seen before,* she thought as she saw the blade close up. "Tell me... I'm ready to know."

"Doom is darkness." The Old Mother closed her eyes for the very first time. "It floats on the wind, and it walks hand in hand with death. The Mother is sick. She bleeds from her wound, and the corruption's poisonous roots dig deep into her veins." She opened her eyes in such a fashion that it startled Vansa, who had found herself staring at her face while she visualized the Old Mother's words. "There is something you must know, Vansa Ketrien." She grabbed Vansa's hands with both of her own, and leaned close. Her palms were cold and clammy, and the skin hung loose on her thin boney fingers.

"What is it?" Vansa asked.

"Vansa... What I have to tell you, no one knows." Tears clung to her eyes. Those in her left eye were diluted with blood. "Not even the Holy Witches behind me!" Vansa heard their gasps, and was unsure whether to laugh or release her bladder. "Open your ears, both of you! You may listen, but my words are for Vansa alone!" She coughed just then, and did not stop for good while. One of the witches offered her a cup of water, which she took politely, then splashed it back at the witch's face. The witch took the cup back graciously and returned to the shadows.

"I understand," Vansa said. "I am ready to know this secret."

"Vansa... The vision... The prophecy... What I have seen... It is Doom! Doom that comes for us all!" She looked as if her words came as some wondrous revelation. *She really is fooking crazy.*

"I know, my lady," Vansa said politely. "It is no secret that Doom comes. You were just telling us–"

The Old Mother covered Vansa's mouth with her hand to silence her. "You don't understand." Vansa tasted something bitter and sour. *Disgusting.* Her skin crawled and she tried not to gag. She politely pushed away the Old Mother's hand and kept her lips firmly sealed. "Listen. All of you. Doom is upon us. Doom!"

"Yes, mother, we know. Doom," one of the Holy Witches said. Vansa was shocked to hear her speak.

"No! Doom! *True* Doom!" she cried. Their looks of sympathy for her dementia transformed into those of doubt and terror. Vansa felt fear course through her. "The fate that befell our ancestors, what we call the Doom, was not the first. There was one other, many eons ago, when the Ancients themselves were but a glimmer of some unknown imagined future." The Old Mother sighed and drew her hands close to her body. "The first reshaped the world by fire, the second by ice. But the Doom that faces *us* will not reshape the world." Her eyes wept, one clear, one bloodied. "*This* Doom will kill the Mother, corrupt the Castle, and bring darkness to the Kingdom as if the Red Star set one night and never rose again." The Old Mother seemed desperate. Her eyes passed to all three of them. "Don't you understand? Don't any of you understand?"

"My lady, what is it?" Vansa asked. "Tell us!"

"The prison will bleed! I have seen it through the eyes of another!" She screamed in high wretched wails and pulled at her old dry grey hair. "*He* is awake! He *sees* me! He sees *you*! He sees us *all*! Don't you understand? He's *watching* us! He's watching us *right now*... At this very moment!"

"Who? Who's watching us?" Vansa held her breath. *This is not what I expected.* Her fear was mixing with paranoia, and she and the witches alike looked around at the darkness. "Who?"

"Isfet! Isfet! Isfet watches us! He will return, and when he does!" The Old Mother's maniacal wailing and moaning came to a sudden halt. "He will die..." she whispered. "But not before, in his boundless empty spite, he opens the Gate of the Heavens once again. Listen to me! All of you! Listen! If Isfet, mighty Isfet, proud Isfet, is to die, then he will drag everything down to hell along with him."

"How can a god, die?" Vansa asked.

"Because the Doom that rains upon *us*, rains upon *gods* as well. In *this* Doom, even dead gods will die." The Old Mother spoke so faintly that they all struggled to hear. "And when *this* Doom has set it course..." She opened her eyes. "There will be *nothing*..." she said with sadness. "*Nothing* forever, and ever, and ever. The *void* will end *everything* that is. And *nothing* ever will *be* again. *Forever.*"

"Why?" Vansa asked directly. "Why would *this* Doom be any different?"

"The answer to that question, my child," she proclaimed, "is something *neither* of us will *ever* know!" She threw her arms wide and grinned, as if that were the grandest thing ever.

"Then who will know the answer?" Vansa tried not to get swept up in her feverish madness.

"The next Old Mother!" She laughed hysterically, then fell silent. Her eyes glazed over.

"Who will that be?" Vansa whispered in the silence.

The Old Mother frowned, took the strange dagger in her hand, and gave Vansa a look of utter madness. Vansa's blood froze and she felt the frenzy upon her. "Neither of us!" the Old Mother muttered, as she raised up the silvery dagger, and slit her own throat right to left. Vansa's mouth gaped open in terror as blood spurted from the crone's neck and bathed both of them in warm, wet, drapes of it. Vansa, up to now, had suspected the dagger was meant for her, and could not speak or even think in the shock of the Old Mother taking her own life instead. It was in that frozen moment that the Old Mother leapt forward and grabbed Vansa by the throat. She fell back with the old crone on top of her. The hag's mouth exhaled hot breath on Vansa's face, and the blood from her neck spilled into Vansa's mouth and drained down the backside of her throat. The purple glow of life in the bitch's eyes faded, and her limbs fell dead atop Vansa's body. Vansa gurgled and coughed, and she choked on the blood, and threw the Old Mother aside.

"What? What?" Vansa coughed, and spit, and vomited the bloody contents of her stomach onto the ancient black rug that now puddled with the Old Mother's gore.

The two Holy Witches came out of the darkness and fell to their knees. "Old Mother! Old Mother!" they chanted. Vansa thought they mourned for their dead leader.

A third, shorter woman, stepped out from the darkness and approached. Vansa sat up, and watched as the woman lowered her white hood. *Not a woman, but a Southern girl,* Vansa realized. She had blonde hair, and sky blue eyes, and looked not a day over thirteen. The child knelt in the Old Mother's blood, and produced a tiny wooden blue box. "Hello. Who are you?" Vansa asked her.

"I am the Old Mother's holy follower," she said softly in a child's voice, as the Old Mother's blood soaked up her white virgin robes.

The girl gave Vansa the box. She took it and smiled. "For me?" The girl nodded, and Vansa opened it. Inside was a silver chain, with a silver heart locket. "What's this?" Vansa asked as she opened the heart by its clasp. There was nothing inside.

"It is the Old Mother's locket, handed down to her from the Great Prognosticator herself." The girl smiled up at her.

"Why?" Vansa was breathless when she realized how ancient the pendant must be.

"Why am I giving it to you?" The girl giggled. "Because *you* are the Old Mother, and our people look to you to save them." Vansa all at once realized the witches were chanting for *her* sake.

"I can't be the Old Mother." Vansa objected. "You heard her, I'm not related–"

"It is not in the blood." The girl interrupted.

"Is it the locket?" Vansa asked. "Will this ancient locket give me visions?"

"No. The locket is metal and nothing more. The visions are magic," she told Vansa. "With her final breath, a djinni's kiss passed to you at the Old Mother's death, my lady."

"I don't feel any different," Vansa admitted. "The Old Mother said I would never leave."

"Where once I saw Vansa Ketrien, I now see only the Old Mother," she smiled. "But let me leave with you these last words."

"You're leaving me?" Vansa asked her.

"Do not fear," she said, "you will have your own holy follower soon. I promise." Vansa opened her mouth to speak, but the girl covered her lips as the Old Mother once had. "Listen, my lady." She removed her hand. "You must listen."

"Tell me," Vansa whispered.

"The Doom spreads from the North. The Holy Witches will guide our people South. It is not your place to lead us. Our spies have done their task, and have chosen where the fleets that will carry our people shall land. But when that time comes, you will not be with us."

"Then where–" Vansa asked, and again the girl stopped her.

"You *must* listen! There isn't time. The Old Mother grows cold." She spoke quickly now. "Go alone. Go to the Barrows, wherever that might be. It is where the Old Mother saw you, and is all we know of your destiny. The rest will be up to you."

"I don't understand," Vansa cried, as the girl crawled over to the Old Mother's corpse. "What am I supposed to do there?"

"You heard what the Old Mother said, my lady!" The girl picked up the strange dagger. "*This* Doom cannot be avoided, and will mean the end of everything, everywhere, forever." She held the dagger up to her own throat and pleaded to Vansa with her eyes. "You have to stop it, Old Mother. *Save* us. Save us *all*."

Vansa woke in a cold sweat. It was early morning, but the light was shadowed dark grey by the heavy snow clouds that loomed above. She wrapped herself deeper in her blanket, and tried to shake the images from her head. Though it had been nearly two months since that fateful day at Tyr Spar, each night she was haunted by memories of that sweet little girl killing herself in the same manner as the Old Mother. Sometimes in her dreams she would stop her, and rescue her from her suicide, while other nights she would look away, and run from the candles into the empty darkness.

The bite of the cold air seeped into her furs and froze her to the bone. With a grunt of dissatisfaction, she rose from her bedding and dressed for the day. She had been given the strange silvery dagger by the Holy Witches, and told it was very valuable. That first day she relished it as a holy relic. Now, when she fastened her belt to her waist and felt the weight of the blade, she felt like tossing it into the bushes and leaving it to rust. *I was raised a spy, meant to pave the way for our people,* she cursed the blade in her head, *not meant to travel alone to some forsaken castle, the leader of my people, on some mad quest for salvation.*

She was given a large sum of gold for her journey, and had been escorted by those two frightful warriors to the Eastern shores. From there a ship constructed in Southern fashion, but sailed by good Fenrian men, bore her South to Astermount. That city looked glorious from the sea, and just as she had been taught, held towers that rose as high as the eagle climbed in the sky. But it was not in her fate to explore that grand new place as she had dreamed she would. She cried as Astermount's white harbors disappeared from view. A day later she was rowed to a barren shore, and left there alone. She stood still and watched as the tiny rowboat made its way back to the ship, which then unfurled its sails, and glided across those cerulean waters back the way it came. She thought of home and stared until it crossed the horizon, then, with mind set towards the future, made her way South across the plains.

A thousand doubloons could buy me dozens of horses once I reach the Barrows, she mused as she searched through her backpack for some dried fruit. *But with all my gold, and all my horses, where would I even go?* She ate her meager meal and drank some water. *If the Doom comes from the North, why travel South to stop it?* The fire she'd set in the night had long gone out, and she scattered it to cover traces of her passing. *The Barrows are my destination, I know that much. Am I to rally allies against an unknown foe, or simply wait for some sort of sign?* The uncertainty and madness of her being sent so far South, alone, had driven her to wits end weeks ago. But she'd cried all the tears she could shed, and had chewed her nails to the bone many times already. At least here, and off the ship, she was free, and her spirit brightened with each day she'd walked that cold foreign wilderness.

That particular morning was her favorite, and as she hiked into the forests, the snow fell for the first time from the sky and turned the world to a miracle of white. Vansa had only seen the snow a few times in her childhood, back when she'd traveled with her mother to the Wellspring Mountains. But that was a lifetime ago, and in more ways than one, she was not the same person as the sweet Ketrien girl who still had a mother. *I am a mother with no children,* she thought coldly as she squatted to take a piss in the snow. *How could a mother be a virgin?* The thought struck her fancy, and her mind lingered on fantasies of sex as her footsteps left imprints on the virgin snow. For the Fenrian people, sex was something that happened freely, and was not constrained by any laws or taboos. Here in the South, however, Vansa knew that those of noble families valued virginity as a morally upward attribute in unwed women. As a spy, it was necessary for her, and all others like her, to remain chaste, and keep their virginity as advantage. *Am I still a spy?* she wondered. *Or is the girl who was a spy, no more?*

By that afternoon the snow had accumulated to nearly half a foot, and the storm gave no sign of stopping. She quickened her pace and made for the top of a nearby hill. *I should not be far from the Barrows by now,* she told herself. *It was smart of me to come by empty land.* She had been six days in the South, and in all that time had not seen a single person. She had crossed barren fields, and skirted along the ledge of a valley that descended into rocky badlands. From there she entered the forests, and now, from the top of that hill, she ventured she would spot Little Moore's Run. It was a tributary of the Bear Trap River, and that would lead her straight to the Barrows. She knew her map was accurate, and was confident that her skills at navigating the strange terrain were about to be proven. There wasn't much wind and the snow fell straight down from the clouds. The only sounds were endless echoes of snowfall, the occasional owl, and the crunching of her steps. In those few moments that she neared the crest of the hill, she felt sure of herself in a way she never had before. For the first time in her life she felt an endless world of possibilities opening up before her, and no matter how great her burden was, she felt truly alive. The very last thing she expected to feel when she finally reached the summit of that hill was absolute fear.

Stretched out before her ran Little Moore's Run. "I was right!"

She chortled as she marveled at the river... before her gaze was drawn upwards towards what lay beyond. The sparkling camp fires of several thousand men and their horses twinkled along the plains, and there, in the center of their army, was the shadow. It rose over a hundred feet in height, and stretched out like a dome draped of darkness. It was no physical thing, and snow that fell upon it disappeared, lost into its empty void. Vansa's blood froze, and the fear was full upon her. *Is that the Doom?* The questioned burned at her mind. *The Old Mother said the Doom floats on the wind, and walks hand in hand with death,* she pondered. *But this shade seems fixed in place, and those men seem well enough.* It was, in fact, more people than Vansa had ever seen gathered in all her life. Still, she knew the fleets that would carry her people would hold hundreds of times their numbers. *An army walks hand in hand with death,* she riddled, and felt the fear of it.

What concerned her most was how visible her tracks would be in the snow. *Armies have scouts,* she worried. Due to the storm she could not see it, but all the same knew that the Barrows was less than ten hours walk along the river. If she braved the snow and made the journey, the snow might cover her footsteps after an hour, but in that hour a scout might track her position, and that would be an unpleasant encounter for both of them. She considered staying put and seeking shelter, and entertained the possibility of retreating back to the forests, but with so many men she could not risk setting a fire. Furthermore her food was running low, and she rued the thought of turning back so close to her destination, just to scavenge and live wild until the danger passed. *No,* she told herself. *No. I must make haste. The shadow and its army may be the herald of Doom, and I cannot escape my destiny.*

Vansa gathered her strength and her courage, hurried down from the hill, and pressed on into the snow. She kept the river to her left and for the remainder of the day stayed out of sight of its edge. Thankfully she saw no sign of men, and not once feared she was spotted. When night began to fall the world slipped into a bleak darkness with the Silver Star hidden behind grey clouds. The snow had stopped, but not before laying a blanket that reached past her knees, and Vansa knew she could not risk getting lost in the forest. She followed the sound of the river and emerged onto its embankment. Though distant, the fires of the army's camps sparkled on the horizon, and the shadow still lingered, a blacker darkness than even the night sky. *The Barrows must be warned of this danger, if they are not alerted already.* She quickened her pace.

After several hours, when she ventured she was nearing her destination, the world flashed with a hellish red light. It illuminated everything as if some great godly candle was held in the sky then blown out. For an instant, Vansa saw the cliff walls of the Barrows' castle a few miles away, and the masts of a ship anchored on the river. Instead of celebrating, Vansa turned with shock, and looked back upon the camp. A swirling vortex of fire had erupted in the army. It was an unnatural inferno whose flames leapt hundreds of feet into the sky, then flickered out as if its fuel was spent. In its place a thousand little fires remained, and Vansa saw the twinkling dance she knew to be panicked men set aflame. *What was that?* she gasped silently. *Is this the way of war in the South?* She marveled for a moment at the great flame and what may have caused it, before she gave in to her baser fears. She gripped her backpack tight and ran away from the army, the fire, and the shadow with fear for her life.

By the time Vansa neared the shore of where Little Moore's Run and Bear Trap River ran together, she was a mess of fright and exhaustion. The ship was in the center of the river, with three flat rafts each twenty feet across, tied up against the beach. A half dozen armed men wearing the colors of an unfamiliar House watched her warily by lantern light as she approached. One stepped from the raft and placed his hand on the hilt of his longsword. "That's far enough!" he shouted.

Vansa slipped the backpack off her weary shoulders and stood tall. "I am Colette of House Shellspear, bannermen to the O'Briens," she declared, hoping that this, one of her many prepared backgrounds, was the wisest choice. "I come from Harkness Cove by way of Astermount."

"I don't give a fook who you are," the man laughed cruelly. "The way's closed. Now get the fook out of here and don't come back."

"Please!" she begged. "You can't make me go back."

One of the other men pushed forward. "Why are you traveling alone, m'lady?" he asked. The first man shot him a dirty glance, but stepped aside.

"I hired sell swords to take me," Vansa forced tears, "but one glimpse of the army and that shadow, and they fled. They took my horses and all my things, save for what treasure I kept on my person." She wiped her eyes dry as she pleaded with them.

"Listen, if it was up to me, I'd give you passage," he sighed, "but we've got our orders."

"Orders from *who*? Who *are* you anyway?" Vansa asked accusingly. "Those *aren't* O'Brien colors."

"That's because they're *Gracious* colors, and–" The first man smacked him on the back of his head, and interrupted.

"Quiet you!" he told him. "You've told this barbarian spy enough already."

"Spy!" Vansa feigned outrage to cover her fear. *Was my ruse that poor?*

"You're on the wrong side of the river to have come from Astermount," the mean man told her. "Now get the fook out of here!"

"By what right do you intend to prevent my crossing?" She stood tall.

"This right!" He half drew his sword, then slipped it back in its sheath. "Now start walking back to wherever you came from, before you taste the courage of my convictions."

"Walk back! From *here*?" she cried. "But I have no horse! It'd take weeks!"

"As if the likes of you, could ever have afforded a horse!" He shook his head and spit.

I have him now. Vansa opened her backpack, and pulled from it a leather pouch. "Can't afford a horse? *Me?* A Shellspear?" She laughed, and threw it at their feet. The nicer man picked up the pouch and opened it.

"There must be over a hundred doubloons in here!" he gasped.

"And they have cousins!" She gave her backpack a little jingle. "Now are you going to let me pass, or will I have to send raven to Lord O'Brien, and tell him of how *Gracious* men refused me in my time of need?" Doubt crept over their faces, and Vansa tried to contain her smile. *If they are bandits, I am doomed.* Her fear was ever present, and she wondered how her meager dagger might fare against chain and leather.

"Riders!" a third man cried. "Riders!"

Vansa turned and saw the men approaching. There were two dozen of them, all ahorse magnificent steeds, and they rode along the river's edge from the direction she'd come. Vansa's blood froze, and she found herself wondering if these men were part of the army she'd seen. The river guards did not seem startled, and they stood by patiently as the riders came upon them. The group came to a stop, and all dismounted their horses. The guard who had given her trouble pointed at one of the horses, where a hooded and bound man was being taken hold of by two of the riders. "Who's that?" he asked.

"What's that Warren? Did you say who?" One of the elder knight laughed. "This ain't no *who*. This here's a *Davenport*!"

The guardsmen cheered at the news and dragged the man onto the raft. Vansa stood to the side meekly as she watched and waited. She knew that the Davenports were a wealthy and influential House pledged to the Dravens of the East, but so too were the O'Briens. The delicacy of their strange Southern politics confounded her, and she prayed that the Shellspears were not an unlucky House to declare. Three of the riders had their eyes on her, and when they dismounted, approached her directly. "Who is this?" one of them asked.

"Girl claims she's an O'Brien bannerman, Lord Commander. She tried to bribe her crossing with this." Warren took the pouch of gold from the kindly guard, and tossed it to him.

"That's a lie!" Vansa objected. "But it *is* my gold."

The Lord Commander shook the pouch in his hand and frowned. "Axe. Check her arm."

The man called Axe stepped forward and grabbed her by the arm. "What's the meaning of this? What are you doing? Get your hands off me!" Vansa objected as a lesser noble lady of the South might. All the same she was surprised to find Axe's grip firm, but exceedingly gentle. With a strength impossible to counter, he ripped the sleeves of her arms open, and examined her bare skin. "What are you looking for?"

Axe glanced back and shook his head. "She doesn't have one."

"Have one what?" she asked, all the more confused.

The Lord Commander carried a sickle across his belt, a bedeviled weapon, but his eyes seemed kind to her. They were dark and peaceful like the night sky, but not so black as the shadow that lurked in the distance. "You want to seek shelter in the Barrows, my lady?" Vansa nodded. "Then answer this one question truthfully, and you shall be given safety."

"Ask me anything, my lord," she said. *He wants the truth... But which truth shall I give?*

"You are magic," he said, and she contained her surprise. "Do not try to deny it. I can see the glow of it all around you. Do not lie to me as you have these men," he warned. "You cannot expect me to believe that a magic noblewoman would be traveling alone." *How can he see magic?* she wondered. *And what magic is that? Is it the djinni's kiss? Does it have a light I cannot see?* "Go on. Out with it."

I cannot risk a lie, nor can I risk the whole truth. Vansa puzzled before she spoke. "I'm sorry for the deception." She bowed her head. "I am from the far North, from Fenria. A black Doom spreads from the North, and my people are worried. As for the magic..." She looked up and pleaded with her eyes. "I was born this way. My people chose me to venture South, to beg the O'Briens for help from the coming Doom."

Vansa was pleased to find that her words were met with authentic fear and interest. The Lord Commander and his two men shared silent looks, and the third spoke. "This black Doom," the man who was neither Axe nor the Lord Commander said. "What does it look like?"

"It floats on the wind." She frowned. "And walks hand in hand with death."

"You were *born* magic?" Axe asked her.

She nodded. "The priests said I was special, like a white kavolia."

The Lord Commander tossed her back the pouch of gold. "Good enough for me."

"And who exactly *are* you?" she asked as they escorted her onto the raft. They introduced themselves as Clique, Collin, and Axe, three members of the Royal Huntsmen, a ranging group from Midgard sent to investigate the Doom. Vansa was struck by the synchronicity of it, and decided she would have to carefully judge their character before deciding to reveal the real truth of her coming. *At the very least, they might come to respect me if they knew I was the leader of my people,* she considered. *But if they knew the sum of my people would soon be following in my footsteps, they might think of it as invasion.* She soon learned that they discovered the barbarian army gathered to their North when they'd arrived at the Barrows, Collin's ancestral home, as a waypoint for a greater quest. They admitted to scouting the army out, but when she questioned about the fire and the shadow, she was met with silence.

"That is not for you to know," Clique explained. "At least not yet." She was told that they would parley with her in detail about the Doom, her magic, and the fate of her people, but first had to deal with more pressing concerns, such as the thousands of men now gathered across the river. The tactics of the coming battle were a matter of great debate between the Royal Huntsmen, and she listened intently as they argued while the ship took them to port. She learned that all the men charged with defending the Barrows, and as such, all the fertile lands South of the river, were in an army two months march away. If the barbarians were to cross the river, they could pass the castle by and raze the countryside with no opposition. But to meet the barbarians in the fields would be certain defeat. Their numbers were simply too many. However, if the men they had, outnumbered more than five to one, were able to somehow draw them to attack the castle directly, then they might be repelled.

Axe suggested a wall of stone be raised across the field to drive them to the castle gates. Then it would only be a matter of meeting them with resistance on the river, to lure them to cross inside the walled passage. One of the Huntsmen laughed and said it was impossible. He scolded Axe that even their four hundred men couldn't build a wall that long in a fortnight, let alone in the six hours they had before the army reached the riverbanks. He claimed it couldn't be done, but Axe said it could, and motioned towards Collin. Soon a strange silence had overtaken them, and all looked to Collin, then to Vansa, where she felt exposed, as if she'd heard or witnessed something not meant for her. *How can they see magic, and why will they not discuss the fire or the shadows? How can a wall be built so fast?* The questions tore through her mind and she wanted nothing more than to beg for answers, but instead consigned quietly to being led below deck for the remainder of the voyage.

It did not take them more than twenty minutes to sail round the edge of the cliffs and reach the castle's port. The docks had one other ship of equal size to the one she was on, and both were over three times the length of the meager vessel that took her from Fenria. *Large ships for a river,* she thought, and wondered just how far away this Midgard was. She had only ever studied the Realms, and half cursed her luck that her first encounter rendered her carefully devised backgrounds worthless. When Vansa stepped from the ship and onto the wooden dock, she was amazed to find it was much less spectacular than Astermount. Instead of fine marble walls that glistened by day and must have sparkled with reflection by night, the walls of the Barrows were crumbling and dotted with moss where not covered by snow. Still they were tall, over a hundred feet so, and when she passed through the main gate and into the gateway, she discovered they were nearly just as thick. Three portcullis doors were lifted for their entrance, and the thick banded iron gate was wide open. Dozens of holes dotted the ceiling above, and through them she saw the eyes of men who watched her.

The grand courtyard was larger than even the largest camps of Fenria, and the wall surrounded all of it. To her right was the castle itself, where great buildings of stone, and scores of towers both tall and short, attached themselves to the central palace. To her left were hundreds and thousands of smaller stone buildings, each one larger than even the biggest huts of her people. Where the snow had melted it hinted at streets of bright red brick. Far across the yard, almost a mile away, a second gate rose from the wall. There, near the gate, a veritable city of crude tents and shelters were set up, and the shanty town was illuminated by just as many tiny campfires to keep away the cold night air. Nearest to her, dozens of soldiers wandered the walls set to numerous tasks. Barrels and satchels were being brought up to the top of the walls, bales of hay were being stacked, and rocks of all sizes were piled. Groups of old men, young boys, and women of all ages assisted in preparations for the coming battle.

Collin brought a kindly old woman in green and blue robes to Vansa's side. "Lady Vansa, this is Ciara O'Brien, my mother's sister." The woman bowed her head and smiled. "She will see to your needs. I am sorry you have come in such dangerous times, but rest assured my lady, there is no place in the Realm more secure. You will be safe here."

"Thank you, Collin." Vansa hugged him. "Good luck."

Collin turned back towards the gate and met with the Huntsmen, while Ciara took her by the arm and led her towards the castle. "Collin tells me you have come from the far North. You must be used to all this snow."

Vansa frowned. "Actually, where I come from it is quite hot and dry. Tell me..." She pointed to the city of tents. "Why do those people live in tents, while others in such tall castles? Is there no room?"

Ciara smiled politely. "They do not live here, child. They have been given shelter here, because they fear the barbarians. We have spread the word with as many riders as we could spare, and have opened the gates for all seeking asylum. The castle has been opened to some, but we do not have the guards to watch over so many people." She rubbed Vansa's arm. "You are very kind to be concerned for them. Rest assured there is more than enough food and supplies to take care of them. Most are women, children, and the elderly." She sighed. "Most of our men had gone away to war, and gained hard won peace, only to have war besiege their homes while away. But do not worry. Everyone here is safe. It is those who have not made it here that I fear for the most." Ciara led her out of the courtyard and into the castle. "Come child, enough of this sad talk. Let us get you bathed and fed after such long journey."

Ciara took Vansa to the top of one of the smaller towers, where she was offered the most luxurious room Vansa had ever been in. There was a bed with a mattress of feathers, silk pillows, and fine oak furniture. The stone walls were draped with brightly colored tapestries, and the floor was a plush carpet of purple wool. Ciara left Vansa in the care of two young women who acted as servants for their family. One ignited the fireplace and filled the room with warmth, while the other brought buckets of hot water and filled a tub for her to bathe. She was told she could change into whatever clothes she found in the chests and armoires, and was given a hot meal of eggs and oats, honeyed wine, fresh fruits, warm bread, greasy meats, and salted nuts. For her it was a much welcome feast after months of poor rations on her journey, and she thanked them kindly and locked the door when they left.

Vansa savored every minute of her soak in the waters, and experimented with the foreign assortment of soaps and oils and perfumes they'd left for her. When clean, she changed into a beautiful violet dress she found in one of the closets, and ate to her heart's content by the fire. There were a thousand thoughts that clung to her mind, but since that first moment she'd slipped into the tub, she forced herself to put her worries aside, and take advantage of her respite, however brief it might be. When her hunger and thirst was sated, she crawled into that opulent bed of feathers, and immediately fell asleep, wrapped in its silken indulgence.

That night she dreamed of the girl standing over the Old Mother's body. Both corpse and child stared at her with their fearful, begging eyes. "Save us," the girl whispered as she ran the silvery blade across her milky skin. Vansa ran to her, and covered the girl's neck with her hands, as if trying to keep the blood inside her throat so she would not bleed. The girl stared up at Vansa as the life left her. Her blood flowed through Vansa's fingers, and as the girl gave her last dying breath, the hot sticky wetness of her blood grew cold, and froze over Vansa's hands. Vansa felt the icy presence of death, and her own blood chilled with fear. The candles flickered out and left her in darkness. In the black void of the Old Mother's chamber, Vansa felt eyes on her, leering at her from some hidden abyss. A clash of thunder sounded from some unseen distance, and when Vansa turned, she saw a range of shadowed mountains. There, in the dead space between her and the horizon, some primeval horror lurked. She could not see it, but somehow knew it was out there, watching her. A freezing wind blew upon her face. *Isfet...*

Vansa awoke shivering in a cold sweat. The fire had long since gone out, but a bleak grey daylight hinted behind the heavy curtains and fastened shutters. Vansa closed her eyes and tried to push aside her fear as she did each morning after dreams of the girl. Vansa was shocked further to consciousness when a loud crash sounded from outside like thunder. *That was no dream,* she thought, as she stood and rushed to the windows. She threw the curtains aside, opened the shutters, and drew her arms close to her chest as the cold wind blew over her. She was several hundred feet above the ground and her window held a view of the fields and the rivers. Her fear rose like never before and chilled her to the bone as she witnessed the spectacle below.

The barbarian army was at the riverbanks and had brought with them an endless supply of rafts and wagons. The shadow had reached the river, and cast darkness across water and field alike. The two ships that belonged to the Huntsmen were aflame in the river, as they rammed barbarian rafts, and soldiers met in combat on the ship's decks. Archers on the Barrows' side of the river were fleeing back to the castle gates as the barbarians approached. Dozens of rafts crossed in the distance, and further beyond crossed the shadow. The cries of battle carried on the wind, and a light snow fell from the cloudy sky. Vansa's mouth gaped in awe as she saw a wall of stone raised forty feet in height extend from the castle and cross the fields for miles. *The wall,* she marveled. *They did it.* Her fear peaked. *They must have a magic of their own... Collin,* she puzzled. *Collin has it. Some power over the land.*

Vansa decided she did not have time to think on the matter. The battle approached, and she would not hide in the corner like a frightened child when a duel of magic was about to take place. *Darkness and Stone. Does Eldaria herself rise up to fight this Doom that's upon us?* Vansa closed the shutters, then changed from her dress into pants and the two black woolen shirts she'd found. She fastened her belt with a pouch of gold and her treasured dagger, then covered herself with a heavy black cloak. It was too long for her, and dragged on the floor, but would be more than adequate to conceal her appearance. *The few men that guard the walls will be more concerned with the enemy outside, than the passage of a stranger,* she told herself as she slipped into the hall and made her way down the tower's spiral stairwell. *But better I watch, than interfere.* And she knew the perfect place to watch from.

It took her the better part of an hour as she lost her way through the maze of halls and passages of the enormous castle, but eventually she came to the corridor that ran inside the wall itself. It opened into a wide hall that sat atop the main gateway. Dozens of cauldrons were heated by fire with bubbling oil cooking within. Hundreds of barrels of stones were stacked everywhere, and no more than a dozen men scrambled to prepare themselves. Vansa was ignored, and she made her way to a tiny window that overlooked the fields outside the gate. She slid the metal cover that hid the window aside, and felt dizzy with fear as she looked out into a daytime world as black as night. Hundreds of barbarians were lined on horseback with torches drawn a few hundred feet away. Darkness had replaced the light of day. *They are here.*

Six barbarians upon chain mailed horses approached the gate. One carried a large iron lantern that illuminated the black flag another man waved. Vansa heard the clinking of heavy iron chain, and felt the tremblings of the portcullis being raised and the gate being opened. She shut the window and clambered over to the nearest murder hole, as the men were calling them, and watched. The horseman with the flag, the one with the lantern, and a third waited outside the gate, while three of them entered the gateway below her. The drop was fifty feet, and Vansa, while she knew she was not in danger, felt some aura of terror somehow emanating from one of the men below. He wore black leather armor, and had an iron helm with three spikes upon its crown. His only weapon was a long black iron bar slung across his back. Her skin crawled as he passed, and she ran across the hall to look down from a better position.

Collin, Clique, and Axe walked calmly into the hall, and all six men stopped ten feet from each other beneath the gateway's center. "I am Collin O'Brien, acting Lord of the Barrows. Who are you? And why have you crossed our river?"

"Swine! Do you not know a god when you see one?" one of the horsemen said. "Here before you is Drathos Dogon, the Lord of Life and Death, and you should all kneel before his glory!"

Drathos raised his hand to silence his man. "All men must kneel before god, but these are no men, Kalios!" Drathos laughed. "Before us stands three gods. *Lesser* gods, to be sure, but gods all the same."

Gods? Vansa wondered. "If you have come for our crystals," Collin said, "then you will not find them so easy to take." *Crystals? What madness is this?* Vansa was amazed by the accuracy of the Old Mother's prophecy. *This is why the she has sent me here... But to what end?*

"I have not come for crystals." Drathos grinned. "I have come for the castle."

"Why would barbarians need a castle?" Collin asked. "Your people have never made war with us before. Why now?"

"Fool. Doom is upon us, and I will not leave my people defenseless when it arrives." Drathos crossed his arms and spit. "We have been promised a castle, and we will take what is owed."

"Davenport's promises were empty, Drathos," Collin told him. "The Barrows have been defended after all. Your plan is finished. If you march against us, every last one of your men will die. If you cross the rivers and raze our lands, our armies will crush your people and scatter their ashes to the wind. Is that how you will protect them from the Doom, Drathos? With their deaths?"

"What would you propose?" Drathos asked.

"Join us." Collin raised his hand into a fist. "We will give your people shelter, so they are protected. Then... Us *gods* can work *together.* Together we can combine our strengths and combat this Doom directly. What faces *your* people faces *mine* as well. If we cannot work towards common purpose, then what hope does humanity have?" Collin took a few steps forward. "Drathos. Heed my words." Collin took off his right gauntlet, and rolled up the sleeve of his arm to reveal a brown crystal that shone with some inner magic. "The fates have given us this gift for a reason. If we do not unite against the Doom, then we turn our backs on our own *destiny*. Peace. Drathos. It is the only way."

"No." Drathos laughed. "There is another way." Collin looked back to Clique and Axe.

"And what way is that?" Collin asked.

Drathos coughed, and took a long drink from his wineskin. "You are correct about one thing, Collin O'Brien, Lord of the Barrows." He spit. "There is no need for men to die." Drathos took another gulp, then tossed the skin aside onto the floor. "The stench of O'Brien honor assails me, even now. But your people live and die by their word as much as mine, and such word can be trusted in honorable combat. *Here* is your *destiny*. Face *me* in combat that our men do not die. Just *you* and *me*, little lord. If I win, then your crystal is mine, and so is the castle. Your men will surrender, and leave, and none of your precious blood will be spilled."

Clique and Axe spoke to him in whispers that Vansa could not hear, but Collin shrugged them aside. "And if I win?" Collin asked.

Drathos laughed. "*If* I die, my crystal is yours, and my men will take what is owed from Garvin Davenport's own Castle Montague. I trust you will not oppose the march on the castle of the man who sold your people out to death."

Clique and Axe continued their whispers, but Collin's blood ran hot. "Silence! This is *my* decision, not *yours*. You may be Lord Commander of the Royal Huntsmen, but inside these walls I am lord over my family's castle! I have a responsibility, and their honor to uphold! Besides... I will not lose." Collin took his other gauntlet off and tossed it aside. "I accept your challenge Drathos Dogon. Step down from your horse, and we *gods* will duel for the fate of our people."

Drathos unhorsed, and commanded his men to wait outside the gate with the others. Collin commanded Axe and Clique to do the same. Every man in the hallway above the gate waited with bated breath for the duel to begin. Some whispered that even if Collin fell, there was no way the Barrows would be surrendered to a bunch of barbarians. When someone said that Collin's O'Brien honor would demand the conditions of the duel be met, another laughed and said that's *O'Brien* honor. He was a Gracious man, and it was *mostly* Gracious men that were defending the castle. He claimed that if their history had taught them anything, it was that Gracious men held little honor when it came to battle. Victory was everything. *Victory was life.*

Drathos ripped the cloak that covered his right arm away, and revealed the jet black crystal embedded in his skin. Vansa and the men who watched gasped. It pulsed with a strange light that reminded her of the Dead Star's aura. Here she was so far South that she doubted any of these men had ever even experienced its abyssal shade. Even the lands of her people were too far South, but as a child she had journeyed with her mother, and their path took her as far as the Wastes, where ice and snow had forever reclaimed what once was the jungle of her people. With Doom came the Dead Star. Her ancestors lived and died beneath its glow before they fled South, and here it was as if a piece of the Dead Star's magic was frozen inside his arm. *So that's what makes the darkness,* she mused. *I see. It is not Doom, but a piece of death itself.*

Drathos readied his iron staff, Collin unsheathed his longsword, and with a nod their duel had begun. Collin came to a defensive stance and lured Drathos to bring the fight to him. The man took several slow deliberate steps forward, then with a flurry of speed, swung his heavy metal staff down at Collin's body. He raised his sword to parry, and the clash of steel on iron brought more than sparks. A brown energy coursed through Collin's blade and corrupted the black staff, while vile tendrils of effervescent darkness snaked along the outer edge of Drathos' staff and struck into Collin's chest like vipers. The energy disappeared with the strike, but their bite passed through Collin's leathers, and he winced at the pain as his blood dripped from his flesh to the cold ground. Collin stumbled backwards, and took wild swings with his sword. *He's been blinded!* she realized as he attacked the empty air. Even so, Collin kept his sense of direction, and lured his opponent further towards the courtyard.

Vansa and the others left their murder holes and scrambled down the hall to get a better view as the battle shifted along the gateway. Drathos swung his staff, and again Collin blocked it. Once more the black magic snaked its death into Collin, but this time as the brown light of Collin's magic corrupted the iron staff, the weapon disintegrated into ash and fell away to the wind. In that singular moment where Drathos was surprised, Collin pressed his attack, but in his blinded state struck three times harmlessly against Drathos' armor. Clique and Axe shouted to Collin, bidding him to follow their voice. As Collin made his blinded escape Drathos gasped in further awe as his armor turned brittle from where Collin's corruption was snaking a way of its own. His robes, cloths, and leathers melted away to nothing, and his belt fell from his waist when the straps disintegrated. In that moment he stood naked as the day he was born, with his metal helm, and a dagger he'd drawn in his hand. Drathos removed his helm and tossed it into Collin's legs. It was not the force that tripped him, but black ethereal vines of magic that wrapped around his ankles, and disappeared by the time his face had hit the floor.

Collin stood and swung blindly, but Drathos nimbly avoided his swing, then stabbed Collin in his side with the dagger. Blood pooled from his wound as he stumbled out of the gateway and fell into the courtyard. Vansa's heart raced with furor, and she began to act without thinking, as if some lunacy had overtaken her good sense.

She tasted something bitter and salty in her mouth, and remembered the madness of the Old Mother. Her eyes had fallen upon a spool of rope nearby that was wrapped round a wheel for hoisting supplies up from the courtyard below. She ran to the spool, grabbed the end of rope in her hand, and tested its resistance. *Good enough,* she resolved in her madness.

With the rope in hand, she ran to the window and looked out to the courtyard below. Collin was on his back, his sword raised in defense. *He's helpless,* she thought. *Fook the honor these people hold sacred.* She pulled the silvery dagger out of its sheath and held her breath. *I will put an end to this myself.* But as Drathos stepped from the gateway, with his dagger raised ready for the killing blow, the skies above cracked open, and a bolt of lightning erupted before her. It was so close that it blinded Vansa from its flash, and though she felt its heavenly heat, she was not its target. The bolt of lightning struck Drathos. Golden energy zapped through him and the lightning vanished. A second bolt struck again, but Vansa had covered her eyes, and regained her sight. When she looked down from the window she saw Drathos unconscious on the ground beside a bleeding and confused Collin. Vansa held her breath once more, and jumped.

The rope spun from its wheel just as she predicted. She tumbled dextrously to the ground unharmed, and came to a stop beside the Lord of Light and Death. Vansa heard shouting from every direction, but did not hesitate as she knelt by Drathos Dogon's side, and slit his throat left to right with her silvery dagger. She felt both sweet relief as he seized with death, and a curious satisfaction that her treasured blade had taken another life. *Destiny itself caused lightning to strike the man,* she thought, *and destiny allowed me the killing blow.* She rejoiced that the creature of death and war and shadow that he was, was dead. *Good riddens,* Vansa cursed.

"No!" she heard a man scream, as the black crystal jumped from Drathos Dogon's arm, and entered Vansa's. None were more surprised of the event than she, who alone heard the words echo in the recesses of her mind. *I am... Darkness,* the voice told her, as night disappeared and daylight returned.

CLIQUE

Clique sat down and poured himself a goblet of wine from the table beside him. Collin was asleep in bed with a wet towel over his forehead. Axe sat in a chair beside Collin's right arm. His eyes were closed and he seemed to be asleep. A priestess puttered about the room tending to her duties. Clique took a long drink from the goblet, and leaned back, savoring his first chance to relax. It had been three days since Collin had fallen in battle, and since then Clique had been swarmed with endless tasks and responsibilities. He had been given little time to reflect on whether a different choice could have been made, and whether he was in the wrong for allowing Collin to take part in that pointless duel. *He was blinded by his family honor. I cannot make the same mistake.*

Clique and Axe had tried to talk Collin out of it, but he was just as stubborn as he was foolish and bold. *He didn't even use his power. With one thought he could have collapsed the stone hallway and struck him dead without a single swing of his sword.* That thought angered him most of all. *You have let your sense of knightly conduct be the death of you.*

Clique was aware that Collin's refusal to fight dirty had mortally cost him, but there was more to it than that. Collin knew, just as well as Clique, that Axe could not be defeated in combat by normal means. From the moment he chose to fight for himself, rather than allow Axe to be his champion, he had given in to weakness. *It is not unjust, or immoral, to champion a cause with a man who cannot be killed. His advantage is ours to use. If we don't use it, then what is the point of him?* Clique could slap Collin right now for his arrogance. *Our task is one against Doom itself, if that woman, and those barbarians are to be believed. And you would squander your destiny on selfish pride!* Clique threw his goblet across the room, where it splashed wine across fresh linens, and clanked upon stone. Axe's eyes opened, and the priestess gave Clique a sad look that replaced his anger with grief. Clique collapsed back into his chair, and cried.

After that girl, Vansa, had gained possession of the crystal of Darkness, the barbarian Kalios rode his horse through the gate. "Drathos Dogon is dead," he had declared. "I am Drathos now! The terms will be met. I will lead my people to Castle Montague, as agreed."

"Your people will never succeed in taking a castle, Drathos," Clique had said. "You have no siege weapons. Fighting a wall is not the same as fighting an army. You'd be lucky–"

"It is you who should count yourself lucky!" the man interrupted. "God, or no god, no walls would have saved you. Nor will theirs save them." He reared his horse and looked down upon Vansa. "You are the Lord of Life and Death now," he told her. "And you will always have a place among my people." He laughed. "Call upon us when we have our castle!" With that, the newly proclaimed Drathos rode through the gateway and led his army back across the river, where they marched East towards Davenport lands.

Clique could have strangled the Fenrian girl when she claimed the crystal. It was the second time such a treasure was snatched away by greedy hands, but by then it was too late. He would not bring harm to an innocent, especially one who was special, and the chosen ambassador for her people. Still, Clique could not leave the girl to her own devices. In private audience with her and Ser Ringley, he and Axe revealed their crystals, and explained their purpose in investigating the Doom. She was rightly shocked, and in the spirit of full disclosure, was later left with Ser Ringley, who would explain all the finer details of the eight crystals, and the events that led to their coming to the Barrows. She had been told that her life as a nomad was over, and that if she was to possess such an artifact, she was now conscripted into the Royal Huntsmen, and would travel with them for the duration of their quest. She was more than happy to agree to their terms, and said it was destiny that brought them together, to join forces against the Doom. Drathos could not see the wisdom in it, but she was no barbarian, and pledged to follow the Royal Huntsmen to the ends of the world if need be. Clique and Axe were satisfied.

The more pressing concern now, for Clique, was what was to be done with Collin's earthen crystal should he die. His fate was all but sealed, and it was undoubtedly the magic of the crystal that had allowed him to linger for as long as he had. If only it were the wounds from magic viper and steel that threatened his life, then proper care and the healing arts might save him. But the wounds he had suffered were minor, and they'd inflicted injuries upon the flesh but nothing more. "He has been poisoned," Howser O'Brien, the head priest of the Barrows, had told them after his first inspection. Collin had been carried from the field, undressed, and placed in bed for tending, and Howser needed only to sniff the dagger's wound, before he suspected a toxin. He demanded the dagger be brought to him at once, and when he and his priests performed tests on the vile substance that coated the blade, they were saddened to discover it was the venom of the manticore. Such a thing was incurable, and would eat away at him from the inside out. There were stronger, more potent poisons that would kill a man quickly, Howser explained. When ingested, manticore venom would kill a man in seconds, but infect a wound with it, and death comes after long painful hours. Clique cursed Drathos for his barbarian cruelty.

Collin was given only a day to live, but two nights in a row he defied the priests and lingered ever at death's door. There was nothing to be done save for making him comfortable. Sadder still, there was no talking with the man. He would come to consciousness, but his tongue was numbed by the venom, and his fingers were too weak to grasp a quill. Even bits of rock dust held on paper struggled to form into letters. The best they could manage was a small stone, that he would tumble to one side for yes, and another for no. His wits had not completely left him, and he understood his fate, and was permitted visitors. On that second day, one by one every last man, woman, boy, and girl inside the Barrows came to pay their respects. They would enter, and look into his eyes and thank him, then leave so the next could do the same. The most emotional goodbyes were those of the Royal Huntsmen and his squire Samuel, who took their time in recounting stories of their adventures together. By way of the rock for communication, and Axe's good sense, Collin revealed his intention to knight his squire before he died. Ser Ringley performed the act in Collin's stead, and Samuel was finally given his knighthood.

Ser Thomas was the most broken up of all, and was even brought to a fury when told he could not stay at Collin's side to the end. That honor was reserved for Axe alone. Ser Thomas objected most vehemently, but ultimately came to know the right of it, and pledged instead to stand guard outside his door. Once he stood, the others did as well, and when not asleep, or tending to duties in the castle, the

Royal Huntsmen took their place guarding the room where their brother was meeting his end.

Clique's grieving was interrupted when the door opened, and Ser Thomas admitted an O'Brien castle guardsman into the room. The man had a scar on his right cheek, and something about him made the Aspects seem imbalanced. Clique ignored the feeling, and played it off to his own heightened emotional state. "He says he has letter for you," Ser Thomas said.

"Aye, a raven arrived from Stormbreaker with message," the guard said. "I came straightaway from the rookery to deliver it, Lord Commander."

"Yes. Give it here." Clique took the tiny parchment and unraveled it.

"Have you been to our rookery?" the man asked. "The Barrows boasts the largest one in the Realm. It is a sight to see, m'lord."

Clique tossed him a doubloon. "That'll be all."

"Duncan. The names Duncan, m'lord." He bit at the coin, and pocketed it happily.

"That'll be all Duncan. You may go." Clique turned to the priestess. "You too my dear." She bowed politely, and after a moment Clique and Axe were left alone. Clique poured himself a fresh goblet of wine and sat back down. He unfolded the paper and squinted his eyes in the dim light.

"Would you like me to read it?" Axe asked.

Clique snickered. "Yes, actually. That would be of great help." He handed the note over to Axe, and sat back down with a thump. He emptied his goblet, and poured himself a second. "Go on. Out with it."

"You'll be pleased to hear that Lady Keira has given birth to a baby boy. He is named Davik the second, and has taken the fashion of *The Undying* by the people."

"That is wonderful news! I have another cousin." Clique rejoiced. "Though not exactly unexpected, and not enough to warrant a raven..."

"There is more. It is unpleasant to hear, Clique. You had best brace yourself." Axe frowned, and Clique felt unsettled that a man like Axe would take the time to buffer the news with politeness. Clique sighed, took a long drink from his goblet, and nodded. "Your brother Kevin is dead," Axe told him.

Clique whimpered. *Poor Kevin.* "Does it say how he died?"

"Yes. He was squired to Havik Davenport. Your father received a letter from him, the contents of which said that Kevin sacrificed his life to save Havik from a pack of wolves. It was his bravery that resulted in their ranging of the gate being a success. Havik awarded him a knighthood in his passing, and regrets his bones could not be saved from the winter lands. If not for Kevin Gracious, Havik Davenport would be a dead man."

"Such wonderful news," Clique groaned. "One Gracious is born, one Gracious is dead, and another Davenport yet lives."

"Do you suspect some kind of treachery on Havik's part?" Axe asked.

"No. I doubt it," Clique admitted. "He may have been a mad fool to go so far North, but I'd see no reason for him to betray a squire's oath. My lord father said the boy's a good lad, and such oaths held sacred, even by Davenports."

"Is that why you haven't taken a new squire?" Axe asked.

Clique had knighted Janson the morning after the celebration, before they left for Cliffwatch. The boy had the gall to even refuse, saying he'd rather squire a crystal bearer than be a knight. For the jest Clique gave the boy one of his honors, and knighted him all the same. He could have taken a new squire, and with so many armies gathered had pick of the litter, as Ser Ringley had called it, but

Clique refused the offer. *I cannot be burdened by a squire, now that I have crystal,* he had thought. In truth he feared that any man he could not completely trust might try to kill him in the night to steal away his magic. The *only* people Clique could truly trust were Axe and Collin. And Collin would soon be gone.

"I'm tired." Clique rose and made for the door. "You have the box?" Axe nodded, and held up the small leaden chest. "When the time draws near..."

"I know what to do." Axe set the lead box down, leaned back, and closed his eyes.

Clique exited. He saluted the Huntsmen who stood watch outside, and climbed the tower. He was even more exhausted by the time he'd reached the top and entered the chamber he'd claimed as his own. It was near to where Collin was kept, but high enough to have a view of both the fields and the courtyard below. Clique set the lock on the door, and within seconds was asleep in his bed.

That night he was haunted by the memories of his arrival at the Barrows. Captain Marcus had been given his choice of ship as reward, and had chosen a mighty Corsair that was the fastest in Robert's fleet. They would need ships larger than his to take their army to the Barrows, but Clique could think of no one better suited to the task of Captaining their mission than the man who'd sailed the Central Sea for him. With a second ship offered as his reward upon return, the good Captain could not refuse the honor of it. And yet, Captain Marcus came to damn the voyage as cursed when they first spotted the dome of darkness on the horizon. Clique's arrival with his army was heralded as the saving grace of the Barrows, and they were heartily welcomed by all. The few dozen men that met them at the gateway were all that remained of the once mighty guard which had once populated the castle. All of their soldiers, guards, and men of suitable age had been conscripted by the army. In so doing they exposed themselves to the onslaught of the barbarians that threatened to cross the rivers. It was clear that the heads of the O'Brien House never considered the barbarians a true threat, and they would have been right, if not for the crystal bearer that Clique knew must have organized their numbers. *If a crystal does not make that magical darkness,* Clique had thought, *then I fear what does.*

The shadow had arrived North of the fork first, and for the ten days that followed, barbarians gathered in its shade. Every day that passed their numbers swelled. Ravens were sent everywhere asking for help, but all who could fight, both East and West, were away with the armies, and months on the march. Rumor of the barbarian horde quickly spread, and people fled the countryside for fear of them. Many made their way to the Barrows to seek shelter, but the gates had been closed by order of Lochlan O'Brien, Collin's ten year old nephew. The boy was the eldest son of Collin's older brother Liam, and had remained at the Barrows to protect the O'Brien line should it have come to war. He was too young to rule, and a steward handled the normal goings on of the Barrows, but it was not too large a city, and politics were a minor concern while so many nobles were away. When Lochlan saw the gathering shadow, he grew so fearful that he acted upon his authority, and sealed the Barrows shut.

While Lochlan was one step closer to the Proper Lordship of the Barrows than Collin, Collin's age allowed him to claim acting rule, and until his family returned, the Barrows were his. Collin's first act was to open the gates to admit everyone that had been turned away. He ordered riders to send word in every direction to seek shelter at the Barrows before it was too late. Though it had been nearly a fortnight since the army's arrival, it was that afternoon that the barbarians first blew their horns, and everyone feared the invasion was imminent.

Will Tarnell, the Prince of the West, had joined the Royal

Huntsmen on their journey. Though he was to be a Royal Huntsman, and the ships would carry no more than five hundred men, the Prince would not travel without procession of his own. One hundred soldiers sworn to the King of the West, a dozen of which were heavy cavalrymen, came as Will's personal guard. As such, one hundred Gracious solders were left at port, and of their five hundred men, twenty percent were Tarnell. Clique thought the precaution was fair, but only when you took into consideration that Will possessed the crystal of Water. Otherwise it would have been an insult that he implied his life could not be trusted in the hands of the men of Midgard. A squire or a few good men would have been one thing, but a hundred soldiers as an attachment was outrageous. And yet, the politics of crystals seemed to turn that notion on its head, and Will's demand could not be refused. *I should have refused him,* Clique swore as he dreamed. *I am the Lord Commander of the Royal Huntsmen, and it was in my right to put him in his place.*

Axe and Collin suggested they take the Royal Huntsmen North to scout out the barbarian horde. After all, it was clear the barbarians possessed a crystal of their own, and it would be unwise to proceed without getting more information about who they were, and why they might be there, if not to simply besiege the Barrows. The matter was agreed upon in seconds, but Ser Ringley could get no further than suggesting they discuss the strategy of their approach, before Prince Tarnell objected. "We knew there would be the risk of barbarians this far North, and that is why I brought my men," he had said. "I came with you to search for answers regarding the black plague. I did not come North to scout armies and fight in battles. And I most certainly did not come to see good Tarnell men die defending O'Brien lands." His comments erupted in a frenzy of argument between all men present, and was cut to silence when the Prince ripped off his Royal Huntsmen badge and tossed it onto the table. The badges were a new honor, devised and forged at Cliffwatch by Clique's father, and before they left for the Barrows, were presented to the Huntsmen by the goldsmith who made them. Each was a golden shield with silver steed and steel sword plated upon the badge. They symbolized everything the Royal Huntsmen stood for, and when Will Tarnell tossed his carelessly aside, every one of them held their breath. "I will not be party to this madness. When you are finished with these barbarians, you can summon me back to your ranks. Until then, you are on your own."

The Prince stood with some of his knights, and turned to leave the meeting hall. Ser Ringley shouted after him. "And where is it you're running off to hide?"

"Castle White Stone," he said. "Where they have even taller walls than here." That was the last time Clique saw Prince Tarnell, and just like that their numbers were cut to four hundred.

Dozens of their soldiers were sent East along the river with instructions to circle back and patrol for enemy scouts. The majority of their men were ordered to organize the Barrows defenses, first and foremost by conscripting the people who were were arriving to take shelter, and setting their labor to purpose. Meanwhile, the Royal Huntsmen and a contingency of a dozen extra knights crossed the Bear Trap by ship and raft, and headed North along Little Moore's Run. When North of the army, Collin created a narrow stone bridge for them to cross. By then their crystals had become legend amongst the Huntsmen, and the knights were awestruck by the power that Collin possessed. They left their horses by the bridge, and snuck through the forest. Night had fallen, and the storm clouds hid the light of the Silver Star, so they were able to make their way unseen to a small hill that overlooked the army.

"I estimate there to be thirty eight hundred men," Axe told them. "More importantly, I have identified the Commander's tent." Axe pointed to the dome of darkness that was visible in the glow of the camp fires. "It is in the shadow's center."

"You can see through it?" Clique asked. "Why am I not surprised?"

"It only absorbs a small spectrum of light," Axe explained. "And emanates from a man who holds a crystal. I can see the glow of it. There are near a dozen men with him, but as luck would have it, the tent is easily accessible if we enter through the shadow's Eastern side."

"You can't mean to attack him directly!" Ser Ringley was shocked. "In the middle of their army? It is too dangerous!"

"What would you have us do, retreat?" Collin asked.

"I have an idea," Axe smiled. "Allow me to distract them. I will draw their attention, leaving you and Clique to scout their command tent, to see what you can learn."

"What sort of distraction do you have in mind?" Clique asked. "And how will we know when it is time?"

"You will know it..." Axe took off his badge and handed it to Clique, "... by the fire."

Axe crept off into the shadows, and Ser Ringley seemed befuddled. "Why did he give you his badge?" he asked.

"I think he didn't want it to melt." Clique laughed and handed him Axe's badge. "Keep it safe, Ser Ringley. Watch from here, then meet us by the river."

Clique and Collin made their way around the encampment, and drew near the Eastern side of the shadow. They waited no more than five minutes, when an inferno flared up in the heart of the army. The column of flame and fire showered hot death in a great ring around it. Collin gasped and Clique laughed. "How did he?" Collin cried. "Was it his crystal alone?"

"You remember that green fire oil the bastard pirate used against us?" Clique rubbed at his face where it had once been burned, and Collin nodded silently. "Axe had a cask of the stuff in his backpack." They watched the blazing fire dwindle down into a scattering of lesser flames and burning men. The shadow itself began to move towards the fires, and Clique started forward. "Come on."

The two of them skirted along the edge of the shadow, and eventually it had moved far enough that the command tent was visible. It was larger than the rest, and was constructed of fine black silk, uncommon for barbarians. They reached the back of the tent, and lifted its skirt to peer inside. A man of nobility in blue and purple silk clothes was chained to a post in the corner. His face was blackened with bruises, but otherwise seemed in good health. A seven foot tall giant of a man with black leather armor and a two handed greatsword stood eating a leg of mutton near the tent's entrance. One other barbarian sat picking at his teeth with a dagger. The dinner feast Axe had interrupted lay half eaten on the table, and of the dozen men, only two were left. *Axe has done it.* Clique smiled. *We can handle these two easily enough.*

Clique motioned that the giant was his, and Collin understood. Collin readied his longsword, and Clique his scythe, and at the count of three, both burst into the tent to take their foes by surprise. Collin's man was nearest, and though Collin's swing was blocked by the man's dagger, he soon found it turn to dust in his hand, and he scrambled backwards across the room while Collin pressed his attack. The giant grunted at Clique, and tossed his mutton aside. "Who the fook are you?" he asked.

"Your death." Clique smiled through his teeth as he raised the battle scythe up in the air. It did not feel the same in his hands as the black steel to which he was accustomed, but that weapon had been damaged in battle and left at Stormbreaker as there was no time for him to have it repaired. This scythe was uncovered in Cliffwatch's armory, and would serve its purpose, but was not as strong nor sturdy as Clique's old one. In that moment he felt naked, and wondered if Collin felt the same. The battles he and Clique had thus far shared, afforded Collin the use of Starsinger, one of the finest blades known to man. Collin now wielded a simple sword of common castle forged steel. Made for the Huntsmen, it had been emblazoned with the mark of their order, but he imagined it was no comparison whatsoever to the feel of an Ancient sword in one's hands. Still, they had magic at their side, and it would be difficult for a mortal to stand up against such a force. Clique's scythe blade was blocked by the giant's mighty sword, but he coursed his power through it, and electrified the man with a pulse of his lightning. The barbarian's body twitched, and Clique smelt the burning of tiny hairs on his flesh, but the man was such a colossus that he seemed undisturbed by the force of the magic. If anything, it only served to drive him into a frenzy.

Clique's attacks with his scythe quickly transformed into a series of desperate blocks as the barbarian charged forward. His mighty muscles wielded the heavy blade with such vigorous speed, that Clique could barely defend himself, let alone stand against the strength of the blows. Clique was driven to his back, and felt the fear course through him as the giant held the point of his greatsword over Clique's head and started to plunge it down. Clique slid to the side, and barely avoided the strike. Out of the corner of his eye he saw Collin engaged in a dire battle of his own, as his man had recovered an axe, and was making a fight of it. The colossal barbarian's greatsword dug deep into the dirt, and he dropped to his knee with his large body towering over Clique's meager physique. Clique's scythe was of no use in close combat like this, and he tasted the salt and fat of the mutton grease that dripped from the barbarian's chin into Clique's mouth. The giant stepped onto Clique's chest and pinned him flat. In that moment Clique's eyes fell upon the dagger in the barbarian's boot. "Goodbye little man," the barbarian boasted as he pulled his sword from the dirt. Clique did not hesitate as he slipped the dagger from its sheath, and split the tendons of the giant's ankle apart.

The man screamed as he fell to his back, and Clique was atop him before he hit the ground. The dagger slid across the barbarian's throat, and split that flesh just as easily with its sharp steel edge. When Clique stood over the corpse of the dead giant, he saw Collin standing equally victorious. Clique's heart was racing, and he still felt the fear of the battle, but Collin gave him a confident smile and a cool stare that put Clique strangely at ease. *Collin...*

They caught their breaths as the purple energy rose from the bodies of the dead, and was absorbed by their crystals in the strange magic ritual that proceeded every death in a crystal bearer's presence. When the magic had run its course, they turned their attention to the nobleman chained in the corner. He had seen everything, but seemed oblivious to the souls of the dead. "Who are you?" Collin asked, as he struck his blade on the chains and disintegrated them, freeing the man.

"The name's Garvin," the nobleman said as he rubbed at his wrists. "Garvin Davenport."

Clique awoke to the sound of knocking at his door. He did not know for how long he'd slept, but it was still dark outside and his body ached for lack of rest. He wrapped himself in a fur robe and opened the chamber door to find Axe standing outside. The lead box was in his hand.

"It is done," Axe whispered. "He's gone."

May you rest in peace, Collin O'Brien. Clique prayed silently. *You will be remembered.*

"Come in." Clique shut the door behind Axe, and opened the lead box. Inside was Collin's brown crystal. Though solid, it felt as if it had no weight, and could be made to stand perfectly on end by its point. The crystal still shimmered with its inner light and it vibrated with the tiniest of high pitched shrieks. When placed against Clique's bare skin, the crystal made no effort to join itself to either of his arms. Collin placed it back in the chest, closed it, and fastened it shut with its latch. "Are we sure this will hold it?"

"Yes." Axe took back the chest, and placed it in a pouch that hung from his side. "Ser Thomas held the box to no effect."

"Good. That's good." Clique poured himself some water.

"What are we to do now, Clique?" Axe asked. "Shall we travel to Astermount, or retrieve Prince Tarnell from White Stone? Perhaps we should warn the Davenports of the army that rides to face them? Or even take our lovely Lady of Life and Death with us, and seek the barbarian's council. It seems all they want is a castle, and with this," Axe patted the pouch with the earth crystal inside, "a castle could be raised up for them in days, whereas once it would take a century. We've no shortage of castles, but the Doom that faces us won't be stopped by walls. Of course, so Kalios claims, neither will they."

Clique sat down and listened to the man. *He has a point.* "Perhaps..."

"What have you learned from Garvin's inquisitions?" Axe asked.

Clique sighed. "He's an idiot." Clique shook his head. "His caravan was attacked by barbarians, and because of his nobility was taken to Drathos Dogon. Garvin was so awestruck by the crystal, that he persuaded Drathos to let him live. In exchange he promised Drathos a castle, that he might have a kingdom to be made King of." Clique laughed. "He played on the barbarian's greed and won out, but was certainly not just going to hand over his *own* castle to them. That would have assured him of life, but lost him his wealth." Clique tossed his goblet aside and started to get dressed. "He knew the

Barrows was empty of men, and led them to the rivers. He was an honored guest of theirs until their scouts saw our ships arrive with *us* aboard. Drathos was convinced Davenport betrayed them, and chained him up. And *that* is how we found him."

"It seems logical," Axe frowned, "but I am convinced his tale is a lie."

"Why's that?"

"Because it is based on the presumption that a Davenport could be an idiot," Axe answered coldly, and that sent a chill down Clique's spine. "We have learned their family prides itself on a superior intellect, and the ability to plan strategy. Plus, you said it yourself when you told Kalios that his barbarians stood no chance at taking a castle. Davenport must have known the same thing. They had no siege weapons. No towers. No ladders. He would have known that if he led them into even a single failed assault on the wall, his life would have been forfeit."

"So what are you saying?" Clique asked.

"He either had spies in the Barrows, that would open the gates from the inside and allow the castle to be taken," Axe explained, "or he knew the barbarians possessed some further advantage that could overtake the walls. Kalios had lost their army's dark crystal, but was still confident that no walls would stop them. Either the crystal created some form of advantage, one that persists even though the crystal's no longer in their possession, or they have something else in mind."

"Then that settles that," Clique said as he put on his boots.

"What do you mean?"

"First we will pay Garvin Davenport a visit, and see if he sings us a new song." Clique fastened an O'Brien short sword to his belt and slipped it round his waist. "Then we will see if Vansa Ketrien has learned any more of the crystal's secrets."

Axe opened the door and was about to leave, but Clique stopped him by the arm. "Axe. There's something I've been meaning to ask you."

"What's that?" Axe turned back to face him.

"When you set that fire..." Clique whispered. "The souls of the dead... the purple aura... did it–"

Axe nodded solemnly. "I took in hundreds of them."

"Did it... change you in any way?"

"Not that I am aware. But I will keep you apprised if it does."

Clique and Axe descended the tower and ventured deep into the dungeons beneath the Barrows where their prisoner had been jailed. The dungeon entrance had been properly guarded by two O'Brien men, but the halls and cells below were empty. "Are there no other prisoners in this dungeon?" Axe asked.

Clique sighed. "Lochlan had every last prisoner put to death when the shadow arrived."

"Why?" Axe asked.

"Where are the guards?" Clique cried as they turned the corner. "There should be men on Garvin's cell!" They both groaned in disbelief when they discovered Garvin was dead. The cell door was still locked, and Axe was forced to pry it open. They found him chained by manacle, with three crossbow bolts in his body. One struck his heart and he had bled out quickly. "The work of those Davenport spies of yours, Axe?"

"Just what I was thinking, Lord Commander," Axe agreed as he pulled a bolt from the corpse. "And from the look of it, O'Brien men, and not our own." He rubbed blood from the side of the iron bolt and pointed at the O'Brien blacksmith's seal. "These Davenports must have spies in every House in the Realm."

"This... poses a very dangerous problem. A very dangerous problem indeed."

"How so?"

Clique started pacing. "Think it through, Axe. If we leave with our army, North, or East, or South, or wherever we decide to go, the Barrows will be left virtually undefended. The O'Briens have only a handful of men, any number of which might be spies, and the streets are littered with Eldaria's Lost Children."

"Who are they?" Axe pocketed the iron bolt and covered Davenport's body with a sheet of cloth.

"Haven't you seen them?" Clique asked. "Oh, right." Clique sat on the cot laid out for Davenport and caught his breath. "You've been with Collin at his bedside... They're these religious fanatics, Axe. They came to see the miracle of the magic shadow, and now the song has spread, not just of our crystals of Lightning, and Fire, and Stone, but also of the Fenrian girl who is heralded as the Lord of Life and Death. Tale of the crystal and how it joined with her upon Drathos Dogon's death will soon be legend across all the Realm."

"Why is it bad they know the truth?" Axe asked.

"First and foremost, it means everyone will know that a crystal can be stolen upon its bearer's death." Clique snickered. "We may as well just paint targets on our armors."

"You fear for our safety..." Axe whispered.

Clique laughed. "No, Axe. I fear for the Barrows, *and* the Realm. Opposing groups of religions have sprouted up like weeds. Some worship Flame, while others Lightning, and so on. These Lost Children have abandoned the Goddess and the djinn for more tangible manifestations of god. *Us*, and our crystals. Their numbers have grown each day, and they preach their sermons at every bench in the city."

"But where is the harm in it?"Axe did not understand.

"Religion is a dangerous thing, Axe Treefort," Clique told him. "More will make pilgrimage here, to where the shadow's song began. And unless some measures to keep the peace are taken, it will undoubtedly come to arms. Even if *we* leave, more of *them* will come *here*. The Barrows doesn't have enough men to handle any such disturbances."

"We could leave half our men here to keep the peace," Axe suggested. "The barbarians pose no threat to us. We don't need the numbers anymore."

"You're missing the point of it, Axe. Think." Axe scratched at his chin, and shook his head. Clique went on. "If we were to leave even all of our men here at the Barrows, and left on our merry way, our men would take their orders from who?"

"From Lochlan O'Brien," Axe answered.

"Yes. And we already know how much the boy fears. He acts in haste, without thinking of what is best for his people," Clique told him. "Collin said as much. He's only a boy, Axe. A boy who first locked out his people, before killing all his prisoners."

"What about his advisers?" Axe asked.

"They could be spies!" Clique raised his arms. "It may have been their influence that forced the boy to shut the gates in the first place. Best not have too many peasants inside! Else they might try to stop the gates from being raised to welcome inside Garvin Davenport and his barbarian horde. For all we know, they wanted to keep the small folk out to protect them, knowing full well the barbarians might kill them *inside* the castle, rather than from without."

"So what's the alternative?" Axe asked. "We stay here until Ronan and his family arrives? That will take months."

"No. We cannot waste time where Doom is concerned." Clique stood. "The situation calls for drastic measures." He patted Axe on his shoulder, and whispered. "The only way to protect *both* the people's peace *and* the castle, until the O'Briens arrive... is if Gracious soldiers were in control of the Barrows. Only then would the spies influence be rendered moot, and with our soldier's presence, peace assured."

Finally Axe understood. "So what you're saying is..."

Clique nodded. "We have to take over the castle."

Clique and Axe's first step was to interrogate the two guards at the dungeon entrance. A few questions revealed that they had been placed on task there by Ser Beribold of the Royal Huntsmen. He had seen the dungeon doors undefended, and moved them there from the main gates. Both were shocked when Clique revealed that Garvin Davenport, the only living prisoner in the dungeons, was dead. "You have either utterly failed in your duty, have arrived on the scene too late, or are the murderers yourselves," Clique told them. "If you don't want to be flogged for your incompetence, then I'd suggest you follow my commands."

"What would you have of us?" they asked, shocked by the magnitude of the situation.

"Gather all of the O'Brien soldiers and guards from without and within the castle," Clique commanded. "Everyone needs to be properly informed of Davenport's murder, so we can attempt to find the perpetrators of this heinous crime. Have everyone brought to the Hall of Oak. I will give speech there to discuss the investigation."

The two guards rushed off to perform the task. "You mean to lead the investigation, Lord Commander?" Axe asked.

Clique shook his head. "No, Axe," he whispered. "I mean to gather their men in one place."

"Ahh..." Axe nodded and smiled. "A tactical deception."

Clique sighed. "Come, we must find Ser Ringley immediately."

They got no further than the entrance hall of the Barrows before they were stopped by Lord Chase in a state of panic. "Axe! Lord Commander!" he cried as he rushed over. "Thank the Heavens you're here, Axe. We need your help right away."

"What's the matter?" Clique asked him.

The fear in Chase's purple eyes was plain to see. "It's the black plague! Come! Quickly!" Lord Chase led them through the halls of the castle with great haste. He stopped when they reached a large iron banded door. The priestess that attended to Collin's passing was in a state of feverish fear beside the fastened door.

"Oh! Lord Commander! It's horrible. Horrible!" she sobbed.

Clique caught his breath. "What's happened? Tell me."

"I was tending to Lord O'Brien's body, and noted a strange black tint to his veins." She chewed at her fingernails. "I thought it was the poison, but... but..."

"Go on. It's alright." Clique comforted her.

"Something moved inside his chest... and... when I touched it... It popped!" She shuddered with fear, and sobbed into Clique's shoulder. "Black powder filled the air, m'lord! It was everywhere!" Clique released her from his arms and backed away. Her eyes were wide with fear. "I breathed some of it in!" She sobbed, delirious. "Am I... Am I?"

"My lady." Axe took a step forward. "I have to ask you to follow my orders. It's very important. Do you understand?" She nodded. "Take off all your clothes, then go straight to bathe in a tub. Clean yourself thoroughly, then cover the tub, and burn the towels you used to dry yourself with. Can you do this for me?" The priestess nodded again, quickly disrobed, then ran off set to purpose. Axe picked up the girl's clothes, and handed his Huntsmen badge to Clique. "Wait here, both of you."

Axe took a torch from a nearby sconce, and it ignited into flame. He opened the banded door, slipped in, and shut it behind him. "How is it the plague has spread?" Clique asked Lord Chase. "Collin showed no signs of sickness before he was poisoned."

"I do not know, Lord Commander." Chase shrugged. "But maybe

Axe will."

After ten long minutes a knocking erupted from the inside of the door, and Clique and Lord Chase stood back while Axe stepped through. A gush of warm wind carrying a cloud of ash and smoke followed him into the hall. All the cloth on his body was gone, and his leathers were black crisps from the heat of the fire. His belt was chain, and his dual axes hung without problem, but his boots were ashen shells. Axe's hair was amazingly unharmed by the flame.

"What happened in there?" Clique asked. Axe reached out and took his badge back.

"We have a fooking problem, that's what happened," Axe exclaimed, and both Clique and Lord Chase gasped at Axe's unusual use of profanity. "The room was thick with the black seed," he told them. "There was so much of it that it obscured my sight. I pushed through a cloud of it to reach Collin's corpse and..." The pause made Clique's blood run cold. "It had transformed him."

"What?" Chase and Clique both asked together.

"His chest was torn open, and some kind of black organic mass was growing inside his body." Axe stared into their eyes. "It rose when it saw me... and his corpse glowed blue with magic, while the black seed itself does not."

Clique was aghast. "What does it mean?"

"Two terrible things, my lords." Axe sighed. "First that we are, all three of us, already infected." Chase lost his stomach and retched onto the floor. "We Huntsmen were exposed by the kavolia. That was the only time Collin was even near the stuff."

"Will it kill us?" Clique asked.

"I do not believe so," Axe explained. "But if those who have been exposed die, then the black seed will blossom."

"But it killed the kavolia," Chase protested between coughs. "Wouldn't we be next?"

"I do not think the kavolia were killed by the plague," Axe said.

"Then how?" Clique asked.

"They died from exhaustion... and fear."

"But this thing... You said it transformed him?" Chase gathered himself and stood.

"I suspect that was the result of Collin's magic," Axe said.

"But his crystal was removed when he died," Clique pointed out.

"Yes, but when he *did* have it, so too did he have the black seed inside him." Axe frowned. "What I'm saying is, it fed on his magic like a parasite. And when he died... it took over."

"And if Collin's crystal was never taken from his corpse... What then?" Axe had no answer for the question, and the thought of it twisted at Clique's mind.

"Where is it now?" Chase asked.

"Burned. Everything in the room is ash. I made sure of that," Axe said. "But from now on, when a Royal Huntsman dies, he must be burned immediately. That priestess included."

"And when a crystal bearer dies..." Clique whispered.

"Vansa has not been exposed. Nor has Prince Tarnell. And I believe I am immune." Axe frowned. "That leaves only–"

"Me." Clique laughed. "Very well then. If I die, make sure I am put to the fires... But what about Drathos Dogon?" Axe shrugged. "Where is his corpse?"

"It was buried in the courtyard," Lord Chase said. "I could have him dug up to check..."

"Later," Clique grunted. "We have more important fish to fry."

Clique ordered Lord Chase to summon the Royal Huntsmen and their knights together, then led Axe out of the castle and into the grand courtyard. It was early morning, and the Red Star had just risen over the horizon. The storm clouds were gone, and the sky was awash with pinks and blues. Clique met with a group of Gracious soldiers and gave command to bring the army together for general orders. Men ran and horns sounded. It was not long before all the Huntsmen, save for Ser Beribold and Ser Thomas were present. Clique stood before his Huntsmen, and their gathering of knights and soldier Commanders, and in hushed tones, Clique explained the situation. He told them of his reasoning behind taking the castle, then issued the orders to take control of the Hall of Oak first, and imprison every last O'Brien man in the dungeons. "Do it with such large a show of force, that it would be madness for any to rise against us," Clique told them. "And try not to kill anyone. It's possible someone might martyr themselves for political motivations, so don't let them get the upper hand."

"What about Lochlan?" Ser Ringley asked.

"Let the soldiers deal with taking the castle. Lochlan should be taken by the Royal Huntsmen and our knights. Make sure no harm comes to the boy, but lock him in the dungeon just the same."

"In the dungeon!" Lord Haren was shocked. "But he is high nobility! The O'Briens–"

"Will be happy he is alive when they return," Clique interrupted. "And a dungeon defended by Gracious men, and Gracious men alone, will be the safest place for him. We cannot trust O'Brien servants, but I will leave it up to their family to weed out the rats. All we need to do is secure their castle, their people, and their lineage until they return. An easy task! For we are Royal Huntsmen and good Gracious men!" Clique shouted. "And this is what Collin would have wanted." Clique raised his fist. "We will keep the peace, for him!" With Collin gone, there was no question as to who was Lord Commander of the Royal Huntsmen, and Clique felt the energy of Collin's great speeches coursing through him as he spoke. The Huntsmen hooted and stamped their feet, and moments later, his army and his men set off to take control of the Barrows. *The most defensible castle in the world,* Clique laughed to himself, *and it has all but fallen twice in four days.*

"Ser Ringley!" Clique shouted after him. "One other thing."

"Yes, Lord Commander?" Ser Ringley asked as he approached.

"What did you learn from Mickey O'Brien?" Clique asked.

"Ahh. He has been most helpful." Ser Ringley smiled. "He and his wizards have been reviewing their materials on djinn. I spoke with him last night, and he says they've prepared for us several maps where he thinks the djinni of life might be found. There are other djinn just as intriguing to consider finding, or so he says. He has maps for those as well. Some even lead to Fenria."

"Excellent!" Clique smiled. *At least one thing has gone right for us.* "And what about the Fenrian girl, Vansa? Where is she?"

"Fountain Street." Ser Ringley pointed across the courtyard. "Talking with the Children."

"Not alone, I trust," Clique said.

"No. She's with Ser Thomas, Ser Beribold, and Harold Wood's brother," Ser Ringley said.

Axe was shocked. "Korvin is here!"

Ser Ringley nodded, as if this were some uncannily interesting news. "What does it matter?" Clique asked, confused. "If he's an O'Brien, should we imprison him as well?"

"It's his bastard twin," Ser Ringley explained. "There's some bad blood between the two."

"Why's that?" Clique asked.

"Harold's brother's the better fighter, but he refuses to join the Huntsmen, or even serve anyone at all," Ser Ringley told him. "Still, he's as good a man as his brother, and is no threat."

"He's not *just* a better fighter," Axe said, excited. "He is a master of a secret style of combat that has been passed through the ages to a select few. Forms of fighting that go back as far as the Ancients!"

"What's so special about it?" Clique asked, and Ser Ringley laughed.

"It's the only thing Axe Treefort *isn't* good at!" Axe blushed. "You should have seen him. Kicking and waving about like a madman trying to imitate his moves." Clique did not quite understand, and Ser Ringley tried to explain further. "He fights... like a dancer."

"Ahh..." Clique laughed when he tried to imagine Axe dancing. "Alright Ser Ringley. That'll be all. Go see to Lochlan's capture. I will fetch the girl and keep her at our side while we seize control."

Axe and Clique made their way to Fountain Street. It was still quite early, and most people were either in their houses, or in the shanty town that had grown even further overnight. Vansa and her knightly guards were in plain sight on the street, and stood beside a group of six men in brown robes. All six turned and stared at Clique as he and Axe approached. When Clique drew close, his stomach whirled with annoyance. Each man had bolt of lightning tattooed on their forehead in red and yellow ink. *Not more of them...* Clique groaned. "This is him." Vansa laughed, and all six men dropped to their feet.

"Lord of Lightning!" one of them declared. "Where once we were Lost Children of Eldaria, now we have found our way. We—"

"Yes! Yes! Yes!" Clique waved them off. "Be silent in my presence, monks." They quieted themselves. "You may rise, and please, take a few steps back. Thank you." The six rose and stepped away obediently. Still they kept their eyes on him.

Axe was shocked, and the man Clique assumed to be Korvin Wood clapped his hands together with delight. "They obey your commands?" Axe asked.

"They think he's a god," Vansa said. "Well, they think all three of us are gods. Only he's *their* god. Or something like that. I'm still not really sure." Vansa laughed. "I think the problem is they're not sure themselves. Everyone has a different take on it. I've made sure *my* followers stay out of sight."

"You've ordered them to, you mean," Ser Thomas added.

"Yes, well," she pointed down the street, where men in black robes seemed to lurk in the distance, ever watching her, "they'll do whatever I say, but they won't leave me completely. *Ever.* Creepy, I know. That's why my good knights are with me. And soon I intend to acquire protection of my own."

"Ser Beribold." Clique eyed him. "A word." Clique and Axe took the man aside, and questioned him regarding Garvin's murder. It seemed he only noticed the dungeon was unguarded while passing by with Vansa. He didn't wish to leave her unprotected, and ordered the next guards he saw to stand watch. His explanation seemed satisfactory, and Clique returned to the group. "Vansa, it is time for us to go back to the castle. There's something we must discuss. Ser Thomas, Korvin, you two come as well. As for the rest of you." Clique eyed the monks. "Gather together all those who follow Lightning. I wish to address all of you later today."

The monks were thrilled by his words, and pledged to serve him to the best of their abilities. Ser Thomas and Ser Beribold escorted Vansa, while Axe walked beside Korvin and chatted with his friend. Clique turned from his monks and came face to face with a beautiful woman with fiery red hair and ruby eyes. She wore a red woolen robe, and had a red flame tattooed on her forehead. "Clique Gracious, avatar of the crystals." She stared at him without smiling, and spoke softly, with sweet, almost seductive undertones to her voice.

"You're a Child of Fire?" Clique asked.

"Yes... I am." *Now* she smiled, and seemed all the more beautiful for it.

"Then Axe is the one you'll be wanting to talk to." Clique

grinned. "I'm Lightning." He tapped on his right arm.

"I know who you are, my lord." Her smile disappeared. "And I have seen your future."

Clique's smile faded just as quickly. "And just what do you think you have seen?" he asked pointedly.

"You will die in flames." After his recent conversation with Axe, the words cut down to his darkest fears. He pushed her out of the way and ran to catch up with his companions. "Do not be afraid!" she shouted after him. "Through Fire you will be *reborn*! I have seen it!"

Clique cast the madness of her prophecy aside, and joined the others. While they walked back to the castle, he explained their situation, and told Ser Beribold and Ser Thomas to bring Vansa to the wizard's tower where Mickey O'Brien might have some use of her knowledge of the North. She requested that Korvin join her, and Clique agreed. It seemed the man had caught song of the shadow, and made his way with the Lost Children to the Barrows. "You could imagine my surprise when I saw Ser Thomas!" Korvin laughed as he talked, and it was plain to see he was quite drunk. "I never thought I'd see a Huntsman so far North of the wall. For a good minute, I thought I was going crazy! Ha ha!"

They parted ways at the castle entrance, and Axe escorted Clique to the throne room, where Lochlan was to have been summoned before his official capture by their knights. When they reached the top of the steps and entered the chamber, they saw the deed was done, but not without blood spilled. Three O'Brien guards, and one of their knights, whose name Clique could not recall, had been slain in the combat. *At least it wasn't a Huntsman,* Clique thought, then felt cruel for thinking it. The battle must have happened recently, for spilt blood still steamed, and captured men still struggled in complaint. There were near twenty men and women who had come to court. All were being bound by rope and prepared for travel to the dungeons. Lochlan stood flanked by Ser Lawrence and Ser Montgomery. He spit at Clique's feet when he approached. "You will *die* for this."

"Lord O'Brien." Clique knelt so he could address the boy at eye level. "What I do is for your own good, and the good of your people."

"You steal *my* castle, and have the nerve to say it's for *my* benefit! You're insane..." The boy laughed, while the faces of nearby ministers and advisers drained of color. "My father and my grandfather will not stand for this!"

"Your father will be glad enough you are not dead! I do not expect you to understand." Clique sighed as he looked at him. "You're just a boy." Clique rose and made eyes with the other men in the room. "You will all be kept safe in the dungeons until Ronan returns. It will be *his* responsibility to sort this all out. It's *my* responsibility to see the Barrows safely back into Lord O'Brien's hands."

Clique stepped back and allowed for the prisoners to be removed to their cells. *If Collin were here, he could have ordered the transition peacefully,* Clique lamented, *instead of it having to come to this.* As the room cleared, Clique beckoned Ser Ringley and Axe to speak with him in private. "Axe. Go with Ser Ringley and dig up Drathos Dogon's corpse. Take note of whether he has been corrupted, then burn him to be sure."

Ser Ringley nodded, but Axe narrowed his eyes. "What do you intend?"

Clique patted him on the shoulder. "Nothing devious, Axe." He laughed. "It's time I wrote a letter to my uncle, our King, and inform him of all that has happened." Axe nodded. "Starcrown and Starspire must be warned of the black plague's potency as well. Meet me in the wizard's tower when you're done. I mean for us to decide what our next destination will be."

Axe and Ser Ringley left for the courtyard, while Clique made his way to the rookery. He knew the location of the tower by sight from outside, and was confident he could find the way himself. It took him no more than two failed attempts, but he soon found himself at the top of the correct tower. The rookery held the castle's ravens, and as he pushed his way into the room, he was beset by the sounds of the incessantly chattering birds and their flapping wings. There were hundreds upon hundreds of them, all housed in dozens of separate cages. Each bird held differently colored bracelets on their legs, all with unique markings of their own. Clique spotted a man nearby, and cleared his throat. "Excuse me..."

The man turned, and Clique recognized him as Duncan. "Ahh, Lord Commander. You've decided to visit the rookery after all."

"Yes. Duncan, isn't it?" Clique smiled at him. The man wore leather armor and had a short sword at his side, but held a bag of corn in his hands that he'd been using to feed the ravens. *It seems my soldiers have overlooked the towers,* Clique thought. *Not every O'Brien guard has been accounted for.*

"Yes, m'lord. Yes. Duncan's my name!" The man bowed politely. "Kind of you to remember."

"Where are the wizards in charge of the ravens?" Clique asked. "I mean to send a letter."

"Oh, it's still too early for the likes of them." Duncan laughed. "Rookery's usually empty in the morning. New birds don't come in til evening hours, m'lord."

"What are *you* doing here, then?" Clique asked.

"Oh me? Why I just like to feed the birds." Duncan tossed some corn into a nearby cage. "Sending a letter to Stormbreaker Stronghold, are you?"

"Yes. Exactly." Clique smiled. "Can you tell me–"

"Which raven you'll be needing? You'll find them over there, with the rest of the Midgard birds." He pointed to the corner cell. "Now if you don't mind, m'lord, I think I'm gonna get myself a warm meal. All the birds are fed, and I think it's about time Duncan had *his* fair turn at the table, if you catch my meaning, m'lord. You'll find all the supplies you'll need over there." Duncan gestured towards the desks then backed out of the rookery.

"Thank you, Duncan!" Clique called after him. "Shut the door on your way out!" Clique waited until he was gone, then found himself some parchment, some ink, a quill, and laid them all out on a clean section of table. *Poor Duncan will be captured by soldiers before he gets his breakfast,* Clique mused as he prepared his letter. *But better him miss a meal, than inconvenience me with having to take a prisoner. The last thing I need is the distraction.* Clique sighed as he dipped his quill in ink and considered all that he needed to write. *This will be a long letter,* he thought. *Perhaps I should write it in parts, and send two birds.*

Interruption came to him not one second after he set quill to parchment. The door opened, and he glanced back to see Duncan walking in. Clique sighed. "What's the matter Duncan, forget something?" Clique turned to put his quill down, when he felt the waves of a change in the Aspects. Clique's heart raced, and as he stood his hand dropped to his sword hilt, but his reaction came too late. The crossbow bolt impaled itself deep into the right side of his chest, where he felt it burrow into his lung. Clique gurgled with pain, angered at his stupidity for not taking the man prisoner from the start. *Why did I not sense the change earlier?* The sting of his incomplete training almost hurt as much as the wound in his chest.

Duncan tossed the crossbow aside and drew his short sword, while three other O'Brien men entered the rookery and flanked

Clique's sides with daggers drawn. "Don't make a fuss about it," Duncan eyed him coldly, "and it'll be over quick, I promise."

Clique drew his short sword, and backed towards the open window. His mind raced, and in that moment he felt his magic surge through him. A bolt of lightning arced through the window and struck his sword, then erupted forward and blasted one of the men in the chest, who flew back and smashed into a nearby cage, which sent ravens flying free in a panic. The man struck by lightning was a charred corpse, but Clique felt the exhaustion of the act alongside the pain of his wound, and knew he could not handle another such attack, let alone three. "After he's dead, back the fook away!" Duncan grinned. "Just like I told ya!"

Time seemed to slow as the three men neared with their weapons drawn. A silvery liquid dripped from their daggers, and Clique recognized it as poison. The bolt in his chest burned something fierce, and he suspected it was poisoned as well. His mind reeled with the possibility of his death. *If I am not killed with flame, the black seed will spread....* The lunacy of the thought, and the red woman's prophecy, was only outweighed by the horror of it all. Clique's eyes focused on the ravens fluttering about him. *And the ravens would carry it everywhere...* Clique's thoughts crystallized in final decision. *That cannot be allowed to happen.* Clique backed to the window's ledge and glanced down. The drop was a sheer three hundred feet, as high as any tower in Stormbreaker, and was angled along the edge of the cliff wall. This meant the drop led down to the freezing waters of the Bear Trap, and not the courtyard.

"Don't do it!" Duncan cried out, but now it was him who was too late. Clique leapt from the window without looking back. He took as deep of a breath as he could muster, and braced himself for the impact with the waters below. As he fell another bolt of lightning descended from the heavens and struck him with a resounding crackle of thunder. Clique figured it was his fear and desperation that summoned the bolt, but his thoughts were wrestled from him when the cold water crashed over his face, and he tumbled into the icy darkness.

Clique pulled at his heavy leather doublet, but it was difficult for him to see or move as his body sunk deep into the river. He tore at his sleeve and revealed his golden crystal. Its magical light illuminated the murky depths, and as Clique's eyes came into focus, he saw the corpses of three wizards in the waters beside him. Their grey robes drifted with the current, but their bodies were fastened by chain to heavy stones that clung to the river floor. They had been there no more than a day. The fright of the vision caused Clique to foolishly scream, and he felt the deadly chill of the river as it surged into his mouth and filled his lungs.

Havik's world was frozen darkness. He did not know if he was alive or dead, or even where he was, or whether it was a dream or reality. What he did know was that he hurt. His body felt awash in cold pain, and when he tried to open his eyes he became deathly aware that they had been frozen shut. From within his blackened prison, he pried his right arm up, and felt snow and ice crack and give way as he lifted it. *I have frozen,* he managed to think, but his mind was a cloud of ice and mist. He pulled himself up from the snow and pawed at his face until again he could see. His fingers were wrapped in crude cloths that were frozen so tightly he had to remove them. Havik sat for several minutes just breathing. His wits were slow to return to him, and he felt as if even his mind had froze. Before him lay a white snowy wasteland seared purple in the Dead Star's aura, and a light snow fell from clouds above. But there in the distance the black sky was marred by a red glow. *The signal fire,* he remembered. *The ship.*

Havik turned and felt for his leather straps. They led into a mound of snow where his sled and its passenger had been covered by the snowstorm. *How is it I'm not dead?* he wondered, and as he thought the question his thawing tongue tasted a hint of the white seed's foam that once had graced his lips. *The foam's magic, it must be.* Havik did not want to think anymore. His head throbbed with ache and his stomach roiled with hunger and nausea. He clawed out the sled from the snow, and dug from its depths what little remaining food he had. He sat there eating his rations until even the crumbs of the cold stale bread were gone, then sucked on pieces of ice to water his mouth. *It is a blessing I have not lost my fingers,* he remarked to himself, but the sweetness of it turned bitter as he regretted not saving some foam for Jhev. Havik had planned on giving him some, but by that time it was lost to them, and Havik chastised himself for eating all that had remained in his pocket in that moment on the fiery cliff.

Havik felt his memories of the events that took place in the Barrens returning to him. Somehow he had managed to block it all out, even forget, in the week he had been pulling the sled. *No,* he reminded himself. *It was my uncle who told me to forget, and I was too weak to make my own choice.* All at once Havik's fear returned to him as he heard the howling of the wolves. *They did hear me... And now they have come for me. Last of the rangers, and last of their prey.* He looked all around him, but in the dark purple wastelands the wolves were nowhere to be seen. Havik grabbed the leather straps and fastened them to his chest.

No! his uncle screamed in his ear when he took those first few steps with the sled in tow. *I told you to leave him! What the wolves want is blood!*

Havik felt like tearing at his ears to silence his uncle, and wanted to shout to the wind in argument. But even in his madness he would not allow himself to make any noise that the wolves might hear. *They may be close, but perhaps they have not found me.* Havik wondered whether he should count himself fortunate he had awoken before they were upon him, or whether it would have been kinder for him to die in his dreams than be chased to a fear filled bloody end.

Fool! Leave Jhev behind and they will be sated!

Havik cursed under his breath and pushed forward. *I will not let them take us!* he swore as he pressed on into the violet flat-lands. Every step he took ended with his feet buried beyond his knees in the snow, and the sled was heavy and didn't ride as easily as it should have. His back burned with pain. Still, Havik would not be deterred and each step was a hard won victory that led to further struggle.

Havik didn't know how far he'd marched, but the wolves had never once ceased their relentless howling. At times their cursed moans seemed to linger in some unseen distance, whereas other times he thought they would soon be upon him. The Dead Star's glimmering light played tricks with the shadows in the wind blown snow, and many a time Havik thought the wolves were right there. He'd drop the straps and swat his arms at invisible opponents, only to find himself stifling laughs of madness when no wolf appeared. Eventually it came to pass that Havik felt his will to carry on leaving him, and felt it sweeter to sleep in the shadow of his sled, and rest for the remainder of his mortal life, than endure another painful second of his endless march. His food was gone but his hunger was far from sated, and the howling of the wolves seemed closer than they were before. The signal fire loomed ever at some unreachable distance, and cold and hunger were beginning to take their toll. *The magic of the foam will not last forever,* Havik warned himself, *and if I sleep again it will be the death of me.*

Fool! Leave Jhev behind, and you can rest while they feed. If you stop now, you will die.

But Havik no longer had the strength within him to press on. He felt hollow inside from hunger and thirst, and whatever hope he'd held out for had left him. The howling of the wolves saw to that. And so, when he found he could take not one single step more, Havik

Davenport cast aside his uncle's warnings and demands for obedience, and knelt for rest and for prayer. Havik exhaled warmth into his freezing hands, then placed his palms together, and looked to the dark skies for guidance. *Ma'at, my Goddess, your grace doesn't shine in this dark place. I know that now. Shall I pray to your brother, Isfet? Or shall I pray to your Mother, who sits below me and not in the Heavens above? I do not even truly know how to pray. I have always cast worship upon the altar of Scientos. But please. Hear me now. Ma'at, please. I beg of you. Give me some sign that I am not forsaken. If I am not to be Prince's, am I to be nothing? Please, I beg of you Ma'at, Eldaria, and yes, even you Isfet. Give me a sign!* Havik wept salty tears, and the chill of the water upon his cheeks made him shiver. He covered his palms over his face and wept into his hands, overcome with his grief, faith, and madness.

At first he did not know if it was madness or magic that made him go blind. A brilliant gleam of white light shone first through the cracks of his fingers, and when he removed his hands the glare of it took away his sight. He raised his palms and cupped at the dazzling illumination until his wits and his eyes came to focus. *The Silver Star rises, and the false day is upon me.* Sure enough, when Havik squinted his night blind eyes and removed his hand from the glare, his eyes focused in on the Silver Star rising from the Sea of Secrets. *Isfet,* Havik could not help but wonder, *have you answered my prayers from within your timeless prison?* But Havik shrugged the thought aside as absurdity. He told himself it was coincidence and nothing more. Even so, he found himself gazing upon the Silver Star as he pondered of Isfet, and Prince's warning that Isfet's minions and dark influence fought for his freedom, even now. *Could the wolves be Isfet's minions?* Havik mused, as Isfet gave him further sign. There before him, lurking at some halfway point between himself and the signal fire, twinkled a light. The white beams of the Silver

Star reflected upon a standing stone that rose from the flat shores like a tower in a field. It was at least fifty feet tall, and it had a rough shape, but Havik had no other choice. *It is something I can climb, and I must make for it. If the wolves will soon be upon me, then it's there that I will make my stand.* He almost dared to thank Isfet for his guiding light, but found himself cursing at his uncle instead. The man would not stop telling Havik to leave Jhev behind, and Havik feared it would soon drive him mad.

"I have made my choice, damn you!" Havik found himself shouting after several hours of march towards the stone. "Will you not leave it be?" *You must leave him,* his uncle would say, again and again. *The wolves want his blood.* "They cannot have him!" Havik yelled. He stopped himself and spun in circles looking every which way, as if he knew his uncle were right there but could not find him. The wolves howled in the distance. "Can't you just leave it be?" Havik continued to spin, searching for his uncle, and found himself dizzy. He collapsed alongside the sled, and retched. *I'm going... I'm going mad.* He caught his breath and his bearings. The wolves howled again. *They close in on me, like a noose.* Havik came to a knee and looked. There, coming up along his tracks was the pack of wolves. Havik always knew they were there by their cry, but he had not seen them once since before Jhev died. Some part of him hoped that their infernal howling was only the sound of him losing the last shreds of his sanity, but when he saw their grey and black forms visible in the light of the Silver Star, he knew that they were real.

Havik cast argument with his uncle aside, and grabbed hold of the leathers. *I will not let them take you, Jhev,* Havik swore. *I have made my choice, and I will have my honor. Your sons will have your ship, and your wife will have your bones, Jhev. I swear it.* Havik had made it too close to the standing stone to give up, and he found it approaching faster than the wolves. *I will make my last stand.* Havik smiled at the thought of it. By the time he reached the lee of the stone he felt as if he might pass out from exhaustion. It rose a good fifty feet from the ground, just as Havik had estimated, and was covered top to bottom with snow. He gave himself a few minutes to rest, but all the while kept his eyes on the wolves. *Ten minutes and they will be upon me.* Havik groaned with frustration, but knew if he could just manage to climb the thing, then the smallest bit of hope remained to him. *The ship is not far, and there is the chance their looking glass shall fall upon stone as marker. If I can reach its top, I may be safe from the wolves, and visible to my crew.* Havik pondered for a moment. *But what of Jhev? If I bury him in snow, the wolves will surely dig at his scent.* Havik knew there was no other way. *I would never be able to lift him up this rock. It will be marvel if I can climb it myself.* Havik grieved at the thought of leaving his friend to the wolves, but his choice had brought him to the stone, and it was at the stone he would face his fate. *I'm sorry Jhev.*

Havik pulled the sled close up to the rock and disconnected his strap. He slung the leathers over his shoulder, then removed from the sled a long stick he had prepared should it come to blows with the wolves. In truth it was a part of the sled, but he had no further use for that now. He fastened the leather straps to the stick, then quickly set about piling snow over the sled, and with it, Jhev's body. It was all he could do in those few precious minutes to cover it fully, and soon he had consigned Jhev to his own lesser fate. After one last prayer over his friend's grave, Havik took hold of the stone and dug his fingers into snow and rock. It felt ice cold as he pressed his palms upon it. When at last he found his handhold, he started his ascent. The stick hung loosely from his shoulder, so that he might climb with both hands and carry his weapon with him. *If it comes to it, I will poke their eyes out,* Havik planned as he climbed.

He had only gotten a man's height above the ground below, when

Havik made attempt to lift his leg higher, and felt it snag. For half a second he thought it hooked on rock, but when he felt a downward force tugging at his foot, he nearly lost his handle on the ledge. *The wolves are upon me already!* he thought with horror, but when he turned his head left he saw them still approaching from the distance, and the snow bore no tracks that might have marked a lone wolf which had run ahead. A mortal terror replaced his fear of wolves, and he found his sanity leaving him in full. *What grabs hold of my leg? Shall I look below and find the darkness of my Prince or the salvation of my crew?* With his breath held and his heart likely stopped, Havik looked, and felt what little urine remained to him freely drain down his breeches. Jhev's arm had reached out from its snowy grave, and grabbed hold of his foot.

Havik screamed. It was a death howl that he thought must have been heard across the leagues between himself and the sea. Havik hung from his fingers that pressed into a crack in the stone, and shook his leg in terror. Jhev's hand released him, and Havik pulled himself up onto an outcropping where he found place to stand. As he grabbed at his leathers and wielded his makeshift staff, Havik watched with open mouth as Jhev's corpse began to rise from the snow. Havik saw an opportunity and swung his stick up at the caked snow that clung to the stone above Jhev's body. With each thwack of the stick snow came loose and spilled down on top of him. *Is it my Prince? Or is it some fell dark life brought into being from the black seed's corruption?* Jhev's corpse found itself buried in the small avalanche, but Havik knew that Jhev was dead, and this abomination would not be stopped by snow alone. Havik laughed as the irony struck him. *Jhev may yet be the instrument of my salvation! If the wolves take to Jhev as they took to Prince, I may be passed over.* Havik felt his head throb with ache and his stomach churn with nausea when he further puzzled Jhev's resurrection. *Jhev was lost to the corruption. What if it was him they chased, and not me? Was my uncle right all this time? Have I doomed myself by bringing Jhev's corrupted body with me?* Still the thought did not sit right. Havik knew that the wolves were already corrupted, or at least knew that those he killed by the lonely tree had burst with black seed after their dying. *Are they carriers of it like some disease? Or are the wolves simply crazed with insanity brought upon by the corruption within? Rabid with ungodly madness. Crazed beasts that murder and devour man and god alike.* The thought chilled him, and he relived Brownbeard's dying one more time. *His was no fate for a Davenport that has spilt the blood of god.*

Havik's fear peaked to impossible heights as he felt the once sturdy standing stone shake. It nearly threw Havik from the ledge, and when it shook for a second time he grabbed hold of the wall. The foul beast below was pounding upon the base of the stone. Whether by madness or anger or some cold logic, it did not matter to Havik. All that concerned him was holding on, and even that proved useless when the snow caved way above him, and an avalanche of the stuff threw him to the ground below. Everything was lopsided for Havik as he struggled to climb out from his snowy tomb. As he cleared snow from his face, he thanked the Dead Star's aura, which permeated the thick snow so that he could still see. He wadded up some mucus, and spit. The fall of the spittle told him which way was up, and Havik started to dig. Soon he emerged from the mound of snow and gasped for much needed breath. Nearby the wolves howled and he knew they were almost upon him. *I have to climb!* Havik told himself, and when he rose to his knees, he looked upon the standing stone, and was taken by the shock and awe of it.

The standing stone had lost its cloak of snow and was laid bare to the light of the Silver Star. It was not stone at all, but was a mighty piece of jagged ice that jut up from the ground as a large crystal, and it sparkled like a million cold diamonds in the starlight. Frozen deep within the icy prison Havik could make out a dark crimson shape that stood near the height of the crystal. Though he had never seen this rock before, it was all too familiar to him. The eerie blue of the ice. The way it glittered wondrously. The faded clarity through which he could see color and shape but not detail. *A djinni! Here!* Havik marveled. *Frozen Magic... Could this djinni be the crystal's child, as Prince said? Or has Isfet led me to one of his minions?* Deep inside the ice, Havik thought he saw a shining light. Some part of the djinni seemed to reflect the light of the Silver Star in a way the dead ice did not, or perhaps the djinni still had some inner luminescence of its own.

His time spent awestruck by the djinni had cost him. Jhev had risen from his snowy grave not ten feet away, and when Havik turned the man stood there before him. His eyes had become solid onyx just as they had when the obsidian horror took Flint and Jaxon, but his face was a spiderweb of corrupted veins. "Prince?" Havik found himself ask in Ancient. *Can you hear me, my Prince of Darkness?* Havik briefly considered taking a knee to beg for his Prince's forgiveness, but when Jhev's mouth opened, it was neither intelligent word nor deafening shriek that left his pale dead lips. Jhev's corpse moaned a guttural groan that gargled with congealed blood and wet bile. Bits of black seed floated from his mouth as he wailed, and the obsidian puffs lingered in the air all around him.

If this is my Prince, then he is some abomination of himself. If a god can die, can a god not also be corrupted? Havik was almost upon it. *But how can a god corrupt himself?* He choked at the thought. *Or is it Eldaria which corrupts him? He did not mean for the tree to grow here. The seed was dead, and it was meant for dead ground.* He knew it was his fault the tree was allowed to take root. If Havik had not listened to his uncle, he never would have slit

Nimmet's throat, and he would have had a Prince now instead of this madness. Perhaps even Jhev would still be alive. Whatever stood before him, and whatever might happen from there on out, Havik felt solely responsible for it. *But it was my uncle who bid me to do it,* Havik argued with himself. *Is it my uncle's fault in truth, or mine for listening to him?* A colder thought passed his mind. *Was Prince's game won the moment the white seed was tainted? In taking from him his rightful victory, have I brought some fresh Doom upon the world?* Havik did not know. He was frozen with indecision, thought, and fear, so it was Jhev that made the first move. He tightened his left hand into a fist, and smashed it against the ice wall as if taken by some ungodly rage. Havik knew no iron nor steel nor heat could puncture the dead ice of a djinni's prison, so he felt felt the sting of disbelief as the beast's fist made cracks in the ice that split its surface in tiny fissures. *The djinn are frozen, because crystal and god are frozen as well. How can this be? Is this what Prince meant by Isfet's dark influence? Or is this Prince's doing?*

Havik made no move to run, nor attempt to climb the ice while it shook so violently. Jhev turned to face the wall full on. He grunted with rage, and with both hands together, pounded it in one mighty bash. The outer layer of the massive ice wall vibrated and shattered. Great pieces of crystal chipped away and fell. Large sheets tumbled and exploded into millions of glistening shards. Havik shielded himself with his arms, and felt only the light dusting of an icy mist splash against him. Not one foot from his chest a splinter of ice the size of a javelin embedded itself in the snow. Jhev let forth one more guttural howl and spewed a wave of black seed across the ice. Bits of the seed took hold here and there across cracks on the wall's surface, and within seconds tiny roots seemed to be expanding across the ice crystal. *Does it mean to corrupt one of the djinn?* Havik dreaded the possibility as a Doom for his age, and he thought it might even be better for Prince to possess a djinni than for one to be crazed with madness.

"Prince!" Havik cried in Ancient. "Prince!" he shouted again. He didn't even know why he was shouting his name, but he hoped what stood before him was of familiar intelligence, and not some mindless monstrosity that meant to unleash Chaos and hell upon Eldaria. *Chaos. Isfet?* "Isfet?" Havik found himself ask in Ancient. "Isfet!" he shouted.

Jhev lowered his hands and turned from the ice wall to face him. The look he gave Havik had no color, and the sly smirk of Prince's knowing gaze was absent. "Isfet!" Havik said again. Whether it understood him or not, he did not know, but he had gotten its attention. Havik felt his stomach drop, and when he instinctively reached for a weapon, he found even his crude stick was lost to him. Jhev took one step forward as if to charge, and Havik was prepared to turn and run as well, when a wolf leaped into Jhev and knocked him to the ground. The beast's maw bit down on his chest, and it tore at his frozen flesh in a wild madness. Havik fell to his back in fright. Jhev's hand grabbed hold of the wolf's snout, and with godly strength crushed bone and flesh alike into a meaty pulp. The thing backed away with a horrible wail as blood spewed from its broken face. Jhev did not have time to stand, for another wolf was soon tearing at his leg.

Six more wolves were approaching and would be there within seconds. Havik knew he could neither fight nor outrun a wolf, so he dropped flat on the ground, and covered himself up with snow. The wolf that tore at Jhev's leg soon found its spine shattered when Jhev's heavy frozen fist came down upon its back. The wolf howled one final time as its life left it. Jhev looked and saw Havik. Their eyes connected in a way that made Havik feel terribly exposed. But instead of acknowledging the look with screech, or smile, or charge,

Jhev instead turned to the approaching wolves. Jhev picked up the sled that had carried him all the way from the gate, and when the wolves made their assault against him, he threw it. It took one of the wolves head on, and sled and beast alike exploded in a shower of wood and gore. *The corruption strengthens him, but he does not grow as Prince did. Is it strength alone which breaks the dead ice, or is it something more?* The battle between Jhev and the beasts must have been a grizzly one by the sound of it, but Havik would not risk being seen by the wolves. He covered himself full in the snow, closed his eyes, and even held his breath. He paid attention to the fight, but listened more carefully for the sound of any wolf that might come closing in on him.

Fortunately for Havik he went unnoticed, and one by one he heard the wolves die at Jhev's hands. When it seemed as if three were left, and there was a pause between the killing, Havik thought they might have felled their man. But that thought vanished when he heard the sound of ice break, and with it another one of the wolves fell silent. Havik dared to look now, and he lifted his head from its white blanket. Jhev's chest was torn to shreds, but his body did not bleed and was as if frozen to the core. His right arm's flesh was nearly completely gone, but icy blood and bone together were bound by veined black corruption, and the cursed arm made lifeless swing at one of the wolves. The limb hit the wolf square on, but did not deter it. The animal grabbed at the bone and gnawed. With a great crack it snapped, and black marrow and noxious plumes of smoky black seed escaped from its depths. The wolf throttled its neck and tore his right arm from its shoulder, leaving Jhev with only his left. The second wolf leaped and gripped upon Jhev's stiff neck, but the man was unfazed. He thrust his remaining fist into the wolf's chest and tore from it its beating heart. The organ was crimson and bore no sign of corruption. *So the wolves are not truly corrupted.* The thought terrified him. *Then is it loyalty to the crazed pack, or something else beyond corruption that sets these wolves to purpose? Perhaps they are Eldaria herself, fighting against that which taints her, be it man or god.*

The battle was over now, and the undead thing before Havik had won. The final wolf was seizing on its side from its wounds, and Jhev was standing victorious over their dead bodies, draped in the fluids of his carnage. Behind him the standing stone was growing corrupt veins of its own that were seeping through shallow cracks and fractures in the dead ice. The tentacles were making their wicked way deeper towards the djinni. *I do not want to be here when this thing awakens,* Havik laughed. *Or do I? Either way...* And Havik found his thoughts pulled from concern when a strange thing happened. The pools of blood that stained the virgin snow and steamed with heat began to boil and glow. As if a weak cinder being stoked to brilliance, a crimson aura began to radiate from the djinni. The blood at Jhev's feet and upon his body took the glow as if it were its own, and soon the whole of the carnage was effervescent with lavender light. The energy seemed to swell and in a moment it was all gone, consumed by the djinni as if it drew the light from outside the crystal, down through the cracks, and into its frozen form. Havik felt icy terror grip him by the throat, but instead of a scream he could only gurgle in disbelief. *Magic is born again.*

Jhev stared at Havik, and neither smiled nor shrieked. *It is not Prince.* Jhev's black eyes bore down on Havik, and the thing started walking. Its leg was in ruins, so it tumbled down to the snow. It only had one arm, and it seemed unstable. Havik stood, and found that beside him was the javelin of dead ice, and a collection of smaller shards. Havik took a sharp piece of crystal and slung it in his belt, then took the javelin in hand. It was surprisingly much lighter than he expected. *It is no simple water.* Havik turned back to face Jhev, who was floundering on the ground, unable to stand. Havik thought Jhev might never even get up, but when their eyes met once more, Jhev started crawling towards him. His strong leg pushed his body forward, and he hopped on his good arm with alarming strength. Havik briefly considered whether he might try fighting the thing, but the image of the heart being taken from the wolf filled him with such horror that he dreaded being anywhere near its terrible reach. And when the thing began to crawl at an increasing pace towards Havik, he was taken by his fear, and ran.

Havik leaned on the spear of dead ice with every step, and pushed himself to the limit of his exhaustion. It was mostly adrenaline that was carrying him the extra distance, but even that was bound to run out soon. The signal beacon was growing closer. He saw it now as clear as day. The crew of the ship had been ordered to fell lumber and light the beacon every day after three weeks had gone by. It was Brownbeard's idea, and though Narvis and Brackens assured everyone they would be able to navigate the icy North without it, Brownbeard was insistent. For two weeks before they arrived at the cove, he had repeatedly explained just how important the beacon was to every single member of the crew that meant to stay behind. There were all sorts of dangers that might befall them in the North, and a beacon for home could mean the difference between all men living or all dying in the freeze. Havik could kiss his wizard now if he weren't dead. *If I did not betray my Prince, would he have protected us from the wolves? Would then Brownbeard still be alive, and I have all the star metal in my possession?* Havik knew the answer was uncertain, for the tree might still have taken root. He could only hope that what he did to Prince was of benefit to the greater good of all mankind, and not the first falling domino in a chain of events that would mean the death of them all. *If this curse were to infect the Realm... No, I cannot think of it,* Havik swore. He would return home straight to his uncle and sing the song of all that had happened. He knew Lord Hubert Davenport of Witchblood Stronghold, of all people, would know what to do with such information. If need be a whole armada of ships could sail back up the Sea of Secrets to their hidden cove and set all corruption to flame. *Black seed took to the wind...* He remembered that dark cloud of it sailing over the ridge wall, and the thought murdered his hope. *Still... While it cannot be contained, it is the tree which is the heart of Prince's darkness.*

Havik enjoyed his mind games. They helped him pass the time when he would rather give up to his failing body. And each time his mental acrobatics failed, and he felt as if he might not be able to go on, he would just look over his shoulder. There in the distance was Jhev, ever crawling. *He is gaining on me.* Havik outpaced him for hours fueled by his fear and his hope for the ship, but with each step his pace now slowed, and the fell thing was relentless. Havik knew Jhev would overtake him eventually, but all he needed to do was get close enough to the ship. *They will see me,* he told himself. *They'll see me and they'll come to my aid.* But the thought ended when he tried to take another step and his legs would not obey. He turned to lie on his back, and groaned for breath. "Ma'at, help me." But Havik knew Ma'at could not see him here. This foreign land was the domain of Prince and Isfet alone. With the Red Star's warmth ever lost to this place, he knew his prayers to the Goddess would go unanswered.

The fires of the beacon were close. He was less than a few hundred feet from it, but he didn't have the breath to yell, and saw no men round the fire. He could only whisper his prayers to the wind. "Jhev, I'm sorry. Your sons won't even have your ship, let alone your wife your bones." The thought infuriated him. *Will I die shamed as well from my failed promise, beyond merely being the cursed*

Davenport that brought Doom upon our age? Is it to be the Age of Corruption that men will sing of in a thousand years? Havik laughed. *What men? It will be the end of ages, and the end of men. Even if my sailors get away, the truth of what happened here will never be known. It will only be known that a Davenport went into the woods, and what emerged was death and darkness and despair. Davenport will be synonymous with Doom until the end of days, and I will have been its herald.* That thought shamed Havik the most. Havik lifted his head and watched Jhev slowly approach. *Ten minutes... No longer.* Havik leaned his head back and closed his eyes.

Havik dreamed... He dreamed he had become a block of ice in an endless frozen field of white. He saw Isfet in the Silver Star as a dark shadow that pecked at the inside of its shell. He saw the Red Star glowing with fire, and its warmth bathed over him. Ma'at was inside of it, her beauty too glorious to behold. He melted beneath her radiance, and transformed into a pool of warm water. Havik's fear was gone. He relaxed and gazed up into a clear blue sky. His eyes fixed in on the Red Star, and he thought of Ma'at, and Isfet, and Thoth, and the legends of his people. *When man is gone, will the Delvers and Devilkin remember us?* But Havik knew the answer did not matter. The Red Star went dark, and Havik felt himself frost. In the sky the Silver Star grew closer and closer. Where once it was a small egg, it had become a mighty crystalline moon that lingered so near he thought the tree of trees might kiss its corrupted heights. The Dead Star was nowhere to be seen, and Havik felt his Prince's absence. *If Isfet's cell swings open, it will not spell the end of man alone. Prince's words were clear. It will mean the end of the Castle. That is man, Delver, and Devilkin alike. The end of all Eldaria... The end of Ma'at, my Goddess... Even my Prince...*

Above him the Silver Star cracked, and the wind that swelled was infernal. Mountains and forests blew to dust, and Havik witnessed a winged beast with curled horns emerge from the Silver Star. It spread its wings and stretched in celestial yawn at its antediluvian awakening. *Poof,* he heard Prince whisper in his ear, and all at once the world turned black. Only the terrible presence of Isfet, the beast, could be felt. Havik saw eight beacons of light rise to the sky. They were rainbow in color, and spun hand in hand as if in dance. All at once they collided and transformed into a swirling vortex of golden energy. The light pulsed outward and became a great circle, through which a million million points of light emerged to cover the black sky. *The Gate of Heavens.* For the first time in his existence, Havik saw all the stars of the Kingdom laid out across the Heavens in celestial display. Havik wept as he saw the universe. *This is no dream, but a vision.* It's then that the fear took hold. Between Havik, and a patch in the sky, was the black outline of Isfet's winged form. One by one the lights went out around him. He flapped his wings, and stretched his monstrous arms, and soon the universe was dead, and only Isfet remained. The golden circle shattered to eight colored pieces, and they fell at Isfet's feet.

This is the end of all creation.

Havik woke to the sound of a guttural moan. He sat up and saw Jhev's frozen corpse crawling towards him not thirty feet away. *There crawls the death of me.* Havik sighed as he waited for death's embrace, but the memory of his dream haunted him. *No... There crawls the death of everything...* Havik found himself make a choice. *I cannot die.* Havik stood. *I am the only one that knows what is at stake. If I do nothing, then everything is lost. There may be nothing left for me to do but die, but I will not do it lying down!*

Havik picked up the spear of dead ice, and aimed its jagged tip at the undead thing lumbering towards him. "I refuse to be afraid. I refuse to accept the fate that has come for me. I am Havik Davenport, and I am an Eldarian! The blood of the Ancients pumps from my heart! I will not let the Mother die, not while I can still stand!" Havik dug his feet into the ground. "Do you hear me? Isfet? Prince? Whatever the hell you are! I'm the only thing that stands between you and the Kingdom! If you are the abyss of color, then I am the light in the darkness! You don't frighten me! Come on! Do your worst!"

Havik screamed and he found himself charging. He ran at the thing and it reared back like an angry horse. Havik plunged the spear deep into the thing's heart and out its frozen back. But it was not dead, and the groan it gave was neither angered nor wanton for revenge. It was a dead moan that spit black seed in the air. Havik held his breath. Jhev swung his arm at Havik, but the reach of the spear was too great. So, in a move that toyed with Havik's resolve, Jhev grabbed the spear and pulled it deeper into himself. *It is relentless.* Havik took the dead ice flat with both hands, and lifted with all the might his weakened body could provide. In one great push Havik turned Jhev onto his back, with the dead ice spear pointing upwards to the sky. *Do not hesitate!* his uncle commanded him. Havik drew the sharp ice blade from his belt, and knelt over Jhev's face. "Jhev! Ah! Die! Die! Jhev!" Havik screamed repeatedly as he stabbed the thing again and again and again. His shouts of rage soon became intermingled with screams of pain. Blood ran from his hand where the edge of the bladed ice cut himself in the wielding of it. Jhev's head was turned to icy ruin, and his corrupted body had fallen still. Black seed lingered in the air, and Havik was unsure if he had breathed any in. His blood was red hot, and it was the fear of the seed and the pain in his hand that led him to sheathe the makeshift dagger and run.

Havik ran and ran, never once looking back to see if he was being pursued. When at last he reached the pit of burning lumber that was his beacon, he stopped. He gasped for breath and turned around.

Jhev's body was naught but a corpse a few hundred feet away. Havik strained his eyes and waited, but it never rose, and remained as still as a grave. Havik knew better than to count his victory won. He had experienced gain and loss side by side in the cruel North. And now all Havik had to show for it was his life, a song, and that piece of dead ice. *A marvel in itself, if truth be told. It will never melt, and will give credence to my tale. Without it, men might think I've gone mad.*

Havik looked about, but there were no sailors by the fire. He walked around the pit, and his heart beat faster when his eyes came upon that sweet sight. Three men in a rowboat were heading his way. One held a long metal cylinder and was using it to spy on him. *The looking glass. That must be Niles, our stalwart old crow's man. He saw me, and he commanded my rescuing. Bless him.*

Havik stripped from his layers of fur and cloth, and tossed them to flame. *Though black seed may yet spread, I will not bring any onto the ship in my furs.* When he was down to only his small clothes, he retied his leather belt around his waist, and belted the dead ice dagger. Finally, he kicked off his bloodied frozen boots into the flames, and walked barefoot to the beach. He sat down just before the water met sand, and waited for them to come ashore. His right hand burned from its cut, and he held it close to his chest. In the distance the red and green sails of the Wandering Turtle waved gloriously. *There is wind to take us from this evil place, and the sooner we sail from the Sea of Secrets the better. But can a ship outpace the wind?* Havik wondered if the same winds that would carry his turtle to the Realm would also carry with it the black seed. *One of the eight winds has been corrupted. How long until the other seven turn black with seed?* Havik remembered Narvis and mourned for her. He suspected the salt may have protected her and Brackens from the saplings, but the speed with which the tree had grown was a terror, and even if they survived its growing, there would be nowhere to run. Havik glanced back in the direction of the Barrens, but even by the light of the Silver Star the tree was hidden by mountains, and the terrible black cloud was hidden by grey storms of snow.

Where would they go? Across all of Fenria? They are lost forever, and should they be so fortunate as to reach the shore, they'll find the ship long gone. They are dead, or soon will be, unless they can brave the months or years it will take for men to mount a return. Havik knew it did no good to pretend any of his party had survived. He knew in his heart that it was a Doom which now spread across Eldaria, and no man or woman, no matter how gifted her sight might be, could stand under the shadow of that fell tree and live. *Or will she become dark minion?* Havik tossed the speculations aside when the rowboat reached the shore. *I will have months to speculate. I must prepare a volume of notes before I reach my uncle. There is paper and ink aboard the vessel, and I should prepare testimony for the many wizards and chancellors and lords that will be called to council.*

Niles had folded up his spy glass. He stepped from the boat and onto the snowy sand. "M'lord Davenport, is that you?" he asked as he approached. *Why do they have their knives in hand?*

Havik stood and approached them. "Yes. It is I." Havik did not quite feel the chill in the air so much as before, even though most of his clothes had been removed. *Is it the foam's magic that still courses my veins, or am I half dead?* Still, even in his weakened state, Havik felt more alive than he ever had.

Niles removed his cloak and meant to wrap his lord with it, but Havik shrugged it away. "I have been without warmth since beyond the gate. I can survive a trip in this boat." Havik stepped onto the boat and sat down. The sailors lowered their blades and sheathed them, though their eyes still sparkled with suspicion.

"M'lord... Where is the rest of your party?" Niles asked.

"Dead. They're all dead." Havik sighed. "Take me back to the ship. I will tell the tale once I've bathed." For the moment that was what Havik truly desired. A lesser man might have gone straightaway for a meal dripping in butter and fat upon arrival at the ship, but not a Davenport. He could already taste the sweet and sour of the honeyed wine he would take, as he knew that after such meager rations for so long, it would be wiser for him to break his fast gently than feast like a fool. The wine would do him well, but it was a brief soak in warm water that filled him with anticipation.

"Aye m'lord," Niles said. With a nod to the other two sailors, they shoved off. It was a twenty minute ride to the ship, and not one word was spoken in the length of it. Havik was too tired to speak for the moment, and he assumed their silence was in sadness from hearing the fell news.

The Wandering Turtle was stained a faded green that was outdone by the radiant emerald of the algae that now grew around its hull. The growth was not there when they arrived at the cove, and when he saw it Havik was quick to wonder whether it was a normal growth, or whether something more sinister might have been afoot. "That algae. Did it grow very quickly?"

"No. It has grown since first we took anchor," Niles said.

"Good... Good." Havik thought more on it. The boat came beside the ship, and soon it was hooked to pulleys, and drawn up the side of the larger vessel. The ship had three large masts, and at the moment their sails were not fully raised. Two of the sails were red, but the central and largest was a brilliant green. The remaining four crewmen had gathered on deck at his returning. Niles stood beside him, and the two men who rowed the boat were securing it to the ship. All together Havik led a crew of seven sailors, down from the sixteen he had when they first set sail. His cargo hold was empty of star metal, and all he had to show for those nine lives was a piece of ice and a story. *All the more reason I set my song to scroll post haste.*

"What happened to you, m'lord? Where is everyone?" asked one of the sailors. Havik struggled to remember his name. *Was it Jon?*

They all looked to Havik for answers, but the two boatmen turned their backs on the question, and Niles seemed quite nervous. "Everyone else is dead." Havik's words unsettled them, and killed their bright eyes eager for news. "Lift anchor and set sails for Astermount."

"What of the star metal?" the same sailor persisted. "What of our share of the profits promised?" Havik was not annoyed at the question. He had a fair concern.

"You will all be paid the same sum of gold promised as if our holds were filled to the brim with the wicked stuff." Havik saw some relief in their eyes. "And a twenty percent bonus if we make it back by the Rat's Moon." *That should appease them.* Havik smiled.

"What of our Captain?" the sailor continued.

"When this cursed shore is beyond my sight, I will tell you all of what transpired," Havik eyed each one of them. "For now, let us make for home with all the speed we can muster." Havik had commanded and his crew obeyed. The two boatmen scampered off somewhere, but Niles remained alongside of him. Havik suspected what he wanted. "Niles. You were in command of the ship and crew while we were on the range, is that correct?"

"Yes, m'lord," Niles said.

"Then you are Captain now," Havik told him.

"Yes, m'lord. I understand." Niles nodded but did not smile. If anything he seemed distressed.

His sullen attitude must be in mourning for the others. For me, the loss has been felt for what seems a lifetime. I must look to the future, lest far more than nine lives will be lost. The Kingdom itself is at stake. "Captain. I want a man in the crow's nest at all times. They are to keep an eye out for a black cloud in the sky."

Niles raised his eyebrow at that. "A storm cloud?"

"No. Something much much worse. A black curse that corrupts the very wind itself." Havik felt the chill in him then, and knew it was time to recover. "All will be explained soon. See to your men, Captain. I'll be below decks."

Havik left him there and returned to his quarters. They felt foreign to him after so long. He took from his trunk a fine Mercantine suit of black silks and leather, and unfolded it. He'd meant to wear it at their victory feast upon returning with star metal in tow. *Instead I will look the part of a noble Davenport when I sing my song to the sailors and set my quill to scroll.* Havik set the dead ice blade inside a cabinet and locked it with a silver key, which he then hid in a jar of tea. He took with him his suit, a bottle of wine, a tankard of water, and a jar of honey, and went to the small wooden room where the tub was kept. Within an hour he had filled it with hot water, and soaps, and oils, and was soaking in the brew with a tankard of watered and honeyed wine in his hand and a smile upon his face. None of the crew disturbed him as he rested for the first time in fortnights. Havik did not sleep, for he was afraid of what dreams might bring. Instead he drank until his bottle was empty, his water was drunk, and the jar of honey licked clean. He intended to wrap his wounded hand in bandage, but after washing the dried blood from his body, found the cut to be quite minor. He instead wore over his right hand a dark glove to cover it.

When at last Havik Davenport emerged from that steamy wooden room, he both looked and felt a noble lord once more. His attire was regal in its cut, and he was fully clean shaven. He was usually accustomed to keeping a neat beard and mustache, but when first he set razor to his face he felt need to be rid of it all. His hair was cut short, and what he kept he'd straightened back with hair wax. Even his scent smelled of nobility. With renewed sense of style and purpose he set out for the Captain's chamber above deck.

When Havik emerged from below he saw that land was still in sight, but knew it would not be too long before it slipped over the horizon. *It will be night soon, and longer still before I see my first true day.* Havik cast his thoughts of the Goddess aside. *I will pray when she is in sight. I have duties to perform.* No crew approached him as he made the walk across the deck and entered the door to the Captain's chamber. The room was used as a common area for those of higher station on the ship. Havik sat himself behind the desk, lit two of the brass lamps with a candle, and set to work gathering quills, and ink, and paper, and other necessities for what he intended to accomplish. By the time he'd cleared away most of the clutter that had collected on their journey and was prepared to begin, Niles opened the outer door and entered.

"Shore will be gone to us soon, m'lord," Niles said. "You are feeling better? Yes?"

Havik was pleased that he'd entered. "Good, Captain. Yes. I feel much better. Thank you. Could you kindly get me some gruel? I have much to do and I would break my fast."

Niles was surprised. "Gruel?"

"You heard me. Gruel. And quickly please, I have a terrible hunger."

"As you wish." Niles turned away.

"Bring it hot!" Havik called out to him as he left.

The first thing Havik wrote was a brief letter to Robert Gracious, the Lord of Cliffwatch and father to his fallen squire. Kevin met a cruel end, and he wished to appeal to the boy's honor before beginning the long process of writing all that had truly taken place. His letter highlighted the boy's many honorable traits, and he wrote of a better end than the one the poor lad had endured. Nothing was said of the obsidian horror, or of the knife Havik had delivered into Kevin's chest. Nor did Havik mention how the young squire was last seen drugged, asleep, and tied to a horse running towards maddened bloodthirsty wolves. Instead the boy had served him well, and died a hero's death protecting his lord from the pack of beasts that killed the rest of his party. And, as further consolation, Havik awarded the boy a knighthood in his passing. If not for Kevin Gracious, Havik Davenport would be a dead man.

This will appease the Gracious family enough that they do not ask unwanted questions. If my uncle means to solidify their cause to ours, he can do so guided by the knowledge I bring him. I will not presume Robert Gracious an ally, no matter how leal one of his sons has been. Besides, some things are best kept secret. In that moment Havik questioned whether he ought to tell the full truth to his men. They were his crew, but would he consider them rangers? They hadn't risked life and limb on the walk, but at least two men had to remain with Wandering Turtle. One for the ship itself, and one for the beacon fires. Instead seven remained. *They deserve to know the truth,* Havik decided. *They have risked enough to earn the hell of knowing the Doom we've unleashed upon the world.* Havik knew the tale would spread, but specific details, such as Prince's very existence, he would leave out. *They should not know of my Prince. That is knowledge for Davenport ears and eyes alone.*

Niles returned just as Havik was signing his name on the letter. The sailor turned Captain placed the steaming bowl of gruel on the desk beside him. Havik took a bar of sealing wax and dripped some onto the folded document.

"There's something I need to ask you." Niles tone was serious.

Havik pressed his Davenport signet ring onto the wax and set the letter aside so he might make room for his gruel. "Go ahead. Ask."

Havik took his first bite of the porridge. He spooned neither syrup nor butter provided upon it, and took it hot and plain. Even so, it seemed to him a savory feast after so long without a hot meal.

"I saw you..." Niles whispered. "I saw you kill a man that was crawling in the snow."

Havik put the spoon down. "It was no man, but a demon."

"I heard you yell Jhev's name."

"A battle cry against the cursed thing, for it took our Captain away from us. That and the wolves killed every last man of our ranging." Havik sighed. "I meant to tell everyone together, but first there is something you must see."

"What's that?" Niles was curious.

"Go to my quarters, and open the cabinet on the left hand side by the porthole. The key's in the jar of tea in my trunk. Inside you'll find a blade of ice. Fetch it, and come back here straightaway."

Niles nodded and left. Havik pushed the gruel aside, dipped his quill in the ink, and started writing on a fresh scroll.

For Lord Hubert Davenport's eyes alone, he first wrote in simple common form. The words that followed were disguised in a basic cryptography his uncle had taught him. To any man who did not know their secret, it would appear as meaningless scribble. In truth it was not unbreakable, not by far, but it would still be effective enough to keep its true meaning hidden from prying eyes.

I do not know if the Prince of Darkness is alive or dead, but I can only assume that since the Dead Star's aura yet shines above us, some form of him persists. The Dead Star IS Prince, or Prince is the Dead Star. I do not know if one can exist without the other, but while the obsidian horror that is Prince still remains, his godly wits and intelligence have been lost. Prince has been taken by some cursed madness, not one as a man would lose his sanity, but in such a way that a god would lose control of himself and become unchecked.

Whatever Order remained to the god seems to have been taken by Chaos, and I wonder if it is Isfet's dark influence. The corruption of the world tree seems to be a thing of its own however, and Prince himself panicked and dropped his guard at the horror of the seed being planted. By his own devices the seed was corrupted and was meant to be grown upon the Dead Star. Yet now it grows instead in the Barrens of Eldaria and from there spreads its black seed to the winds. These realizations and this testimony may seem strange uncle, but as you read of the events which took place, you will come to understand that gods walk among us and magic has been reborn. Even now Isfet and his minions threaten all of creation. All members of my ranging team have been lost, including my wizards, my squire, our spy, my Captain.

Havik lifted the quill and paused. *Jhev... I cannot deliver his bones, but I can ensure the ship goes to his sons. I told him it would, and a half honored promise is better than nothing.* Havik set the scroll aside and rose. He found the deed to the Wandering Turtle in a chest that held bills and other lists of expenses for the journey. It had all been neatly cataloged by Jhev so every doubloon was accounted for. Havik set the deed on the desk and inked his quill. *The vessel is worth a fair sum. And I'll give them a bit of gold as well to ease their way into the business.* Havik knew it was, in part, Havik's own fault that Jhev's fleet sailed the waters they were lost in, and he felt there was great honor in giving his sons the chance to follow in their father's footsteps. The door opened as Havik signed his name on the deed and authorized the transfer of ownership to the sons of Jhev Whitesteed. "Niles, is that you?" he asked without looking up.

"It is, m'lord." Niles approached the desk, and when Havik looked up, saw his new Captain's face was stone cold. "What's that? The deed to the ship?"

"Yes." Havik set the quill down. "I mean to give it to Jhev's sons, in fulfillment of a promise I once made." Havik rubbed his hands together, while Niles seemed lost in thought. "Well?"

"M'lord, we're no longer in sight of land, and the crew would have words."

"Excellent." *It will be a hard tale to tell,* Havik thought, *and a harder tale to hear.* "Get out a keg of rum." Niles turned and meant to exit the room, but Havik stopped him. "Captain! The blade, did you retrieve it?"

Niles paused, but did not look back. "The crew would have their words." He exited and closed the door behind him.

Something about the way he said it unsettled Havik to the bone. *Perhaps they are afraid of the demons and curses I've hinted at. As right they should be.* Havik had prided himself on being a man who knew no fear of man nor beast, but one lesson he'd learned on his range into the Barrens was that *only a fool would not fear magic, for magic is the realm of gods and Doom.*

Havik took two last bites of gruel, and followed Niles out onto the ship's deck. All the men that remained in his crew stood waiting outside. Niles, the two men from the boat, and the four sailors. All were Gulgari except for Niles, who looked of the Western Realm, but he was old, and hair that might have once shone gold had long since gone grey. Some part of Havik always found it funny that the Gulgari, a people who were known to sail the Central Sea, were his sailors on this Northern voyage, but Jhev had told him it was for just that reason he'd suggested the purchasing of Wandering Turtle in the first place. "Gulgari men are my folk," Jhev once told him over a jar of rum. "They're the only ones I would trust with such precious cargo. The Sailor's Law is written in their blood." Havik remembered the words now, as he saw that the keg of rum had already been fetched, but it was untapped and stood upright, underneath a rope noose that hung from the boom overhead. Havik's mind reeled and all his thoughts left him.

That familiar feeling of fear coursed through Havik. "You can't mean to!"

"Oh, but we *do*, m'lord," said the man Havik thought was Jon. "We *do* mean to."

"But I chartered this voyage and I *bought* this ship!" Havik protested. "Without me you'll never get your gold."

Jon smiled. "Ah, but there's a mouthful m'lord. Seems we won't be needing gold where we're going."

Havik did not understand. "What are you talking about?"

Jon started to speak but Niles stopped him. "It's my brother," Niles explained. "He told us about a pirate fleet out past Blackport, and any that turns over their ship voluntarily like, gets honored position in their ranks."

"Those are Kefka's shores," Havik laughed. "Piracy wouldn't be tolerated. Your brother's sold you a false bill of goods. Go there and you'll be hanged."

Jon laughed back at him. "You'll be the one doing the hanging."

Niles frowned. "Sad to say, it's Lord Kefka himself that sits Admiral to the fleet. He means some mad merchants war, and the plunder to be had puts the pittance of Davenport consolations to shame."

Havik could not believe it. "Lord Kefka is my father's friend. When he hears of this–"

"He'll never hear a word, m'lord." Jon shook his head. "Shame you were half mad when we found you in the cold."

One of the boatmen spoke now. "And not half a league from the shore."

The other boatman spoke. "A tragedy you died soon after." He took his hat and set it over his heart.

"Just enough time to write your last words," said Niles.

"And eat your last meal." Jon smiled.

"The gold, *and* the pirate's ranks, you can have them both!" Havik argued as the two boatmen took him by the arm and walked him towards the barrel. He briefly tried to struggle against them, but he was in a weakened state and their muscles were well kept. Havik knew if he were to turn them, it would be by words alone. "Deliver me to Astermount, and I will shower you with riches! You can take that with you to the fleets!"

Niles shook his head. "They take the gold too I'm afraid. Wood and wealth together's the price."

"Then bury it somewhere! Or give it to someone you trust to keep it for you!"

Jon laughed. "Neither map nor men can be trusted. But we all trust the dead to stay silent."

If only that were true, Havik thought cruelly. "I invoke the Sailor's Law!" Havik demanded. "You are Gulgari, and it is written in your blood, or have you meant to betray us all along?"

"We wouldn't betray one of our own, it's true," Niles told him. "We would have sailed all eight seas beneath Captain Jhev. He was a good Gulgari man... But you ain't."

"You cannot kill your commanding officer!" Havik protested.

"You don't command us," one of the sailors said. "Niles is our Captain now. You promoted him yourself!"

"You returned without our old Captain m'lord," Niles said. "Might even be he was the man you killed before you reached the shore." The sailors made eyes with each other and nodded in agreement.

"He was a demon, I told you!"

"Maybe he was, and maybe he wasn't. Either way he's dead." Niles sighed. "Lift him up."

Havik was hoisted up onto the barrel. "But I bought this ship! It's mine! You can't betray the man who gives you leave to sail his ship! I have owner's right! Make me walk the plank by some shore near the Realm and I'll swim for it. I won't seek revenge, I swear! By the House of Davenport, I swear it!"

The two boatmen pulled the noose over his head, and slipped it round his neck. Havik found it hard to breathe.

Niles seemed to have walked off, but he returned now with something in his hand. If ever some of the men seemed unsure of themselves, when Niles held the thing aloft they nodded with approval.

"You signed over the ship, and your owner's rights along with it." Niles held up the deed for all to see.

"That's just a technicality! I could have waited until we reached Astermount to sign it." Havik spoke, but his words were softened by the rope.

"You could have," Niles frowned, "but you didn't... And thanks to that our consciences will be ever cleaner for it... I'm sorry m'lord. We even voted on it, we did. It was unanimous. Things were a bit dodgy at first, but the transfer of title was the final nail in your coffin."

"Wait. Wait. Just wait. What of the blade from my cabinet? Did you get it? That stone out there was a frozen djinni. The dead ice broke and I took a piece of it. It will prove–"

One of the boatmen tightened the noose, and Havik hated him for it.

"Sad to say, I did m'lord." Niles shook his head sadly. "But all that were inside was a puddle of water and blood." Niles turned his back on Havik. *The dead ice melted. Of course. Why wouldn't it? It had already been broken.* "Best leave all this talk of demons and curses as the fevered words of a dying man... Madness and nothing more." Niles nodded his head to someone Havik couldn't see.

They did give me my words. Havik hoped that short preamble, to what was meant to be an epic testimony of his journey, would suffice in giving his uncle sufficient warning of the Doom that all men faced. *I pray they mean to send them.*

Havik felt the barrel get kicked away from beneath his feet. Then he felt his neck snap beneath the weight of his falling body, and his world went dark. His thoughts were of the Goddess, and how he wondered if the nightly caravan were real, and whether it would still take him to Ma'at if he died in this foreign place, where the Red Star never shone.

"Go get his trunk for the body," Havik heard Niles say in the darkness. "His father would want his son's bones. That's the noble thing to do."

"*Uncle*, I think it was." It was Jon's voice, but it was growing fainter. "He was always going on about his *uncle*."

Havik meant for his final thought to be of his Goddess, or Eldaria the Mother, or even his uncle or father. Instead what he saw in the shadows of his death was the onyx outline of Isfet and his terrible flapping wings.

Havik felt the fear flow through him.

www.ingramcontent.com/pod-product-compliance
Lightning Source LLC
Chambersburg PA
CBHW060240030726
47493CB00024B/1434